The Weaving

A Novel of Twin Flames
Through Time

Books by Cheryl Lafferty Eckl

Non-Fiction: For Times of Dramatic Change

A Beautiful Death:
Keeping the Promise of Love

A Beautiful Grief:
Reflections on Letting Go

The LIGHT Process:
Living on the Razor's Edge of Change

Poetry: For Inspiration & Beauty

Poetics of Soul & Fire

Bridge to the Otherworld

Idylls from the Garden
of Spiritual Delights & Healing

Sparks of Celtic Mystery:
soul poems from Éire

A Beautiful Joy:
Reunion with the Beloved
Through Transfiguring Love

Fiction: For the Love of Twin Flames

The Weaving: A Novel
of Twin Flames Through Time

Twin Flames of Éire Trilogy
The Ancients and The Call
The Water and The Flame
The Mystics and The Mystery

The Weaving

A Novel of Twin Flames Through Time

CHERYL LAFFERTY ECKL

Revised Edition

FLYING CRANE PRESS

To twin flames
everywhere in time & space
and beyond

THE WEAVING: A NOVEL OF TWIN FLAMES THROUGH TIME
Copyright © 2018, 2020 by Cheryl Eckl | Cheryl Lafferty Eckl.
All poems and epigraphs are © 2015-2018
All rights reserved. Flying Crane Press, Livingston, Montana 59047
Cheryl@CherylEckl.com | www.CherylLaffertyEckl.com

Library of Congress Control Number: 2020907882
ISBN: 978-1-7346450-4-0 (paperback)
ISBN: 978-1-7346450-5-7 (e-book)

Author's adaptation of "Amairgen's Hymn" taken from multiple translations of
Lebar Gabála Érenn (*The Book of Invasions*).

Excerpt from *The Ancients and The Call: Twin Flames of Éire Trilogy - Book One*
Copyright © 2020 by Cheryl Eckl | Cheryl Lafferty Eckl

Cover and interior design: James Bennett
Publishing support: Theresa McNicholas and Paula Kennedy Kehoe
Author photo: Larry Stanley

Printed in the United States of America

Dear Reader,

The calling of a novelist is to write what her characters inspire. I wrote *The Weaving* because I was prompted to tell the story of why the path of reunion for Sarah and Kevin, who are twin flames, demands all of their depth, all of their strength, and all of their selflessness.

And why, despite having a deep inner knowing that their souls were created in the beginning as two in one—the great T'ai Chi of masculine and feminine—in lifetime after lifetime, they have experienced enormous difficulties in remaining together.

On occasion, they have even pursued separate paths.

They promised they would always return to each other. But, like many other twin flames, they have not succeeded as they intended. In fact, the consequences of their choices may have been more effective at keeping them apart than in bringing them back together.

And, circumstances have a way of changing people, even those for whom love-at-first-sight is a reality. Such is the case with Sarah and Kevin. When we meet these two lovers in modern-day New York City, life—and their response to it—has challenged them to the core of their beings, as individuals and as a couple.

I hope you will find reading their story as compelling as I did writing it. Following the journey of these two souls took me to places and events I never could have imagined—including to ancient civilizations where many seeds of their present difficulties were sown.

For that experience, I credit the magic of Ireland, which sparked *The Weaving*—the story of twin flames Sarah and Kevin through time. Their path is arduous because staying together will mean rekindling the spiritual fire of union that was theirs in the beginning, regardless of any obstacles that might oppose them.

I invite you to come with me now to discover if this lifetime will be the one in which they finally overcome those obstacles.

Cheryl Lafferty Eckl

P. S. To help guide you through Sarah and Kevin's past-life adventures, I have included a Glossary and Pronunciation Guide on pages xi-xii.

CONTENTS

PART ONE
Time Will Tell

PART TWO
Reaching for the Sun

PART THREE
Journey into Mystery

PART FOUR
Putting Down Roots

Glossary & Pronunciation Guide

Names	Pronunciation	Meaning
Ah-Lahn*	ah-LAHN	*Var.* Alan, noble, rock
Alana	ah-LAN-uh	Dear child
Amairgen	A-mer-geen	One of wonderful birth
Arán Bán*	rahn bahn	White bread
Bleddyn	BLEHTH-in	Wolf (W)
Brigantes	bri-GAN-tez	Pre-Roman Celtic tribe
Carwyn	KAHR-oo-in	Fair, blessed (W)
Casidhe	KAH-seeh	Clever
Cróga	KRO-guh	Brave, hardy
Dearbhla	DAR-vla	Daughter of the poet
Eog Bach	AY-og bachk	Little salmon (W)
Enfys	EN-viss	Rainbow (W)
Fflur	FfLEER	Flower (W)
Gareth	GEHR-eth	Gentle, watchful (W)
Gormlaith	GOORM-luh	Blue princess
Gréagóir	GRAY-uh-gor	Watchful
Huw	HUE	Lullaby, drowsiness
Joha-lihn*	jo-ah-LIN	Atlantean priest
Khieranan*	KEER-uh-nahn	Atlantean priest
Laoch	LAY-ochk	Hero
Lile	Leel	Lily
Madwyn	MAHD-oo-en	Forthright, practical (W)
Naimh	NEE-av	Luster, sheen
Nhada-lihn*	nah-dah-LIN	Ascended Lady Master
Óengus	O-en-gus	Singular strength
Riordan	REER-duhn	Royal poet
Seanait	SHA-net	*Var. seig*, hawk
Sorchae	SUH-ruh-ka	Bright, radiant
Tadhgan	TIE-guhn	*Var. Tadhg*, bard, poet
Treylah*	TRAY-luh	Atlantean priestess
Una	OO-nuh	*Var. uan*, lamb

Where possible, spellings are Old Irish. Names with * are the author's invention.
Letters *ch* (written phonetically as *chk*) are pronounced as in *loch*.
(W) following the meaning denotes names that are Welsh in origin.

Place Names	Pronunciation	Meaning
Afon Menai	AV-ron MEN-ay	Menai Strait
Albion	AL-bee-on	Island of Britannia
An Bhearú	un VA-roo	The River Barrow
An tSiúir	un TOOR	The River Suir
Buaicphointe	boik-FWEE-tuh	High point
Cois Abhann	cush OW-enn	Riverside (túath)
Éire	AY-(r)	Ireland
Muir Éireann	moyr AY-(r)enn	Irish Sea
Tearmann	TAR-a-mun	Place of refuge (túath)
Ynys Môn	en-nis MOHN	Anglesey Island (W)

Terms	Pronunciation	Meaning
A chara, mo chara	uh CHKAR-uh	O friend, my friend
An Síoraí	un SHEE-uh-ree	The Eternal One
Ard-Druí	ard DREE	Archdruid
Ard mháistir	ard WOHSH-ti(d)	Grandmaster
Bandruí,	bahn-DREE	Druidess
pl. Bandruíthe	bahn-DREE-hyeh	Druidesses
Banfháidh	bahn-OYG	Female seer, healer
Bealtaine (festival)	bee-YOWL-tin-uh	May 1, Bright Fire
Beannacht	BAN-acht	Blessing
Ceann-Druí	KYAHN-dree	Chief Druid
Currach	KER-uchk	Traditional boat
Druí, pl. Druíthe	dree, DREE-hyeh	Druid(s)
Fáidh, pl. Fáidthe	foyg, FOY-hyeh	Seer(s), shaman, healer
Féath Fíadha	fay FEE-a-duh	Mists of invisibility
Imbolc (festival)	IM-bolk	Feb. 1, Ewe's Milk, Brigid
Lughnasa (festival)	LOO-nuh-suh	Aug. 1, Harvest, Lugh
Mo chroí	mu CHKREE	My heart
Mo mhuirnín	mu WOOR-neen	My darling
Ollamh	AH-luv	Master poet
Samhain (festival)	SOW-in	Nov. 1, New Year
Seanchaí	SHAN-chkee	Storyteller
pl. Seanchaithe	SHAN-chkee-hyeh	Storytellers
Toísech	TEE-shuchk	Chieftain
Túath, pl. Tuatha	TOO-uh, TOO-ah-huh	A territory, its people

PART ONE

Time Will Tell

Your ancient calling beckons,
the voyage has begun.

A Matter of Appearances

Sarah relished the sound her high heels made as she briskly crossed the marble-tiled lobby of the high-rise office building where she worked. She liked to imagine their click-click, click-click announcing to the world that here was a person of consequence.

Even today, when she had on her casual slacks and simple linen blouse, she wore high heels. Wearing these shoes boosted her self-assurance as well as her height.

You've arrived, Sarah, she told herself, pushing out of her mind the reason she had gone after this job as a communications writer for a prominent politician. She made her way through security screening and hurried into the elevator that let her out on the thirty-third floor.

As she swiped her key card and pulled open the heavy glass door to the reception area, Sarah looked around with pride at where she had landed not quite a year ago. Every piece of custom-made furniture and carefully selected artwork spoke of influence and power.

"Nothing but the best for A. B. Ryan." Sarah said aloud, repeating her boss's mantra that applied to everything and everyone within his purview. Visitors waiting for an audience with A. B. would be aware that, once admitted through the dark walnut doors that led to his domain, they would be facing a formidable person.

Sarah loved being part of this world. She worked hard and had even received a few compliments from A. B. himself—although she wasn't certain if he was commenting on her work or her figure. He was that kind of man.

Nevertheless, she was thriving on the fast pace demanded of A. B.'s staff. The constant whirlwind of producing timely press releases, fund-raising mailers, and frequent letters to his constituents was a tonic to Sarah. She was learning more about current events and political influence than she ever could have imagined. Witnessing the flow of important people in and out of the office was thrilling.

And, she had to admit—like her co-workers who were chatting over their morning coffee more casually than usual—she was glad that today would be less stressful than most.

As of yesterday, A. B. was out of the country for a month-long international tour. To everyone's relief, he had taken his haughty assistant with him, so the remaining staff could get caught up without the boss issuing new directives.

The good news is: I'm not late today, Sarah congratulated herself. For the past week she had been having trouble getting to work on time.

A few of her fellow writers were already in and waved or nodded as she walked by. No matter what happened in the office, this was a team that had each other's backs, and Sarah was delighted to be part of it.

Each writer had an office with a door that could be closed for privacy and a full expanse of windows that looked out on the city. The interior glass walls that instantly showed who was at their desk also let in natural light that made the central collaboration area a pleasure to work in.

Sarah entered her own office and admired its designer furnishings. One thing you have to say about A. B., she commented to herself, he doesn't mind spending money to create a professional physical environment—even if his detractors do say he runs an "up-tight" ship.

She stowed her purse in a desk drawer and went to the employee break area where she planned to make herself a latte on the restaurant-grade espresso machine—one of the many perks of working for A. B.

Debbie, who assisted the communications team, was there wrapping up a discussion about mailing deadlines with the team's senior writers, Gwen and Tony.

As those two rushed off to take an unexpected call from A. B., who was phoning from Dubai, Sarah asked, "Debbie, do you have a minute to stop by my office?"

"Sure, I can come now. Bring your latte. I'll drop this off and be right there," Debbie answered, gesturing with the pot of specially-blended tea she kept at her desk.

Sarah smiled as she walked next to the efficient young woman who was becoming a close personal friend. She was intrigued by Debbie's long blonde hair that she wore down and straight or, like today, tied up in an intricate knot. Her manner of dress tended toward the artistic in an effortlessly colorful style that Sarah tried not to envy.

"What's up?" Debbie asked cheerfully as she entered Sarah's office. She closed the door and took a seat across from her friend.

Sarah went straight to the point she had been mulling for several days. "Have you ever had an animal repeatedly show up in your dreams, acting like it's trying to tell you something?"

"You mean like an animal spirit guide?"

"Is that a real thing?" asked Sarah.

"Uh-huh." Debbie grinned and nodded.

Sarah's face brightened. "Then I suppose you won't find this strange. A few weeks ago, I started dreaming about a huge female cat. I know she's female because there's a mothering presence about her, even when she's far off in the distance. She sort of glides in and out of the foliage that's part of the atmosphere in these dreams.

"Lately, I've heard her making this deep, purring sound. And last night she was rubbing against my legs and nudging me toward something. When I woke up this morning, I could still feel her pressing against me. What do you think this means?"

"What color is she? Does she have any markings? Describe everything you see when she appears," Debbie asked with the intensity of a sleuth.

Sarah closed her eyes for moment. A clear image came quickly into focus. "She's completely black with a silky coat that ripples like waves when she moves. She stands about thigh-high on me. She's very powerful, but she's not frightening.

"Or at least she's not frightening now," Sarah admitted. "The first time I saw her, I woke up feeling shaky. Now that I'm more accustomed to her appearing, I can tell she's quite benign where I'm concerned.

"The thing is, she's becoming more insistent, as if she's trying to get me to recognize something. Do you have any idea why she keeps coming to me?"

Debbie thought for a minute, remembering one of her own dreams.

"I believe your spirit guide is a panther. When a panther appeared to me years ago, the meaning I found at the time was:

> Embrace life's mystery.
> Flow with the unknown.
> Don't worry about the future.

"From what you've told me, I believe your panther wants you to flow with a mystery that's unfolding in your life. Does that make sense?"

"Yes, I suppose so, although I've never thought of myself as someone who would have an animal spirit guide," Sarah said, then chuckled. "I can't quite imagine myself strolling around the Upper East Side with a panther on a leash."

"Probably not the best idea," agreed Debbie with a grin.

"Well, you've certainly eased my mind," said Sarah as the two young women stood together.

"Let me know if you have any other questions," Debbie offered. "I'm very comfortable with the idea of animal spirit guides. Ask me anything."

"I'm going for a walk. I'll grab a bite to eat while I'm out," Sarah called to Debbie at lunchtime. "See you later."

"Okay, have a good think." Debbie knew she had given her friend lots to consider.

Sarah did not have to plan where she was going. Her feet knew the way to her favorite spot in Central Park, although she hadn't been there in months since—well, since the losses she did not want to think about today. As soon as she arrived, she kicked off her high heels, sat down on a shady patch of grass and leaned against a very old oak tree.

Debbie had said that a panther could portend a mystery, but she had offered no clues as to what that might be. Sarah's mind was brimming with questions.

What mystery was she supposed to embrace? What unknown was calling her into its flow? What destiny had she yet to discover?

"I'm sure you know the answer," Sarah said aloud to the big tree she was leaning on as she looked up through its leafy branches that spread out like loving arms. The oak did not feel compelled to respond. This was familiar territory for both of them.

Listening for the unique wisdom of trees was something Sarah had done since childhood, though she could never quite seem to retain their messages that tended to fly out of her mind like autumn leaves blowing in the wind.

She stood up and put her arms around the tree's thick trunk. Letting out a deep sigh, she rested her cheek on the rough, weathered bark. She inhaled the oak's familiar woody scent and listened. It seemed to say:

Remember your love.
Think of Kevin and discover what is true.

Kindred Spirits

*A*h, Kevin. Sarah's thoughts turned to her husband. Life had seemed crystal-clear when they were first together. There had been no need for stressing over destinies in those days.

Their relationship had been all about being together in the present moment, Sarah reminded herself, as she sat back down under her oak tree, absorbing its strength into her back. She stretched out her legs and wiggled her toes, sighing into the firm foundation of earth beneath her.

She caught the scent of wild roses that trailed along the rustic fence ringing this secluded spot. Inhaling deeply, she smiled as a soft breeze played with her unruly auburn hair that had gone curly in midsummer's humidity.

At last, infused with Nature's relaxing sensations, Sarah let the memory of her early days with Kevin carry her back in time—and was surprised at the unbidden tears that sprang into her eyes when she recalled the deep caring that had sparked between the two of them on their very first meeting.

Seven years earlier, Sarah's editor friend, Gillian, had invited her to the annual gathering of colleagues from the major book publishing firm where Gillian worked. The event was being held at a recently restored, hundred-year-old mansion located on Riverside Drive overlooking the Hudson River.

"If you show up, I'll introduce you to a couple of the acquisition editors who'll be there. You can pitch them your book idea," Gillian had enthused. "I know you don't like parties, but this one could be a life-changing opportunity for you. At least come to see the house and try the food."

Sarah was almost sorry she had mentioned that she was working on a book. She wasn't ready to tell anyone about the ideas that were just beginning to take hold in her imagination.

And Gillian was wrong about her and parties. She enjoyed socializing with people she knew. Crowds of people she *didn't* know were what made her nervous. In this case, she really wanted to see the mansion, and she knew the gourmet hors d'oeuvres would be fabulous.

Convincing herself at last, Sarah put on her silky green party dress and took a chance. And, just in case she did meet someone to tell about her book, she tucked her journal into her purse.

Might as well be prepared, she assured herself as she headed for her neighborhood Metro station.

On the way, she decided to get off the subway one stop early so she could treat herself to a short stroll through Riverside Park before braving the party. The hour would be late enough that she would miss the warm glow of October's golden tree tops, but walking in the crisp night air would be invigorating.

Sarah knew she had reached her destination when she approached a stately, five-story limestone and brick Beaux Arts townhouse. Every window was aglow with light from the festivities going on inside. As she walked up two steps from the street, the butterflies in her stomach calmed slightly when the beauty of scrolled stone corbels and wrought-iron balconies above the front entrance caught her attention.

"Why, thank you," she said with great dignity when a uniformed doorman opened the etched-glass doors and ushered her into an exquisite, rose-colored marble lobby. He nodded and replied with fluid ease, "Mademoiselle is most welcome. Please proceed upstairs."

Once inside, Sarah stood a moment, taking in the sumptuous scene. She could easily imagine elegant ladies dressed in their fine lace and satin gowns, their trains flowing gracefully behind them as handsome gentlemen in white tie and tails escorted them up the sweeping central staircase. They would have spoken in refined tones as they reached the second floor that opened into a series of spacious rooms.

No doubt, they would have nodded approvingly at the expensive furnishings—the dark woods, rich velvets, heavy brocades, and decorative moldings that were to be expected in all the best houses. And they would have paid particular attention to the imported Persian carpets that covered the hardwood floors of every room.

Clearly, I was born in the wrong era, Sarah thought. She sighed as she ascended the stairs—unaccompanied—and looked around.

As she had feared, the place was wall-to-wall strangers, except for Gillian. Sarah spotted her in the central reception room's far corner, ensconced in a lively discussion with several smartly dressed men and women. Gillian waved, but showed no sign of introducing her friends.

I told you I wasn't good at parties, Sarah grumbled to herself, though she had to admit the food was worth the discomfort of facing a crowd. The savory canapés awakened taste buds she didn't know she possessed. The expensive Pinot Grigio she chose was sublimely zesty and light.

After eating alone with barely a word of greeting from the clusters of guests who were obviously well-acquainted with each other, Sarah decided she was too old to be a wallflower.

Gillian had told her the house was a must-see. Surely there's no harm in exploring, Sarah thought as she turned down a hallway with a lush, maroon and gold wool carpet running the entire length.

She immediately kicked off her high heels to experience the deep pile beneath her feet. Shoes in hand, she gingerly opened an intricately carved wooden door at the hallway's end and stepped into a book lover's paradise.

The library took her breath away. "Oh!" Sarah exclaimed as she ran her fingers over delicately grained mahogany paneling. The wood felt steeped in history, aged in the smoke of ancient fires that had crackled in the green-tiled fireplace where cheery flames now danced as if recently lit.

The sight of expensive, leather-bound books drew Sarah's eye up and down the floor-to-ceiling bookshelves that held what appeared to be centuries of well-cared-for classics and an equal number of modern works. There was even a rolling ladder for reaching the gilded volumes nearest the top. Sarah could hardly resist clamoring up that ladder to check out those lofty treasures.

The chocolate-brown leather sofas begged to be touched—which she did while checking over her shoulder to make sure a white-gloved butler did not step out of a corner to scold her. She had never felt leather that was this perfectly soft. Someone had taken great pains to keep the upholstery well conditioned and supple.

Sarah wanted to curl up on one of those sofas. She almost did, until she spotted two, red-velvet wingback chairs that all but spoke their invitation for her to laze before the fire in the warm glow of Tiffany lamps and read a bit of Jane Austen.

The room was Sarah's fantasy library come to life.

After long minutes of indecision, she finally selected a couple of newly published hardbound volumes and crossed to one of the velvet chairs. Rounding its tall corner, she suddenly leapt back with a cry of surprise and dropped the shoes she still carried.

She was not alone. Occupying the other chair was a man in his late twenties. He wore his dark wavy hair long enough to touch the top of his royal blue cashmere turtleneck. The soft sweater fit snugly, outlining broad shoulders and muscular arms.

His mustache was full, yet well trimmed—his smile instantly friendly. She looked into his blue-green eyes and imagined falling into two deep pools.

He had been watching her from behind his chair's conveniently placed wing. Intriguing, he thought, observing her apparent guilty pleasure as her delicate fingers explored the library's luxurious furnishings.

At first, she had stood with her back to him—a view he found quite appealing. Her long auburn hair glistened in the firelight, reflecting hints of red and gold.

Her appearance suggested an affinity for color and texture. Dangling rhinestone earrings flashed tiny rainbows as she moved about the room. When she stretched up to reach some books on shelves above her medium height, her emerald green dress flowed easily with her, showing off a pair of trim legs and a compact feminine form.

When she turned around, he was not disappointed. Youth and vitality sprang from her rosy cheeks and expressive mouth that ooh'd and aah'd over each new discovery.

He had stifled a laugh when she turned a circle and gazed blissfully around the library. She was hugging an armful of books and breathing in deeply as if she were trying to inhale every single word of wit and wisdom that filled the room.

Here is a kindred spirit, he thought. Anyone who appreciates good books that much was someone he'd like to know.

"Hi. Sorry to scare you," he said easily as she eyed him warily. "Are you hiding from someone?"

"Everyone, I guess," she admitted, feeling the color rise in her cheeks. "I'm not very good at meeting lots of new people."

"Neither am I. My girlfriend dragged me here, but then she left. Apparently, I wasn't the date she had in mind. She texted a while ago to say she had run into an old friend and was leaving with him. I could go home if I wanted. I guess that makes her my former girlfriend."

He smiled ruefully. "By the time I noticed her text, I was comfortable here. I decided to stoke the fire and stay a while. Care to join me? My name is Kevin."

"Sarah," she said, shaking his extended hand. His grip was warm and confident and vaguely familiar. "Thanks, I will," she added, sinking into the chair that wrapped cozily around her.

"What are you reading?" Kevin asked as naturally as if they had been friends for years.

"Actually, I'm not sure." Sarah glanced at the volumes she had managed not to drop when he surprised her. "I'm working on a novel and I wanted to see what other people are writing. These books looked like a good place to start."

"Are you an author?" Kevin inquired.

"I write for my boss, but I haven't published anything of my own. The novel is just a hobby. What about you?"

"I work for an accounting firm, and I write a little for fun. That's what I was doing when you came in. There is something about being surrounded by all these classics that inspires me." Kevin looked around the room with an appreciative smile.

"Would you read me something you've written?" Sarah ventured. "I'm always curious about how other writers use language."

"Okay, but first I want to hear about your book."

Sarah was surprised. She had not expected him to be interested. Since he was, she pulled out her journal. Was this conversation the reason she had brought it along?

"I've barely started, but I can read you some of my notes. Are you sure you want to hear about this? My ideas are still pretty rough."

"Rough is fine." Kevin didn't care what she said—as long as she kept talking to him.

"Okay. When the story opens, we meet a young woman named Glenna who lives in New York City. Might as well start with what I know, right?"

They both laughed. Sarah opened her journal and began to read the notes she had made about her book's main character.

Glenna has always wanted to go to Ireland, but she can't afford it. She has distant relatives there, but none that her family in the States knows well enough to arrange for her to visit. Then one day, she receives a letter from an attorney in Galway.

Sarah paused. "How about I read you the letter? It sets the stage for the story to unfold."

"Whatever you like. A trip to Ireland sounds great," Kevin beamed.

Dear Ms. Glenna Morrissey,

I am authorized by my late client, Mrs. Caroline Rooney, to send you the enclosed check for three thousand euros and a one-way plane ticket to Shannon Airport in County Clare, Ireland.

Mrs. Rooney was the wife of your father's third cousin, Seamus. The Rooneys had no children of their own and died owning few possessions. However, they had accumulated considerable savings which they willed should be divided among their distant relations, of whom you are the last to be contacted.

The only requirement is that you use the one-way plane ticket as-is. Once in Ireland, you may spend some of the euros to purchase a return ticket or you may use them all for an extended stay in our fair country.

Whether you choose to remain or return is up to you. The Rooneys lived in Dingle and would have been delighted to welcome you to their home. Perhaps you will visit the area.

Feel free to contact my office if you have any questions about this gift.

Congratulations and best wishes,

Gerald H. Breathnach, Esq.

"Interesting." Kevin drew out the word. "I can imagine Glenna having all sorts of adventures. Does she have to leave Ireland or can she find a way to stay there?"

"That's not clear yet," said Sarah, shaking her head. "The story is only now beginning to take shape. Other than a few pieces like this letter, I have lots of ideas, but that's about all. I haven't shared the concept with anyone. The story has felt too unformed to talk about except to say, 'I'm working on a book.' "

"Then I'm honored. I'd love to read your book whenever you finish it," said Kevin sincerely.

"Thanks. I'll make sure you get a signed copy."

Sarah felt herself blushing under this attractive man's very attentive gaze. She quickly put her journal back in her purse and faced him.

"Your turn. What are you going to read for me?"

"I like to experiment with different genres," Kevin began. "Mostly prose, some essays, occasionally poetry. I've also been known to compose some 'rhyme-y' lines for birthday and holiday cards.

"These days I find a conversational tone most appealing. This piece is written in that style. I was working on it when you tiptoed into my sanctuary," he said with wink. "Anyway, here goes."

I see you as you have never seen yourself. How could you not know who you are? Except we often do not recognize our True Self unless another holds up a mirror of unwavering affection.

You let me be myself—the greatest gift. For basking in your acceptance, I learn to love my frailties and the shortcomings that do not seem to trouble you.

With you I am made whole, as with me you are also healed by promises kept and ancient puzzles solved.

United in this love that dissolves separation in Eternity's timelessness, I am forever and always yours. One, one, one, one.

Sarah was touched by the beauty of Kevin's words. They flowed from him with a quiet strength she found profoundly intimate. His voice was resonant and full of feeling.

There was something familiar about listening to him, as if she had been comforted by that voice many times in the past. His recitation was creating an ethereal atmosphere. She could almost hear an Irish harp playing while he repeated, "One, one, one, one."

Kevin looked up from the page and into Sarah's hazel-green eyes. They were wide and glistening with a far-away expression, as if she were gazing into another realm of existence.

She appeared to him as if frozen in time. And then he knew: He had seen that look on the face of another auburn-haired beauty. And his heart was galloping then, too.

Kevin pulled his mind back to the library. "Did you like the piece?" he said quietly.

"Your reading was a beautiful meditation that made me feel that I have known you for a very long time," Sarah said dreamily. Then she added with a nervous laugh, "And I don't know why I said that."

"I know why. I feel the same." Kevin spoke with a certainty that surprised him, considering his girlfriend had dumped him earlier that evening. Smiling, he said, "Maybe I was writing those lines for you."

Minutes slipped into timelessness as Kevin and Sarah talked non-stop for the next few hours, comparing likes and dislikes, discovering they both had Irish roots and marveling at the happy coincidence that had brought them to a party which neither had been eager to attend.

At two in the morning, the cleaning crew discovered them in the library and asked them to leave. Not in the least offended, they gathered up their belongings and called out a giddy, "Goodnight!"

Hand in hand, they practically floated away into the chilly autumn air. Though neither spoke the words aloud, each silently vowed to stay with the other until the end of their days.

Early Days

After that night in the library, Sarah and Kevin were inseparable. The more time they spent in each other's company, the more certain they were of having been together many times in past lives.

"When you know, you know" was the only explanation they could offer to skeptical friends and family members who were astonished when they immediately got engaged to be married.

"Are you sure you know what you're doing? You hardly know Kevin." Sarah's mother had questioned her daughter vigorously while they were shopping for bridal gowns.

"I believe we have been working on this wedding for centuries," Sarah had answered without reservation. "I know Kevin's soul as well as I know my own."

The wedding had taken place in a fortnight, and thus began the happy task of the couple creating their life together.

For Sarah, life with Kevin included learning to appreciate the many sports he enjoyed, in part because he had played most of them in high school and college.

"What events do you like to watch?" he asked on the evening they became engaged.

"Not many," Sarah admitted. "Although I enjoy the Olympics and I do like NFL football—but only on television in a warm living room. No cold stadiums."

"That's good," Kevin readily agreed. "I've played plenty of football in cold stadiums. These days I want my feet up with warm slippers."

Sarah was delighted to learn that Kevin enjoyed movies, theatre, live music, and eating in restaurants as much as she did. Though, sadly, he balked at opera, ballet, and sushi.

"Well, nobody's perfect," she'd kidded him.

Actually, Sarah believed she had married the perfect man. Whenever she and Kevin embraced, she could feel the strength of him that made her think of safe harbor from life's storms. He was amazingly at ease in his own skin, which made her hope that one day she might learn how to be comfortable in hers.

Married to Kevin, Sarah also had somebody to be silly with. Like the time they spent an hour snickering behind fake trees and tall dressers to avoid a furniture salesman who insisted on following them around the store where they were just browsing. Sarah loved that her husband told her jokes, and he loved that she laughed at them.

For Kevin, his marriage to Sarah meant he had found the partner he had longed for since he was a teenager. His love for her was astonishingly deep. He frequently found himself overcome by the sheer immensity of joy that welled up in his heart and left him wondering how to express such enormous emotion.

Giving voice to his passion in daily conversation was beyond his skill as a naturally quiet man. Writing he could do. So he composed verses for his wife and wrote her notes and cards, hoping she could feel how much she meant to him.

In the depths of her soul, Sarah did feel his meaning. Her favorite of his compositions was a rhyme he wrote her on Mother's Day, the first time she conceived the child they were trying for.

Sadly, the pregnancy did not last. Happily, the poem did. Sarah kept it as one of her most precious possessions.

As I sit here by the hours,
At my window cold and gray,
Should I buy her pretty flowers?
What to do on Mother's Day?

Make her happy on the morrow
In the dreary month of May.
August weather we would borrow,
That would surely help us play.

So with joy I give you flowers
From my heart, and I will pray:
In angels' care and in their bower,
Keep us on this Mother's Day.

You are my once-in-a-lifetime love. —*Kevin*

With Sarah as his wife, Kevin was no longer alone, which was a blessing he had never expected. For as long as he could remember, he had thought of himself as a solitary wanderer.

In his youth, part of that wandering had made him an avid outdoors man. Sarah was not much of a naturalist, but she was game to try. Camping in a small, unspoiled forest in Western Massachusetts gave her an entirely new experience of Nature's quiet beauty.

She found exploring the Catskills in the warmth of autumn's rich golden leaves and crystal blue skies thoroughly invigorating. Unfortunately, and much to Kevin's chagrin, hiking a portion of the Appalachian Trail in late April turned out to be a very short walk in very deep snow.

Urban excursions to visit Kevin's family in Poughkeepsie and Sarah's in the Boston area were among their favorite holiday outings. Extended road trips by car were the best. With no other travelers to interrupt their conversations or peaceful silences, they cocooned in the unified presence that was their greatest joy.

On weekends, Kevin focused on creating the handmade cabinetry he had designed for the home they were remodeling. He was surprised when Sarah resisted some of his initial ideas.

"Why can't you trust me?" Kevin asked her after a rather heated discussion about his plans for the kitchen.

"I don't know," she answered, as bewildered as he. "I want to trust you, but for some reason my first impulse is to object. I'm sorry. I guess I'm not able to visualize what you describe. Or I'm afraid something won't turn out right."

"Don't worry, I'll start small," he reassured her. "I know what I'm doing, Sarah. You'll see."

And after the first project, she did see. Everything Kevin built was beautiful, sturdy, and functional.

As her husband was creating their dream home, Sarah discovered an unexpected pleasure in cooking and taking care of domestic chores. She enjoyed being a wife and hoped to one day be a mother. Her career remained important to her. And yet, as time went by, Kevin became more and more the center of her universe. She was surprised to notice how happy that made her.

She also appreciated his spiritual nature, which sparked her own. He did not reveal his inclination toward the mystical to just anyone, yet he seemed intent on sharing this very personal side of himself with her. They soon began to rely on the deep conversations that emerged from this connection as the essence of their relationship.

Little did they know how seriously they would need that bond in years to come.

Flying Solo

Kevin had measured the same board three times and still could not bring himself to put blade to wood and make the cut. His mind kept wandering and that bugged him—a lot.

Woodworking usually calmed him. Creating something tangible with his hands helped relieve the mental tension of his nine-to-five job. Although the regularity of a forty-hour workweek suited him, he was sometimes desperate for a break from other people's needs and opinions. His building projects usually provided that respite.

Not today.

Kevin stood still—his eyes not registering the array of tools and woodworking equipment that surrounded him in his shop. He was thinking about his marriage.

He knew that two miscarriages had taken a toll on Sarah. After the second one, over a year ago, a sadness that he could not fathom had clung to her. He hoped she would eventually come out of it.

He wanted a family as much as Sarah, and he was also mourning the loss of their babies. After the first miscarriage, they had been able to comfort each other. However, after the second, Sarah had closed herself off and was no longer willing to talk about it.

Kevin honestly did not know how to support her in her grief—if grief was the only problem. He was beginning to think that Sarah was dealing with more complicated issues than even she knew.

Nowadays, she seemed to need constant reassurance and outward expressions of love that, frankly, seemed fearful or desperate. When she was like that, he found himself wanting to retreat.

Clearly, something else was going on with his wife, and he was at a loss as to how to unravel that mystery.

Kevin woke with a start. He had been dreaming that he and Sarah were in the mountains in winter. They were each on their own bobsled, careening down a wide, icy slope toward a divided path that led to permanent separation. He shouted for her to take his hand, but she turned and slid away from him as if he did not exist.

Wide awake now, Kevin ran his hand through his hair and tried to clear his head. Cautiously, he stood on legs gone weak and padded quietly into the kitchen, wracking his brain. Why would Sarah not come to him as she used to, either in a dream or real life?

Maybe he'd never understood her, he thought as he stood leaning against the counter, drinking a glass of water. And maybe she didn't understand him either. Why didn't she seem to appreciate how hard he worked and how tired he was at the end of the day? He probably should have told her.

His job in a mid-sized accounting firm was becoming frustrating. His fellow employees were pleasant enough, but they were generally resistant to process improvements he considered essential. Many were grateful for the help he gave them, yet they were not willing to change the habits that had caused their problems in the first place.

But he wasn't a complainer. Grumbling about his co-workers would show a lack of character.

Of course, Sarah also worked, and she seemed energized by her job. After the second miscarriage, she had thrown herself into a whole new career. These days she came home eager to talk about politics and activist issues she had never been interested in before.

Kevin found those conversations tiring, though not because of the topics. The sarcastic tone Sarah had picked up from her boss was distasteful to him and unlike the woman he had married.

Despite those differences, he continued to look forward to Sunday mornings when they read inspirational books together or listened to uplifting music. Their philosophical discussions went deep and created a connection he cherished.

Does Sarah still feel the same? he wondered. The possibility that she didn't sent a wave of nausea rolling through his stomach.

Early in their marriage, these Sunday mornings had reinforced their belief that their souls were two halves of the same whole—"twin flames" as some people called the relationship. Kevin was beginning to question if that belief were true.

Recently, Sarah hadn't been in tune with him or the material they were sharing. She often seemed in a hurry. Last Sunday, when he had posed a philosophical question he wanted to discuss, she had given him a perfunctory answer that made him sorry he'd raised the subject.

"Are we finished for this morning?" she'd asked. Not waiting for Kevin to answer, she had popped up from her easy chair after barely an hour. "I need to get ready for tomorrow's big meeting, which I assume you're not interested in hearing about."

"Not really," he'd answered quietly as she turned away. "I'd thought we might go for a drive this afternoon. But if you're going to be working, I'm going to watch the Yankees game. I'll be in my shop until it starts."

What if we are about finished? Kevin asked himself, closing the door harder than he meant to. He didn't see Sarah turn at the sound and follow him with saddened eyes. On opposite sides of the barrier that divided them, they were thinking the same thing:

How could we have come to this? We loved each other instantly. Now we're sniping, snapping, not connecting, with no idea of how to mend the barrenness that's spreading where real tenderness once bloomed.

In their own ways, Kevin and Sarah were skilled communicators, but they were woefully inept when a difficult conversation was needed. So they maintained a brittle silence until their failure to understand one another came to a head.

For Sarah, the final exasperation took place the following Saturday. She was putting away leftovers in the kitchen after lunch. Kevin was getting a bottle of water from the refrigerator before he went out to his workshop.

Because they had actually had an engaging conversation about politics during their meal, Sarah happily threw her arms around her husband. He started to hug her back, then, with a sigh, let his arms fall to his side.

"What's wrong with you?" she demanded.

"I can't do this, Sarah," Kevin said.

"You can't do what? Hug me when I show you genuine affection?" she retorted, feeling the anger she had been holding in for weeks start to get the better of her.

"No, I can't pretend to know who I'm hugging. I don't recognize you, Sarah. You've changed since you took that job in the city. Your clothes are different. You wear those spiky heels all the time. I'm pretty sure you're not running for office, but you're beginning to sound like a politician."

"I am not," she said defiantly.

"Let me finish. I've needed to say this for a long time. You get worked up about other people's causes, but you seem to have forgotten the cause you vowed to honor above all others—us.

"Worst of all, you're shorting our Sunday mornings together, which is about all we have since you don't get home in time for dinner at least three nights a week. I feel like I can't talk to you."

"Well, you don't want to talk to me." Sarah was losing the battle with the resentment she had hidden from them both.

"I would if you didn't talk *at* me," said Kevin, feeling his frustration rise. "Listening to you repeat slogans or other people's opinions is not my idea of conversation. I don't know what you've done with the woman I married, but I wish you'd bring her back."

"You're just jealous because I'm working for important people while you spend your days juggling numbers for people who don't appreciate you," Sarah was practically shouting.

Kevin's eyes narrowed. He fixed her with a steely gaze and said with a cold control that stunned her, "If that's what you think, Sarah, you don't know me at all."

She forced herself to look at him. "And I feel like you don't want to know me. I'm finally doing work that makes me feel smart, admired, competent."

"You don't need a fancy job for that," he said quietly. "You're all those things and more."

"You've never told me that."

"Well, I'm telling you now."

"You're too late." Sarah fled upstairs to her home office before the hot tears that were brewing behind her eyes betrayed her.

Kevin turned and strode out the front door. He meant to slam it this time. If he had grabbed his bike, he would have ridden twenty miles to burn off the agony that gripped his heart like a vice. Instead, he walked the few blocks from their house to the beach. There he sat, surrounded by happy families frolicking in the waves, and pondered what to do.

We're not two ships passing in the night, he thought as he watched the afternoon tide roll in. We're not even sailing on the same ocean.

He didn't feel he could ask Sarah to quit her job. Would he do the same for her if she asked? Maybe. Maybe not. Sometimes the future just had to be lived to be known. He guessed that's the way life was now for him and his wife. All he could do is let things run their course.

An hour later, Kevin walked home. He was still exhausted from the fierce emotions that had whipped through him, but at least he was calm.

When he came back into the house and turned on the baseball game he had told Sarah he was going to watch, he could hear her stomping around upstairs. He hoped she would calm down by bedtime.

But Sarah didn't calm down. This was the last straw. Could Kevin really be so clueless? Couldn't he see that she was desperately unhappy? She had to do something—and fast.

Half an hour after she heard him open and close the front door, she marched downstairs, strode over to his chair, grabbed the remote that was lying on the side table, and switched off the television right in the middle of what was promising to be a spectacular triple play.

"What the hell are you doing?" he demanded, making a grab for the remote as she jerked it up over her head.

"I'm leaving," she declared.

"What?" He couldn't believe his ears.

"I said, 'I'm leaving,' " she repeated as she slapped the remote back on the side table.

"For good?" Kevin suddenly remembered his icy dream.

"No. For two weeks, maybe three. I've been wanting to resurrect my book, which has been moldering for too long in a box of notes. My boss will be gone for nearly a month, so this seems like a good time to get away.

"I went online and grabbed the last spot on a tour of Ireland for writers. My flight to Dublin leaves next Thursday. And don't worry, Kevin, I'm not asking you to go with me. I know you don't like to fly across oceans."

"Thanks, I guess," he answered. Sarah was right that he didn't like flying over large bodies of water, but he figured that was not her reason for leaving him out of her plans.

"Have a nice time," he offered, doing his best to be conciliatory.

"I intend to," she said in a sarcastic tone she immediately regretted. "We both need some space. I'm seeing that we get it."

Without giving her husband an opportunity to respond, she turned and tromped back upstairs to the bedroom she knew they would not be sharing any time soon. That night Sarah cried herself to sleep in their bed, and Kevin slept fitfully on the sofa in the living room.

He had dared not ask if she planned to come back. If he had any hope of their staying married, he knew he couldn't stand in the way of his wife's going on this trip. The thought that she might not return was tearing him apart.

Less than a week later, Sarah was off to Ireland and glad to be on her own. If she didn't gain some perspective on herself and her marriage, she was going to lose her mind or leave Kevin for good. She couldn't bear the thought of doing either.

The Call

Sarah sighed and nestled into her comfy, business class seat. The upgrade had wiped out her frequent flyer miles, but the expense was worth it.

Knowing she would arrive rested instead of wrung-out from no sleep was important. She would be meeting other writers, many of whom were probably very accomplished. She wanted to make a good impression.

She quickly donned an eye mask to avoid being distracted by the action movie flashing on the seat-back screens all around her.

The better to dream about home, she thought. For landing anywhere in the British Isles—as she had done on a couple of London business trips for her previous job—had always felt like coming home to a land that some deep part of herself knew very well.

Ireland was still the most compelling destination. Probably because her father's family had originally hailed from County Clare. And because of the experiences she had shared there with her parents and younger brother.

Their family of four had traveled together as a high school graduation present for Sarah and as a chance for all of them to connect with their Irish heritage. The luminous green of the Emerald Isle, the dramatic sites like the Cliffs of Moher and The Burren, and the generous hospitality of Ireland's people had deeply touched all of them.

The only cloud for Sarah—which she had never mentioned to her family—was the inexplicable sadness she had felt when their plane first landed in Ireland. At the time the sensation had made no sense to her, and it had passed nearly as quickly as it had come. But now that she was once more on her way to this land that held an almost mystical fascination for her, she wondered:

What was that sensation she'd felt ten years ago? Would she feel it again when she landed this time? She had no way of knowing.

As her thoughts drifted back to the present and the anticipation of new experiences, she suddenly perked up. She could hear a chorus of voices intoning the word "home," as if calling her to a place or time she ought to remember.

The sound was definitely not coming from anyone's movie replay. Those passengers were all wearing headphones. Rather, the chorus seemed like a far-off whisper that was emanating from the midnight stillness outside the plane. At first, the sound was soft as a whisper, and then grew more distinct and insistent.

"Come home, *mo mhuirnín*, my darling," the voices began to repeat, until the words became a chant that gave Sarah a sense of inner knowing, though of what, she could not be sure.

Come home, *mo mhuirnín*, discover yourself.
Come back to where your journey began,
Far away in time and space,
Yet not so far as your memory can reach.

Come back to life and learn what you will.
Come to a thin place where destiny waits.
Come home. Come home. Remember us.
Come home. Come home. Remember us.

All the way across the Atlantic, the chant continued like a lullaby. Sarah eventually fell asleep and only noticed that the voices had stopped when the pilot announced their descent into Dublin Airport.

She gave the experience no more thought as she cleared customs and joined a lively group of thirty-five men and women, each of whom was a writer. They all eagerly boarded a bus for the short ride to the picturesque village of Wicklow, where they would be staying.

After an hour's drive along the dramatic cliffs and coves of Ireland's eastern coast, Sarah and the other travelers had most of a day free to get acquainted, walk along the seashore, and explore the local shops. Several in the group were also avid photographers who could not wait to capture images of the land and its people bathed in Ireland's misty luminescence.

"Isn't this grand?" Sarah gushed to her fellow travelers. "I already feel like a new person."

"We do, too!" they agreed as one voice.

Following a satisfying dinner that evening and a good night's sleep in the quaint thatched cottage that was to be her base for two weeks, Sarah awoke the next morning, refreshed and eager to explore every facet of this part of the country known as Ireland's Ancient East.

Their tour's first morning program included a presentation by a local historian who regaled them with stories of the area's past. The afternoon was dedicated to the initial meeting of Sarah's writing group. They were a talkative bunch, but no one wanted to read first.

May as well get this over with, Sarah urged herself. She took a deep breath, stood up, and volunteered to read part of Glenna's story that she had beguiled Kevin with years ago.

Her hands were still clammy when she finished, but the others had applauded. The little rush of pride that followed their encouragement helped her shove back the nagging memory of her parting from Kevin. She promised herself—again—that she would not think about him.

That evening, the entire group trekked to a nearby pub where some very talented local musicians were playing soul-stirring traditional Irish music. Sarah's toes were tapping wildly to the lively tunes. She could hardly stay in her seat.

"C'mon, lass, let's put those feet to work!" offered an Irishman twice her twenty-eight years of age. His blue eyes twinkled with mischief.

Are all the Irish this charming? she wondered.

"I haven't danced in a long time," she tried to object as the man whisked her onto the dance floor, then easily guided her into the steps.

Soon she was flying around the room, her hair streaming behind her, feet not quite touching the ground.

"You're a natural!" her partner shouted over the irresistible sounds of fiddle, drum, and Uilleann pipes. Apparently others agreed. Out of nowhere, a half dozen lively gents, some younger and a few considerably older, began cutting in. They continued swinging Sarah around the dance floor until she had to escape, breathless, back to her chair.

"I feel so alive!" she declared later to her tour group friends as she practically skipped back to her cottage. "This is the Ireland I came for!"

Each day of the tour produced its own fascination. The guides were brimming with interesting facts about local history, good restaurants, shops with the best prices. And there was plenty of free time to write.

Sarah found the excursions to ancient sites particularly engaging. The most memorable day trip took the group to the passage tomb of Newgrange. The energy inside the five-thousand-year-old structure was peaceful, yet invigorating. When the guide asked everyone to be silent and then turned out the lights, Sarah felt a profound familiarity, as if she had spent time in that same total darkness, though she could not imagine when or how.

Later in the week, the writers spent a spectacularly sunny afternoon at the ruins of a serene medieval village called Glendalough. During the return bus ride to their cottages, the tour leaders announced that a surprise guest would be presenting the following day.

Many of Sarah's new friends went to the pub after dinner, but she opted for an early night. She sensed that the special event promised a unique opportunity. She did not know why, but she wasn't going to miss a minute of whatever was being offered.

The next morning, her eyes popped open as soon as the birds outside her window starting urging the sun to rise. She jumped into the layered clothing and sturdy hiking shoes that were essential in Ireland's changeable weather and hurried through her breakfast of strong black tea and creamy oatmeal.

Other early risers joined her in the first van. Though most of the group was still breakfasting, the driver took his passengers up to the trailhead where a narrow path led across a wide, gentle mountain and back down to their village. Even from the carpark, the panoramic views were spectacular.

As Sarah and her companions waited for the others to arrive, her eyes hungrily absorbed the scene. Open fields, gently sloping valleys, and tidy farms bordered by hedgerows and stone walls lay for miles in all directions. The patterns they created reminded Sarah of the patchwork quilts her Irish grandmother used to make.

"I could stay here forever," she whispered to the land she sensed was listening.

As soon as the other travelers arrived, everyone began what would more likely be termed an amble than a hike. Sarah usually preferred being at the front of a long line of walkers. Today, however, she lagged behind.

She felt compelled to kneel down for a better look at tiny mosses and lichen that carpeted even rocky places with muted greens and browns. She took her time skimming her fingertips along the tall, soft grasses that shimmered in the rays of sunlight now breaking through the most Irish of morning mists.

Sarah relished every step upon the glistening green landscape that quite literally hummed with history and mystery. She was happy to be trailing the group today and gladly followed some other stragglers as they clamored over a stile in one of the area's ever-present dry stone walls.

She could barely make out the path they were supposed to follow. The faint track was almost completely hidden by a profusion of vivid wild flowers whose variety of color and fragrance took her breath away.

At last, the hikers arrived at what their guide said was a sacred oak grove. Sarah could see that the space had once been a larger clearing, though now it was partially overgrown with enormous oak and hazel trees, ferns, and mosses.

The foliage was kept vibrantly green by a clear, cool stream that ran through what felt to her like a sylvan cathedral. The tallest oak trees linked their branches overhead in imitation of a vaulted ceiling.

Today's guest presenter was a renowned local storyteller, called a *seanchaí.* He was of medium height and strongly built, with his wild, red hair pulled into a ponytail that flowed down his back.

Leaning comfortably against one of the hazel trees, the man looked to Sarah as if he had grown out of the forest. Dressed as he was in an olive green shirt and khaki pants, he might have completely blended into his surroundings, had his brilliant blue eyes not flashed as he spoke.

He was obviously ready to begin his talk, so the group quickly found places to sit on large rocks or stand near the wall of a ruined chapel that hugged a moss-covered overhang at the back of the grove.

The storyteller had been invited to recount the history of the mysterious men and women who had used groves such as this for their ancient rituals and healing practices, and to instruct their students.

He began with a bit of Gaelic. "We call them *druíthe* in Old Irish. *Druí* for a man and *bandruí* for a woman. I use the old terms so you can hear the sound of the language that carries their essence."

Explaining no more, the man began to beat his bodhrán drum as he repeated an ancient chant known as "Amairgen's Hymn."

Pa-PUM-pa-pum, pa-PUM-pa-pum—the rhythm went, sending tingles of energy up the listeners' spines, until all felt their bodies merge with the beat, as if they themselves were the storyteller's drum.

> I am a wind within the sea.
> I am a sea-wave on the land.
> I am the sound of the deep sea.
> I am a stag of seven tines.
> I am a hawk on the high cliff.
> I am a teardrop of the sun.
> I am a turning in a maze.
> I am a boar of great valor.
> I am a salmon in a pool.
> I am a lake on a fair plain.
> I am the excellence of art.
> Who, but I, knows mountain's stones?
> Who, but I, calls ages' moon?
> Who, but I, knows what lies West?

As the seanchaí continued intoning line upon line, the sound of his drum and voice bathed the grove and swirled around the group, growing stronger and stronger until they felt the tug of the invisible world that Amairgen's words invoked.

Once the chant was complete and its purpose achieved, the man spun out his tales of the wise ones who had frequented this place.

"No one knows for certain where the druíthe came from, though their origin is older than most will say. Some claim they were Egyptian priests or Persian magi. Perhaps astrologers from Babylon, or students of the ancient Greek, Pythagoras."

Sarah sensed the truth in every word the seanchaí spoke. When he said the druíthe came from Egypt, she felt a moment of intense clarity. The grove's atmosphere went all shimmery before her eyes, and she heard her voice of inner wisdom declare:

He's telling my soul's story.

Later her mind would recall only snippets of the fascinating stories. Her heart remembered every word.

The afternoon shadows lengthened, and the lowering sun began to transform a few thin clouds into fingers of radiant purple, ruby, and gold. Mindful of the time, the seanchaí concluded his talk.

"Remember friends," he said with sparkling eyes and a sly smile, "the druíthe placed great importance upon dreams. Perhaps one night your slumber will be graced by a visitation from the ancients."

Gazing out at his audience, he scanned the gathering as if he were looking for someone. When his intense blue eyes met Sarah's, a flash of recognition shot between them like a tiny bolt of lightning. The power of that connection almost knocked her off her rocky perch.

The man smiled and briefly continued looking out at the others. Then he gave a slight bow to his enchanted listeners and walked briskly off into the trees. Later, those who sat where they could watch him go swore they had seen what looked like fireflies flickering in his wake— though none could be certain, he had disappeared so quickly.

The travelers were unusually quiet as they made their way back to their lodgings and a welcome meal.

Sarah joined them for a family-style dinner of poached salmon, cold lentil salad, and boiled potatoes, but she hardly noticed the abundance of the spread. She was still feeling the impact of her experience in the grove. On other evenings, the generous meal that had been carefully prepared by local cooks would have earned her full attention. Tonight she could not eat.

"I'm exhausted," she explained to her new friends. "I need to go to bed." Several nodded. They, too, were still caught up in the numinous atmosphere the seanchaí had created.

"Good night," they called after her. "Sleep well."

Once Sarah was back in the cozy peace of her private room, she stretched her arms over her head. What should she be doing? She felt the seanchaí's stories beckoning, though to what end, she could not say.

Deciding the time was actually too early for sleep, she kicked off her shoes and sat on her bed. Throwing a homey comforter over her feet, she fluffed up her pillows and leaned back to reflect on the day's events.

"I should record what I felt in the grove," she said out loud.

But the minute she took up her journal, she could not pen a word. She could not even remove her clothes. Instead, she curled up in the comforter and sank into her bed's downy softness.

As slumber began to overtake her, Sarah felt and then heard the full-bodied purring of her panther guide. Enveloped in the animal's vibrant murmur, she slipped into a dream that, in days to come, she would realize had been a visitation, as the seanchaí had foretold.

The scenes she was about to witness would extend far beyond her imagination into worlds of mystery and wonder.

PART TWO

Reaching for the Sun

*We all play our roles with passion
in this idyllic web of life,
as we reach for the Sun
that calls us to itself.*

Éire

Ynys Môn

Afon
Menai

An Bhearú

Brigantes Territories

Muir Éireann

An tSiúir

*Tearmann

Cois Abhann

Albion

Alana

A barefoot young woman walked carefully along the water's edge, avoiding a patch of broken shells and bits of seaweed tossed up on the coarse sand by the latest high tide.

Hardly any of the other residents, who were called tuatha—people of the túath or territory, frequented this slice of beach. The shore was a bit rough and extended only fifty yards until it abruptly ended in the rugged dunes she had scrambled down earlier.

She needed a quiet place to consider the burden upon her. The seclusion here gave her that peace. Better still, this morning the breeze was gentle and the waves were calm at low tide.

Her name was Alana. She was twenty-two years old and troubled about her new life in the land of the Brigantes tribe. The clear future she had grown up expecting was lost to her in this foreign place.

Gazing wistfully toward the east, across the grey waters of Muir Éireann, she longed for home. The home that beckoned her to fly as a gull over the sea and return to her roots.

Surely, if she could go home, the deep, steady part of herself that lived there would answer all her questions and calm her troubled mind.

But that home was no more, except in her imagination.

She had a strong imagination. And, though she was not as skilled at shape-shifting as the druíthe who had raised her, Alana found great pleasure in using what skill she did possess to become any number of creatures that lived along the strand.

As relief from her worrisome thoughts, she turned into a diminutive sand piper, dancing close to and then away from silvery waves. She was having a grand time, skittering around on spindly legs, snatching her meal of sea worms and tiny crustaceans before they buried themselves in the sand.

Slipping further out into the sea, she became a rón glas, a female grey seal. She was frolicking with her pup, peeking her head up out of the water, and then diving down to capture some fat herring that handily swam by.

As the powerful spirit of the tides brought her back to shore, she was a wave, sliding back and forth upon the sand, lacing foam with sea-weed fronds. Moment by moment, she wove upon the beach a tapestry of elegance that would be pulled back into the bosom of the deep when the sea rose again to its full height.

When Alana let her imagination rest, all of Nature's elements moved easily through her body that was, of course, only human.

Her feet registered every texture of the earth as she walked back to drier land. When she sat down amidst the tufts of sturdy grass that dotted the dunes, she caught a wisp of the elemental conversation that went on here in this threshold place where land and sea and sky lost all sense of separation.

She turned her face to the wind as it picked up and wrapped her shawl closer around her shoulders in the air's sudden chill.

"Oh, to be as free as sea breezes that blow wherever they wish!" she cried aloud to the gulls that wheeled overhead, cawing, chirping, and squawking back to her in the fresh, salty air.

As if to tempt her into flight, a playful gust tossed her long auburn tresses, curling them around her head like a halo. The tiny lizard that streaked across her toes brought her back to earth.

She looked up as April's mid-morning sun slanted between moody clouds, its light rays sparking the clarity of her hazel-green eyes that flashed now with a fervent inner fire.

That fire burned in her as an intense desire for knowledge and the more refined skills she knew she was lacking. She longed to join the company of the druíthe and fulfill the destiny her home across the sea had promised.

Suddenly overwhelmed by the traumatic manner in which that promise had been ripped from her, she turned into a gull and flew home.

"I will not think of Ynys Môn as it exists now," she declared as she flew. "I will not let it be all black and scarred from the horrendous battle and fires that killed everyone I ever loved."

The vow spurred her on as she sailed across Muir Éireann toward the once-magnificent island where she had grown up with her family of druíthe—her grandfather, Ard-Druí Bleddyn, and her parents, Carwyn and Enfys.

Much sooner than she expected, Ynys Môn appeared, glowing like a disc of amber, floating in all its glory between the blues of sea and sky, protected by the tides and sands that had blocked invaders for centuries.

Immediately, her seagull feet touched down on a pristine beach and she was once more a child, skipping along the sand that sparkled with a million tiny crystals. Grandfather Bleddyn held her little hand in his big, strong one and answered her questions as if he were speaking to another sage.

As he faced her and swung her around, she saw their hands grow older. When he set her down, she found herself singing with bards of all ages, learning their stories, and playing her harp.

She turned around and found herself making herbal tinctures with the healers known as fáidthe. Then she was absorbing their unique wisdom through her senses that tingled in their garden that was redolent with the fragrances of myriad rainbow-hued flowers.

She turned again to stroll through a thick, cool forest, its sylvan floor paved with gilded leaves. Soft, loamy soil cushioned her feet, and autumn sunbeams caught her eye as she looked up through a golden-boughed ceiling that glittered with touches of red and green and orange.

She reached up into a gnarled old fruit tree and plucked a ripe red apple from its heavily laden branches that nearly touched the ground. She bit into the tender fruit and savored the crunch that came before the juice that had never tasted this sweet.

Beckoned by the fairy voices she was certain called to her from above, she climbed high up in the tree to let her eyes feast on the distant sight of golden fields of wheat ready for harvest and meadows of wild grasses waving under early fall's clear blue sky.

As if gliding on her own fairy wings, she fluttered down to a nearby stream and plunged happily into the flowing water where she became her favorite form—a salmon.

There was her father, Carwyn, the master shape-shifter. He flipped his own salmon tail in welcome and off they swam, leaping and spiraling until they came upon Enfys, Alana's mother, who was sitting on the grassy bank, watching the sunlight create diamonds on the water.

Enfys was dressed in a bright yellow gown with her red hair spilling over her shoulders. Her finest gold torc, delicate rings, and the jewel-encrusted brooch Carwyn had given her flashed in the sun.

She laughed as father and daughter splashed up in their human forms to sit beside her, as dry as can be. She was a gifted seer as well as a bandruí who kept a watchful eye on her loved ones, wherever their adventures might take them.

Alana kissed her parents and scampered off while they embraced each other. She could see the rosy light of their devotion radiating all around them. She believed that love would hold them together forever.

She was running now, eager to meet her friends, Huw and Fflur. The three of them had been staying in one another's homes to learn how others lived and worked. One week they were all going to be farmers like Huw's people. The next week they were certain that making swords and shields, as Fflur's family had done for generations, was the best possible occupation.

And now they stood together, clasping hands and declaring as a single voice, "I am going to be a druí! My inner guidance told me! This means we will be together always!" They trusted they would continue to thrive in one another's company while they absorbed the ancient mysteries of the druíthe.

Alana turned again and was nearly grown as she made her way to the Ard-Druí's wisdom grove where she knew many druíthe would be gathered. The clearing was incandescent from the glow of stately birch, yew, and oak trees whose leaves were burnished like the golden rings, brooches, torcs, and other ornaments the men and women wore in appreciation of beauty and as a sign of respect for one another.

The entire assembly—young and not-so-young, apprentices and mentors, Alana's parents and childhood friends—emanated an aura that she knew arose from their dedication to the flow of inspired wisdom from An Síoraí, the Eternal One.

She remembered being a youngster who took that aura for granted, until one day Bleddyn had asked her what she thought it meant.

"An Síoraí's wisdom means we know things without knowing how we know them," she had answered with a child's clarity.

"That is true," her grandfather had agreed. "And our calling as druíthe is to project that light of wisdom throughout the Earth. We must push back the darkness, *Eog Bach*." For "Little Salmon" is what he called her, after her favorite shape-shifting form.

Bleddyn's violet eyes smiled at her now as she entered his grove. She knew that, as his granddaughter and as one of his most dedicated students, she was always welcome here.

The Ard-Druí wore a wreath of oak leaves on his youthful head of chestnut hair. His white robe was made of the finest linen that had been interwoven with crystals forming arcane symbols known only to master druíthe. The robe's borders and beltings were elaborately embroidered in threads of gold and silver.

Bleddyn's thick, gold torc glistened like solid sunlight. The jeweled rings he wore flashed rays of ruby, emerald, sapphire, topaz, and diamond light across the grove. He had never appeared more resplendent.

Alana thought her heart would burst with the love she felt for this luminous assembly. She would stay with them forever, if only . . .

Suddenly the wind gusted again, instantly returning her to her seat upon the dunes on the western shore of Muir Éireann.

She gazed once more across the water to the east and felt her eyes mist in the knowledge that only in her dreams would the community of Ynys Môn's druíthe exist as it had been.

Saddened by her memories and a bit unsteady from shape-shifting, she rose slowly to her feet and made her way to an easier path she had discovered that led up from the sea.

The sun shone brightly overhead, letting her know that Tearmann also glowed with the light of wisdom. She looked up and smiled ruefully as she walked back to the cottage where she now lived with her mother's sister, Banfháidh Dearbhla, the master seer, healer, and prophetess of all the Brigantes.

Alana's visit to the beach had given her a vision of what had been, though she had no clearer picture of what might be. Still, she was hopeful that an answer to that question was on the horizon.

One thing she knew for certain: Although she had never needed a formal mentor before, if she was going to become the bandruí her life at Ynys Môn had promised, she needed one now. And only a master druí would do.

"I will not stop looking until I find that person here in Tearmann," she declared, for vows must always be spoken aloud.

If she had listened carefully, beyond the sound of waves that rolled in with the rising tide, she would have heard the voice of her mother, the seer and bandruí, Enfys, telling her that she was about to embark upon a series of adventures that not even Alana's determined mind could have known to hope for or imagine.

The message did not reach her ears that day, but it soon would.

Mutual Admiration

*A*lana assumed she had met every type of druí—that is until she caught sight of the remarkable figure of Arán Bán. He carried himself with an air of uncommon dignity and radiated a magnetic allure she had not experienced before.

She had first noticed him two weeks ago when she was walking across the central green. At that time, he had been in deep conversation with Toísech Cróga, the powerful chieftain who ruled Tearmann. They appeared to be exchanging important information. Cróga was asking Arán Bán questions which the druí answered without hesitation.

From the way they raised their chins and looked each other in the eye, Alana could see they were well matched in authority and confidence. They reminded her of two stags vying for supremacy.

Before Alana's first view of Arán Bán, he had been away from Tearmann in advanced study with Ard-Mháistir Óengus and had returned only a few weeks earlier. He was now serving as Acting Ceann-Druí in place of Old Quin, Cróga's former chief adviser who had died in early March.

Once she was aware of Arán Bán's presence, Alana had embraced every opportunity to observe him as he went about his duties in and around the túath. She had learned from one of her aunt's apprentices that his nearly thirty years of intensive study and practice had made him an accomplished master druí. As Cróga's Acting Ceann-Druí, he wielded considerable influence in Tearmann.

Throughout Éire, the druíthe were as powerful as the tribal chieftains they advised. The druíthe held sway in the supernatural and the chieftains were in charge of civil authority. Each group could use their power against the other, but at their own significant peril. Cooperation with an eye to justice was the wiser course, and most took it.

To Alana's mind, Arán Bán was one of the most impressive of his class. She smiled to think that some of the senior druíthe she had known at Ynys Môn would have raised an eyebrow at his grand manner, but the residents of Tearmann were clearly impressed with his abilities.

Alana happened to overhear several of the local túath residents talking about Arán Bán as she strolled by their fields.

"His rituals never fail to transport me," one of the flax farmers commented to her female relatives as they worked together, carefully tending the precious crop's first month's growth. Weeding helped the young plant stems develop tall and straight to produce the long fibers their family was known for.

"My husband says Arán Bán knows the Brehon Laws better than anyone," offered a cousin.

"No wonder Una's so proud, being wed to such a man," sighed her younger sister, referring to the black-haired woman they all envied and disliked. "I would have married him myself if he had looked my way."

Alana agreed with her new neighbors. Arán Bán was an imposing figure. Standing more than six feet tall, he overshadowed most of the other men in the túath, including the stockier Toísech Cróga.

The druí's appearance was striking. He had a chiseled jaw, thin nose, and full lips that curled slightly to one side when he smiled. Only in his mid-forties, his thick, prematurely grey hair glistened like spun silver in the sunlight, making his midnight blue eyes appear even darker and more penetrating than they might otherwise have seemed.

He had long, artistic fingers and hands that he used to great effect when summoning the energies of the invisible world during the various rituals over which he presided.

Unlike most other druíthe, who wore simple linen or woolen garments for everyday activities, Arán Bán never appeared without a finely woven cloak of his own design.

He had been born into a family of master weavers who taught him the art while he was still a youngster. When he became a druí, he had created a design for a cloak, and his older sister, Casidhe, had woven it for him.

Like her talented brother, she was gifted with a bit of magic in her fingers, which gave her fabrics a vibrancy that surpassed the work of other weavers.

During Arán Bán's ten years as a master druí, Casidhe had woven him several cloaks of wool or linen. These elaborate garments billowed around her brother when he wore them, almost as if they contained a life force of their own.

Each of Casidhe's creations was unique in its intricate pattern of spirals and interlaced knots that she wove into the fabric or embroidered with threads of real gold and every color of the rainbow.

With his physical appeal impressively enhanced by his attire, Arán Bán was resplendent, and Alana was utterly captivated by him. In her eyes, he was the most exceptional druí in Tearmann.

She would have been thrilled to know that he was soon to become equally drawn to her. Until now, his studies and duties had prevented him from noticing Alana. All that was about to change.

To help Alana feel at home in her new community, Dearbhla had encouraged her niece to join the bards and other musicians, singers, and dancers who would perform on the second day of the annual Bealtaine festival.

Alana had mulled the invitation and agreed to sing one song. She had been brooding all winter, which was unlike her. At first she had claimed to be hibernating as befit the season. But when springtime's bouncy lambs failed to lift her spirits while they gamboled next to their mothers, she realized her aunt was right to nudge her out of the doldrums.

Wintry despondency was not the problem—Alana's worry over her future was. At the moment, the destiny she had grown up believing in often felt like a half-truth, a mystery left for her to unravel.

She had no one to help her resolve why some days she felt betrayed by the ones she had loved most. Not because they had left her alone, but because they had shielded her from understanding the dangers of the world they lived in.

Her only hope was to find a mentor who would tell her the truth.

Now is the time, she promised herself as she practiced the song she had agreed to sing for the Brigantes, who were now her people.

The fire festival of Bealtaine had always been Alana's favorite. Yesterday, when the druíthe lit the giant bonfires on the Buaicphointe, the túath's high point where festivals were held, she had felt the power of that fire moving through her, even as it cleansed the land of winter's darkness.

When the cattle herds were driven between dual fires for their purification, she had felt herself relieved of a portion of the sorrow she had carried since losing her home and family last summer.

Bealtaine sparked the new beginnings that Alana was seeking.

Now she only needed a mentor to guide her. Perhaps springtime's fires would send her that person.

Alana was not the only one with high hopes for Bealtaine. The entire túath was ebullient as they gathered on the Buaicphointe for the day's festivities. Wearing their finest gold ornaments, most colorful clothes, and flowers in their hair, men and women—from the very old to the very young—greeted each other with glad hearts and open arms.

No one could tell which shone brighter—the Maytime sun or the beaming tuatha themselves.

A bodhrán drummer's sprightly rhythm called all the merrymakers to attend, and a jolly piper sounded the first notes of a gathering tune that carried the vibrancy of fire itself.

Immediately, dozens of tuatha, including bards, fáidthe, and druíthe, joined hands in a circle dance they had learned as children. As they spun 'round and 'round, the light of youth burned in their breasts, elevating their spirits and renewing the unity of kinship they felt for their fellow residents of Tearmann.

The dancers clapped and cheered as the song ended. An elderly shepherd then stepped forward, and the crowd grew quiet. The fellow was the best whistle player in the territory. In his entire seventy-plus years, he'd not missed a single Bealtaine festival, and he had played his whistle at most of them.

As he began a stirring melody, Alana took her place beside him to sing about a young girl's longing for her beloved. She was dressed in a sky-blue dress with a circlet of deep blue forget-me-nots on her head. Her cheeks blushed rosily against milky white skin, and her long curly hair glowed in the sun like an auburn halo.

Taking up the ethereal tune, her clear soprano matched the whistle player's soulful expression, instantly capturing the attention of the spectators. They nodded to one another in knowing approval of this new addition to the community.

Every member of the túath was blessed with some sort of musical ability, and they all appreciated an excellent singer. They could tell that Alana had a special gift.

Arán Bán detected more than talent.

The girl carries herself like a bandruí, he said to himself, as the audience greeted her performance with enthusiastic applause. The only people he knew who displayed such natural mastery were druíthe.

Who is she and what is she doing in Tearmann? He had to find out.

Arán Bán made his way through the jubilant crowd that was once again singing and dancing and taking full advantage of the huge tables of food and drink that had been laid out on the far side of the Buaicphointe. He caught the eye of his sister and waved her over.

"Casidhe, what can you tell me about the young singer?" Arán Bán asked when she joined him. He appreciated that he could be direct with his sister and that, being an intelligent and well-informed woman, she likely could answer his inquiry.

His sister looked at him and smiled. Nearly as tall as he, she was slim, with flaxen blonde hair that glistened in the light like the silky fibers she spun for weaving. She was proud of her brother and his quick rise to prominence in the túath. She was also aware of his reputation for recognizing exceptional abilities.

"Her name is Alana," answered Casidhe, matching her brother's tone. "She is Dearbhla's niece. She came here last summer with her mother, who died not long after.

"Alana was bound to capture your attention. She is descended from some powerful druíthe who perished in the massacre at Ynys Môn. Anyone can see she's a talented singer. However, given her background, I expect her family was grooming her to be a bandruí. Will you take her on, brother?"

"I may do exactly that," answered Arán Bán thoughtfully. Without another word he turned and hurried away from his sister, leaving her looking after him. She took no offense. He had always been abrupt when confronted with an important decision.

Arán Bán had not assumed responsibility for mentoring any new students for over a year. But seeing the obvious promise that Alana possessed, he knew he must convince Dearbhla that only he could properly guide her niece to her full potential.

Alana could be his greatest protégé yet.

He had long dreamed of being Ceann-Druí, regardless of who ruled Tearmann. He knew he deserved the permanent position. He was certainly the popular choice in the túath.

Without a doubt, his success in developing Alana's talent would prove his worthiness to Ard-Mháistir Óengus—the powerful leader of the hundreds of Brigantes druíthe and the only man authorized to bestow Ceann-Druí status within the tribe's sizable territory.

A strong breeze ruffled Arán Bán's fine linen cloak. In that moment, he realized that his future was inextricably linked to this slip of a girl with the golden voice.

He must see Dearbhla immediately.

Dearbhla

A lock of fifteen-year-old Madwyn's wild brown hair blew into his face in the soft spring breeze that swirled through the garden he helped tend as one of Banfháidh Dearbhla's apprentices. He ran his hand through his hair and focused his attention on his mentor.

Though she had not asked him to, he was observing her from his perch high up in a sturdy apple tree. If she saw him, she would probably tell him to get back to his studies. He was willing to take the risk.

The other apprentices had gone deep into the forest with their tutors to gather herbs that grew only in shade and loamy soil. Madwyn had asked to stay behind in a nearer wooded area of the garden where he cared for the bluebells, one of the many healing plants the fáidthe cultivated.

However, instead of taking his usual shortcut to the woods, he had been prompted to stop and climb the tree where he now sat and watched Dearbhla. She was walking slowly along a path that followed a dry stone wall covered with a profusion of violet wisteria flowers.

The garden was a glorious place, bursting with springtime's exuberance. Madwyn breathed in the sweet scent of pink and white apple blossoms that surrounded him as he instinctively laid back on the thick bough that supported him.

Effortlessly, he let his vision carry him up, up, up through branches covered with such ethereal beauty that, before he realized it, he was standing in the invisible world that was as much a home to him as the material world.

He would take only a moment, he said to himself, as he greeted the apple faeries who were working carefully at the base of each blossom, creating tiny buds that would grow into delicious fruit in Éire's soft, warm summer.

"You have outdone yourselves this spring," he complimented them, admiring their handiwork.

"Wait till you see the apples," laughed Rósach, one of Madwyn's fairy friends. "We will have a bumper crop this year. Stay and watch. These buds will be double stems."

"I cannot right now," said Madwyn reluctantly. "I am looking out for Dearbhla, but you know I will be back."

"We are always glad to see you," said Rósach, planting a fairy kiss on her friend's cheek. "Off you go now. Dearbhla needs your attention."

Madwyn had been visiting the invisible world since he was very young. When his widowed father brought him to Dearbhla six years ago, she had taken on the lad as a novice because she recognized his natural ability as a seer. He was not much of an herbalist, but he could perceive things that even fáidthe with more experience did not detect.

"Develop your discernment and use your gifts wisely, Madwyn, and you may become a master seer," Dearbhla had encouraged him.

Madwyn loved her like the mother he had never known. He knew that his own mother had loved him dearly. He would liked to have grown up with her, but she had died when his little brother was born barely a year after his own entry into this world.

"Thank the gods Dearbhla took me in," Madwyn whispered to the apple tree as he returned his gaze to his mentor.

Dearbhla was a graceful woman who seemed to glide rather than walk with her long, white-blonde hair spilling down her back like a waterfall. She was tall and willowy and radiated a luminous quality of peace and strength.

A person who could see such things might easily mistake her for one of the elemental devas with whom she easily communed. These spirit beings infused the garden's plants with special healing properties they gathered from the most refined domains of earth, air, fire, and water.

Madwyn knew from his own experience that the devas enhanced the meditations of anyone who sat among the secluded alcoves and bowers that they and gifted healers had planted centuries ago.

Dearbhla's ability to work with these spirits, and her own mastery as a seer and prophetess, had made her the most respected banfháidh in all of the Brigantes territories.

And that was saying something, Madwyn thought proudly as he watched her. For the Brigantes were a large tribe and their influence was significant, even beyond their own many tuatha in the southeastern part of Éire.

Madwyn thought Dearbhla's finest quality was her dedication to her novices and apprentices. She had never borne her own children, so she doted on the young people of both genders who worked and studied at her school for fáidthe in Tearmann.

The young seer knew he was a product of her ability to provide wise guidance to a variety of minds and talents. She tailored her instruction to bring out the special gifts of each of her pupils.

However, after her niece, Alana, had come to stay following the trag-ic death of the young woman's mother, Dearbhla had seemed uncharac-teristically anxious.

The Banfháidh was not quite herself this morning. Madwyn could tell because he could read auras. Most days the light energy surrounding her form scintillated in vibrant greens, purples, pinks, blues, and golds. Today those colors were muted, the waves of light flowing more slowly than usual.

Madwyn was not sure why Dearbhla was unsettled. Perhaps she was troubled about her orphaned niece. He had overheard Alana telling her aunt that she did not want to study with her.

The young seer decided to cheer his mentor by telling her how much he was learning from her. But then he noticed Arán Bán enter the gar-den, wearing that very purposeful expression he often assumed around the túath. He was gesturing toward the spacious thatched cottage that served as Dearbhla's home and workroom, and he was calling out that he would like to speak with her.

Madwyn knew he should not intrude his awareness upon that conversation, so he quietly climbed down from the apple tree and sought out a meditation spot amidst a clump of gorse bushes. The exotic scent of their vivid yellow flowers always inspired him.

Dearbhla was more than a little surprised that Arán Bán should appear in her garden. She had considered sending him a message about Alana, but had hesitated, knowing he was most likely busy.

He must have sensed her request because here he was, sitting in her cottage with his exquisite cloak draped casually over the back of his chair, chatting like an old friend.

They had known each other for many years, but Dearbhla had never considered that she and Arán Bán were close. He had never been an easy person to know—apparently, until now. Today his manner was unusually open. She found herself speaking freely.

"My niece has the blood of druíthe running in her veins from both her parents," Dearbhla confided to Arán Bán as he sat drinking one of her hot herbal beverages and observing her with keen interest.

"While not all children of druíthe parents follow their family's heritage, Alana's gifts are fairly bursting out of her. Sadly, her education was interrupted by her flight from Ynys Môn and her mother's death. My niece lost everything last summer. She does not know where she fits into our community.

"Before Alana's mother died, she told me that her daughter would expect to be treated as a bandruí, even though she has not completed certain aspects of training she would have received, had circumstances been different. Her grandfather, Ard-Druí Bleddyn, trained her to follow the flow of An Síoraí through her inner guidance, which she has done with some rather striking results."

Arán Bán agreed. "Her performance at Bealtaine was impressive."

His ready approval encouraged Dearbhla to continue.

"Last fall, I invited Alana to spend some time with the fáidthe in our meditations and workshop. She would be exposed to some of our particular skills that enhance a bandruí's art, and I was certain that working with Nature would help heal her grief. However, my niece declined the invitation.

"Then, I suggested she might like to work with Ollamh Gormlaith as a tutor for some of the young bards, but she rejected that idea as well. Yesterday, she declared that the only person she believes can help her is you, Arán Bán.

"I know you are very busy as Acting Ceann-Druí, but could you be of assistance to our family?"

Arán Bán's face shone with instant pleasure. Here was an unanticipated turn of events. His original intention for disrupting his early morning ritual of quiet study had been to discover more from Dearbhla about the sudden arrival last summer of Alana and her now-deceased mother.

However, hearing that the Banfháidh's niece had asked specifically for his guidance cleared the way for him to go straight to the point of his visit. He would learn all he needed to know about Alana's background from the young woman herself.

"Of course, I will be more than happy to help you, Dearbhla," Arán Bán offered sincerely, his deep blue eyes focused on hers.

"I am certain you know of my success with gifted young bandruíthe like your niece. Alana is a perfect candidate for my methods, and you will not have to worry about her while she is in my care. My wife, Una, will be pleased to have her stay with us while she studies with me."

"You are a godsend, Arán Bán," Dearbhla exclaimed. "I know you will find my niece eager to learn from you. She has some specific concerns which she says only a master druí will understand."

"I assure you, her concerns will be my own," said Arán Bán, taking Dearbhla's hands in his. "With your permission, I will see Alana this afternoon."

Dearbhla agreed without question. "You may leave word with Madwyn as you go. He has been following me around this morning and should have returned from his meditation by now. He will send Alana to you today."

Arán Bán rose and plucked his cloak from the back of the chair where he had been sitting. He bowed deeply to Dearbhla and stepped outside.

Indeed, Madwyn had felt his mentor calling him from the garden only minutes earlier. He was now waiting breathlessly outside her cottage as the Acting Ceann-Druí paused to deliver precise instructions for Alana to attend him after midday.

Arán Bán smiled to himself. He gracefully swung his cloak around his shoulders and strode to the oak grove where he would receive his new student.

Initiation

*A*rán Bán's energy feels as clear and sharp as a finely honed sword, Alana noted to herself as she entered the wisdom grove that was normally reserved for only the highest rituals of the druíthe.

Thinking of her family and their peers, she recalled that each druí was possessed of a unique vibration. She had never experienced such a flash of intellectual prowess as now rippled through her upon coming face-to-face with Arán Bán.

She had felt the force of his attention when she noticed him watching her as she sang at Bealtaine. Meeting him in person, with his mind focused on her in such close proximity, was a stirring experience.

"Welcome, Alana." Her new mentor's tone conveyed a dignified presence. "Are you prepared to embark upon an accelerated course with me as your guide?"

"I am," she answered, greeting him with the respect a master druí deserved. "Thank you for accepting me as your student."

"You may not always thank me, for I am a demanding mentor. However, by the time your studies with me have concluded, I am certain your gratitude will know no bounds."

"There is a matter about my studies I would like to discuss with you," Alana ventured.

"We will do so later, if necessary. Do not worry about the past or the future, my dear. Any worries you have now will dissolve as we work together. Come, walk with me."

Arán Bán ushered Alana out of the grove and guided her toward the sea. As they made their way past the cliff that overlooked the beach where she and her mother had first come ashore, the master druí walked close to his new pupil. She could feel the heat of his body.

How thrilling, she thought. He was purposefully radiating his energy directly toward her. Most druíthe were not so open with a new student. Arán Bán must consider her worthy of such an honor.

They stopped on a windy promontory that offered a dramatic view of land and sea and sky. Arán Bán gently placed his left arm around Alana's shoulder and swept his right arm in a graceful gesture that encompassed the entire expanse.

In the smooth tones of one who has practiced refined speech, he spoke to her with great intensity, "Let yourself absorb the power of this place, my girl. Do you feel its majesty, its grandeur?"

"I do," she answered. The ocean's thundering presence never failed to move her.

"When you are fully trained as a bandruí, all of this and more will be your domain. Others will respect you and your considerable gifts. Do you want to fulfill your destiny, Alana? Do you wish to live according to your highest dreams?"

"I do," she answered again, already pleased that she had asked for Arán Bán's assistance. "Do you believe I am ready?" Personally, she believed she was more than ready to work with him, but she wanted him to agree.

"Absolutely!" Arán Bán exclaimed. "There are no limits for you, my girl. Not with me as your mentor. I will evaluate your skills in our first session together, and then you will progress swiftly to become the great bandruí your talent already predicts. Is this not what you truly desire?"

A ray of hope glimmered in Alana's imagination. "I do wish for greatness. I am grateful to speak my mind to you."

"Indeed, and may it always be so. Tell me your hopes and dreams, and I will help you realize them."

Satisfied that this first step in winning Alana's trust was so easily won, Arán Bán released his arm from around the delicate shoulders of his protégé and firmly turned her to face him.

He removed from the index finger of his left hand an immense gold ring in which was set a blue-grey stone that had been polished to a high sheen. The stone began to pulse like a heartbeat as soon as he held it in the sunlight for Alana to study.

"This ring comes from the land of your ancestors. The stone is rarely seen here in Éire. It carries the vibration of our primordial forebears who created the great monoliths we revere as sites of immense power.

"The blessing I am about to give you through this ring will enhance your native abilities. Its energy may even help you unlock the mysteries of your past lives."

Placing the stone on the center of Alana's forehead and holding it in place, Arán Bán chanted a lengthy prayer in a language that sounded familiar, though the young woman could not make out its meaning. He steadied her as she swayed under the stone's powerful transmission and carefully returned the ring to his finger.

"Absorb this initiation, Alana," he said, his voice assuming an authoritative tone. "Your lessons have officially begun, my girl. It is now time for you to meet my wife, Una, who eagerly awaits your arrival."

As Arán Bán led Alana away from the cliff edge and back to the roomy thatched cottage that he and his wife shared with their nearly grown children, the druí remained close to his new student.

He wanted his new student to become comfortable in his aura. He intended to intensify his unique vibration in coming days, gradually weaving her into deeper connection with him and his personal approach to the arts of the druíthe.

The Ollamh's Tale

A dozen girls and boys, ages six through twelve, waited anxiously for their master teacher to arrive. They were gathered in the túath's practice hall—an oval-shaped thatched building with a high ceiling. There were stools, chairs, and benches for seating and a platform at the front of the main area where students could practice their lessons.

This wonderful space, which offered the best acoustics of any building in Tearmann, was also a place where accomplished bards and those hoping to attain advancement could work out their latest compositions of story, chant, or song.

Today was a special day because Ollamh Gormlaith was presenting. These youngest bards-to-be had only met her in person when she had welcomed them on their first day of training. Yet, whenever they passed her in the túath—which was often, as her school was located adjacent to the central green—she was unfailingly friendly and always greeted them by name.

Unlike Banfháidh Dearbhla's school, which was set further back in the forest beyond any family dwellings, or the cottages of Toísech Cróga and the Ceann-Druí, which overlooked the green from a rise on the south, Ollamh Gormlaith's school for bards was a visible part of the landscape of Tearmann.

Gormlaith had promised the youngsters an event solely for them. They could not help fidgeting with the excitement of being with her. Their tutors had told them to pay close attention because they would be asked to speak their own versions of the Ollamh's presentation during their afternoon of practice.

Suddenly the children sitting closest to the back of the hall shushed the others. "She's coming!" they cried. "We can hear her golden bells. Be quiet, everyone!"

The six-year-olds clapped their hands over their own mouths in amazement. They were too young to be pupils, but those who lived in Tearmann were sometimes allowed to accompany their older brothers and sisters for special occasions.

All ears perked up at the sound of delicate golden bells, now tinkling faintly in the distance and becoming louder every second. Only the most accomplished master bards carried birch or apple tree branches with tiny bells attached that sounded as the boughs moved.

The youngsters turned and watched the back of the room, for that is where the sound was coming from. Then, suddenly, the bells were louder at the front of the room. The children turned again, and there was Gormlaith shaking her birch bough, a gentle smile playing about her lips.

For today's event she had worn her finest garments. A long, deep blue linen dress with soft folds graced her diminutive form. Though she was not tall, whether she was standing or sitting, she always gave the impression of considerable stature—inner height, as one of her students had quipped some years ago.

Gormlaith's family were goldsmiths who produced the territory's most exquisite ornaments. As much of Éire's gold trade passed through Tearmann's seacoast, everyone in the túath had access to at least one piece of the luminous metal.

The Ollamh always wore an exquisite gold torc. If anyone asked why she was never without it, she explained that the metal's refined energy protected her throat and enhanced her voice's musical tone.

This torc was especially fine, created as it was from multiple strands of gold wire that had been twisted together like a rope and secured at the ends with small orbs of gold. Each orb held a dark blue lapis stone that was reputed to have come from Egypt.

Gormlaith's dark blonde hair was pulled back from her face so the torc glistened in the light of torches that had been set around the room for illumination and warmth on this unusually chilly morning.

Her woolen cloak had been dyed the same deep blue as her dress and was secured on her shoulder by a large gold brooch, inlaid with blue lapis and green stones made from marble that came from Éire's west coast. The garment flowed around her with the softness of a baby duck's down.

"Good morning!" The Ollamh merrily greeted her pupils and their tutors as they all clapped and cheered her appearance. "Are you ready for today's surprise?"

"We are!" they answered together.

"Lovely. Let us begin with a song." She cast the warmth of her smile into each hopeful face until the entire room was aglow with happy grins.

Taking up her harp, which had been placed on a wooden stand next to where she stood, she played and sang a familiar tune that set her audience's toes to tapping and filled their hearts with joy as they sang along with her.

Gormlaith finished the song and set aside her harp. Then she began to speak in the clear voice of a master seanchaí.

"Your surprise is a story that I learned from Ard-Mháistir Óengus himself. Only this morning, he said to me that, if he were here, he would tell you the same tale. It conveys a message for each of you. See if you can catch its meaning."

Some of the younger children wondered how Gormlaith could have spoken to the Ard mháistir, who lived miles away in another túath, but the question evaporated from their minds as the story began:

Once upon a time there was a young man who had been born under a fortunate star. That is what his mother had claimed ever since he could remember. She told him and everyone she knew that he would grow up to be a great man.

But the youth—who was a natural teller of tales and singer of songs—did not want to be great. He wanted to be happy. So he left home at the age of twelve and became a roving seanchaí. He recounted stories old and new, chanted the praises of any chieftain who would give him a dry place to sleep, and mucked out stables on the few occasions when no one was interested in his offerings.

One day, as the afternoon shadows lengthened, he found himself in a dark wood—one he had never entered before. The forest was strangely quiet. Then, all of a sudden, he heard a terrific noise. A rumbling growl and the sound of something crashing through the trees unnerved him as no experience had ever done.

The young man peered into the dark, but could see nothing. Then, without warning, a beast was upon him, snarling and breathing its hot breath into his face. He feared it would bite him with the sharp teeth it bared or that it would tear him with its horrible claws.

However, the beast only threatened. It did not wound the young man. Instead, it pinned him to the ground.

He was a strong youth. But the bear—for the beast was an enormous brown bear—was too much for him. It simply rested its furry bulk upon him until he wore himself out struggling to escape.

At last, fixing his captive with a stare from its huge brown eyes, the bear spoke:

'Will you give up?'

'Never!' croaked the young seanchaí who could hardly breathe under the heavy paw that rested on his chest.

'Then I will wait,' said the bear.

'For what?' asked the youth, still gasping for a full breath.

'For you to wake up,' said the bear simply.

'But I am awake,' protested the young man. 'No dream was ever this heavy—or this talkative, considering you are a bear.'

'I have been talking to you for a long time, but you have failed to listen. I have addressed you in the wind, in a child's cry, in the hoot of an owl, a mare's whinny, and a wolf's howl. Every sound has been a message that you refused to hear.

'Now that I have your attention,' the bear continued, 'what would you like to talk about?'

'I thought you were speaking to me,' answered the youth, now more puzzled than frightened.

'I was,' answered the bear. 'But your head is so full of your own thoughts, there is no room for mine. I suggest you empty your brain, and then we will see what I might add to our conversation.'

Realizing he had no choice, the youth acquiesced. 'As you wish. May I sit up, so I can breathe?'

'Of course,' said the bear. He removed his paw and seated himself across from his gasping captive. 'But do not try to run. Obviously, there is no point. Tell me, what fills your mind?'

Being very wise indeed, the bear had been right. The young seanchaí talked for hours. His recollection of every hurt, question, pleasure, accomplishment, or dream he had ever entertained came rushing out as the bear listened.

As is often the case with life's most important matters, the seanchaí's most serious burden was not revealed until he had nearly finished his emotional discourse.

'I do not know what I am meant to be,' he admitted wearily. 'I am nagged by the feeling that I am not in my right place.'

'You are in exactly the right place at this moment,' stated the bear with a knowing grin. 'Though, naturally, you do not wish to remain here permanently. Trying to find your destiny, are you?'

The young man nodded. 'I know I have a destiny, but I cannot seem to find it.'

'You are searching in all the wrong places,' explained the bear. 'Look back the way you came and tell me what you see.'

When the seanchaí turned around, the trees seemed to part, creating a pathway that was illumined for what appeared to be many, many miles behind him.

'I see home, family, people, animals, the land. And I feel this yearning, deep in my soul.'

'What do you yearn for?' asked the bear, focusing his own strong will in support of the youth before him.

'I long to serve them as each one needs to be served. How shall I do that?'

'Sometimes to move forward, you must go back and pick up what or whom you have neglected to love,' said the bear, looking wistfully along the path that had led the young man to this place of encounters.

The bear waited for a moment, then said softly, but firmly, 'Go back. Walk with each creature on its path. Attune with the land. Discover what each one needs most and offer them that gift with all the love in your heart.'

That is exactly what the young seanchaí did, one person, animal, plant, and plot of land at a time. He forgot about destiny and thought only of serving with love.

Very soon he found himself able to become who or what he had neglected, until eventually he had bonded with all things seen. And, in not too long a time, he also bonded with unseen beings as well.

The land and creatures thrived in his care, and he flourished in their gratitude. For all living things long to be appreciated for themselves.

The seanchaí is a good deal older now, though he has told me himself that he has not finished loving life. As he looks across at his túath and far beyond where his daily blessings are carried on the wind and the water, his blue eyes twinkle. His laughter can be heard echoing across the land where everyone calls him 'Uncle'.

"Can you guess who this story is about?" Gormlaith playfully posed the question to her enraptured audience.

"Uncle Óengus!" cried several of the children who were acquainted with the Ard mháistir.

"Indeed," answered Gormlaith, pleased at their ready response to her story.

"And why did Uncle Óengus want you to hear this tale today?"

The room was silent until a tow-headed brother and sister, ten-year-old twins, popped up from their seats, speaking in unison.

"So we will know how to find our destiny?"

"Exactly. Well said," answered Gormlaith, nodding for them to sit.

"Life will respond to your best intentions by pointing you to what or whom needs you most right now and in the way you are most needed. Whatever your calling, remember that destiny is not only what you are doing, but also how you are being in the process.

"Tend life with your whole heart. Someday a seanchaí may even tell your story to her students to inspire them as they pursue their own unique path.

"Remember: Anyone who tells a story needs an intelligent, receptive audience such as you have been today. And every audience needs to receive what is lovingly told. We are nothing without each other."

Gormlaith's clear voice caught slightly in her throat as she felt deep affection beaming back to her from the tender hearts of her pupils and their tutors. Bowing graciously to them all, she picked up her Ollamh bough and departed out a side door, returning to her own thatched cottage at the center of the school grounds.

The children were certain they could hear her golden bells tinkling joyfully throughout the remainder of the day.

Óengus

*A*rd-Mháistir Óengus rested comfortably on the sturdy wooden bench that admiring residents had placed for him.

He loved sitting here among the fragrant golden gorse bushes that grew profusely in this patch of rough, grassy land that overlooked his túath of Cois Abhann. From this vantage point he could cast his presence across those lands and surrounding territories.

As he looked out over the gently sloping banks of An Bhearú, the river that sustained his túath, he hummed contentedly. The water appeared as soft as the early morning mists that hugged its verdant channel.

Óengus liked soft weather. There was something about an overcast day that lent itself to his stepping into the realms beyond the earthly where he did his most intriguing work.

At the moment, he was enjoying listening to Ollamh Gormlaith tell the story he had suggested that she share with her new pupils. The fact that she was standing in a practice hall at her school on the eastern coast of Éire while he was sitting by a river many miles to the west was natural to them both.

His gift of clairaudience allowed him to hear far-off conversations. And Gormlaith could project herself to another location to visit with him as skillfully as any druí—as she had done earlier this morning, .

"My Amairgen," he had dubbed her, for she was uniquely gifted in all the bardic arts as poetess, singer, and seanchaí. He had encouraged her to study with him and become a bandruí, but she had declined.

"I love my stories too much, Uncle," she had explained.

Of course, he understood her preference. He would have remained a seanchaí himself had he not been called elsewhere. Once he had set his able mind to the task, he had so quickly mastered the essential skills of the druíthe that he could do naught but pursue the advanced studies that had led him to becoming the Ard mháistir he was today.

As he heard Gormlaith conclude the story and, with his inner sight, watched her return to her cottage in Tearmann, Óengus stood and stretched, preparing for his own day's service in Cois Abhann.

Early this morning he had wrapped his broad-shouldered, seventy-year-old form in his warmest white wool robe and cloak and had laced his leggings and sturdy leather boots securely against the springtime damp. He knew he would be outside for several hours and planned to stay dry in the misty weather.

A large man of simple tastes, Óengus appreciated the durable fabrics his túath weavers were experts in creating. As he looked out across the expansive flax fields where tall green plants bloomed with delicate blue flowers, he considered how busy they soon would be.

The crop would be ready to harvest in another month and then the laborious process of transforming woody stems into luxurious fibers would begin anew, as it had for centuries, reaching all the way back to ancient Egypt's lands along the Nile River.

Óengus was aware of many aspects of antiquity. Better than most, he understood the history of the druíthe and the role those like them had played for thousands of years in the lives of many civilizations.

He breathed in the subtle aromas of barley, wheat, and oat fields that were ripening upriver. He never tired of the varied fragrances of Nature's summer greenery or of the rich scents of cattle and sheep that grazed contentedly nearby.

Mindful of his many responsibilities as Ard mháistir and head of the Brigantes school for druíthe, Óengus stood at last and prepared to send his blessings up and down the vibrant waterway that gave life to all the creatures that lived in and along its considerable length.

Raising his staff and his booming voice, he intoned the ancient words of beannacht that were a vital part of this service to his people. Looking first to his right, the Ard mháistir visualized his invocations traveling north to the river's source in the distant mountains, far beyond the borders of his own Brigantes tribe. Speaking with a master druí's power, he prayed:

> *O spirits of creativity and inspiration, in the name of An Síoraí, the Eternal One, I call for blessings upon all who live along An Bhearú, even those who might raid our herds. May all be safe. And may the gods grant us the wisdom to live in harmony with each other as we do with the land.*

Óengus felt the power of An Síoraí expand further as he sent his benedictions to both sides of An Bhearú's long channel where all manner of animal life, both wild and domestic, were busy raising new generations in Nature's rhythmic cycle of birthing, growing, and maturing.

Many months remained before winter's chill would return again, the Ard mháistir reflected with pleasure. Much dedicated labor and several welcome seasonal celebrations would be accomplished well before then. He relished officiating at the important rituals that marked the passing of each quarter of the year, and he always managed to join in the festive songs and dances.

Óengus now shifted his awareness downriver to where his túath of Cois Abhann sat at a bend in An Bhearú's wide, tranquil channel. Here the swifter, salmon-rich An tSiúir added its abundant flow to the rivers' combined run to the sea. Óengus thanked the gods that his túath was thriving in the active trade that plied these waters in traditional currach boats of many sizes.

Those who built the boats and those who piloted them held a special place in the Ard mháistir's heart. These sturdy vessels carried agricultural goods, natural materials, and handmade items to and from neighboring tuatha along the rivers and out to sea to lands beyond Éire's fair shores.

Feeling Óengus's blessing and knowing of his high regard, several crews waved and shouted their greetings as they sailed by. These were strong men who rowed up river and, on the return trip, welcomed the current that took much less effort, though no less skill, to travel down to the sea.

Óengus blessed them all and visualized them reaching their destinations safely, buoyed by the fair winds he sent them.

At last, sensing a profound flow of mutual gratitude between the one who blesses and those who receive the blessing, Óengus concluded the ritual and chuckled at the scene around him.

As he had been praying, a dozen small children had gathered at his feet on the promontory by the river. They were laughing and begging for stories of his adventures.

Their innocence reminded him of why he had spent the past thirty years of his life perfecting his skill as a master druí: He was here to guide these precious souls and their families, to settle their disputes, answer their deepest questions, and support those who would protect them so they could fulfill their destinies.

He wondered if they had any idea how tenuous life was these days. Then, shaking off his concern for now, he gave the children his full attention.

"What story will you have this morning?" He stooped down to ask the youngsters who peered hopefully into his twinkling blue eyes.

"Have you heard about when I turned into a butterfly? Or when I stopped the rain from falling on the Bealtaine fires? Or, would you rather hear about . . . hawks!"

As soon as he proclaimed the word, Óengus stood up and crooked his left arm as a perch for the keen-eyed, blue-grey hawk that came sailing in with a great flutter of wings to land on the master's arm.

"Hello, a chara," he said softly to the bird as he stroked its silky head feathers. "What messages do you have for us today?"

"What is he saying, Uncle?" asked the children eagerly.

Óengus held his ear close to the hawk's beak and listened intently.

"Hawk says he has been flying into your dreams and that you must pay attention to your surroundings. Are there omens in the wind or treasures in the clouds? What magic is about to land on your out-stretched arms? What can you learn from your animal friends? And he says to listen for the new ideas he may be sending you."

As the majestic bird pointed itself toward the sun and lifted off, Óengus smiled at the children's wide-eyed expressions.

"Hawk has flown back to his other business now, my dears, and I must fly on to mine. But I will see you again soon. And next time we meet, I want to hear some of your stories. I know there must be a sean-chaí or two among you. Am I right?"

"Uncle says we are seanchaithe!" the little ones exclaimed as they scurried off to explore their own imaginations.

"You can never start practicing too early!" Óengus called after them with a hearty laugh. All the Brigantes were steeped in song and story, and they cherished the oral histories their bards chanted. Many of the druíthe were also masters of word and song.

A few of the older children already imagined having such a destiny and had told Óengus they felt called to become druíthe. One and all, they said how glad they were to live in his túath so they would not have to travel to study with him.

Those who decided to become fáidthe or bards would travel, as soon as they were old enough, to apprentice with Banfháidh Dearbhla or Ollamh Gormlaith at their schools in Tearmann.

Other young people would find their perfect livelihoods working on the land or at sea or in any of the vitally important arts and trades. And everyone would raise their families in the knowledge that all were essential to sustaining the túath's alignment with Nature's rhythms.

At least for the present, the web of life was secure with the Brigantes, Óengus assured himself as he removed his wool cloak in the warming, late morning sun and strolled back to his cottage. But how much longer would he lead the druíthe of the Brigantes? Who would take his place when he was ready to pass out of this world?

Even now, he sometimes longed for the peace of Tír na n'Óg, Land of the Ever-Living, where the pressures of guiding the Brigantes would not weigh on his still very strong, seventy-year-old shoulders.

For how long would any of Éire's druíthe be safe from overthrow?

Óengus could not help being concerned. Over three decades ago, when he had completed his intensive studies with Ard-Druí Bleddyn at the community of Ynys Môn, his mentor had commissioned him to start his own school at Cois Abhann.

"Your túath is in a more secure location than Tearmann," Bleddyn had assured him. "We must have a place for druíthe to continue their studies in case anything happens to us here at Ynys Môn."

At the time, Óengus had been puzzled, though he was obedient to the Ard-Druí's direction, which had proved prophetic. Only last year, the community of Ynys Môn had been viciously destroyed.

Óengus still grieved for all the lives that had been lost, and he remained ever more grateful that his own school for druíthe continued to thrive.

Choices

Meditating on a stone bench cushioned with woolen blankets at the far side of his wisdom grove, Óengus contemplated the task before him. He had delayed longer than he should have done. Today he must make the decision whose consequences were bound to reverberate to every corner of the Brigantes territories.

Old Quin, the stern Ceann-Druí who had served the tribal chieftains of Tearmann for more years than anyone could remember, had died last March.

The power vacuum his death had created was significant because Toísech Cróga, the chieftain who ruled Tearmann and its adjacent lands in southeastern Éire, had ambitions of expanding his influence within the Brigantes territories.

Cróga was an intelligent, though slightly headstrong leader who, like his father before him, had valued Old Quin's advice. Cróga knew that every toísech, especially a man like himself who tended more toward confrontation than diplomacy, needed a strong Ceann-Druí to guide him wisely. He welcomed Óengus's role in choosing a successor to his former adviser.

As Ard mháistir of the Brigantes people, Óengus was responsible for designating a Ceann-Druí for each of the chieftains who ruled the many tuatha within the tribe's lands. He took the task seriously.

Throughout the more than thirty years he had been a master druí, he had watched with deep regret as some very able colleagues had fallen prey to their ambitions. More than ever, dependability and balance were vital in any Ceann-Druí he might appoint.

The ancient oaks that surrounded him in the grove understood his burden. As Óengus gazed at them, he could see the wizened faces of friends long departed in body, yet ever present in spirit, looking out at him from the trees' weathered trunks. He felt their support and was glad of it.

At last, Óengus was prepared to conduct the interviews that would determine which of three worthy candidates he would choose. He stood and began walking rhythmically around the center of the grove where he had set a lively fire burning on a stone-lined hearth.

Beating his well-worn bodhrán drum to focus the energy demanded for this ritual, he chanted the arcane words of invocation that he would one day pass on to his own successor. After several revolutions around the grove, he stopped before the fire.

As he gazed into the flames, three crystalline orbs appeared before him. Each contained the image of a master druí he was considering as permanent adviser to Toísech Cróga.

Óengus stepped into the first orb to speak with one of his most able druíthe. "Well met, Riordan," he said to the youngest of the three candidates. The man, whose dark gold hair gave him a perpetual glow, stood and warmly greeted the Ard mháistir.

Clapping his former student good-naturedly on the back, Óengus went straight to the point. "Tell me, my son, why should I name you to manage our friend Cróga?"

"You honor me, Uncle," replied Riordan with an affectionate handshake. He would always be grateful to this generous man who had encouraged him to become a druí while he was yet an inexperienced bard.

"However, I do not believe you should name me. Do you honestly expect Cróga to listen to me when, inevitably, I must advise against his wishes?"

"Likely not," Óengus answered thoughtfully, stroking his full grey beard. "Still, I want you to know of my confidence in you. You have done well these past several years.

"I am aware that some of your fellow druíthe may consider you too sentimental, but your heart is pure, Riordan. The depth of your spirit comes through in your invocations. Do not lose that tenderness or the presence of An Síoraí within you. Others may yet come to rely on you in difficult days ahead.

"Be well, my son."

Óengus embraced the man who, he realized with regret, did not have the tough political instincts to be Cróga's next Ceann-Druí. He closed the orb and returned to his grove.

Óengus could feel his love for each of the druíthe increasing as he stood once more before the flames. He allowed his attention to rest on the second orb and stepped into the presence of Arán Bán.

The candidate was wearing his finest robes and gold torc in honor of his mentor's presence.

"Greetings, Uncle."

"Good day to you, my son. Are you ready for our discussion?"

"I am, and I want to tell you how honored I am to be considered as Cróga's permanent Ceann-Druí. I believe I enjoy the high esteem of the people, and I have worked hard to apply the advanced skills you taught me when we were last together. I feel confident that you will find my service more than acceptable."

"That I have already," Óengus answered with a nod. "I received very positive reports about your service as Acting Ceann-Druí while Cróga was away from the túath. And Quin always told me he thought you would make an admirable adviser. I know he appreciated your affection for the details of the office that matched his own.

"Tell me, my son, now that you have had some direct experience with the job, what do you consider to be the Ceann-Druí's most vital duties toward his or her people?"

"There are three things," said Arán Bán, feeling his enthusiasm rise.

"First, to instill in the people respect for the office of Ceann-Druí through well-executed rituals and powerful invocations. Second, to ensure their understanding of the Brehon Laws. Third, to guide the toísech away from war whenever possible."

"You have given much thought to the role of Ceann-Druí," observed Óengus.

"Indeed I have, Uncle. And I feel strongly that a well-administered tribe is a safe tribe. Our neighbors will not take advantage of our weaknesses because we will have none."

"Thank you, Arán Bán" said the Ard mháistir. He warmly shook the second candidate's hand. "I can see that you have worked hard to win the permanent position. I will let you know of my decision as soon as I have made it."

Back in his grove, Óengus sat and meditated for a few minutes before approaching the third orb. He knew that times were changing. Threats from both foreign and domestic invaders were increasing. And the various Brigantes tuatha were having more than their usual trouble getting along with each other.

Perhaps Arán Bán was right in believing that more structure was needed to protect the tuatha, from themselves as much as from outsiders.

Rising at last, the Ard mháistir stoked the flames on the hearth. Gazing into the fire, he breathed deeply as the third orb came into focus.

He prepared to enter and then halted with a merry grin. The third candidate was seated on a wooden chair outside his simple cottage. His eyes were closed as one who was meditating, but his mouth was moving. He appeared to be composing with great concentration.

Ever the philosopher-teacher, Óengus chuckled as he observed the man whose friendship he had valued for more than twenty years.

Here was a person for whom ambition meant increasing his attunement with the world of the unseen in order to bring its blessings into the world of the seen—particularly to the young druíthe he enjoyed guiding until they were ready to study with Óengus.

The Ard mháistir eased gently into the orb, knowing his decision rested upon this final interview.

"Good day, Ah-Lahn," he said as quietly as his big voice allowed.

"May I interrupt you?"

Ah-Lahn looked up and blinked in the sun. Or was that light the radiance he often detected around his mentor?

"Of course, Uncle. Please, join me." Ah-Lahn indicated a chair he had placed for the Ard mháistir in anticipation of their conversation.

"I was just working on a new story for young druíthe as a lesson about the demands placed on an adviser who campaigns with his or her toísech. The tale conveys the pitfalls quite dramatically."

He paused. "But you are not here to talk about mentoring young druíthe or military campaigns, are you?"

"That I am not, my son. We need to discuss the position of Cróga's Ceann-Druí. Have you given the opportunity much thought?"

"I have. Many hours of thought." Ah-Lahn drew in a long, slow breath. "Uncle, I will accept the position if you believe I must, but I do not seek it for myself. You know the people prefer Arán Bán."

The Ard mháistir nodded in agreement. "They appreciate his precision. Arán Bán is a man of impressive abilities, as are you and Riordan. If I could toss the three of you into a pot and stir you into a single druí, I believe I would have the perfect candidate."

Óengus chuckled at his own joke, then furrowed his brow.

"Riordan has the heart of a wise leader, but he lacks the strength to stand up to Cróga's ambitions. Arán Bán is smarter than either of you, and he certainly possesses the drive to lead.

"You, my son, handled Cróga well on the campaign you recently completed. And you have a loving heart that can become wiser with experience—if you will keep your eyes and ears open. Choosing one from the three of you is not an easy task."

Óengus paused and closed his eyes.

Ah-Lahn waited in silence. The Ard mháistir's deep, even breathing told him that his mentor was searching the depths of his soul for the best choice that could be made at this time.

After several minutes, Óengus opened his eyes and spoke. He had felt the answer come to him as a profound knowing that he recognized as inspiration from his own inner guidance.

"Ah-Lahn, I must look to the future of all our druíthe. Whenever my

days on earth run their course—which is no time soon, I assure you—
our order will need a rock-solid leader. The presence of An Síoraí tells
me you can be that person.

"I know that taking on the role of Cróga's Ceann-Druí is a challenge.
He is not always an easy man to work with. Yet, I must insist. You are the
only master druí whose combination of character and skill I can trust
today and in the foreseeable future. Not even the master seers seem to
know what may be coming upon us."

From the apologetic expression on his mentor's face, Ah-Lahn saw
that Óengus regretted having to force a decision.

"Will you take the job, my son?" the Ard mháistir asked.

"I will, Uncle. And I pray the gods will grant me strength to do what
you need of me."

Both men stood and clasped hands in the double handshake of true
affection. Each druí knew the other trusted the man before him, and
each silently vowed to uphold that trust.

Óengus dissolved the final orb. Once more in his grove, he stood before
the fire and leaned upon his staff in deep concentration until only
embers glowed at the center of the sacred space.

Before walking back to his dwelling for a meal and some rest, he said
a heartfelt prayer for the outer safety and inner guidance of Ceann-Druí
Ah-Lahn, his loyal friend on whom much depended.

The old trees watched Óengus depart and nodded to each other at
the wisdom of his choice.

Ah-Lahn

As Óengus believed would happen, now that Ah-Lahn had been Ceann-Druí for several months, even the most reluctant residents of the túath could not help but embrace him.

Whether he was teaching, singing, chanting, or praying, Ah-Lahn could raise the energy of a gathering with the sheer power of his voice and the presence of An Síoraí that coursed through him.

In recent years, his natural gifts had only increased under the Ard mháistir's careful guidance. For Óengus had initiated Ah-Lahn into the most occult mysteries of the druíthe—secrets he had been prompted to share with only a few students during the many years he had been Ard mháistir.

As the tuatha enjoyed market day before Samhain, men and women alike compared their experiences with Ah-Lahn.

"I was transported by his invocations," declared the local master chandler as she laid out the tallow soaps and candles she had made.

"He conducts the rituals with sincere reverence," observed her cattle-herding friend who supplied the tallow. "Since Ah-Lahn has been leading them, I have gained insights I had not experienced before."

"My cousin has met Uncle Óengus," interjected a potter who joined the conversation from the adjacent stand where he was displaying his wares. "He says that Ah-Lahn is cut from the same cloth as the Ard mháistir. We should respect the new Ceann-Druí and heed his advice."

"Well, I like the look of him," blushed the chandler's young female apprentice. "That handsome face, dark hair, blue-green eyes, and broad shoulders. I would marry him in a trice."

Others added their comments as they admired the fruits of one another's labor.

"Ah-Lahn treats people with equal respect, no matter who they are."

"He judged my dispute fairly without prejudice."

"When he passes, he always speaks and asks about my family."

Had Ah-Lahn heard their comments, he would have been relieved to know of their acceptance. He had been concerned that the residents of Tearmann would be disappointed that Óengus had not chosen Arán Bán as permanent Ceann-Druí.

However, Ah-Lahn's mind was on other matters today. Wrapped in his heavy wool cloak against the chill of this crisp autumn morning, he was focused intently on the song that was forming in his mind. He planned to give the tune to the bards in case they wanted it for their Samhain presentations.

Despite his many duties as Ceann-Druí, he enjoyed creating songs and verses and welcomed their occasional inspiration. He celebrated the appearance of An Síoraí in any of its manifestations.

As was his habit, he had been up and dressed before daybreak, ready to greet the dawn with prayers for his people. The sun had matched his mood, rising cheerfully and casting a rosy glow upon the landscape that lay serenely under the October sky, the fields now cleared from a bountiful harvest.

Without Ah-Lahn's notice, the morning's remaining mist had drifted off down the hill, through the túath, and far away from the spacious thatched cottage where the Ceann-Druí sat, singing new stanzas as they came to him.

Éire! How you call to me
Awake or in my deepest dreams,

Beloved isle, you have nourished me
since birth, through youth,
and you bear me still
along the road I walk as a man.

I love you to the depth and breadth
of my soul's yearning to be free.
The shimmering green of your fields and dales,
the presence of earth and rock and tree,
hold me like a mother does,
embracing her most precious child.

Your wild, eternal sea does speak
to me of far-off distant shores,
as it once called my ancestors
to sail away to this bless'd land,
to sail away to this bless'd land,
to sail away to this bless'd land.

I glory in your atmosphere
of mists and birdsong in the morn,
and midday's warm, fair-scented breeze.
Even stormy winds do thrill
my very soul when I am home,
the place where I most long to be,
the place where I most long to be,
the place where I most long to be.

Satisfied at last that his new song was well anchored in his memory,
Ah-Lahn decided to visit his friend and colleague, Dearbhla. They had
known each other since childhood and still enjoyed an ease of associa-
tion that never failed to cheer them both.

As youths they had teased each other about their preferences—

his for words and philosophy, hers for plants and prophecy. Now that they were adults, they were grateful for the different perspectives that informed their shared affinity for mysteries of the human soul.

And they inevitably discovered new insights into challenges they each faced in service to their people.

Ah-Lahn looked forward to a stimulating conversation with his trusted friend. And, truth be told, he was eager to see her niece, Alana, again.

He needed to discern if the spark of recognition he had felt for the young woman a year ago was still present. Would he again experience the same thrill of attraction that had rippled through him on that fateful day? Or had he simply imagined a connection between himself and Dearbhla's niece because he was travel weary?

Ah-Lahn resolutely made his way to his friend's cottage and pondered all these questions. As he walked, he remembered the stunning sensation that had bloomed in his heart when he first encountered Alana—almost exactly a year ago, not long before Óengus named him Ceann-Druí.

First Glimpse

*A*h-Lahn breathed deeply of autumn's crisp air and rubbed his hands over his face. He had recently returned from one of Toísech Cróga's frequent skirmishes with a neighboring Brigantes chieftain. The past several weeks had been difficult, and Ah-Lahn needed to clear his head.

Always a creature of the morning, he had decided to take a stroll in the garden that Dearbhla's young apprentices tended as part of their training in the healing arts. Unbeknownst to him, the Banfháidh's orphaned niece frequently walked there.

Dearbhla's garden was tucked behind a thick stand of hazel trees, so Ah-Lahn heard Alana before he saw her. He was soon to learn why even seasoned bards in her homeland had often paused to listen, enthralled by the bell-like tone of her voice.

The druí was dazzled by the natural genius he heard in her singing. He was deeply touched by the depth of sorrow she expressed. His heart wept with hers as she sang of losing those she loved. He, too, had suffered great loss, though many years ago. Her emotional outpouring moved him as none had done for a very long time.

> Wind-tossed waves on Muir Éireann
> Dark ahead, no light behind.
> Family, friends, what shall befall us?
> Will we ever meet again?
>
> Sail, oh sail, my soul flies onward.
> Mother, safety, all are lost.

> Orphaned woman, child no longer.
> I will survive at any cost.
>
> Lonely stranger on an island.
> Songs of love lie hollow here.
> Learn to live in secret places.
> Destiny's call may yet be clear.

Ah-Lahn stood still as myriad thoughts tumbled, one after another, through his mind:

Her passion arises purely from An Síoraí, he thought. Such purity must be protected—though from what, he could not say. Still, in this moment, he knew he must shield her from some unknown threat that he could feel breathing down his own neck.

If he were able to stay at home in the túath, he would personally see to her safety. But he and his fellow druí, Arán Bán, would be leaving immediately after the Samhain festivities to study for several months with Ard-Mháistir Óengus.

"Let her be, Ah-Lahn," he quietly chided himself. There was little he could do for the young woman at present.

Yet, what was this profound affection that quivered within him as he watched and listened to her?

He was old enough to be her father. She and his son, Tadhgan, were likely close in age. How could he justify being instantly attracted to a young woman who was nearly two decades his junior?

But he could not deny the feeling that, for the first time since his wife's death nearly twenty years ago, the stirrings of love quickened within his breast.

Without warning, he found himself whispering—for he dared not startle the young woman by singing aloud—a spontaneous ballad of deep affection.

> She drifts by me like gentle mist
> that nestles in and 'round the roses
> still flourishing within this garden,

a place of soil and sky's pure union,
with birds and trees and softest grasses
that thrive in this bless'd sanctuary.

She comes here for her heart's renewal,
to grieve and offer fervent praise
for blessings of peace to feed the soul,
abundance of food for bodies' sake,
all lovingly sown and gathered in,
secure to last all winter long.

Nature offers life's deep wisdom
to those who learn to read the signs.
This lady tends a lush grove garden
where I am bidden to observe
the sowings of her nimble hands,
nourished by her honeyed tones.

I am lifted up in her soul's song.
I am lifted up in her soul's song.

Desiring not to disturb Alana's meditation, Ah-Lahn had quietly withdrawn to Dearbhla's comfortable dwelling, a thatched cottage similar
to his own, though much roomier. The Banfháidh's main living space
included an adjoining workshop area where she guided her apprentices
in the herbal arts essential to their healing practices.

"Greetings, Dearbhla."

"Ah-Lahn, a chara. I am pleased to see you."

They exchanged the pleasantries of old friends until Ah-Lahn felt he
could pose the question that was begging to be asked.

"Who is that striking young songbird in your garden?"

"She is my niece, Alana. Her mother was my younger sister, Enfys.
You were away when they fled here this past summer to escape the threat

that turned into the massacre at Ynys Môn."

Ah-Lahn frowned at the mention of that terrible event.

"Incomplete reports reached us on campaign. Several of us druíthe were with Toísech Cróga in place of Old Quin, who, I understand, is still under the weather. We have only now returned home.

"I gleaned a bit more information from some seamen who brought refugees here, but they were still too shaken to relate the full story. What they did tell me was beyond comprehension. Did I hear correctly that Alana's mother died here in Tearmann?"

"Enfys participated in the battle, and that is what killed her." Tears welled up in Dearbhla's large grey eyes.

Ah-Lahn looked puzzled. "I thought your sister and Alana were safe here."

"They were, but Enfys experienced the entire event in her finer body. She was a gifted seer and bandruí who was determined to act as a shield for her father-in-law and her husband. That determination proved her undoing."

Ah-Lahn's spine tingled as he once again felt the energetic reverberations of the massacre. Druíthe all over the world had experienced that tremor and feared for their lives.

He willed his attention back to Dearbhla. "Your sister must have been a remarkable person. How is her daughter faring?"

"May I tell you their story?" Dearbhla asked somewhat tentatively.

"Of course," Ah-Lahn responded warmly.

"Thank you, mo chara. Speaking of them helps me, and you are the only person I feel comfortable telling the whole of it."

Tragedy's Legacy

Dearbhla gathered her shawl around her shoulders as she prepared to explain the tragic events surrounding Alana's arrival in Éire not quite three months earlier.

"My sister, Enfys, was beautiful and incredibly intuitive, though not at all practical when she was young. She had a habit of wandering off into the invisible world, communing with deceased relatives, faeries, and other spirit beings. I am certain that is why she was kidnapped by raiders."

"How and when did they take Enfys?" Ah-Lahn asked.

"When she was eighteen and I was twenty. She was off on one of her wanderings in a secluded cove not far from Tearmann when a band of raiders drew up in a small currach boat. They were retrieving some of their booty from previous inland raids on their way back to Albion.

"Apparently, they saw Enfys walking along with that dazed look her family knew well. The raiders snatched her and rowed off to the larger boat that would return them to their base. Naturally, they planned to sell her into slavery as soon as they landed.

"Fortunately, before they could reach Albion's shore, they were waylaid by a band of fierce local seamen. Ard-Druí Bleddyn's son, Carwyn, was on board. As a druíthe, he was exempt from fighting, but he was good with a sword. In Albion, if you did not fight, you did not survive.

"They had sailed out to support other warriors who were searching for pirates that troubled the rich trade along their coast of Muir Éireann. Carywn had planned only to offer prayers for the warriors, but they came upon the thieves by accident, and his swordsmanship was needed.

"He and the seamen swooped in on the raiders and quickly dispatched every one of them. Fortunately, they had spotted Enfys in time to save her from a pirate who was about to toss her overboard.

"Years later my sister described for me the thrill she felt when Carwyn rescued her. Her words are as clear in my mind now as the day she told me the story."

Carwyn was incredibly powerful, standing on deck of the raiders' boat with his bloody sword, looking around for any pirates who might still be alive. And yet he was kind to me, a frightened young girl. As soon as I looked into his dark brown eyes, I knew I was for him.

I wanted only to be at his side. I begged to stay with his tribe and soon became his wife. Alana was the child of our union. Both her father and grandfather cherished her, and she grew up determined to become a bandruí.

Ah-Lahn was full of questions. "How did Alana and her mother get here? And how exactly did your sister die?"

Dearbhla continued: "The community of Ynys Môn was large, with its own renowned school where druíthe could focus on the areas of expertise that most suited their talents. For decades, our great master druíthe have traveled there for higher learning."

"I myself had hoped to study at Ynys Môn," commented Ah-Lahn, "but with Uncle Óengus's school in Cois Abhann, travel was unnecessary."

The druí paused. His eyes grew wide.

"Dearbhla, do you realize that my staying here in Éire most likely saved my life? If I had gone to Ynys Môn, I might have been tempted to stay there and teach. I was interested in the theories of the Greek philosopher, Pythagoras, which had been handed down through the lineage of the druíthe and were a specialty of Bleddyn's school."

"I am grateful you are still here, mo chara," said Dearbhla. "I know you would have been loyal to the community, and I fear things would not have gone well for you."

Dearbhla drank deeply from a cup of water and resumed her story.

"The druíthe of Ynys Môn were prosperous because they controlled a large portion of the gold trade between Éire and Albion. Of course, wealth made them a target.

"However, the real threat they posed was their profound inner knowing. They did not rely on outer structures to comprehend the mysteries of life and death. Those whose power is built upon separating entire peoples from their land and culture are threatened by those who live in the unifying flow of An Síoraí.

"Capturing the gold was an excuse the enemy used to justify their attack on Ynys Môn. The real reason was fear of the otherworldly power wielded by the druíthe who taught that the soul's nature is freedom.

"As a community gifted with many seers, the leaders knew trouble was brewing. Also, refugees from Gaul reported a build-up of heavily armed legions moving west through Albion. An attack on Ynys Môn was inevitable and came to pass three months ago.

"Enfys was determined to remain with her husband, to support him and his father, Bleddyn, who for over twenty years had been Ard-Druí of Ynys Môn. But Carwyn forbade her. He feared that he, and even his father, would be fighting as much as praying.

"My sister told me the whole story when she and Alana first arrived. I can still hear the anguish in her voice as she relayed how she and her daughter were separated from their family."

'You must leave, Enfys,' Carwyn commanded me, though I knew saying so wounded his soul.

'Take Alana and sail to Éire while there is time. You are my legacy and Alana is our future. See her safely to your sister's care and be at peace.

'I must remain here to take this stand against the invaders' tyranny, but you and our daughter must go. Time is running out for you to escape. Please, do as I ask.'

Oh, Dearbhla, I knew I would never see him again in this life, and I could not bear the thought. I could hardly stifle the anguished cry that rose up in my throat.

I desperately embraced Carwyn as he clasped his strong

arms around me. I knew he would not demand this sacrifice of me unless our daughter's future depended upon it.

At last I acquiesced. Rising up on tiptoe to whisper in his ear, I told him, 'Alana and I will sail to Éire, but I will not leave your side. I will be with you, come what may.'

Dearbhla paused briefly. Ah-Lahn could see the great effort required for her to calm the emotions she still felt acutely.

"Two days later, Enfys, Alana, other mothers and children, and the sick or elderly who could travel slipped away from Ynys Môn in the company of some seafaring gold traders. They sailed across the rough waters of Muir Éireann in several large currach boats, eventually arriving here in the land of the Brigantes.

"The attack came only weeks later. Enfys was distraught as she kept a vigil of prayer for her husband and father-in-law as they prepared for battle.

"As soon as forces began arraying on both sides of Afon Menai, she could not be dissuaded from trying to protect Bleddyn, Carwyn, and the other druíthe and bandruíthe who would be giving their utmost to repel the onslaught.

"She made me vow not to tell Alana what she was doing to protect her loved ones. She said that her daughter, as yet untried, should not face such an initiation. And she placed around her own consciousness an orb of invisibility that she believed Alana did not have the skill to penetrate.

"Enfys begged me to leave her alone as she traveled back to Ynys Môn in her finer body, but I could not. I stayed with her physical body that she left sleeping as she lived through the awful event in its entirety. Through my inner sight, I witnessed everything.

"I will never forget my sister's fierce expression as she stood for hours, holding her hands aloft and crying to the heavens the prayers of protection that she hoped would help turn back the violence of invasion and destruction.

Dearbhla paused again and shuddered in recollection of the terrible event she was about to relate.

Ah-Lahn placed his hand on her arm. "I am here, mo chara. You do not have to go on if the memory is too painful."

"The memory is very painful, but I must tell you," Dearbhla insisted, squaring her shoulders. "Future generations must know the truth of how a great community of learning was wiped out by ignorance and fear. Their story is part of the legacy I feel honor-bound to share.

"Ah-Lahn, promise me you will preserve this truth for those who come after us."

"I will, I promise."

As Dearbhla prepared to recount the full extent of her sister's courage and her own experience as witness, Ah-Lahn opened his mind to memorize the narrative as master bards and druíthe had done for centuries. He must remember every word of the story that came to be known as *The Sacrifice of Ynys Môn*:

The druíthe were able to observe the foot soldiers before they noticed our force. Our magicians had conjured the féath fíadha mists in order to listen to the enemy's conversation.

There were hundreds of them, like an army of ants, ready to swarm across Afon Menai's treacherous currents in their flat-bottomed boats. They were afraid, mumbling among themselves the lies they had been told about us since childhood.

'They practice human sacrifice and drink the blood of their enemies,' they were telling each other. 'If we do not kill them first, they will cut our throats and eat our hearts.'

Such hideous lies, but also useful ones. Our leaders believed they could use the soldiers' fear against them.

Our brave male and female warriors arrayed themselves on our side of the strait. Their bodies were painted blue and some of the fiercest were naked save for their boots and weapons. They were shouting threats, banging their swords on their shields, brandishing spears, and waving flaming torches.

Carnyx players added to the cacophony with weird and frightening sounds blaring from their massive bronze horns.

The enemy had never seen trumpets as tall as a man with bells shaped like wild bores or fantastical animals that looked as intimidating as the terrible noise they created.

Armed volunteers joined the warriors' ranks at strategic intervals while the druíthe and bandruíthe stood in rows behind the warriors. From that position they could direct their prayers and invocations into the most critical locations once the battle began.

Bleddyn and Carwyn were in almost constant motion as they moved among our defenders. The two men would pray and fight wherever the need was greatest.

Gradually, the druíthe dissolved the mist to reveal the spectacle of our warriors. The commotion our force created was frightful. I can still see many of the foot soldiers paralyzed with fear, unwilling to face the magical powers of our people.

For a while, the enemy ranks continued to falter. As they hesitated, the druíthe intensified their prayers. They raised their hands and voices to the sky, invoking the spiritual and elemental powers that have kept our tribes safe for centuries.

Enfys was with them in her finer body, standing at the side of her husband and father-in-law. The three of them had never appeared more powerful.

Our show of force was working, and our warriors began to cheer. But suddenly, from behind the army's right flank, their commander and his cavalry came riding, furiously splashing back and forth through the shallows, threatening their foot soldiers with gruesome death if they did not board their boats and cross the narrow strip of water.

Fired by their leader's exhortations, the soldiers proceeded as other enemy fighters remained behind, launching huge boulders from the war machines they had set up on the shore they controlled. These projectiles landed with devastating effect on our defenders. Nevertheless, those who were not injured hurled their spears with great accuracy, killing many soldiers and cavalry that were swimming next to their boats.

Eventually, the invaders landed. As their ranks reformed, they began a steady march forward, the clank-clank of their armor creating the rhythm of inevitability that their armies have used for hundreds of years to conquer and destroy.

Many enemy foot soldiers continued to fall, but the columns behind them simply stepped over their wounded comrades, inexorably closing the distance between themselves and our people.

'Hold the line!' shouted our leaders. But even our best fighters were being infected by the blood lust and fear that was emanating from the invaders.

Without warning, in a moment of tragic chaos, many of our frenzied warriors rushed forward, shouting and cursing at the soldiers. They were determined to engage the enemy that I could see from Enfys's expression the druíthe now realized they could not defeat.

No one was thinking, only acting. The armies clashed, and the bloodbath began with crazed ferocity.

'Retreat!' I heard Bleddyn shout. The gruesome battle was waning. The druíthe had to move to higher ground to continue praying. The vicious army had decimated our warriors and was descending upon the living areas.

The army's leaders had commanded their soldiers to take no prisoners. No one was spared. Men and women, old and young were butchered, their homes torched, their bodies piled and burned.

I did my best to follow Enfys in case I could pull her back from the fray. But she would not leave Bleddyn and Carwyn. They were still fighting while urging others to flee.

The three of them were faithful to the end, which I could see was fast approaching as the invading leaders ordered their final act of savagery against our people.

The wicked red tongues of fire rising up in the distance could mean only one thing: The sacred oak groves had been set aflame, killing all those who thought to be safe among their sweeping branches, but were now caught in the inferno, unable to escape.

I stood transfixed, seemingly for ages, witnessing the final destruction of that most sacred sanctuary. Unfortunately, as I watched the flames, I lost sight of Enfys.

With my inner vision, I frantically searched the awful scenes of carnage, at first to no avail.

Finally, I found her. She was still in her finer body, running behind Bleddyn and Carwyn. They had been captured by a group of soldiers who were brutally wrestling them to stand at attention in front of the enemy leader.

I could not believe what I was seeing. The man's bloodshot eyes were filled with inhuman hatred. Snarling a curse at Ard-Druí Bleddyn, the crazed commander killed him with a single thrust of his sword and then maliciously faced Carwyn.

But Carwyn was smiling. He turned away from the commander. As his eyes met those of Enfys, who was beside him, I saw him tell her one last time, 'I love you.'

An instant later, he fell to the ground as the commander maniacally plunged his sword into the brave druí's back again and again, as if he were afraid that a single blow would not kill a man who smiles in the face of death.

Ah-Lahn and Dearbhla clutched each other's hands for a moment and then sat back as she wearily finished the tale.

"The moment the enemy leader killed Carwyn, Enfys uttered an anguished cry and hurtled back into her physical body. She immediately lost consciousness and collapsed into my arms, as limp as one already departed from this world.

"In the same instant, Alana rushed in. She had felt the attack on her family and knew something was terribly wrong.

"For several days Enfys lay as if dead. Although Alana, the fáidthe, and I did our best to rouse her, she was beyond our ability to reverse the outcome she herself had set in motion.

"On the third morning, she awakened and weakly called Alana to her side. I will never forget my sister's final words to her daughter as she spoke in a ragged whisper.

'My beautiful Alana. Please, do not be angry with me for returning to Ynys Môn. I could not leave my men alone to make the ultimate sacrifice.

'We were buying time, mo chroí, for you and for all who might escape to Éire and beyond these shores. Even now, the enemy commander has been recalled to fight our kinsmen in Albion. Many have risen up against his senseless brutality.

'Alana, my daughter, you must carry on. Complete your studies with your aunt and the druíthe who live here. They will care for you. Embrace their people as your own and serve them well. You have the gift to become a great bandruí.

'Remember us with love, mo chroí. Honor your heritage and follow our path. Your father awaits me in the invisible world. I have delayed too long.

'Farewell, Alana. I will love you forever.'

Dearbhla paused for a moment and then gathered herself to complete the telling of the traumatic story.

Ah-Lahn sat in silence before his friend, his eyes wide in amazement. He had never been more impressed with her courage or her ability as a seer. The woman was formidable. He vowed never to underestimate her ability to face the most difficult of challenges.

"That is the end of the story, Ah-Lahn. Enfys died immediately after speaking with Alana. My sister believed she could survive the battle in her finer body. Unfortunately, she had expended so much of her own life force in trying to shield her husband and father-in-law that, when Carwyn died, she could not live.

"Alana has been here with me ever since. She spends many hours in the garden, which I pray will help heal her grief. She seems to be adjusting, but I know she feels isolated and alone."

Differences

*A*h-Lahn's mind snapped back to the present, though his head still swam with memories from a year ago.

Now that he and Cróga had agreed to remain in Tearmann through the winter, he was intent on visiting Dearbhla and her niece as soon as possible. Once and for all, he must determine if his attraction to Alana was real or imagined. And, was she in need of his protection?

Despite his eagerness to clarify his feelings for Alana, Ah-Lahn followed a round-about path to Dearbhla's cottage so he could think.

His son, Tadhgan, was also on his mind. The young man was studying to be a bard and aspired to one day be an Ollamh—a master bard—like his mentor, Gormlaith. However, the son had stated emphatically that he wanted to be nothing like his father.

Born to a mother who had died at his birth, Tadhgan was a wiry eighteen-year-old. He was brash, sure of his intellect and brooding good looks, and, to his father's mind, entirely too cocky. Though blessed with impressive talent for a bard's dramatic delivery of story, song, and chant, Tadhgan's character made him a difficult person.

The boy's impetuosity was one of the reasons Ah-Lahn had requested permission from Gormlaith to conduct a few mentoring sessions with his son. He wanted to help the lad in any way he could, and he believed Tadhgan would benefit from the unique direction that he, as a master druí who was also a lover of language, could provide.

Unfortunately, the young man was strongly resistant to his father's influence, which had doubled Ah-Lahn's determination to help set his son on a path that would bring out his best qualities. That task would not be easy.

Ollamh Gormlaith understood why the Ceann-Druí hoped to help his son. She also wanted the best for Tadhgan. He was one of her most promising apprentices and would surely earn his bronze bard's bough in the coming year—if he maintained his harmony.

She could not help being fond of the lad. She had been cousin to his mother, Lile. The day before Tadhgan was born, Lile had surprised her cousin by begging her to watch over the baby—should anything go wrong with the birth.

Gormlaith did not press her family connection with Tadhgan. But throughout the years of his apprenticeship, she had let him know that she believed in his talent. She also believed that his immersion in a bard's communion with An Síoraí would eventually heal him of the unknown burden that made him restless, easily offended, and prone to self-pity.

As kinswoman and Ollamh, she gave Ah-Lahn her full support in his efforts on behalf of his son, but she feared their interactions would not turn out well.

Ah-Lahn approached the central green on his way to the school for fáidthe that was located some distance away. There he saw Dearbhla and Gormlaith. They, along with Arán Bán, were watching a rehearsal of a dramatization that apprentice bards, including Tadhgan, were to present at tomorrow's Samhain festival.

The Ceann-Druí was surprised to discover that Alana was also performing. Because he had learned from a casual remark made by his fellow druí, Riordan, that Arán Bán had assumed the role of Alana's sole mentor, he secluded himself behind a stand of hazel trees where he could observe without being seen.

He had been puzzled by the disquiet that had rippled through him when his friend told him the news, though he could not say exactly what troubled him. Yet, as he watched Alana practice her song, he detected a reason for his concern.

He maintained his distance until the rehearsal concluded and the young performers dispersed. He did not attempt to speak with his son. He had more pressing matters to address. He came out from behind the trees and called to Dearbhla as she said good-bye to her colleagues and turned toward her school.

"Dearbhla, may I walk with you?"

"Of course, mo chara."

Ah-Lahn embraced Dearbhla warmly and commented casually as they walked together. "I did not expect to see your niece among the young bards. I thought her skill would have exceeded that of an apprentice long before she arrived here."

"Oh, Alana is not studying with the bards," Dearbhla explained. "Gormlaith asked if she would like to join in the presentation because everyone enjoys her singing. Arán Bán gave his permission, but only if she was given a featured song and only if he coached her. I thought her rehearsal went well."

"I see," said Ah-Lahn, although he thought it odd that Arán Bán would be directing his protégé's vocal performance.

"Can you tell me how Arán Bán came to be Alana's mentor? I would have expected you to assume that role. Surely, spending time with the fáidthe would have aided her ability to hold her grief gently."

"Alana asked to work with Arán Bán," Dearbhla stated plainly, a tinge of disappointment in her voice. "She told me that only a master druí could guide her. She has not discussed her studies with me, other than to say that Arán Bán determined she needed more training in the Brehon Laws. She seems happy with that arrangement, which I find reasonable. She always enjoyed discussing the law with her grandfather, Ard-Druí Bleddyn."

The two friends entered Dearbhla's cottage, but Ah-Lahn could not sit. He paced as the Banfháidh prepared one of her hot herbal drinks.

"Ah-Lahn, what is bothering you?"

"I am not certain," he said, finally taking the seat Dearbhla offered and furrowing his brow. "I agree that Alana sang well today. And yet I noticed a subtle difference from when I observed her a year ago.

"When I first heard her sing in your garden, there was a freedom to her spirit, a depth in her expression. Her voice rose and fell easily, where now it seems constrained, as if she were afraid of something. Her technique is flawless, but when I watched Alana perform just now, I could not help imagining a caged songbird. Have you noticed a change in her recently?"

"I have not had much occasion to observe Alana," said Dearbhla. "I know that Arán Bán has been preparing her to eventually study with Ard-Mháistir Óengus, but that is all. My niece and her mentor have said quite clearly that I am not to interfere with his methods.

"Of course, I would like to engage Alana in some skills of the fáidthe that will be useful to her as a bandruí. Perhaps she will be open to working with me later if Uncle Óengus encourages her."

Dearbhla and Ah-Lahn became lost in thought. As was their habit when considering a complex situation, they settled into An Síoraí's intuitive inspiration, allowing their own inner guidance to suggest a solution. A way forward was not long in appearing.

"I have an idea!" they said in unison and then laughed at the unity of mind they had enjoyed for many years.

"Go ahead, Ah-Lahn," Dearbhla invited, "although I am certain I know what you are going to suggest."

"Of course you do." Ah-Lahn chuckled. "Can you arrange for Alana to come to your cottage this afternoon? I would like to interview her without Arán Bán present. As you are her only family and I am Ceann-Druí, I believe we have an obligation to ensure that she is being guided as her parents and grandfather would have wished."

"I agree," said Dearbhla. "I do wonder about Arán Bán's approach with Alana. Although she is accomplished in many of a bandruí's arts, she was sheltered at Ynys Môn. She is intellectually mature, but while she was living with me I noticed an emotional innocence about her that made her easily swayed by the strong opinions of others."

"We know that Arán Bán can be very persuasive, especially when his audience is receptive," Ah-Lahn added. "He holds strong opinions about the duties of a master druí that may have influenced Alana.

"Or she may have simply mistaken flawless technique for An Síoraí's perfect flow. Many druíthe have gone through that phase on their way to developing true mastery."

Ah-Lahn embraced his friend and returned to his own cottage.

Dearbhla immediately sent word to Arán Bán requesting that Alana visit her that afternoon for what she described as an important family matter that could not wait.

Alana's mentor grudgingly agreed. He would insist that his protégé rehearse doubly hard that evening. They both expected her Samhain performance to be perfect.

Confrontation

Alana was halfway across the threshold of her aunt's cottage when she halted abruptly in mid-step. Standing before her was the Ceann-Druí himself, the very person Arán Bán had recently warned her about.

"Beware Ah-Lahn's apparent kindness," he had said pointedly in response to her remark that she had never met the Ceann-Druí.

"His words are smooth, but his charm has fooled many who only later discovered that he prevented them from rising any higher than his own position. Even as a young man, he was ambitious for power. More than once have I been on the receiving end of his schemes. Do not trust him, my girl, no matter what he promises you."

Alana gathered herself to the fullness of her medium height, entered the cottage, and planted herself before the man she suspected of being a threat. She and Ah-Lahn eyed one another, steadily taking the other's measure and reaching very different conclusions.

His eyes are kind, but that could be a trick, Alana surmised. She must be cautious and read between the lines as Arán Bán had taught her.

Why does she look so defensive? Ah-Lahn wondered. Had her mind been set against him? He must proceed carefully.

Stilling his own mind, he said cordially, "Welcome, Alana. Please, come in and be seated."

She did not move. "I prefer to stand. I am expected shortly for my afternoon tutorial. Arán Bán insists that I be prompt." She made a point of emphasizing his name.

"I am aware of your mentor's punctuality," said Ah-Lahn, smiling to

himself. He remembered how Arán Bán had scolded him for being late
to a session with Uncle Óengus when they were studying with the Ard
mháistir last winter.

"Alana, your aunt has secured your release for the remainder of the
day, so please, be seated. The three of us have much to discuss."

Seeing she had no choice but to comply, Alana sat in a chair nearest
the cottage's entrance. At least she would be close to the exit in case she
felt the need to escape to Arán Bán's grove.

Ah-Lahn stifled a smile. He could practically hear her strategizing.
Her mind was impressive, though she would be appalled to know how
loudly her thoughts spoke to him.

"We are interested in your studies, Alana. I happened to see your
rehearsal this morning. You appear to be doing well under your mentor's
guidance."

"Arán Bán says that my technique is beginning to match my talent."
She answered in the confident tone he had told her she must use with
people who might not appreciate the extent of her gifts.

"I see," continued Ah-Lahn. This behavior was new. He had observed
nothing arrogant in her demeanor a year ago.

"Indeed, you are gaining a reputation for excellence," he agreed.
"Yet, I sense you may be carrying a burden you have not felt safe to
share with your aunt. You are protected here. No one can make you do
anything against your will. What is troubling you, Alana? Has someone
frightened you?"

Alana stared at Ah-Lahn. How could he know such things? She had
barely admitted to herself the internal conflict she had been wrestling
with for weeks.

Her first three months with Arán Bán as her mentor had been very
satisfying. They had agreed that she needed more training in the Brehon
Laws, and he had introduced her to more precise interpretations of the
law than she had ever received at Ynys Môn.

But recently, the man had, indeed, begun to frighten her.

If she failed to express the law in the exact manner he preferred, he
became cross and threatening. He accused her of not taking her studies
seriously. And he had drilled her relentlessly on how she should perform

her song at Samhain.

His behavior toward her was becoming erratic. Alana was beginning to wonder if his original reason for agreeing to mentor her no longer applied.

At the beginning of their relationship, he had expressed his pleasure that she had grown up surrounded by illustrious druíthe. But nowadays, he treated her heritage less like the advantage he had extolled and more like a thorn in his side that made him very angry.

Then he would catch himself and apologize, expressing unusual affection for one in his position. At first, he had done nothing more than give her a peck on the cheek. But more recently he had ventured to cup her face with his hands and look deeply into her eyes.

She was finding him increasingly difficult to resist, as each new tenderness awakened in her a disturbing sensation that drew her to him. She knew that, as her mentor, he should not attempt to seduce her, yet that seemed to be his intention. She worried that her own desires were beginning to match his.

All of these thoughts flashed across Alana's mind in an instant. She willed her expression to remain neutral so as not to betray the confusion that was bubbling up in her mind.

"I do not know what you mean."

"I believe you do, Alana," Ah-Lahn said evenly. He realized he had been holding his breath while she leveled a cool stare at him.

"You have nothing to fear from me. Your aunt and I merely wish to evaluate your current studies. Would you be willing to sing something for us? Perhaps one of your own compositions?"

"I am not working on music. I am learning to be an accurate interpreter of the law," she objected. "In any case, I did not bring my harp."

"Every subject has its inner music, Alana. And every melody harmonizes with every other melody to create a symphony that is the great work we aspire to perform in whatever capacity we are called. From what I know of your homeland, I feel certain that harmony would have been part of Ynys Môn's culture."

It was, but she was not going to agree with him.

Alana scowled, and Ah-Lahn caught her meaning—very clearly.

"Your aunt and I understand that the Brehon Laws flow from the music of justice, as a bard's offering is improved by years of practice of their forms. Therefore, your voice alone is sufficient for whatever you would like to share with us."

"Very well," Alana agreed, though she continued to eye the Ceann-Druí suspiciously. She would run if he threatened her.

Alana stood and faced Ah-Lahn and Dearbhla.

"I call this piece 'Fatherhood.' I wrote the lines in the voice of my father, Carwyn. This is the story he told me about his experience of seeing me for the first time, right after I was born."

"I am eager to hear your song," said Ah-Lahn as he recalled the difficult circumstances surrounding the birth of his son.

"My heart broke open today . . ." The first line caught in Alana's throat. Get control of yourself! she fumed silently. She had better not be blushing. Swallowing hard, she summoned her determination and sang.

My heart broke open today,
on the day you were born,
on the day I became your father.

How could a being so tiny create such an earthquake,
shattering my defenses, rendering me helpless,
vulnerable, ridiculously and blissfully in love
with you and your mother?

I sense a strength I have never felt,
as if a noble power had descended upon me.
I stand up straighter and walk with new confidence
to greet my fellow men.

My heart expands
with a joy unparalleled in worldly deeds.
All because your infant fist grasps my finger

with a persistent determination
that speaks right to my soul:
'You are my father and I will never let you go.'
In this moment, I am not ashamed of my tears.

Alana fought back the flood of emotion that now threatened to undo her. Furious at her weakness, she turned and headed for the cottage's entrance.

"Alana, stop!" Ah-Lahn was on his feet in an instant. "Please return to your seat. You have not been dismissed."

She turned around, but did not move from the door.

"I would like to discuss your song, which has moved your aunt and me," Ah-Lahn said firmly as Dearbhla held her hands to her heart.

Alana's temper erupted.

"You tricked me, as Arán Bán said you would! He warned me about your manipulative ways. Now I know he spoke the truth. You have made me forget my hard work, but you will not turn me against him, even though you are Ceann-Druí. Punish me if you like, I am loyal to my mentor!"

"Have you done something to deserve punishment?" Ah-Lahn was genuinely surprised by Alana's explosive response. Why would she expect reprisal for what had been a touching performance?

"Arán Bán gets angry when I lose control of my delivery. Once he threatened to strike me."

Alana instantly chided herself. Why had she said that?

"Did he strike you?" Ah-Lahn took a deep breath and waited. The room bristled with the tension between them.

"Arán Bán would never do that. After he loses his temper, he apologizes and becomes . . .I suppose you might say, 'tender'." Alana searched for a word that would not reveal the extent of her mentor's amorous behavior, or her own unwitting response.

Every muscle in Ah-Lahn's body was on edge. Do not frighten her, he cautioned himself.

"I see," he said evenly. "Let us leave that subject for now. At the moment, I am most interested to know how you would describe your experience in singing your song."

What was the Ceann-Druí up to, and why was she trembling?

Alana felt as if she were about to step off a cliff. Instead, she took the seat across from her aunt, sat up straight, and gripped her hands in her lap. "Arán Bán and I agreed that I am not to get caught up in my emotions."

Dearbhla leaned over and rested her hand on her niece's knee. "He is not here, Alana. You can talk to us."

The young woman said nothing, so Ah-Lahn continued, though her expression warned him to tread lightly.

"I am certain your mentors at Ynys Môn demonstrated that, regardless of our roles as bards, fáidthe, or druíthe, we must at all times retain some awareness of our own emotions. Our gift is to welcome An Síoraí's inspiration, and our service is to inspire our listeners."

"Do not speak to me of An Síoraí!" Without warning, Alana shot to her feet, her eyes flashing at Ah-Lahn and Dearbhla.

"Arán Bán says that too much reliance on An Síoraí is the problem. The druíthe of Ynys Môn followed inspiration and imagination to their deaths. They were innocents living in a naïve world of inner knowing, and what happened? They were slaughtered because they did not pay attention to the outer world!"

"Alana, my dear . . ." Dearbhla began.

"Do not try to placate me, Aunt Dearbhla! I saw what happened. I watched Bleddyn and Carwyn fall! My mother thought she could prevent me from seeing her return to Ynys Môn on the inner, but she could not block my tie to the community. I knew every one of those people who perished. They were all my family.

"Enfys should have told me what she was doing! You should have made her tell me! At least I could have prayed for her while she was in the battle. If I had been with you from the beginning, she might have survived. You and I together could have lent her enough life force to save her when she rushed back into her body.

"Instead, you and my mother trusted An Síoraí to inspire you, and my family died! They all died!"

Uncontrollable sobs shook Alana's body. She could not stop the hot tears streaming down her cheeks. When Dearbhla went to her side to comfort her, she shook off her aunt's embrace.

For months she had worked hard to attain the precision Arán Bán demanded. Now she had negated that effort in a flood of emotion. And she had likely put herself in danger with a single song she never should have offered to the Ceann-Druí.

Alana's mind was whirling as she glared at Ah-Lahn.

"You would turn me into the same kind of bandruí as my mother, but I will not have it! I will become a druí like Arán Bán. One who knows the Brehon Laws, who speaks with disciplined authority, and who does not succumb to the siren song of An Síoraí."

Alana looked directly at Ah-Lahn and declared, "Arán Bán says that many people use An Síoraí as an excuse for being mentally lazy. I have a strong mind. Let me use it!"

Dearbhla faced her niece, horrified at her outburst. She longed to ease Alana's pain and knew she could not.

"I am sorry your mother tried to block your awareness of what she was doing," the Banfháidh explained. "Enfys was certain the initiation would be too much for you. I regret that we both underestimated you.

"As for our meeting today, the Ceann-Druí and I only want to help you fulfill your calling as a bandruí. We had thought you might be open to spending some time with the fáidthe before going to study with Ard-Mháistir Óengus."

Alana clenched her fists at her sides. "Arán Bán would not like such an abrupt change, and neither do I." She turned to Ah-Lahn who had stood to face her. Her voice was now coolly controlled.

"I do not trust you, Ceann-Druí. I acknowledge your interest and yours, Aunt Dearbhla, but I will decide what is best for me. You may have confused me today, but I will not be so vulnerable in the future. I will decide for myself what studies to pursue."

"Very well, Alana." Ah-Lahn lowered his voice, willing himself to speak calmly. "You are free to choose your path. No one is forced into any avenue of practice in the arts of the druíthe. You may let your aunt know when you have decided how you wish to proceed. Until then, you have my blessing."

Ah-Lahn restrained his impulse to place his hand on Alana's brow.

He wanted to free her mind from the mental cage she had built around herself, but he did not want her to think he was trying to manipulate her. He could not force her to resolve her misunderstanding of An Síoraí.

Instead, he walked to the doorway. He turned, bowed slightly to the two women, and strode resolutely away from Dearbhla's cottage. He did not stop until he reached the reassuring atmosphere of his own wisdom grove.

Ah-Lahn paced back and forth between the grove's ancient oak trees. He ran his fingers through his hair and wondered: Had he acted in Alana's best interest, or had he behaved like a jealous lover?

He was upset to learn that Arán Bán had abused his position as Alana's mentor. There had been rumors about the man's behavior in the past, but Ah-Lahn had chosen not to believe what he considered idle chatter. He had admired Arán Bán since they were boys, and he still hoped to continue in that opinion.

He was astonished to learn the real reason behind the Alana of a year ago and the Alana of today. She had become convinced that An Síoraí, the power of inspiration and inner knowing that was clearly one of her gifts, was the cause of her family's demise.

Why had Arán Bán encouraged her in that belief?

Ah-Lahn knew he was right to let Alana make her own decision about her future. There would be no artifice on his part. He had done all he could for the time being.

He must accept what was and was not happening. If there was to be any relationship between Alana and himself, which at this moment he sincerely doubted, she must come to him of her own accord.

He could pray for her safety and for her communion with An Síoraí to awaken. But without her permission, he could do no more. And that realization weighed on his heart like a stone.

PART THREE

Journey into Mystery

*Let us be travelers together
along the way that leads
from what we see
to where we only dare imagine.*

At a Threshold

*A*lana's song at Samhain did not go as she had hoped. Confused by her conversation with her aunt and the Ceann-Druí the day before, she had doubted herself. The result was a mediocre delivery in her eyes and worse in the opinion of her mentor.

Many of the young bards and other members of the audience had congratulated her on an excellent performance, but she was very disappointed. And so frightened by Arán Bán's anger that she had fled to her aunt's cottage for the remainder of the festivities.

Now that Samhain was over, Alana had sent word to Arán Bán that she was ill. She needed more time before resuming what she expected to be some very demanding instruction.

The November sky was scattered with dark clouds, and the scent of rain hung in the air. Alana's mood matched the atmosphere as she stood atop the treacherous cliffs outside Tearmann, high above the shore where she and her mother had landed over a year ago.

A return to the source, she thought.

The weather had been warm, then, and mild. Not cold and piercing like the chilly blast that swept up from the thundering sea below her. The wind blew sharply through her hair. It whipped her skirts and made her miss her mother.

Alana's heart ached for the family she would not see again. Never had she felt this confused and alone.

The Ceann-Druí's behavior had unsettled her. Why else would she have revealed her fear of An Síoraí or her anger at Enfys and Dearbhla? No wonder her performance had been far from perfect at Samhain.

In every possible way, Alana stood at a threshold. What course should she take? Her thoughts traveled far out into the invisible world, begging for an answer.

Even as rain threatened, there was a lightness in the air here. She could feel it—a glimmering sense of possibility that made a person want to lift off and test the wings that would surely appear if you believed in yourself.

Not yet, she told herself.

She stepped back from the edge and walked on. Following the rugged trail that skirted the cliffs, she found a sheltered outcropping of moss-covered rock where she could sit and think while still looking out to sea. If only someone she trusted could advise her.

She closed her eyes and breathed in a gentler breeze that unexpectedly wafted in from the east, smelling of salt and sea and, strangely, of apple blossoms. The scent reminded her of her carefree childhood on Ynys Môn.

Then she heard him. Floating in on that milder draft was the voice of her deceased father, the druí Carwyn, encouraging her as he always did when she was frightened or troubled:

Alana, mo chroí, to fear An Síoraí is to reject the life force that beats your heart. Life is nothing without imagination and inspiration. Embrace An Síoraí's flow and step into the essence of your True Self.

How do you hear me, if not through An Síoraí? Allow yourself to know that Presence, daughter. And in that knowing, live.

Alana leaned back upon the mossy rock where she had been sitting and pondered her father's words.

Could she have been mistaken about An Síoraí? Was inspiration the essence of the life she longed to live? Why had Arán Bán encouraged her to believe otherwise? Why had he implied that her family had deceived her with simplistic interpretations of the law and the path of the druíthe?

Carwyn pointed to An Síoraí as life, not the cause of death.

Alana looked up and saw the faces of hundreds of druíthe smiling down upon her from the clouds. Here were her friends from Ynys Môn, and standing in their midst were Carwyn, Bleddyn, and Enfys, who beamed a mother's love to her daughter:

Believe in your ability to be inspired, Alana. Though dark forces or well-meaning friends would have you deny the gifts that make you who you are, follow your inner guidance. Embrace An Síoraí and know what is true. That is your way forward.

Though Alana's mind would argue, her heart said her parents spoke the truth. Their words cast a light of illumination that pierced the veil of illusion she had unwittingly embraced.

She got to her feet. At last, her next step was clear. The honor of a bandruí demanded that she let her mentor know she had the Ceann-Druí's permission to decide what she would study.

"I will spend the next several days in meditation at Aunt Dearbhla's cottage," she declared resolutely to the elements. "When I clearly see my way forward, I will inform Arán Bán of my decision."

Arán Bán could not believe his ears. Alana would let *him* know what she had decided. *Indeed!* Though his insides were churning, he smiled benignly, nodding as she excitedly described her pleasure at being trusted with her own life path.

"I do not really trust the Ceann-Druí," Alana said reassuringly when she noticed a dark cloud cross Arán Bán's brow. "I could tell he was just as manipulative as you said he would be."

And why do I not believe what I just said? she thought as soon as the words escaped her lips.

"You do not mind my exploring what I really want, do you? You have praised my potential. I only want to be certain of my true desires. This decision feels like an important turning point in my life."

Arán Bán took in a long, steady breath, willing himself not to react.

"Of course, my dear Alana. You must do what you feel is best. You know where to find me when you are ready. I am certain you will see the wisdom of continuing our work together. After all, we have hardly begun to tap your capabilities."

Flashing his most beguiling smile, Arán Bán gently took Alana's right hand and brought it to his lips, lingering ever so slightly.

"Run along now. I will see you soon."

Clever little charmer, Arán Bán thought as Alana left his cottage. She was using his own words against him. Though she said otherwise, he could tell that Ah-Lahn—that meddling thief who had stolen his rightful office as Ceann-Druí—had gotten to her.

Well, he decided, he would play along with their game for now. He knew he would win in the end.

Spells

Una was furious. "What do you mean, 'He gave her leave to plot her own course'!" Arán Bán's wife stormed around their cottage when her husband told her about his conversation with Alana.

"Who does she think is responsible for her progress? Is this the thanks you get for sacrificing your time and energy to improve her meager talents!"

"I know," replied Arán Bán, treading lightly through Una's outrage.

She was a full-bodied woman, several years his junior, who ruled her two children and her celebrated husband with a capricious volubility that made them all wary of triggering her displeasure.

Arán Bán knew Una's anger also had its uses. He could always count on her to be incensed by the inevitable betrayals of the young women he occasionally pursued. And, of course, Una was fully aware of his seductions. She always made certain he came home to her.

She possessed her own ways of ensuring the girls' departure from his instruction. Somehow their parents never questioned their sudden decision to marry, and the girls remained silent on the subject.

"There now, husband. Have some beer and a bowl of the nice lamb stew I have made for you," Una cooed soothingly. "You will feel better after a meal and some rest. That silly girl will come to her senses. You will see."

There was a part of Arán Bán that melted when his wife coddled him. From experience, she knew he would drink just enough beer to conceal the potion she added to his beverage. The clever herbs would enflame him so she could do a bit of seducing herself.

Una needed one of Arán Bán's treasured possessions for the spell she planned to conjure later in the evening. Once he was snoring away after their coupling, she could steal the lock of Alana's hair he had cajoled his protégé into giving him. That precious token would serve as a perfect talisman.

The little chit will never know what hit her, Una promised herself with a sly smile.

Dearbhla's cottage was pitch black when Alana awoke at midnight, shivering under her woolen blanket, soaking wet with perspiration from the fever that raged within her.

The pain was like a knife in her back. She rose feebly, only to swoon as the room began to pitch and roll. Her stomach heaved as she stumbled outside to the fresh air.

Retching violently, she doubled over as the sickness erupted from her again and again. Too weak to stand, she fell to her knees beside a large cool stone where she could lay her head until the next wave of nausea rushed through her.

She had no idea how long she stayed there, struggling to breathe and desperate for a damp cloth to quell the malicious fire that burned in her forehead.

Eventually, she collapsed into a death-like sleep. She remained next to her aunt's silent dwelling, unseen and unheard, until two apprentices found her at dawn when they came to stoke the fires and prepare the Banfháidh's breakfast.

Terrified, they ran into Dearbhla's cottage, frantically calling as they entered her chamber.

"Mistress! Mistress! Come quick! Alana is dead! We just found her outside! Oh, mistress, she is dead! She is dead!"

"Silence, girls!" commanded Dearbhla, rising quickly and throwing her green wool cloak around her shoulders.

"Where is she? Take me to her!"

All three women reached Alana at once. Dearbhla instantly knelt to check her breathing and her heartbeat. Deftly lifting the young woman's limp body in her arms, she moved swiftly into the cottage and laid Alana on her own bed.

"She is not dead, but we must act quickly. Her life force is very weak. Sorchae, boil water and fetch my kit.

"Naimh, run to the Ceann-Druí. Say these exact words to him— 'Dearbhla says the worst has happened. Please come now.' He will know what that means. Repeat the message, girl, so I know you understand."

"Dearbhla says the worst has happened. Please come now," repeated little Naimh, frightened out of her ten-year-old wits.

"Good," said Dearbhla, embracing her little charge. "Now run fast, and do not worry. You have done well. Alana is not dead. I am depending on you to help me keep her alive. Off you go!"

With Naimh on her way, Dearbhla now took the basin of steaming water that eighteen-year-old Sorchae brought her. Into the liquid she poured a combination of healing herbs and a concentrated tincture reserved for only the most serious illnesses.

Placing her hands over the fragrant potion, she closed her eyes and began to chant her most powerful invocations:

> *In the name of all the gods and by the authority of the Sisters of the Healing Arts, I call forth Light! Light! Light! Spirit of An Síoraí, charge this elixir with your mighty healing rays and reverse the cause and core of this illness that has beset your servant, Alana.*

Continuing to pray in this manner, the healer first dipped some of the mixture into a cup so it would cool to room temperature. Then, using a hollow reed to extract tiny amounts of the elixir, she eased them between Alana's lips so she would not choke.

As Dearbhla continued her ministrations, she instructed Sorchae to dip a pure woolen cloth into the remaining mixture in the basin so she could bathe her niece's now deathly cold brow.

After several minutes, Alana shuddered and drew in a jagged breath. Still, she remained unconscious. Her face was contorted, showing she was in terrific pain somewhere in her body.

Using her highly sensitive hands, Dearbhla felt along Alana's arms, legs, neck, shoulders, and finally her back. As she touched a place between her niece's shoulder blades, a jolt of vicious energy flashed up her arms, striking her heart with a virulence that nearly knocked her off her feet.

"Sorchae, carefully now, help me turn Alana over so I can see her back. Yes, there is the place. We dare not touch it directly.

"Bring me another soaked cloth, and please keep the water warm. We may be here for many hours. I pray Ah-Lahn is close by, but we cannot count on Naimh finding him immediately."

Little Naimh was a good runner and she felt the importance of her mission. The distance was not far, but she was out of breath when she reached the Ceann-Druí's cottage.

She knocked frantically, for she dared not enter uninvited. No one answered. She knocked again. Hurry, please, hurry!

At last, a strapping young man in his late teens stood before her.

Thank the gods! Here was her older brother. Naimh had forgotten he was working as an aide to Ah-Lahn.

"Gareth!" she cried with an anguish he had never heard her utter. "Where is the Ceann-Druí? I have a message! He must hear this! 'Dearbhla says the worst has happened. Please come now!'"

"He is not here, little one. Tell me what has happened."

"Alana is almost dead! Please, Gareth! The Ceann-Druí must come!"

"Do not worry, little sister. We will ride to him this minute. He is miles away, but I know where he is, and he has his own horse. He will arrive in time to save your friend."

Though Alana was no longer dying, she was far from healed. Over many anxious hours, Dearbhla and Sorchae tried every possible remedy with little change in their patient's condition. They were nearly exhausted, and still Alana had not awakened.

She was in great pain, as her moans attested. As the healers prayed for a miracle, they could not have comprehended the ferocity of the battle raging in Alana's mind and body. Her dreams were terrifying. Later she would describe the nightmares as being tormented by demons that poked her with sharp sticks while they laughed at her misery.

At one point, she saw a voluptuous, goddess-like figure with long, flowing black hair. The woman appeared to be coming to her aid. But when Alana reached out for help, the figure changed into a hag, her expression an evil sneer.

The hag's garments flamed up red and menacing around her. She grabbed Alana by the shoulders and spun her around, plunging a sharp, chiseled stone dagger into her back, right behind her heart.

The wound was not fatal, but the pain was unbearable. Alana nearly begged for death. Then, somewhere, coming from a great distance, she heard the voice of her beloved father calling to her:

Endure, my daughter. Endure. This wound is not to the death.
It is for your liberation. Endure.

Instantly, a ray of brilliant blue light flashed from the invisible world directly into Alana's body. The ray was just strong enough to increase her will to live. With all her might, she summoned a surge of energy that caused the demonic apparition to draw back and fly away, cackling with a hideous laugh that said she was not defeated.

Despite the hag's flight, the dagger was not withdrawn. In excruciating pain, Alana slipped even further into unconsciousness.

Healing

Ah-Lahn urged his majestic grey stallion, Toireann, to the absolute edge of the noble animal's endurance. The Ceann-Druí was an able horseman, and his mount was devoted to his master. Together they flew on spirited hooves to reach Alana before time and Dearbhla's strength gave out.

They plunged on through twilight into a moonless night, arriving at last at the Banfháidh's cottage. Ah-Lahn leapt from the horse's back and patted the faithful steed on his sweat-soaked neck. He tossed the reigns to an aide that Gareth had alerted to be on hand as soon as horse and rider should appear.

"Give him a good rub down and extra feed," he called to the lad. "Toireann truly thundered across the earth today."

Ah-Lahn took a deep breath and blew out his anxiety as he eased into Dearbhla's warm cottage. In the light of a dozen candles, Alana lay pale and haggard on the bed where her aunt had placed her hours earlier. She appeared nearer death than life.

"Ah-Lahn!" cried Dearbhla, stiffly rising to her feet. "I had nearly given up hope. Alana is hovering between this world and the next. I have done everything in my power, but the sickness upon her does not relent.

"I have had to be mindful of how much I touch her. The evil in her back lashes out at me from an invisible wound behind her heart. Please, mo chara, you must do something!"

Ah-Lahn knelt and held his hands over the near-lifeless body before him. The same evil flashed out at him, then retreated when it encountered the power of a master druí.

"This is a complicated spell, Dearbhla. Rarely have I felt such dark energy and certainly not in our túath. I am not surprised at its resistance to your treatments, though you have done well to keep its murderous intention at bay. Thanks to you, the spell has not succeeded.

"Sorchae," he said to the senior apprentice who was as nearly exhausted as her mentor, "take Dearbhla to the cottage of one of your sister banfháidthe and get some rest. I will send for you both if anything changes. Please ask the lad outside to bring in my hazel bundle. Gareth will have made certain it was here."

Then laying his hand in great affection on Dearbhla's weary shoulders, Ah-Lahn looked into her eyes in deepest gratitude.

"Thank you, mo chara. One day I hope to tell you how much your service means to me."

Ah-Lahn placed his full attention on Alana. Immediately, he knew that his own life and the lives of many others depended on her survival. He must not fail. More was at stake than he had imagined.

Seconds later, Dearbhla's apprentice, Madwyn, carefully brought in the large bundle of what would appear to those untutored in such things as nothing more than a bunch of weather-beaten hazel sticks.

But Madwyn knew that here in these humble branches was nothing less than the wisdom of the ages, handed down from master druíthe since time immemorial. Each stick was notched and inscribed with mysterious runes and ancient symbols that made no sense except to the most accomplished practitioners.

Ah-Lahn was such a master. He recognized in these marks the recorded prayers, invocations, healing tonics, and arcane spiritual practices that comprised some of the world's deepest knowledge in the ways of spirit and matter that had been known by only a few initiates since antediluvian times.

Dismissing Madwyn with a kind nod, Ah-Lahn sat in Dearbhla's chair next to Alana's sleeping form. He closed his eyes and relaxed his mind into a deep meditation, searching on inner dimensions for the remedy he had never been called upon to use in his many years as a druí.

He remembered that Ard-Mháistir Óengus had given instruction on a series of powerful chants and healing tinctures to be used only in case of the most virulent dark spells. It was the hazel rod containing this sequence that Ah-Lahn now sought.

After several minutes, an image he had never seen before came to him. He stood and, without hesitation, reached into the very center of the bundle, extracting a gnarled stick that was blackened with age.

Resting the other hazel rods reverently in the cottage's corner, Ah-Lahn took the ancient stick firmly in both hands. Holding it horizontally before him, he invoked the presence of his lineage, praying for the master druíthe who had preceded him to overshadow this ritual.

Immediately, inner guidance began to direct his fingers over the grooves, notches, and symbols that ran the full length and circumference of what was taking on the vibration of a wand.

Scintillating energy ran up Ah-Lahn's arms, across his shoulders, down his spine, up to the crown of his head, and back down to the center of his chest where it remained. Spontaneously, he opened his consciousness to the instructions that began pouring through his mind. At the same time, his body merged with the hazel wand. Together, they became a single rod of power.

Sheer determination to save Alana fueled Ah-Lahn's ability to stand in such potent energy. Powerful vibrations permeated his body with a healing radiance unlike any he had ever experienced.

The wand's luminosity prompted him to intone strange words he had never spoken in this life. Yet he knew them as old friends. He had relied upon them more than once in his soul's journey through the ages. Now, as then, he let them flow with the movements of mind and body the hazel wand inspired.

Several times, Ah-Lahn felt the scepter's highly polished end dip and quickly touch the place on Alana's back that he had identified as the source of her pain. Each time, a tiny puff of dark smoke shot up from the invisible wound, decreasing in volume and blackness until the final touch elicited only the tiniest wisp of grey vapor.

Gradually, the energy vibrating through the Ceann-Druí's body abated until he found himself once more holding a simple hazel stick. The only evidence of its astonishing activity was a slight warmth and pliability in the wood.

Ah-Lahn had hoped that Alana would awaken after this ritual. When she did not, he replaced the hazel rod with its fellows and mixed one more tincture in a small wooden cup.

Gently turning her over, he used Dearbhla's hollow reed to slip several drops between Alana's lips before stepping back to observe her still-unconscious form. He was pleased that some faint color had returned to her cheeks. The grimace that had marred her beautiful face appeared to be relaxing. Yet, she did not stir.

While Alana continued to sleep, Ah-Lahn moved to a seat next to his hazel bundle in the cottage's corner where he could keep watch over the young woman. As soon as he sat down, he realized he was exhausted from the superhuman exertion the healing ritual had required of his already fatigued body.

Knowing he would need his strength for whatever happened next, he relaxed into a state of lucid dreaming. Here he could rest while retaining his outer awareness in case Alana should awaken.

Ah-Lahn meant to settle into that familiar plane of consciousness where he accomplished much of his inner work. However, he was soon aware of being in a different dimension than the one he was accustomed to accessing. This realm was not a pleasant one.

Why am I here? he wondered. The atmosphere felt neither safe nor restful. Then he saw her. Alana was dazed and wandering. Her eyes were open, but she appeared not to see where she was going.

"Alana!" he called, though he knew she did not hear him.

She is stuck in the astral plane, he realized with a shock that weakened him. For whatever reason, he had not the strength to reach her.

"Beloved Nhada-lihn, help me!" he cried aloud to the ascended lady master he had known of old and who continued to guide his path from her home in Tír na n'Óg, Land of the Ever-living.

Alana's soul was hanging in the balance. The evil she had absorbed from the hag's blade was so deeply embedded in her mind and body that not even a master druí's skill could fully dissolve it.

She was walking into darkness and would be lost forever, unless a miracle happened.

Into the Future

*A*lana was no longer in excruciating pain. Still, she did not know where she was. She was empty of thought and emotion.

She had no desire, no energy, no will to do aught but walk further into the grey nothingness that was in and around her. As she wandered, she began to hear the faint sound of a human voice coming from far away.

Who calls? she wondered, though she detected no reason to veer from the track she was inexorably pulled to follow—until a ray of pure white light suddenly shot from the sky. It landed directly in front of her, halting her progress on the path to oblivion.

A shape began to materialize before her. Frozen in place, Alana watched as an orb of rose-pink light coalesced around a lady of exquisite ethereal beauty.

The lady's golden tresses flowed behind her like ribbons of silk. A ruby diadem graced her forehead. Her gown of gossamer material glistened with the iridescence of butterfly wings. Her smile banished the darkness that had enveloped Alana only seconds before.

Here, in answer to Ah-Lahn's call, was Lady Master Nhada-lihn. She radiated such tenderness that Alana sank to her knees and began to weep with relief.

"You are safe now," said the lady master in a melodic voice that sounded like angel song. Raising Alana to her feet and placing her arm around the young woman's shoulder, she said gently, "We must leave this place. Your presence is requested in finer dimensions, for you have been granted a boon from the Masters of Light."

"I know you," said Alana faintly, searching her scattered mind for a memory from the far-distant past.

"That is true, my dear, and I know you. Now, come with me. Your druí awaits you in my retreat in Tír na n'Óg, Land of the Ever-Living. He was desperately worried until I let him know I would pull you from the darkness. Close your eyes now. We will meet him soon."

Too weak to be other than obedient, Alana let her heavy eyelids shut in perfect trust of her guide. At once she felt herself rising into the air.

She and the Lady Master were flying among the stars. They traveled fast, so she kept her eyes sealed, daring to open them only when her feet touched the cool marble floor of a glorious temple. The entire structure shimmered with rainbows.

"Welcome to Tír na n'Óg," said Lady Nhada-lihn as she escorted Alana into the temple's interior.

Exotic trees and plants grew around a rose-quartz fountain that splashed joyfully in the courtyard they passed through. Alana entered reverently, for the atmosphere vibrated with the heartbeat of An Síoraí.

She wanted to stop and stare, but the Lady Master urged her into a great hall whose walls were lined with crystals that emanated delicate rays of light in every possible color.

At the front of the hall was a large screen on which images played, depicting scenes of people in various activities of daily life.

"I know this place," said Alana, sitting on a bench that faced the screen. A cup of sparkling elixir appeared in her hand and she drank deeply. She had not realized how thirsty she was.

"You and your druí have been here often, sometimes together, sometimes separately," explained Lady Nhada-lihn. "You are both present now, though you will not speak to each other until later.

"Today you have been called to watch and listen and learn. For the scenes on the screen will reveal what may befall the two of you in the future. Whether or not these events come to pass will depend on decisions you make today and in years to come.

"Now, focus on the screen and let yourself merge with the images. Watch closely, Alana, and remember what you see and feel.

"Receiving this information is a rare grace to you and your druí. You must remember."

Alana eased her consciousness into the images on the screen. Immediately, she saw herself walking across a barren plain that was surrounded by rows upon rows of very tall buildings. Odd-looking vehicles were scattered around the area.

The expanse was covered with some sort of black, tar-like substance that had an almost fluid appearance. Yet it was solid enough to hold her weight as she made her way toward the largest in a cluster of buildings.

The structure was square in a design completely different from the rounded thatched cottages in Tearmann. Its edges were sharp, its framework cool to the touch except for where the sun warmed it. Its bright, clear surfaces shone like quiet pools of water at midday.

Two massive doors suggested an entrance. She pulled on one enormous handle and the door soundlessly glided open, revealing an atrium paved with grey and white tiles that were polished to a bright sheen. The click-click of her oddly shaped shoes echoed as she crossed into the center of the building.

She heard voices coming from further inside. Following the sound of laughter and animated conversation, she carefully ventured down a hallway into a spacious room where dozens of people were gathered for a celebration of some kind.

She knew many of the guests and they knew her. They called her "Sarah," the person she now knew herself to be.

She was chatting amiably with several young women, when one said pointedly, "I saw Kevin today. He said he might stop by. I didn't tell him you'd be here. What will you do when you see him? You haven't spoken since the divorce, have you?"

"And I don't plan to," Sarah said dryly. Her stomach clenched in dread of the confrontation she had managed to avoid for six months.

"I think you should talk to him, Sarah," said a bubbly brunette to her left. "He's as miserable as you are."

"I'm not miserable. I'm tired," Sarah snapped.

She was genuinely annoyed. This whole gathering felt like a set-up.

Which of her friends had decided that putting her and Kevin in the same room was a good idea? Anyway, he probably wouldn't show up. He had never been one for parties.

Then she saw him. He was dressed in his usual tan polo shirt, brown khaki trousers, and casual navy jacket. But his appearance was different. He had cut his hair, and his mustache was shorter than Sarah liked. He looked tired and older, as if the past six months had been hard on him. She knew the feeling.

He had entered from a side door and stood scanning the room, as if he were looking for someone. He had been frowning when he first came in. Then his eyes found hers and locked on.

As they stood studying one another, she shot him a look that said, "I dare you to come over here."

Her heart skipped a beat when he did just that.

"Hello, Sarah," he said casually, though there was nothing casual about the way he crossed his arms over his chest when he reached her.

She instinctively planted her feet and did the same. "Hello, Kevin, I'm surprised to see you here. I didn't think you liked parties."

A strong offense is the best defense, she told herself. Let him leave. She was here first.

"I thought I would try something different. I heard you'd been out and about. Got a new man to push around yet?"

Damnit! He could have kicked himself. That was not what he had meant to say.

"Laser-sharp as always, Kevin." Is that how he remembered the way she had treated him? As far as she recalled, he had been the heavy-handed one.

Sarah returned his sarcasm. "I'm off men for a while. Living with you for seven years was enough male ego to last me a long time."

Frustration rippled through her. This ridiculous conversation had to stop. "Kevin, why are you here? We're divorced."

His dropped his arms and stepped forward, forcing her to face him. He had to say what he came to say.

"I know. You demanded that I sign the papers, so I did. Then the other day I thought I heard you call me. I wondered if you had changed your mind after six months."

"I did not call you, and I have not changed my mind," Sarah said flatly, willing herself to keep breathing.

Kevin eyes went deep and dark as he searched hers for the answer he had never received. "Why did you leave, Sarah?"

Did she detect a plea in that question? "You're kidding!" She spat out the words. "If you don't know by now, I can't tell you. You wouldn't understand."

"Try me. I really would like to know."

"Don't bully me, Kevin. You broke my heart. That's all the explanation you're getting. Now go away. I don't want to see you ever again."

For a minute they stood like two actors stuck in a scene neither knows how to complete.

"Then I guess we're finished," Kevin said at last, his jaw set hard as a stone. He took his ex-wife by the shoulders and fixed his blue-green eyes once more on her hazel ones.

"Don't look back, Sarah, because I won't."

Turning sharply, Kevin strode out of the room. Sarah did not catch the pained look on his face as he left, and he did not see her shoulders begin to shake as a torrent of tears streamed down her cheeks.

The screen went dark and the great hall fell silent. Alana was once more in Tír na n'Óg. Instantly, she doubled over with a stabbing pain in her belly that was far worse than any torment she had ever experienced.

"The confrontation you just witnessed would be the last chance for Sarah and Kevin to reunite," Lady Nhada-lihn said evenly, as she walked from the back of the hall to stand in front of Alana.

"In the beginning of time, Sarah and Kevin were created as two halves of the same whole. However, they had spent so many embodiments apart, developing different interests and preferences, that for them to build a bridge back to oneness was nearly impossible.

"They might have stayed together this time if they had each done their own inner work instead of expecting their partner to solve their problems. Sadly, that is not what we witnessed."

Alana was shaking uncontrollably. The anguish of separation from the man she now recognized as the beloved of her soul was unbearable.

"You said this scene was only a possibility." Alana was grasping for hope. "How do we prevent this prophecy from coming to pass?"

"Only the two of you can determine if Sarah and Kevin will avoid permanent separation," said Lady Nhada-lihn, motioning for Ah-Lahn to join them. He took his place next to Alana.

"You have done well in other lifetimes, both together and apart. For this you have been granted an opportunity to change the future. The world needs your reunion. Only the two of you can ensure it.

"Now, join hands and promise the Masters of Light who guard your lives that you will remember what you witnessed today—for this boon will not come to you again. Do you promise?"

"We do," they said in unison. The Lady Master placed a delicate hand on each of their foreheads.

"I am sealing your minds against a certain portion of darkness that opposes your mission together. More than that I cannot do. Your victory depends on the decisions you make. Remember what you have seen here and choose well."

As Alana and Ah-Lahn gazed in amazement, the radiant lady, the great hall, and the temple all faded from view. Immediately, they closed their eyes and slipped out of dreamtime, each returning to Dearbhla's cottage where their bodies lay deeply, and separately, asleep.

Awakening

*A*lana stirred first, crying out from the edges of her dream, "I'm sorry I left you, Kevin. I promise to do better. Please, forgive me. Please, forgive me!"

Ah-Lahn heard her and woke with a start. He had not meant to sink into deep sleep. He rushed to her side, shaking his head to clear the fog that lingered from the prophetic dream he now vividly and painfully remembered.

Does Alana also recall the prophecy? He begged An Síoraí for an answer. Searching his beloved's face for some sign that she did remember, he knelt, taking her hands in his. Her eyes fluttered open and filled with tears as sobs convulsed her body.

"I am here, Alana," he whispered. "Do not be afraid. You are alive. You have come back."

"Kevin!" she cried, desperately throwing her arms around Ah-Lahn's neck. "How could I have been so blind? I pushed you away, didn't I?"

Before Ah-Lahn could explain that he was not Kevin, Alana cried out again. "I'm so sorry. Please, forgive me." For a moment she looked frantically at Ah-Lahn and then fell back on Dearbhla's bed.

"Of course, I forgive you," said Ah-Lahn through the tears that misted his own eyes. He could see that Alana had not awakened from her experience in the retreat of Lady Master Nhada-lihn.

"Rest now, mo chroí. I will call Dearbhla's helpers to make you some broth. Tomorrow we will talk. We are together now, Alana. We will not lose each other again. I promise."

In reality, Ah-Lahn was not certain he could keep Alana safely near him, though he vowed to try. Unfortunately, when she was fully awakened, she remembered neither their shared dream experiences nor her own passionate declaration of love.

Once or twice, she looked at Ah-Lahn with a quizzical expression, perhaps teetering on the cusp of a memory. But throughout her recovery from the hag's spell, she remained silent and emotionally distant.

Unable to help her, Ah-Lahn deferred to Dearbhla to care for her niece until she regained her strength.

After another week, Alana was strong enough for Dearbhla and Ah-Lahn to bring her a message they were eager to share. She was surprised to see them smiling when they pulled up two chairs at her bedside.

"My dear niece," began her aunt, "the Ceann-Druí and I have some happy news for you. An insight has come to us in our meditations that you have passed through a major initiation in the fáidh training that a bandruí undertakes."

"I did not know I was in fáidh training," said Alana suspiciously. Were these two trying to influence her future again?

"Neither did we," enthused her aunt. "However, our inner guidance confirms that you have been in the company of seers and healers in the invisible world for some time now."

Without thinking, Ah-Lahn clasped Alana's hands. He looked deeply into her eyes and said earnestly, "You nearly died from an evil spell. You were stuck on the astral plane until a great lady master freed you. You have come back to us from the dead. Those events are initiations that fáidthe often require years to complete. Some never do."

Ah-Lahn was so caught up in his fervor that he did not realize he was squeezing Alana's hands. She looked down at them and then up at him, as if to say, "What are you doing?"

His face reddened. He quickly released her hands and sat back in his chair. Dearbhla saved him further embarrassment.

"We are here to celebrate your victory, Alana," she said happily.

"You are well on your way to attaining the skills of a seer that will be helpful if you wish to continue on your path of becoming a bandruí."

"I do wish it," said Alana without hesitation. Nothing was going to stop her from fulfilling her destiny. "What will be expected of me?"

She looked from one eager face to the other.

To Ah-Lahn's great consternation, his palms started to sweat and his heart raced. Why was he suddenly so anxious in Alana's presence?

To still his nerves, he stood and began to address both women in an uncharacteristically stilted tone, as if he were explaining a difficult concept to a large and not very bright audience.

"Normally, seers spend a period of time in total darkness where sensory deprivation triggers deeper intuitive faculties."

Alana glanced sharply her aunt.

Dearbhla flashed an intense look of disbelief at Ah-Lahn and quickly took up the conversation

"Do not worry, Alana. Enduring further darkness is not required of you at this time. Instead, we suggest that you spend the next year in Nature's healing presence."

She looked over to see that Ah-Lahn was once again seated and was currently studying his feet. He had taken her meaning.

Dearbhla continued, "While cooler temperatures are upon us, you may help me indoors. When the weather warms, you may study outside in our healing garden, breathing fresh air, communing with the vibrancy of life itself. After that, we shall see what we shall see."

"How will I know if I am making progress?" Alana wanted to know.

"The abilities of each seer develop differently," explained Dearbhla. "Follow An Síoraí's guidance, Alana. I will be here to support you in this next step of your development."

The Banfháidh was suddenly overcome with emotion.

"Oh, my dear niece!" she exclaimed. "Your family is exceedingly proud of you. I see Enfys, Carwyn, and Bleddyn smiling at you now from the invisible world. Receive their sincere approval, Alana. You have done very well."

Consequences

A full week after Alana's ordeal, Arán Bán was still fuming. That crafty seductress, Una, had tricked him.

How annoying it was to be so susceptible to her charms. He knew they were usually laced with spells or potions designed to render a man either impotent or raging with desire. He hated that he was powerless to resist his wife or her magic.

Una had been well aware that he was saving his ardor for Alana, yet she had seduced him anyway. And, to make his humiliation complete, he had enjoyed it. How revolting!

Now his protégé was out of reach. Without so much as a "by your leave," that interfering Ceann-Druí and meddling Banfháidh had absconded with his prize student before he'd had a chance to enjoy her.

To Arán Bán's extreme consternation, he had also learned that he would not see Alana again for many months. As soon as she had regained her strength, she had begun to study with her aunt and the fáidthe.

Chiding himself for being too slow to fulfill the desires he considered perfectly natural, Arán Bán determined to confront Ah-Lahn for his treachery.

"What do you mean by interfering with my most promising student?" Arán Bán challenged Ah-Lahn outside the Ceann-Druí's cottage. "You had no right to sabotage her progress when I was finally bringing her to a proper reading of the Brehon Laws."

"And you had no right to abuse her, Arán Bán."

Ah-Lahn did his best to speak with the measured tones of a man who wanted only the most positive outcome for all involved. He was acutely mindful of potential disaster if he did not skillfully handle the man seething in front of him.

"I have become aware that from time to time you have misused your position as tutor with some of our female apprentices. The Council of Druíthe is also aware.

"I was forced to apprise them of the attack on Alana. Some members wanted me to banish you for such practices. However, I convinced them that your past service to the community warrants your being given another chance."

Arán Bán tried to protest that his wife, not he, had attacked Alana, but the Ceann-Druí held up his hand.

"The Council has agreed that over the next several weeks you may work directly with me on matters of túath administration. Depending on your actions, I may also include you in some group exercises with our advanced students. But you are not to engage in any direct tutoring, especially of the younger initiates."

The air bristled as the two powerful druíthe stared at each other.

"Will you agree to these terms?" Ah-Lahn broke the silence.

Arán Bán answered flatly. "I will."

Ah-Lahn spoke sincerely to the man he once had trusted. "I want you to succeed, Arán Bán. We have been colleagues. I hope we may be again. You are very talented. You could be a superior druí if you would allow your life to flow with the spirit of An Síoraí that resides within you."

Seeing that he was temporarily defeated, Arán Bán acquiesced in his most obsequious manner.

"Of course, Ceann-Druí, I accept your terms. I meant no harm to the young lady. Like you, I am here only to serve our people's best interests."

"Good," answered Ah-Lahn firmly. "I expect you to be a man of your word. Please meet me at my grove tomorrow after your morning meal."

"Of course, Ceann-Druí. As you wish, Ceann-Druí," Arán Bán muttered to himself as he entered his cottage. He was glad to see that Una was not at home. He swept his cloak grandly around his body and spoke to the image of Ah-Lahn he conjured in his mind.

"Oh, circumstances will proceed, though not in the way you expect," he sneered. "I have plenty of time. And you are right, Ah-Lahn, I am very talented. You and your cronies have no idea how gifted I really am. But you will learn soon enough."

Seer Emerging

Though pride would not let Alana admit her pleasure to either her aunt or the Ceann-Druí, she had been eager to begin the outdoor activities that awaited her as soon as lambing season commenced in early February.

Until then, she had passed her days with Dearbhla and the other fáidthe, immersed in the heady scents of the tinctures, powders, and oils they prepared from the dried and preserved plants they had harvested from their abundant garden the previous autumn.

Simply inhaling those redolent fragrances was healing to Alana. Her mind always felt clearer after a day in Dearbhla's workroom.

As part of their ongoing practice, the fáidthe devoted several hours a day to meditation. When the chill winds of winter blew through the school grounds, Alana and the others would gather around the fire that warmed Dearbhla's cottage. They enjoyed the shared contemplative experience that enhanced each one's intuitive gifts.

When spring finally arrived in Éire's temperate climate, Alana began spending more time outside. Whenever the weather was warm enough, she was drawn to complete her meditation practice alone. Her favorite spot was at the very back of the garden near an enormous apple tree that she loved to climb.

By April's end, the tree was fully leafed out in anticipation of May's sweet pink and white blossoms. Their fragrance always reminded Alana of her home of Ynys Môn, known to some as The Island of Apples.

Every day the garden was more vibrant with scent and color. Alana awoke at dawn each morning so she could run out to the harmoniously interwoven flower beds and vegetable patches to guess how many buds would burst open in the midday sun.

June buzzed with the conversation of bees as they hastened between fields and gardens both near and far, spreading the very essence of life that perceived no separation between the visible world and the invisible one.

As midsummer approached, Alana visited the cottage she shared with two female fáidthe only to eat and sleep. Even then, she did not return each night. Instead, she preferred nestling in soft grasses, resting in Nature's bower in the manner of her new-found animal friends, the rabbits, ground hogs, and foxes that snuggled harmlessly around her.

Since her arrival in Tearmann eighteen months earlier, Alana had also become fond of the birds that lived in the healing garden. Many more visited on their way to and from their wintering and breeding grounds.

These comings and goings intrigued the young woman as she let the landscape's instinctual wisdom permeate her body, mind, and soul. From dawn till dusk and into the rich darkness of nighttime, the movement of sun and moon and stars captured her growing imagination.

One afternoon, as Alana sat leaning peacefully against her friend the apple tree, out of the corner of her eye she caught sight of two bright green eyes watching her from beneath a flowering bush.

When she turned her head to look more closely, the eyes disappeared. There was no sound of an animal in the shrubbery, but Alana was certain of one's presence. She decided on an experiment.

Closing her eyes, she settled her mind and body into a receptive state and silently invited her visitor to come near. When several minutes passed without a response, she slipped deeper into meditation and gave no more thought to the animal.

As a mist began to coalesce around her, she opened her eyes in time to see that on its margins a dozen pairs of green eyes appeared, watching her intently. They displayed no malice and offered no threat. They only watched. Alana was not troubled by their presence. Rather, she felt comforted, accepted, almost known, as if she and whatever stared at her were old friends.

Eventually a figure emerged from the mist as the other green eyes faded from view. A sleek, female panther padded silently toward Alana and stood for a moment at her feet, taking in her scent.

The young woman's eyes grew heavy and closed once more, though she did not fall asleep. Her heart grew warm and seemed to spin as she felt a ribbon of deep knowing pass between her and the silky feline. The stream of affection that flowed between them grew so strong that Alana could no longer keep her eyes closed.

Opening them, she looked around, expecting to see the panther near by. However, she was alone, except for the sound of a throaty purr that emanated from beyond the garden's border.

"To be visited by a panther is an honor," explained Dearbhla when Alana described her experience. "Rarely will she appear to you physically. Her tribe has been hunted mercilessly, more from fear of her power than for any other reason.

"If she showed herself, you can be certain she attends you, whether you see her or not. No doubt, she has been your companion in the past. Now you must strengthen the tie. Whether she appears physically, in your dreams, or in your meditations, her message is the same."

> Go deeper into the mystery of your own soul,
> Embrace the inner wisdom that is yours,
> Follow the path of intimate communion with Nature,
> And do not be afraid of your own inner guidance.
> The seed that matures must first begin in the dark.

As the panther gradually let herself be seen, Alana named the feline "Sprid" and made a point of thanking her for her presence—physical or otherwise.

Sprid was not the only animal to discover the pleasures of lingering in the garden. Earlier in the spring, Alana had discovered a sheltered berm that kept out the wind and encouraged the grasses to grow thick and soft. Here was the perfect spot for her bed.

Soon after Sprid came into her life, on many a night she was joined in her berm by Cróga's giant wolfhound. The dog preferred Alana's affectionate company to that of his owner, from whom he routinely escaped.

Cróga's dog was a courageous beast who, for many years, had fought wolves and dangerous interlopers that threatened the túath's safety. He was reputed to have saved lives more than once and was considered a hero. Still vigorous, but too old for fighting, he became so attached to Alana that Cróga finally gave him to her.

When the hound stood on his hind legs, he was as tall as a grown man and, to Alana's mind, resembled one she had dearly loved. The dog's noble carriage, soulful eyes, and shaggy, silver-grey coat reminded her of her grandfather, Bleddyn. She renamed the dog "Laoch" after one of the most selfless heroes she had ever known. She and the hound became inseparable.

When Laoch first began frequenting her nighttime bower, Alana was concerned that Sprid might not approve. She need not have worried. She often saw the two animals playing in her dreams. She came to see that they each watched over her in their own way.

Alana treasured all manner of life. She immersed herself in the vibrant energy that pulsed like a heartbeat from the garden's plants and the wild creatures that found food and safety in its sheltering borders.

Her soul rejoiced in the solid warmth of the earth beneath her, the sight of the Milky Way above her at night, the sound of the sea booming beyond the high cliffs that protected Tearmann from invaders.

Most comforting of all was knowing that everything she needed to learn was here in Dearbhla's garden and in her growing acceptance of An Síoraí's presence with her.

Weeks and months passed. Without Alana's knowing exactly how, the garden's unhurried rhythms transformed her.

Planting, weeding, watering, singing to the vegetables and flowers, digging with her hands in the rich soil. These simple tasks fed her, anchoring her body, mind, and soul in the wisdom that arises from living and working with the earth.

She learned to detect angel voices whispering through her apple tree's lofty branches. When she listened carefully at night, she could hear faeries sing as they danced in the moonlight. Birdsong became for her a chorus accompanied by a symphony of floral melodies—for every resident of the garden was alive with its own special music.

Alana's visions grew more vivid. Her inner sight awakened as her intuition came vibrantly alive. An Síoraí's spirit of prophecy flamed up in her as she absorbed the deep mysteries handed down by generations of seers.

Her heart bloomed in the ecstasy of contact with finer realms that Sprid's presence encouraged, bringing a flood of new poems and songs that poured through her. Alana could not contain them, so she sang day and night with the great beast, Laoch, at her side. He always paid close attention as if he, too, were committing the lines to memory as quickly as they emerged.

Disturbances

*A*lana was burdened with a secret. Though she tried to push them away, images of the Ceann-Druí filled her mind—pervading her dreams and troubling her meditations.

She often saw them in loving embrace or in heated argument. In other visions she saw Ah-Lahn in combat with Arán Bán, or a person who looked like her former mentor. Theirs was always a violent confrontation from which Alana would awaken gasping for breath, unable or unwilling to view the battle's bloody conclusion.

Brief snippets of scenes from what she suspected of being past lives occasionally flashed across her mind. However, they never lasted long enough for her to discover their location, point in time, or meaning.

Most disturbing of all, the image of Arán Bán sometimes invaded her dreams, appearing as his most beguiling self, tempting her with his subtle logic and romantic whisperings. Sometimes she felt his hands on her, roaming her body as his thoughts intruded upon her mind.

She wondered why Sprid did not protect her in these situations. But then one night she saw Arán Bán throw out a wall of energy that blocked the panther from reaching her.

Alana would fight to rouse herself from most of those dreams, which made the druí's apparition furious. But some mornings she awoke in the terrible knowledge that she had succumbed to his advances, as horribly real in dreams as if he had physically violated her.

She dared not confess these lapses to her aunt, although Dearbhla always seemed to know. Immediately after one of Arán Bán's psychic intrusions, she would ask Alana to work with her for several days. That direct contact with her aunt's masterful presence always transferred to Alana's consciousness a sense of stability and purpose.

Gradually Arán Bán's violations ceased. Alana was not certain if she had grown stronger or if perhaps her aunt, or even the Ceann-Druí himself, had invoked greater protective energy around her. Sprid was also more present now in both her sleeping and waking hours.

Regardless of the reason, as summer increased its heat and Midsummer's Eve approached, Alana began to feel a growing affection toward the Ceann-Druí.

Still determined not to open her heart to him, she focused on her studies. And yet, sweet visions of Ah-Lahn continued to drift into her awareness, as if her soul held its own deep memory of him and of a destiny she was not willing to acknowledge.

Despite her strong intentions to the contrary, An Síoraí's inspiration insisted on composing a meditation about Ah-Lahn and sending the words into the twilight realm of Alana's dreams:

As a child runs to the safety of her parents' arms, so my soul would run to the warmth of your embrace. How I yearn to understand the mystery of silent communion that causes my heart to tremble with the memory of your presence.

Closer than thought, more fervent than desire, is my longing to speak with you of roads not taken and, more keenly, of the one we are on. I know we walk together, hand in hand, heart to heart. And all those meetings are more real than my daily occupations.

A tension builds within me—a fire that kindles, lighting up my soul, yet telling me to hold my peace and wait for insights yet to come.

Where you are leading I must follow, or perish in the longing for our reunion. Though my dreams cost me all I have, I live in hope that the love I am pursuing is also seeking me, and that from such affection one day all our striving will come to sweet fruition in the rosy bower where you wait for me.

Coincidentally or not, soon after this meditation anchored itself in Alana's reluctant awareness, Ah-Lahn appeared at Dearbhla's cottage with an idea whose time had come.

In conference together, they agreed that Alana's studies with the fáidthe were sufficient for now and that she was ready for a new assignment. All that remained was to inform her of the opportunity she was being granted.

"What do you mean, we are going to sea on a diplomatic mission with Toísech Cróga?" Alana's temper flared at Ah-Lahn's announcement. "Aunt Dearbhla, did you know about this?"

"Alana, remember to whom you are speaking," scolded her aunt. "The Ceann-Druí is offering you a great honor."

Alana took a breath and planted her feet on the smooth floor.

"I beg your pardon, Ceann-Druí. I only wish you had asked me rather than telling me. I cannot leave now. The garden is in full bloom. My dog, Laoch, needs me. I am experiencing some profound meditations. Even if others can care for Laoch and the garden, how am I to continue my studies at sea with strange people all around?"

"Alana, please take a seat while I explain," said Ah-Lahn, pulling up a chair opposite to where she finally sat down. Must this woman always be so resistant? he thought, trying to remain calm.

"Your aunt tells me that your skills as a seer have exceeded her expectations. She considers you highly gifted, like your mother, who was an accomplished seer before she became a bandruí.

"Our experience is that spending too much time in the garden's relative seclusion can be detrimental for a bandruí, unless there is equal time in more external application of the skills you have been developing.

"For this reason, we believe you would benefit from discovering how your abilities can be applied in a variety of settings. There will be other women on this voyage, and I will personally guarantee your safety. This is a commission I am asking you to accept."

Of course, Alana had acquiesced. As she prepared to leave the security of the community of fáidthe, she consoled herself with the knowledge that not even chieftains refused the direct request of a Ceann-Druí.

And was she not more than a little intrigued by the idea of going on a special mission? To be chosen was an honor, though the prospect of spending days at sea with Ah-Lahn troubled her.

Another Proposal

Midsummer's morning sun glistened on the colorful riot of dewy petals in Dearbhla's full-bloomed garden. As Ah-Lahn had hoped, he found Alana strolling there, deep in contemplation, softly singing to the plants, her dog, and other animals that gathered around her.

He had decided to approach her in a setting where she felt at home. He took a deep breath to calm the internal quaking he found decidedly unnatural and stepped into the garden.

Alana heard Ah-Lahn approach and looked up from her reverie. She was surprised to see him this morning. She expected that he would be busy preparing for the voyage. She was more surprised by his appearance.

Here was the Ceann-Druí, standing at the garden's entrance with a meek look on his face. Rather than his long white druí's robe, he was wearing a blue bard's cloak over a simple tunic and leggings. His hair was ruffled, and he appeared to have been out walking for some time.

"Alana. Good morning. May I speak with you?"

"Of course. As Ceann-Druí, you may speak to whomever you wish." Alana answered as coolly as she could manage. "However, I do not believe I see the Ceann-Druí before me."

"I wish to speak to you as a man, not from my office."

"Excuse me?"

"Will you sit, a chara?" Ah-Lahn gestured to a bench under a shady tree. When Alana had seated herself, he took the opposite end and forced himself to look at her. "I have matters to discuss with you."

She eyed him warily. What matters had they not discussed? Why was he so obviously uncomfortable? And why was her heart galloping out of her chest?

Ah-Lahn cleared his throat that had suddenly gone dry.

"I understand that you are not happy about going on the diplomatic voyage."

"I am not at all happy about it," Alana stated plainly.

"There are reasons for you to go, if you will hear them."

"As you wish."

Ah-Lahn took a breath and swallowed very deliberately.

"Toísech Cróga and I agreed that we should not leave you behind with Arán Bán at large in the community. He has done nothing of late to warrant banishment, but we need not subject you to his attentions."

"You told Toísech Cróga?" Alana felt herself redden at the thought of the tribal chieftain knowing the details of her personal life.

Ah-Lahn hastened to explain. "I mentioned only that Arán Bán had made advances toward some of female initiates, including you. The others are better protected by fathers and brothers than you would be."

"Thank you." Alana answered truthfully, though she was beginning to feel very uncomfortable. What was the Ceann-Druí up to?

"Your aunt and I believe this voyage will be good training for you. And what better way to advance your leadership knowledge than to observe how druíthe and chieftains conduct negotiations?"

Alana could not help smiling at the thought of watching her túath's leaders in action. Ah-Lahn seized the moment.

"Perhaps now you do not consider our adventure as onerous as you might have thought."

Rarely at a loss for words, Alana was suddenly flustered.

"I do not . . . I mean, thank you. Learning from you and Toísech Cróga is, indeed, of interest to me."

Ah-Lahn seemed pleased with her response and not inclined to take the conversation further. When he abruptly fell silent, as if lost in his own thoughts, Alana decided to put her mind at rest.

"Are there other reasons for my being included in this mission?"

The man had rehearsed a dozen ways to introduce his feelings. Yet now that the time had come to articulate the passionate sentiments he had held in his heart for nearly two years, he could only say, "I love you."

"What!?" Alana shot to her feet. Ah-Lahn also rose and grasped both her hands in his.

"My dear Alana, I have loved you from the moment I recognized you in your aunt's garden not long after your arrival here. I realize you have not trusted me in the past. But now that you know of my affection, I hope you will accept me as a worthy husband so we can be married before the expedition sails."

"What do you mean, you recognized me?"

"I realized that you are my soul's other half. The first time I saw you I knew we were created together in the beginning of our souls' time on earth. Our destinies are intertwined and have been for millennia. For this reason I am emboldened to ask if you will marry me."

"I . . . I . . ." Alana struggled for words that would not come.

Finally, she stammered, "I admit that I have dreamed of you, of being with you long ago. But I have always hoped to be wooed, not presented with political expediency. I cannot accept you this way, Ah-Lahn. I am sorry!"

Alana ran to her cottage as if she were being pursued by wild beasts, while a bewildered Ah-Lahn remained on the bench they had shared— feeling foolish, vulnerable, and damnably exposed.

As the sun began to warm and climb to its midday height, the Ceann-Druí turned from the garden and, berating his stupidity, sought solace in his wisdom grove where at least the old oak trees accepted him.

Proof

Alana paced and prayed for hours, seeking answers that eluded her. The sudden regret that weighed on her heart was excruciating. She would not have felt worse if she had committed a crime or lost her parents all over again.

She was angry, confused, humbled. These feelings she could identify. But was she in love?

Being certain that Ah-Lahn would not bother her, she decided to take her loyal hound, Laoch, for a walk to clear her head. The eager dog bounded down a little-used path, so she followed him.

She soon found herself in a hazel grove that was soft with ferns and moss and vines that overgrew the trees, creating a greenery-roofed shelter that felt sacred in its stillness.

A gentle brook babbled through its midst and poured into a tiny pool whose waters were calm in perfect reflection of the emerald ceiling directly overhead. Curious to learn what created such a perfect mirror, Alana crouched down beside the pool and, leaning over, peered into its crystalline waters.

Laoch was equally curious and stuck his nose in the pool, ruining any possibility of reflection.

Alana laughed and pushed his big woolly head away.

"Go lie down, Laoch. Be a good dog and have yourself a nice nap by that tree."

Laoch ambled obligingly over to a large oak and plopped down where he could watch his mistress as she peered once more into the pool's mirrored surface.

At first, she saw only her own reflection. Then the waters trembled ever so slightly, revealing, not her image, but the face of Ah-Lahn. As she stared, unable to look away, her image came again, and then his, and then hers. Their two faces were dancing in the pool, one becoming the other, and then back again.

Alana did not know how long she gazed at the face of her beloved, for now she knew him to be exactly as he had said. Their souls were two halves of the same whole, their destinies intertwined, their futures united, no matter the strangeness of outer circumstances.

Here was proof, indeed. And yet, she wanted more. He was Ceann-Druí, and she was well on her way to becoming a bandruí. They had both been trained to rely upon their intuition, so she set him a test. Would he respond to her unspoken call to join her here in this secluded place?

Alana stepped away from the pool and seated herself next to Laoch, who sighed as she placed her arm around his sturdy neck. Here she settled into deep meditation, radiating the affectionate feelings for Ah-Lahn she now felt coursing through her. With her full concentration, she beckoned him to come to her.

Ah-Lahn was sitting dejectedly in his grove when his head snapped up. He heard Alana calling to him. He had known this spark of contact in centuries past. How long ago, he did not care. She was beckoning him. Now. Today. In this very moment.

"I am here," he heard her say.

"And I," he replied as he ran out of his grove, following a pathway illumined by a ray of sunlight that beamed directly down to earth from between two clouds.

"Alana!" He cried as he burst into the clearing, startling the sleeping Laoch, who leapt up and began barking furiously. Not even the Ceann-Druí would get past him to harm his mistress.

"*Fan!*" Alana said firmly, calming the dog with a single word.

"Alana," said Ah-Lahn more quietly, keeping a wary eye on her canine protector who was likewise watching him.

"Have I heard truly? Did you call me here?"

She held out her arms to him.

"I did, Ah-Lahn," She gently brushed his dark hair back from his brow where it had fallen during his feverish dash to join her.

"I saw our faces together in the pool. In that moment, a veil was lifted from my eyes. I see you now. I see us. With all my heart, I accept you as my husband."

The Wedding

Uninhibited excitement had flown through the community with the news of Alana's betrothal to their Ceann-Druí.

Of course, there had been a few broken hearts, for no small number of females had cast flirtatious glances Ah-Lahn's way in recent years. But none had ever caught his eye. He had been determined to fulfill his obligations to his people. And, lately, his attention had been held by the belief that he and Alana were meant to be together.

As the wedding day dawned in all of early July's sunny splendor, more than a few ardent young men wished the Ceann-Druí well and thanked him for clearing their way to woo a bevy of new sweethearts.

"Surely the birds have never sung so exuberantly," enthused the people. "Have you ever seen such a sky, perfectly clear and full of promise? Or flowers so radiant, or a more sumptuous feast prepared for after the ceremony?"

Hearts were light and filled with joyful anticipation as the Brigantes gathered from far and wide on the Buaicphointe, where all could witness the union of the Ceann-Druí and his bride.

True to his nature, Ah-Lahn had been up and dressed since first light. After quickly breaking his fast on a bowl of porridge and an herbal drink that Dearbhla had insisted he take to sustain him throughout the day, he stepped outside. Moments later, his best friend, Riordan, came walking through the early morning mist that whispered across the ground.

Ah-Lahn thought his friend looked like a god today. His fair hair waved wildly in the damp morning breeze, and he moved with a lightness that told the Ceann-Druí his comrade had already been at his prayers.

The two men exchanged friendship's double handshake and smiled knowingly at each other. With a mutual nod, they turned and walked purposefully up the Buaicphointe.

At this early hour, neither was dressed for the wedding. Gareth would bring their best garments later. For now, they wore warm cloaks over tunics and leggings, with heavier boots than the soft leather footwear they would don for the wedding.

However, they did wear their ceremonial gold torcs, for they were on a druí's mission this morning. As they reached the top of the clearing where Ah-Lahn would marry his beloved, the men stopped to survey the scene.

To the north and west, far-away mountain tops could be seen peeking up through the mist that was already clearing. Down below lay the túath of Tearmann. Its green hills and valleys and fields, its herds and flocks, and scores of dwellings with their roofs freshly thatched for the summer spread out as if they had been woven into the land rather than resting upon it.

Circling around to look behind them, the men paused and allowed their gaze to drift far out to sea, across Muir Éireann. No conversation was necessary as each said a prayer for the druíthe and their families who had been lost at Ynys Môn.

Riordan turned to his friend. "Alana came from there as well."

Ah-Lahn nodded. "I thank the gods each day that she did."

Putting his arm around his friend's shoulder he laughed. "And now we have work to do, Riordan. Let us see about the fires."

They walked a few hundred paces across the Buaicphointe and noted with satisfaction that their fellow druíthe had already lit the ceremonial bonfires meant to purify the area.

They added more gorse branches to the blazes from nearby stacks and then began the ritual they had agreed was essential for creating a sacred atmosphere for the wedding.

Ah-Lahn and Riordan stood back to back, each in front of one of the bonfires. They headed off in opposite directions, walking solemnly around the perimeter until they reached points across from the fires. Then they turned and proceeded toward the center of the Buaicphointe where they crossed paths, creating a figure-eight pattern in the grass that, thanks to a little druí magic, never grew tall up here.

They traced the pattern three times, all the while chanting powerful invocations to bring more spiritual energy into the clearing. On the final repetition, they broke into song and sang at the top of their voices their praise to all the gods, goddesses, and other benevolent forces they asked to bless today's ceremony.

Taking up a final chant, they once more proceeded to the center of the figure eight. Then, together, they walked in ever-widening circles to create an enormous spiral that encompassed the entire Buaicphointe.

Coming back to the bonfires, they bowed to the center of the clearing, added more branches to the blazes, and waited for Gareth to arrive, which he did shortly.

Gareth was an energetic seventeen-year-old who had found his vocation in service to the Ceann-Druí. The young man had no other desire than to support Ah-Lahn, his colleagues, and soon-to-be-bride to the best of his abilities—which were considerable.

The young man was highly intuitive and had studied to be a bard before meeting Ah-Lahn. He knew then that he had found his mentor and that he would learn everything he needed to know in this life by serving the man he considered the model for all other druíthe.

Gareth arrived as expected. He had come on horseback since he carried ceremonial garments for each druí, along with some food his mother had insisted he bring for the men whom he now helped get ready. The wedding hour was fast approaching.

All three retired to the back of the Buaicphointe, beyond the bonfires, where they would not be seen. The men devoured the food Gareth had brought and blessed his mother for her foresight. They had not expected to be ravenously hungry.

As the young man helped these two vibrant druíthe, whom he

greatly admired, remove their everyday garments and put on the long white robes they wore for the most sacred of rituals, he could feel the Presence of An Síoraí descend upon them.

When he placed the traditional wreaths of oak leaves on their heads, he felt as if he were crowning them with circlets of gold. He could almost see an aura of light surrounding their heads.

Gareth made certain their golden torcs were straight and placed around each man's neck a large gold medallion pendant that was carved with ancient symbols unique to each druí.

By the time they had finished dressing and sent Gareth hastening to the Ceann-Druí's cottage with their belongings so he could return for the wedding, the time had nearly arrived for the ceremony to begin.

As Ah-Lahn and Riordan came out from behind the bonfires, they stopped in utter amazement at the sight before them. The Buaicphointe had been transformed into a garden paradise.

While they had been preparing for the ceremony, a score of volunteers had erected an enormous archway decorated with every possible wild and cultivated flower from the hillsides and Dearbhla's garden.

Never had the two druíthe seen such a profusion of color or inhaled such heady fragrances. Honeysuckle, gorse, clover, foxglove, violets, rhododendron, wild roses, and many more varieties combined their sweet scents to create an ambrosial perfume.

The volunteers had also fashioned a center aisle down which Alana would walk to meet her beloved. For the past few days the workers had been busy intertwining branches of willow, hazel, and birch together. As soon as Ah-Lahn and Riordan had completed their ritual, the decorators had placed their "trees" upright in the ground and then festooned them with ivy and more flowers.

The decorations were not the only unexpected beauty that caused Ah-Lahn and Riordan's hearts to swell as they waited for the ceremony to begin. Every available member of the Brigantes tribe from miles around Tearmann appeared to have made the trek up the Buaicphointe.

The Brigantes never missed an opportunity to wear their finery. Men, women, and children were all dressed in their most colorful clothes and best gold ornaments. Every head was adorned with a wreath of flowers and ivy that many of the wearers had fashioned themselves. Still others had received considerable assistance from flower faeries who flitted around, inspiring fantastical creations.

Ah-Lahn and Riordan took their places beneath the sweet-scented arch, and the ceremony began.

At a signal from Ollamh Gormlaith, who had arranged the wedding music, bodhrán drummers, whistle players, pipers, and harpists danced down the aisle. They played an uplifting melody that echoed across the Buaicphointe as if angel musicians had joined in to amplify the sound.

Two five-year-old girls in matching rose-colored linen tunics came next. Each wore a circlet of ivy and carried a basket of flower petals which she enthusiastically scattered down the aisle and on many of the congregation as she walked.

"Oh!" exclaimed the crowd when Alana followed with Banfháidh Dearbhla at her side. Never had they beheld such ethereal beauty. Alana and her aunt seemed to float down the aisle.

Both women wore their hair in elaborate braids that had been woven with strands of ivy and wildflowers in colors selected to complement their gowns and then arranged like crowns upon their heads. Each carried an elaborate bouquet of the same vines and flowers that streamed nearly to her feet.

Dearbhla wore a smooth gold torc that glowed against her ivory skin. Her dark green gown glistened with gold threads that had been woven in random patterns which mimicked the appearance of sunlit leaves that shimmered and flickered as she walked. More than ever did she resemble her friends, the devas.

Alana was a vision. Her form-fitting linen gown had a wide neck that set off the delicate gold torc Ah-Lahn had given her as a wedding present. Her gown's skirt draped like a bell from the sleeveless bodice and fitted waist. The garment had been dyed in light-to-deep shades of blue, starting with delicate blue-greys and flowing into rich blue-greens and purples that rippled like Muir Éireann on a sunny day.

Most remarkable of all was the nearly transparent, light blue linen mantle that fluttered behind her like angel wings. The garment was fastened at her shoulders by two elaborately crafted gold brooches that flashed in the sun as she walked.

Those who could see such things—which today included almost every member of the Brigantes—noticed that she was surrounded with an aura of golden light and that flecks of fairy dust trailed behind her.

Alana and Dearbhla had just started down the aisle when they stopped momentarily, their eyes wide in amazement at the sight before them. For there, next to Ah-Lahn, were Enfys, Carwyn, and Bleddyn, beaming like the proud family they were.

At that same moment, Ah-Lahn also saw the three druíthe standing by him, surrounded in white light and blessing his union with their beloved Alana.

The audience, who had been hushed to awed silence by the procession, suddenly began to chuckle when a very dignified Laoch trotted behind the bride and her aunt. He was wearing a collar of ivy and wildflowers and appeared to be trying very hard to behave.

Yesterday he had whined like a baby when Dearbhla declared that he could not attend the wedding. To placate them both, Alana had bathed and brushed the great beast, telling him firmly to be quiet during the ceremony.

Sprid had assured Alana that she would help her canine friend keep his composure. So far, the feline support seemed to be working.

At last, Alana joined her Ah-Lahn under the flowered arch as Riordan stepped before the couple and their supporters. Raising his arms, he looked to the heavens and, with a powerful invocation, summoned gods, goddesses, and angels to protect the ritual and all in attendance.

Immediately, the sun brightened and melted away the few dark clouds that had begun to gather just as the ceremony was starting. In answer, a lively breeze swept around the Buaicphointe, swirling the fragrances of sea air and flowers together, setting the crowd's senses humming.

The audience applauded when Gormlaith appeared in her royal blue robes, finest gold torc, and jeweled brooch to sing a soul-stirring love song accompanied by a single piper who played with sincere emotion. The song moved the musician deeply, for he was soon to be married himself.

When the song was finished, Riordan beamed an affectionate smile at Gormlaith and then turned to face the bride and groom. In a voice like warm honey, he recited the blessing he had composed for these friends whom he loved like family.

Ah-Lahn and Alana, may you always know this truth:

The purpose of your reunion is to be One,
to embody unity as unspeakable joy,
to flower in Earth's garden as a hundred blooms
that have no other purpose than to nourish bees
and perfume the world with their fragrance.

Imagine putting down roots,
drinking in pure air, reaching for the Sun,
being washed by morning showers,
while basking in An Síoraí's great Presence
that simply is the essence of being
that holds us all together.

To Alana, Riordan seemed to be speaking from far away on the outside of a sphere of translucent rose-pink light in which she and Ah-Lahn were enveloped. What she heard instead was the ringing of a bell whose tone vibrated in the depths of her soul.

She turned to face Ah-Lahn and knew he was also hearing it. This was the keynote of their twin flames, the tone that had sounded long ago when their souls had been created from a single spark in the heart of An Síoraí. With that tone still resonating in her soul, Alana made the promise to Ah-Lahn that she knew she had longed to keep for centuries:

O, my Beloved, take me to your own sweet self. For today I am completely yours, as I have always been, even across invisible vastnesses or through the trials of far-off worlds.

I am yours forever, joined by a silver cord. I promise I will not fail, for we belong to one another.

I adore you. I cherish you. I am consumed in the fire that binds my heart to yours. Love of my life, this day I weep for the joy of loving you. I am home at last in your powerful embrace, where I vow to remain forever, come what may.

Ah-Lahn choked back the emotion that suddenly made speech difficult. Seeing his friend's dilemma, Riordan gave him a brotherly fist to the shoulder. The gesture worked. Everyone laughed and Ah-Lahn regained his composure. He was Ceann-Druí after all, not some bumbling youth.

He took a breath and centered himself to share his own promise. He looked into Alana's eyes and sang with his whole heart:

We will always have roses
spring, winter, or fall.
And Midsummer, especially,
brings blossoms that call
from the best of the garden's
bright festival display:
'Gather pink for your sweetheart,
and do not delay.'

I will always have roses
alive in my heart
when I think of you, darling,
and how precious thou art
to me now and forever.
My love will not wane,
whether we are together
or separate again.

For our hearts are joined
like two buds on a stem;
we spring from one plant
though we bloom in strange lands.

Our missions may differ
and take us afar
from each other for purposes
larger than we are.
Still, you are flesh of my flesh
and bone of my bone;
with you I am made whole
and never alone.

For I carry your love
in the heart of my heart,
remembering always
that I am a part
of your soul's very fabric,
as you are of mine;
we are woven together
till the end of all time.

There will always be roses
where you are concerned,
for my love is not seasonal
and need not be earned.

Our bond is eternal,
and there lies my faith
that we will stay young forever
like buds in a vase.

The congregation cheered as Ah-Lahn kissed his bride. And then the crowd laughed out loud, for Laoch could no longer contain himself. Leaping up to stand on his hind legs, he embraced the couple with a huge paw on each of their shoulders.

Ah-Lahn could feel the dog's eye upon him as if to say, "Take care of her. She is mine."

Alana saw Sprid simply roll her deep green eyes. She had done all she could to teach the wolfhound some manners. Clearly, dogs were not panthers.

As the bridal party processed out to join their friends and family at the feast on the central green, those who thought to look up saw the sky filled with an enormous gathering of spirit beings. Happiest among them were Alana's family who beamed their fondest blessings to the couple.

All was gaiety and congratulations in the túath, except for the grim expressions on two human figures who hung back in the shadows.

PART FOUR

Putting Down Roots

*A new day is dawning
fresh and pure
as if from long ago
before the world was.*

Adventuring

A solitary figure stood on his cliffside vantage point high above the cove where three large currach boats were being loaded for the diplomatic expedition. No one noticed him there. And he was beginning to realize that few cared if Arán Bán looked down on them.

He frowned and whipped his sumptuous cloak around his neck and shoulders. A vigorous breeze was playing with his finely woven garments and that annoyed him.

Most things annoyed Arán Bán these days—particularly, knowing that that sneaky Ceann-Druí and his ambitious little bride were now the túath favorites. He could see them on the beach below, smiling and laughing with a crowd of sycophantic well-wishers.

He lifted his chin and sniffed indignantly. Arán Bán does not lower himself to participate in such ridiculous displays of idolatry. He had not lost his self-respect. Indeed, he had not.

Were circumstances not sufficiently humiliating that he had not been included in the negotiating mission? Or that he had not been given any authority in the túath or administrative duties to perform while the other leaders were away. Instead, Riordan would temporarily fill the position of Ceann-Druí.

Arán Bán had expected that his assignments carried out under Ah-Lahn's supervision would have gained him some recognition from the Council of Druíthe, at least from Toísech Cróga. But he now realized that no one thought of him. Alana had captured everyone's attention.

And, he grumbled, she would probably find a way to endear herself to his own kinsman, Toísech Gréagóir, the chieftain who was hosting negotiations in Cois Abhann. Arán Bán had hoped to solidify his ties with Gréagóir on this voyage. Now even that possibility had been snatched away.

Nevertheless, he saw the upcoming absence of Ah-Lahn and Cróga as an opening to press his advantage elsewhere, especially with the Ceann-Druí's son, Tadhgan. The lad had worn a perpetual scowl since his father's marriage to Alana—the usurper, as he had labeled her when Arán Bán happened to mention her name.

The druí suspected that, like himself, Tadhgan secretly desired Alana. When she had first come to live in Tearmann, the young man had pursued her in a puerile way that was obvious to anyone who cared to look. The lad's behavior was immature and, therefore, highly susceptible to influence.

A few well-placed insinuations suggested to an excitable mind can cause useful disruptions, Arán Bán assured himself as he descended the steps that led from cliffs to shore. At the last minute, he had detected a strategic opportunity and joined the well-wishers to bid the travelers farewell.

He made a great show of waving and shouting, "Safe travels!"— appearing for all the world as if Ah-Lahn's offering him a second chance had converted him to a positive force within the túath.

Alana was standing with her husband waiting for their boat to be loaded so they could go aboard. She was in no hurry to leave.

Instead, she buried her face in Laoch's thick neck fur and hugged him reassuringly. She was leaving him behind with Madwyn, one of her fáidh brothers, and Laoch did not understand.

"Do not worry, I will take good care of him," Madwyn promised, but the dog's downcast expression nearly broke Alana's heart. She scratched Laoch behind his ears and kissed his giant head as the lad did his best to prevent the hound from leaping onto the boat.

"Stay with Madwyn, Laoch. He loves you, too. I will be back soon."

No other creature had ever adored Alana so exuberantly as this enormous wolfhound. Sailing off without him was almost more than she could bear. Fortunately, Sprid had let Alana know that she would watch over the soft-hearted beast. Personally, she did not need to travel in a boat. She could appear in her mistress's dreams and meditations at any time. Besides, she preferred to maintain her physical form in the familiar shelters of Dearbhla's garden.

As the currach boats got underway and the great square sails caught a strong breeze, Alana pulled herself together. She threw back her head and opened her arms to the exhilarating wind that blew away any cares that might have followed her on board.

She had done little more than huddle with her mother during their terrifying flight from Ynys Môn. Today, every cell of her body rejoiced to be sailing under positive circumstances. The weather was fair, the seamen were the túath's best, and her husband appeared more content than she had ever seen him.

Ah-Lahn was extremely pleased with the flow of events. He was eager for Cróga to become accustomed to Alana's presence at his side. The Ceann-Druí intended that his wife should be present for the nego-tiations that were meant to create a mutual defense pact between two Brigantes chieftains.

Of course, Ah-Lahn's main reason for wanting Alana with him was to introduce her to his dear friend and mentor, Óengus. The Ard mháistir of the Brigantes and head of their school for druíthe would also be acting as mediator for the negotiations at Cois Abhann.

Ah-Lahn hoped that Alana would come to share his fondness for Óengus, a mutual affection that he and his mentor believed had been centuries in the making.

Ah-Lahn and Alana had no thought of future trials as they sailed around the coast. At night, they slept peacefully in each other's arms. And, to Ah-Lahn, a vision of long ago came again.

Here was a scene he had forgotten in the many years since childhood. In those days his imagination had wandered to far-off lands and ages past, to strange experiences and recollections of himself in foreign aspects quite unknown in these times.

And yet it was himself in another life that he had seen as a boy.

I know this land of plenty, Ah-Lahn mused as he drifted into the familiar dream. Our kingdom is the envy of the world and the center of its richest culture.

The exquisite royal barge glides lazily upon the ribbon of blue water, cleaving vast stretches of desert—its sands shimmering in Egypt's blazing sunlight. The only sound is a rhythmic splash, splash of the oars. The rowers keep an unhurried pace as the barge passes spectacular stone edifices and immense statuary bearing likenesses of the gods and the royal couple who are taking their ease on the barge.

Gorgeously clothed are they, arrayed in garments made of finest linen, nearly transparent in their delicacy. Relaxed and laughing, they recline on richly upholstered couches. They turn and gaze across the water at their palace, glittering in the sun and surrounded by massive date palm trees whose fan-like fronds sweep up to a cloudless sky.

Golden armlets grace Pharaoh's sun-bronzed arms, and thick rings set with lapis, carnelian, and ivory adorn his long, artistic fingers. Even these riches pale beside his resplendent pectoral collar, heavily inlaid with precious stones and metals. More gold to reflect the Sun God's rays that are symbolic of his own majesty.

The Queen is radiantly bedecked in golden bracelets, ear-rings, and a pectoral collar that complements her extravagantly pleated gown—all designed to reveal her beauty of face and form. The couple appear as gods, for so are they considered by their people.

The desert air, stifling today upon the shore, is cool beneath their servants' fans and deliciously fragrant with exotic incense. The experience is made sweeter still by tastes that sparkle on the tongue as the royals sample tangy fruits and candied delicacies created especially for their pleasure.

In his dream, Ah-Lahn turns his head. And then he sees her . . . his beloved . . . his Queen . . . though not his wife. She is wed to Pharaoh, while he, the dreamer, is her royal steward. He is a highly favored adviser who frequently escorts his patrons on the royal barge.

The Queen's features are partially obscured by the elaborate wig that trails along her temples to rest upon her smooth shoulders. Yet he knows her as he knows his own soul.

She turns to him with a vague smile, though only her lips does he see. And then her image vanishes like so much fairy dust, waking him gently, as he inhales the richly perfumed essence she leaves behind.

Tantalizing, beckoning, so clearly present is she with him in the scene, yet far away. Just out of reach and impossible now to touch in the ephemeral mist of the dreamscape into which she fades.

Even when Ah-Lahn was a child, whenever the vision occurred, he would reassure himself: I will know her when I see her again.

And, of course, he had recognized Alana the moment he discovered her in Dearbhla's garden. That experience had been immediate and stunning in its power.

His instantaneous regard for her safety and well-being had overwhelmed him. The joy that flamed up in his heart had burned away past sorrows. His desire that they should enjoy a happy union was then, as now, passionate and all-consuming.

Remembering the powerful emotion that flooded his childhood vision, Ah-Lahn now understood his duty to the one he had loved since the beginning of time.

In addition to supporting Cróga's negotiations, he must inform Alana of certain past lives they had shared. Her readiness for future challenges depended on her intimate understanding of who they had been, how they had lived, and the forces that still opposed their union.

Ah-Lahn had no sense of imminent danger, but any druí worthy of the title was aware that destructive forces could lurk behind smooth veneers.

Greetings & Promises

While their little fleet sailed around the southern coast of Éire and then north up the river called An Bhearú, Ah-Lahn and Alana easily kept themselves occupied.

Ah-Lahn happened to be an able seaman, so he gladly joined the crew as they worked the rudder and the boat's bulky sails. Like his own family of fishermen, these sailors were masters of wind and sea currents that fluctuated moment by moment. They functioned as one body to guide their boats past high cliffs, mud flats, marshes, and coves—some of which they used for safe harbor at night. Ah-Lahn relished being one of them, and they were grateful for his company.

Meanwhile, Alana was in her element. She loved the sea. Ever since she was a child, its voices had called to her as surely as the apple and oak trees that created her sanctuary on land. The sea was another kind of sanctuary, one that beckoned her into the deepest recesses of her soul.

Walking on the beach or sitting on the rocks on the western point of Ynys Môn had calmed her restless childhood mind. Sometimes her father or grandfather had taken her sailing, which gave her an incomparable sense of freedom.

More often, she and her mother would walk as far out as land allowed. There they would sit for hours, matching their breath to the rhythm of the waves, easing into profound meditations in the numinous world of the unseen.

In these precious hours Alana had learned about her mother's childhood in Tearmann and of how Carwyn had rescued her from pirates. The stories of her ancestors from the far-distant past thrilled her soul each time she heard them.

"The sea is in your blood," Enfys had assured her daughter. "It will always call you home to your soul's quiet place.

"Let the waves carry you, Alana. Listen for the ocean's messages and heed her warnings. For then you will also gain her blessings. Land and sea and sky will guide you to the next threshold. Your way will be made plain when you embrace the fullness of life in every landscape and every creature."

Which is what Alana did today.

As she relaxed into the boat's motion, rising and falling with the waves, a song came to her. Nature's voice resonated in and around her as one great melody of life. She felt her mother's gentle presence and gave herself over to the joy of living in the sound of many waters.

> Plunge into the deep
> to the heart of the sea,
> said the divers and gulls.
> That heart is your home
> wherever you are,
> wherever you are.
>
> Be one with the whales,
> the bards of the sea,
> keepers of records.
> To find your soul's song,
> you must want to know,
> you must want to know.
>
> Breathe with the dolphins,
> weaving the tides
> with An Síoraí's own breath.
> Bring earth their message
> of Dreamtime's pure peace,
> of Dreamtime's pure peace.

Graceful and loyal,
white swans mate for life.
Spirals of future
call souls to their path.
Surrender to flow,
Surrender to flow.

Reflect on your gifts,
blue heron suggests.
Go far, far within.
Be willing to look
and trust what you see,
and trust what you see.

After five days of fair seas and skies, the small fleet landed safely at the impressive riverside túath called Cois Abhann. Here, at the seat of the Brigantes druíthe, they would engage in several days of negotiations.

With the currach boats secured, the party walked a short distance to the comfortable thatched dwellings where they would be staying. As soon as they were settled, Ah-Lahn took Alana to meet Uncle Óengus.

The Ard mháistir was waiting for them outside his cottage on his school's grounds. Even from a distance, Alana could sense why Ah-Lahn loved him.

His presence radiated compassion and good humor, as did his deep blue eyes that twinkled from beneath bushy eyebrows. His full beard, going grey to white, framed a weathered face that spoke of years well spent with the land and its people.

His long white robe was artistically embroidered with arcane symbols wrought in colorful threads along the borders. The garment graced a body still strong and able to perform the many duties of Ard mháistir and head of his school for druíthe.

Alana could feel joy bubbling out of Óengus as he strode out to meet her and her husband. Ah-Lahn had told her that this giant of a man tamed all manner of wild birds and animals through nothing more than the tenderness of his heart.

When he enveloped Alana in a bear-hug embrace, she understood how those animals must feel. There was something about the strength and affection emanating from the Ard mháistir that made a creature relax and want to be with him.

After a moment, Uncle Óengus held her gently away from him and studied her face.

"Alana, mo mhuirnín, you have the look of your mother."

"You knew my mother? I had no idea."

"Nor did I," said Ah-Lahn. "When did you meet Enfys, Uncle?"

"Many years ago, before you were born, Alana. Your parents were newly married when I arrived at Ynys Môn to study with your grandfather, Bleddyn. How I loved them all! In fact, had Enfys not already been married to Carwyn, I would have taken her to wife myself.

"We recognized each other, you see, from ages long past. We instantly knew our souls were twins, but your mother was deeply in love with your father. I would not interfere with them, and they trusted my knowing that twin souls do not always live and serve together.

"The three of us spent many glad hours in each other's company while I lived at Ynys Môn. They even cared for me when I caught a fever from fishing in a cold rain.

"Leaving them when my studies ended was hard. And I grieved sorely when I learned of the massacre and your sweet mother's death. She was an exceptional seer and was growing as a bandruí. Sadly, she did not know the limits of her skill. That one small gap ended her life."

Here was the question Alana had never dared to ask.

"I have forgiven her for not telling me that she was returning to Ynys Môn, but I still do not understand why she thought she could wade into the battle."

"A fair question that many have asked," Óengus agreed. "Not even master seers are infallible, mo mhuirnín. We take each step with what we are given to know. We may detect what others do not, yet we are always a bit blind as well.

"You see, we are meant to stay humble before our gifts. But sometimes our passion to help others gets the better of us. Then, like your sweet mother, we put ourselves in mortal danger. Enfys did what she believed she must. That is all any of us can do."

"Thank you for telling me." Alana choked back a sense of regret she wondered if her mother had felt. "May I explore your garden now?" she said softly. "You have some very rare plants."

"Take the path to your right." Óengus and Ah-Lahn smiled at each other as they pointed Alana to the same views. As soon as she was on her way, they fell into the easy conversation of those for whom the separation of time and space is no obstacle to deep connection.

"Of course you must use my grove whenever you wish," the Ard mháistir instantly agreed in answer to Ah-Lahn's inquiry. "The place holds special significance for you, my son. You will find its power has only increased since you have been away."

Then he added with a hearty laugh, "Are you certain I cannot persuade you to return here to support me in my dotage? None of the new druíthe quite compare with you. Why not bring your bride to Cois Abhann and make an old man happy?"

Ah-Lahn smiled with no small tinge of nostalgia. "You know if my duties did not lie elsewhere I would be honored to serve at your side, Uncle."

He paused for a moment to watch the love of his life as she wandered contentedly around the Ard mháistir's lush garden. He grinned when Alana stopped to speak to a bed of purple pansies whose petals looked like tiny faces.

When she buried her nose in the fragrant wisteria blooms that hung in profusion from an enormous arbor, he felt his heart expand in remembrance of the first day he had seen her in Dearbhla's garden.

So much had happened since then, and Ah-Lahn expected their future to be even more eventful. He turned to Óengus, a look of concern furrowing his brow.

"If anything should happen to me, will you take Alana into your care? Her aunt Dearbhla is a masterful banfháidh, but she may not be able to protect my wife in more dangerous times."

Óengus placed his hand on Ah-Lahn's shoulder and nodded.

No further explanation was needed. Both men were all too aware of the political and spiritual opposition to the traditional path of the druíthe that was percolating beyond and even within Éire's shores.

Mindful of the hour and tomorrow's obligations, Óengus called out to Alana, "Come, mo mhuirnín, we will have a meal in my cottage where we can relax. Then I will tell you how your husband tested my patience when he was a young druí."

Anticipating the Past

Early the next morning, Ah-Lahn awakened Alana. He served her a bowl of porridge to break her fast and asked her to dress quickly.

She was surprised to see him wearing the long white robe of Ceann-Druí and the ceremonial gold torc he wore only for the most sacred of rituals. When she finished eating, he began speaking with a quiet intensity that caught her attention.

"Alana, the time has come that you should be told certain secrets usually revealed only to advanced druíthe. If you are to work with me as the gods have ordained, you must know who you are, who I am, and what we have been to each other."

"As you wish." Alana consciously matched his tone. Why was he being so formal?

Without further explanation, Ah-Lahn wrapped the green wool cloak Dearbhla had given Alana around her shoulders and led her outside. They walked in silence to Óengus's private meditation grove, a place of greater serenity and power than any Alana had ever seen.

An open circle nearly thirty feet across was formed by a ring of enormous oak trees that extended at least ten feet beyond those on the inside of the clearing. Some of these interior giants were so hollowed and gnarled with age that their massive trunks resembled the bodies of ancient druíthe.

Alana looked at them intently, easily detecting wizened faces in the rough bark. Quietly, a soft energy came over her, making her feel loved and protected, as if these great ones both knew and sanctioned the purpose of her visit.

Turning her gaze from the kindly trees, Alana felt and then saw the true source of the grove's power. At the very back of the circle were three massive, lozenge-shaped boulders lying horizontally on the ground, forming a slight arc. They appeared to have rested in that position since the beginning of time.

As Alana walked closer to get a better view of the intricate spiral patterns carved into the rocks, she immediately felt a buzzing. The air around them was charged like the atmosphere after a rain storm.

She reached out to touch the central boulder and then jumped back as a tiny bolt of blue lightning struck her outstretched fingers before they could make contact with what was clearly much more than mere rock.

For now she noticed that the stones were faintly humming in a deep, sonorous tone, not unlike the chants she remembered her grandfather intoning on profoundly sacred occasions. As she stood transfixed, she could feel a gentle vibration building in the circle until her entire body was charged with the energy of pure life force.

Sensing that the stones had quickly done their work to elevate Alana's consciousness, Ah-Lahn walked up gently so as not to startle her. He carefully placed his hands on her shoulders and turned her around toward the interior of the grove, guiding her to sit before the blazing fire he had built in the center of the enclosure.

"Close your eyes, Alana, and follow my lead," Ah-Lahn instructed. "You are protected in this place. Some of the images you will see may be troubling, but I will be at your side. Do not be afraid."

Placing the thumb of his right hand between her eyebrows and spreading his fingers atop her head, he began an invocation that seemed oddly familiar to Alana.

As her husband's words flowed into deeply resonant tones, Alana felt herself lifting up into the sound that soon included her own voice joining Ah-Lahn's. As they chanted together, her body vibrated with a force that was both in and around her.

She closed her eyes and turned her gaze inward. Mists began to form before her, coalescing into a rainbow-colored sphere that spun, casting off shards of light that suddenly burst with a great flash.

Alana's eyes shocked open. Ah-Lahn was now standing to her right with his left hand resting on her back behind her heart. He was creating a pulsing vibration that caused her to inhale to the very bottom of her lungs.

"Relax, Alana," he said gently. "Gaze into the flames and tell me what you see."

She hesitated at first, then took a deep breath and focused her full attention on the cobalt blue center of the fire.

"The flames are very bright and there are iridescent orbs spiraling around with images forming in them. I can see myself at different ages with different people."

"Step into the scene your soul chooses," instructed Ah-Lahn calmly. "Breathe in and let the story carry you. Treasure awaits in the orb."

The Prince

Princess Meke took the Queen Mother's elegantly ringed hands in hers as they sat next to a cooling fountain in the center of the luxurious palace garden.

"Grandmother, please tell me again about my grandfather," the twelve-year-old asked eagerly. "People say he was a great man."

"Yes, Meke, he was," answered the girl's grandmother, wistfully casting her eyes across the pool's lush reeds and lotuses to the gigantic statues of herself and her late husband that rose up from the desert in the distance.

"Your grandfather was a great man, and he loved you and your siblings with his whole heart. Do you remember him at all?"

"Not really. I was very young when he died. I do remember that he seemed to glow like the sun and he always smelled good. Did he wear perfume?"

"Not exactly perfume," chuckled the Dowager Queen. "He carried the aroma of the Kyphi incense that he and the priests burned in the temple while he offered his daily prayers.

"Even today, if one of the priests walks by, I catch that scent of myrrh and honey and juniper, and then I look around for your grandfather. I have to remind myself that he has been gone for years."

"I am sorry to make you sad," soothed Meke, placing a gentle hand on her grandmother's shoulder. "We do not have to talk about him if you prefer not to. Although I really do want to hear the story of your romance. Did you love him as much as my sisters have told me?"

"Oh, yes, child, with all my heart. Remembering does not make me sad. He actually seems closer when I tell our story. Are you sure you want to hear it again?"

"Yes, please!" exclaimed the princess, clapping her hands.

Meke was the truest romantic of all of the current Pharaoh's children. She guided her grandmother to a more comfortable seat with a cushion behind her aging back, then seated herself across from the Queen Mother so she could catch every nuance of the story she loved to hear.

In later years she would be glad to have taken the trouble, for this would be the last time her grandmother was able to share her fondest memories.

The Queen Mother leaned back in her chair and drifted into the events that led to the happiest days of her long and exciting life.

I remember the first time I met your grandfather. I was about thirteen years old. My parents and older brother and I had only recently arrived at the court of your great-grandfather where I felt very plain in comparison with other girls my age.

"I cannot believe you were ever plain, Grandmother," objected Meke. "You are so elegant. My mother still copies some of your styles."

The Queen smiled and admired the fine linen gown, jeweled rings, and golden bracelets she wore every day.

"What you see here is the result of many years of practice. Your grandfather showered me with jewels and exquisite garments because he loved beauty. Our styles evolved together. Now, do not interrupt, sweetheart, or I will lose my train of thought.

On that glorious day I was seated on a beautifully carved bench in a spacious room with many other women. Most were young, like myself, and a few others were older with children.

Servants had dressed us in exquisite finery. That afternoon some of us newer girls, known in the harem as 'ornaments,' were to be presented to the Prince. He was the second son of the King, who, like your father is now, was known to his people as *Per-aa*.

What an astonishing life I was leading—wearing finely pleated linen garments, jewelry made of gold, faience beads, and precious stones. Perfumes, cosmetics, and fancy wigs were even then part of my accoutrements.

Because I already knew how to read, write, sing, and dance before I came to the harem, I was more accomplished in my lessons than many of the girls. Most of them cared only to primp and gossip and talk about the wealthy husbands they would attract from among the courtiers they would meet.

Everyone understood that not all the new girls would be chosen to remain in the harem, so there was considerable competition among us.

When my family and I first came to the capital, my parents had wanted me to follow them into priestly service like my brother, Anen. But I was eager to advance myself at court. Even as a young girl, I was interested in being at the center of power. One way to get there was as a royal companion.

I was fortunate to make friends with two powerful women who were in charge of the harem. One was the Prince's older sister and the other was his mother. Today I was going to meet her son.

I was so nervous. I had never been in the presence of such an illustrious person as the Prince.

We new girls were taken to an exquisitely furnished chamber to await his arrival. Every wall was painted with papyrus stems intertwined with blue lotus flowers and fantastical images of plants and animals that live along the banks of The River. Intricate designs in red, green, blue, and gold overwhelmed my eyes. The furniture was luxurious, made of exotic woods and inlaid with colorful beads and precious stones.

I had been told that the royal family's quarters put these rooms to shame, but I could not imagine anything more resplendent than this room.

As I gazed awe-struck at my surroundings, I suddenly became aware of the Prince's arrival. Even as a young man, he liked to create a dramatic entrance by surprising his audience. He certainly did that day.

His appearance took my breath away. Surely the gods were not more beautiful. His deep-set grey eyes were penetrating as he surveyed the latest additions to the harem his father had created for him when he came of age.

He was elegantly clad in a finely pleated linen kilt. His sash was embroidered with jewel-toned threads and beadwork, and he wore the blue and gold striped *neme* headdress of his position as Prince. He walked confidently about the room, showing off his muscular, sun-bronzed torso and legs. A slight smile played upon his full lips.

His sandals were of the finest leather, decorated with electrum. He wore a warrior's arm bands that looked like the protective wrist guards my brother used when he practiced archery. Of course, the Prince's were more finely made.

I was not the first of the 'ornaments' to catch his attention. But when he came to me, he stopped and looked me straight in the eye. I was utterly transfixed, unable to move except to return his gaze.

I could feel the color rise in my cheeks. A tingling sensation traveled up my spine. My mind went numb, and I forgot to bow until an attendant poked me from behind.

The Prince seemed amused. This was not the first time his appearance had overwhelmed a young woman.

'Come, sit with me,' he said with the authority of his title. He beckoned me to a richly upholstered bench that was set against a vividly painted fresco depicting the worship of Hathor, goddess of love and beauty.

So dazzled was I by his presence that I did not notice the other girls being ushered out of the room. I heard later that some did not bother to hide their jealousy that I should be left alone with the Prince.

He took my hands in his and said in a voice as calm as a windless day, 'Tell me about yourself, and do not be nervous. I bite only when angry.'

'Then I must be certain never to make you angry, Sire,' I surprised myself by replying with a bit of spunk. When he laughed, I sighed and relaxed.

After that, our time together sped by. The Prince was kind and self-effacing. He put me so completely at ease that I found myself babbling about my life back home. I was especially excited to tell him about our horses and how my brother, who was serving in the temple of Amun, used to take me racing over the desert in one of the chariots my father managed.

The Prince seemed to already know everything I was jabbering on about. He was well acquainted with my brother and my father, who had been brought to court by the Prince's father, Per-aa, to be master of horses and chariots.

The Prince told me he was also an archer and insisted that I feel his muscles. Then I sang him some of the songs my mother had taught me while she was a royal entertainer in the temple to the god Min back home where I was educated.

'I know that temple well,' he declared. 'It was built by my great-grandfather. Perhaps we can visit there sometime and you can show me around. I have not been there in years.'

Suddenly the Prince grew quite effusive in describing how he loved to drive his own chariot at enormous speeds around the palace perimeter. He even suggested that he take me for a ride, an invitation that I heartily accepted.

'Then let's go!' he exclaimed. He took me by the hand and walked so quickly that I had to run to keep up with his long strides. Very soon we came to the stables where two slender stallions were being hitched to the most beautiful chariot I had ever seen.

The chariot was brilliant in the simplicity of its design and decoration, using only a delicate rendering of the Prince's cartouche wrought in electrum. The horses' headdresses were enormous ostrich plumes dyed blue and gold. This was nothing like the rigs my father and brother had taken me riding in.

'Your chariot is breath-taking!' I cried out in amazement.

'I knew you would like it,' he said proudly. 'And I was certain you would want to ride with me, so I ordered the grooms to hitch the horses for us.

'Up you go!' the Prince exclaimed as he hopped into the driving position and swung me in beside him with a quick arm around my waist.

Instinctively, I hooked my knee into the cut-out on the side of the chariot and steadied myself for the fast start I knew was coming.

The Prince laughed in approval. 'I had a feeling you would be well trained. Since you are in the archer's position, will you defend me against my enemies, little warrior?'

Surveying his powerful bow and quiver of arrows next to me, I answered sincerely, 'I fear your weapons are too heavy for me, Sire. But, yes, I will always be your defender. I promise.'

With a victorious shout, the Prince snapped the reins as the horses pranced away from the stables. Once clear of the palace yard, he urged them to gallop. He raced them at full speed across his father's lands, showing off the tight turns and intricate maneuvers that royal charioteers used in battle.

'This is how my great-grandfather defeated his enemies years ago!' he exclaimed as we plunged toward invisible armies. 'Do you know the best thing about leading the charge? No dust from the chariots in front of you!'

I barely heard him as the wind rushed past my head, setting my earrings to jangling as the horses' headdresses bounced before me. I was dazzled by the animals' rippling flanks, the brilliant sun reflecting white light off the desert sands, and the feeling of power that poured through me.

I was riding as if I had always ridden next to my Prince, for I already considered him mine.

Of course, there was consternation in the court over my

lack of decorum. For me to be seen in the Prince's company outside of the palace instantly sparked gossip and raised unwanted suspicion from the priestly class. They and many traditionally minded courtiers expected Per-aa's heir to choose his public companions and wives from other royal families.

We did not care. We were young, in love, and filled with the vigor of youth that often underestimates the consequences of its actions.

Life with Per-aa

Meke could see that her grandmother was growing tired. She helped the dowager walk to the comfort of her private quarters in hopes of hearing more stories about her forebearers.

As they entered the Queen's luxurious apartment, her panther, Mau-Ba, stretched her silky body and purred for her mistress's attention.

"Hello, my beauty," said the Queen as she stroked the big cat's elegant head and body. "Have you been guarding your domain today?"

Indeed, Mau-Ba was the ruler of all she surveyed from the exquisite, elevated perch that had been fashioned for her, at the Queen's direction, to look like a very wide throne. The black panther's emerald green eyes missed nothing.

Over the years, the Queen had owned several panthers, but Mau-Ba was her favorite. She was uniquely attuned to her mistress and exceedingly loyal. Rather than roaming outside, she preferred to remain in their shared quarters, which included a lushly planted courtyard and a fountain. Mau-Ba had been one of the last gifts from the Queen's husband, which made this panther all the more precious. The two royal females were aging together.

Mau-Ba leapt down from her throne and rubbed against the dowager's legs as they walked together to the Queen's comfortable divan. The panther curled up gracefully at her mistress's feet and listened to the story that soothed her. She loved the sound of the Queen's voice and purred in harmony with its timbre that had mellowed as the lady aged.

When the dowager and her feline companion were settled, Princess Meke tried to move the story along.

"Grandmother, will you tell me about the wedding?"

"Ah, the wedding," sighed the Queen, drifting into a particularly fond memory.

I do not recall how many months passed after I first met the Prince. I do know that I grew up considerably during that time. My figure filled out and I was more confident of my place in his affections. The very thought of him made my body tingle as I anticipated becoming a wife and a mother.

On our wedding day we were surrounded by a crowd of well-wishers. The palace was lavishly decorated with oceans of jasmine and stephanotis flowers perfuming the air. Magnificent Nubian slaves waved enormous ostrich plume fans to keep the guests cool.

I was dressed in a delicately sheer linen gown that showed off my new curves. I was wearing bracelets of faience beads on my arms, exquisite lapis earrings dangling from my pierced lobes, and a golden pectoral collar upon my bosom.

My papyrus sandals were expertly woven and trimmed with gold and silver. An intricately braided wig hung to my shoulders. My eyes were lined with kohl, and my lips were stained with precious ointments.

The Prince walked proudly at my side as we processioned through the great colonnade to the open-air court where the festivities were to take place. Two gilded chairs had been prepared for us, though, of course, they were not as grand as those of the Prince's parents, Per-aa and his Queen.

Foreign dignitaries had sent gifts; and our local singers, dancers, and priests had gathered to play their parts in the rituals that would seal our union.

On the celebration's first evening, after hours of feasting and entertainments that would continue for several more days, at last we were alone in our quarters.

My Prince took me in his arms and kissed me deeply. I will never forget his whispered promise. 'My love for you will span the centuries.' As he made me his wife in deed as well as word, I knew he spoke the truth.

"Was he a very tender lover, Grandmother?" asked Meke slyly. She was eager to know how soon the mysteries of human lovemaking would be revealed to her.

"Yes, he was very sweet," said the Queen, remembering her best days with her husband.

He always treated me with respect, especially when I was pregnant, which was often. Fortunately, I bore children easily. I was able to carry out my royal duties into the final week.

I am sure this good fortune contributed to the singular position I held in my husband's affection and the role I played throughout his reign.

His older brother had died unexpectedly, so my Prince ascended the throne to wield Egypt's sacred crook and flail at a relatively young age. By that time I had already given him two healthy sons, and our mutual affection was very deep.

That is when he commanded that I be known as the Great Royal Wife.

Meke smiled. She was pleased to see her grandmother so happy in her recollections.

Although my husband occasionally took other wives in diplomatic exchanges with foreign leaders and maintained his traditional harem, none of the other women were ever elevated above me in rank or in his favor.

The treaty wives had their own apartments, households, and attendants, but he visited them frequently only when I was too pregnant for lovemaking. I remained the only wife to bear him children that he acknowledged as his heirs.

I enjoyed spending time with our sons and daughters, as did my husband, though we both preferred politics to family life. Whenever possible, I accompanied him on state business, as his Great Royal Wife and co-ruler.

In those days I had the honor of meeting foreign rulers and translating for my husband, as I speak a number of languages. I dictated letters on his behalf and offered my opinions on matters of domestic and international relations, which he requested if I failed to volunteer my thoughts.

I relished this work and the influence it gave me. Naturally, some of the other courtiers, both men and women, considered me too influential. But I knew I was fulfilling my husband's wishes as well as my own desires to function in a leadership position.

Our greatest worry was that the High Priest and his army of priests were becoming increasingly hostile toward your grandfather as his reign progressed. Of course, they had always resented me because he placed so much value on my position as co-ruler.

The priesthood's wealth was actually greater than Per-aa's because of the temple taxes that had been authorized by previous pharaohs. We were aware that many priests were also practicing dark arts to oppose my husband and me, though they would smile obsequiously to our faces.

For many years, the state god had been known officially as Amun-Re, but the older priests felt threatened by your grandfather's increasing identification with the Great Sun Disc. His father had begun the precedent of elevating worship of the Sun God Ra. Your grandfather merely elaborated on it.

Many years ago our second son proclaimed to us that he would do away with all lesser gods if he were to assume the throne, which we did not expect at the time. Nevertheless, we worried about his apparent rashness, which concerns me now that he is Per-aa.

"Is my father rash?" Meke could not help but question her grandmother. She was unaware that many of the old priests called the current

Per-aa a heretic and a criminal.

A shadow crossed the Queen Mother's face.

"Sadly, your father has made many enemies by moving the capital city and banning worship of the old gods.

"Your grandfather and I both emphasized the Great Sun Disc in our private worship. And in the last few years of our reign, your grandfather began to identify himself personally with the God Ra. But your father is more outspoken and demonstrative than his father, who was always a supreme diplomat."

"Oh, Senaa, come in," the Queen paused. She and Mau-Ba both looked up to acknowledge the dowager's personal steward. "I am telling Meke about her grandfather."

"Such a superb leader he was," Senaa said with noticeable affection. He nodded respectfully to Meke and then bowed deeply to the Queen before kneeling down to stroke Mau-Ba, who purred approvingly.

Meke was pleased to see the steward, who frequently visited her grandmother. She had always liked the looks of him.

He was a stately man with dark hair and expressive eyes. As was his habit, he was wearing a simple linen kilt and neme headdress that identified him as a royal aide.

Meke knew he was at least fifteen years younger than her grandmother. And, she noticed with particular interest today, he was very comfortable in the Queen's presence.

Directing a look of deep appreciation toward the dowager, Senaa then turned to Meke. "Per-aa practically raised me, you know, and he gave me the great honor of serving your grandmother these many years.

"Forgive the intrusion," he said gently to the Queen. "I can return later if you wish. These matters of finance are not urgent."

Exchanging an affectionate smile with the dowager, he bowed again and backed out the way he had entered.

Troubles

*A*s soon as the steward retired, Meke ventured a question that had long puzzled her.

"Grandmother, do you love Senaa?"

"Goodness, what a question!" the Queen responded, surprised at the girl's keen perception.

"The way he smiled at you seemed more intimate than a mere aide would be allowed. Were you two lovers?"

"Such fantasies you conjure, Meke. We were never lovers, though I admit he is a very attractive man. Senaa was always as devoted to my husband as he was to me. Per-aa trusted him implicitly—trust he has earned many times over.

"I once asked Senaa why he never took a wife, though he has had several women in his life. His expression was perfectly circumspect, revealing nothing. He only bowed deeply and answered, 'I am wed to royal service, my Queen.'

"Senaa continues to administer the lands that support my household expenses. He has always been conservative and sometimes quite stern when I order more furnishings from my workshops than he considers prudent.

"Of course, in the old days, he was as indulgent as any of the other stewards when Per-aa's penchant for lavish expenditures was involved, especially for his jubilees. But Senaa always warned me about being extravagant, lest my own finances not support me in my old age.

"He often counseled me to be careful of my political ambitions, in case they should involve me in foreign intrigues I was not prepared to handle. However, my husband did not share his concerns. I enjoyed considerable influence throughout our reign, and I still do as adviser to your father and mother.

"I find Senaa annoying at times, and yet I cannot fault his advice, which has proved correct over the years. Per-aa loved him like a son. I would be lost without his guidance since your grandfather died.

"Though I sometimes find myself tempted to be too familiar with Senaa, as you noticed, I have learned that he always keeps my best interests in mind. He does not take advantage of his position."

"Uncle Anen does not like him," said Meke plainly. She hoped that her grandmother would explain the tension she had always felt around the Queen Mother's brother.

"I have never understood the antagonism between them. The animosity began many years ago on the very first day Senaa became my steward," answered the dowager. "He is always cordial to Anen, but my brother has admitted to being suspicious of Senaa's motives and often disagrees with his counsel.

"I have learned to ignore my brother's hostility, and I try to ensure that the two do not come into contact, at least in my presence. But the situation is very odd. Neither of them will discuss the other, so I do not broach the subject with either of them."

The Queen Mother fell silent, her thoughts drawn to the conundrum she had never been able to solve.

"Do you miss your home at Grandfather's palace now that my father has moved the court to his new capital? Was Egypt truly more glorious during the days of Grandfather's reign?"

Meke hoped that her pointed questions would nudge her grandmother back into the story. The Queen Mother obliged.

Our family is still blessed with great wealth, and your parents have created a magnificent new capital here between Upper and Lower Egypt. But we were much richer in Nubian gold and other foreign imports in the old days.

Your grandfather lavished me with finery—delicate gold

necklaces and earrings, extravagantly woven wigs, gemlike scarabs that honored me while extolling his accomplishments, and exquisitely carved statuary that celebrated our marriage.

And, oh, how your grandfather loved to build! New and refurbished temples, immense statues, waterways, cities. He even created an artificial lake for me where we sailed in our glorious golden barge. My life was far grander than I could have imagined as a harem 'ornament'.

Suddenly the Queen Mother bent over in her chair, holding her head in her hands. Mau-Ba sat up suddenly, searching her mistress's face.

"I am fine, Mau-Ba. Go back to sleep, my beauty," said the dowager. The panther settled down, but did not sleep. The Queen drank some water from the cup her granddaughter handed her and drew in a long breath.

"Oh, Meke, I miss your grandfather so terribly. He was more than a husband to me. He was my mentor and spiritual guide. I always felt more capable in his presence than when I was alone. He never failed to challenge me to learn and do more in support of our kingdom.

"I try to offer the advice he would have wanted for your father and mother, especially to use diplomacy to keep Egypt out of wars with her neighbors. Your grandfather was very wise in how he created alliances with gifts of gold and our finest linen, and through strategic marriages that he sometimes undertook himself.

"I believe he went to war only one time throughout his very long reign. But circumstances are changing, and I fear we are heading for difficult times."

"How did he die, Grandmother?" asked Meke tentatively. "Did the plague take him?"

"No, that terror had occurred years earlier. We were fortunate to survive the scourge, though many did not. I suppose you are old enough now to hear about it."

Once more, the Queen Mother slipped into the vivid scene she was describing, her voice heavy with the burden of painful memories.

Our land of peace and plenty was decimated by pestilence. Everyone was terrified. Crops failed from lack of farmers to tend the fields. People from all levels of society died, and livestock perished because their owners had passed away or fled.

Disease was rampant, and no amount of sacrifice or prayers to the gods succeeded in turning the tide. They seemed not to hear us until our sins were purged.

My parents succumbed to the grotesque skin eruptions, fever, and vomiting. Their bodies had to be hastily entombed. Hundreds more, even thousands, died as the contagion went on for nearly a dozen years.

Eventually the darkness passed, but it left its mark. Your grandfather had aged terribly and was drained of his vitality. The building projects and carvings he commissioned became more religious in nature in those days. After the plague he began to fully equate himself with the Great Sun Disc.

The old priests were agitated because their ranks had been severely diminished in the plague. Per-aa's most trusted adviser replaced the deceased with younger priests who were more amenable to the new ways. Nevertheless, trouble was brewing, and we were deeply troubled.

Our kingdom remained prosperous, but the glory days were clearly winding down. For the first time in our reign, I did not know how to aid your grandfather, or what action to suggest that he take to combat the intrigues of the old priests.

Despite their shrinking numbers, the darkness of the Amun priests grew, as did their influence. They whispered lies to the people, creating fear and resentment toward our court. They spoke vilely against us, and their hatred began to physically affect Per-aa.

"What happened to Grandfather? How was he affected?" Meke was completely immersed in her grandmother's story, but she could not help interrupting.

Your grandfather was nearly sixty years old and in failing health when he decided to name your father co-regent to assume some of the official duties of Per-aa.

As you know, our first son, your father's older brother, had died of malaria, making your father the one to become co-ruler with your grandfather and me. He was, and is, a very dutiful son and has greatly honored his father by refurbishing some of his temples that had been damaged in the big earthquake that came after the plague.

After your grandfather died, some of our closest allies wrote me letters of support, expressing their regard for my husband and honoring me as his Queen and co-ruler. Your grandfather's priority was always to maintain *ma-at* and to extend that peace, love, and compassion toward all of Egypt and our territories.

Our allies asked me to counsel your father to take a more cautious approach to the changes he was determined to effect, and so I have. But my son says that his time is short and he must act decisively while he is able. That is why he created a new city dedicated to the Great Sun Disc and banished the old religion.

'Mother,' he explained to me some time ago, 'the dark priests do not respect diplomacy. I know you have done much to keep peace in our kingdom, but sometimes a revolution is required. I have had visions of the Great Sun Disc of my father and his father before him. Ra has told me to take bold action.'

'What about ma-at?' I questioned your father. 'Does peace not mean anything to you for your children and your people? That was your father's guiding principle.'

'Ma-at also means truth, Mother,' your father insisted. 'Dedication to truth in art, governance, and religion is what guides me now. The priests have turned even positive deities to darkness. Ra is a god of love and light. We do not worship him in darkness or fear like Amun, the hidden god.

'Ra needs no animals or gigantic idols to placate him. The rays of his brilliance shine upon all of his creation. This we must teach our people to free them from the cruelty and avarice of priests who would steal the last morsel of food from the mouths of babes as taxes to line their own coffers.

'I believe the pestilences and earthquakes that have beset our land are caused by the darkness that has crept into every aspect of society. That is why I have left the old priests behind and forced them to abandon their temples, rites, and sacrifices.

'Upper and Lower Egypt must embrace the One Light if we are to survive as a people and a civilization. This is my dream and Ra's calling to me and my Queen. I cannot turn my back on so great a commission.'

The dowager sighed. "Meke, I cannot argue with your father's fervor. Who am I to say his visions are wrong? I have continued to play the diplomat whenever possible. Still, the priests and many of the people are angry at the dramatic changes.

"I have done what I can, but I am old and tired. I fear your father's revolution will not end well."

"I hesitate to ask again, Grandmother," Meke said with childlike insistence, "but how did Grandfather die? I was very small and all I remember is the harem women keening for days. Only a couple of nurses stayed with us children. We thought another earthquake was coming or Hittite invaders or an attack of giant crocodiles."

The Queen Mother's hands covered her heart.

"My poor child. Adults can be so thoughtless when tragedy strikes. Now do let me continue, sweetheart."

I was beside myself with grief and frustration in your grand-father's final days. The court physicians could do nothing. Their potions and prayers were useless against the pain that racked my husband's body day and night.

He cried out for someone to ease his agony, but the experts were impotent. They said that Per-aa's jaw and stomach had deteriorated from years of indulgence in rich foods and that his body was too old to fight. I believe the illness was more virulent than that.

I am certain the dark priests accelerated his decline with their evil spells and incantations. Their epithets are like poison to anyone they oppose, and they hated my husband for decades.

I believe they also may have gradually poisoned him, though I cannot prove it. Sometimes I myself feel ill. I get stabbing pains in my back and stomach. None of the usual remedies help . . .

"Grandmother?" Meke spoke earnestly as the dowager abruptly grew silent and stared off into space. When the Queen Mother spoke again, it was wistfully, more to herself than to her granddaughter.

"I miss him terribly. Still, I am grateful he is gone now. I am glad my husband no longer suffers, but I feel lost without him and in personal danger. These days, the High Priest is openly menacing toward me, though I am still strong enough to resist his threats.

"Thank the gods, Senaa remains in my service. And your father and mother both treat me with great respect.

"Meke, I am ready to join my Prince in the afterlife. I see him now, waiting for me in all his youthful radiance. Before he died, he promised to reveal a secret to me, but he never did. I have waited long enough to learn the answer to that mystery. If Senaa were not here to support me, I might have died already."

With a sudden surge of will, the Queen Mother pushed herself up from her divan. She grasped the arm of the young princess who sprang to her feet. Meke looked upon the dowager's ashen features with alarm and tried to avoid stepping on Mau-Ba, who had also risen suddenly.

"Help me lie down, Granddaughter. I must rest now."

Meke eased the Queen's frail, though still-regal figure onto the sumptuous ebony bed she had shared with her husband.

"You are a good girl, Meke," said the Queen as she rested her hand on the head of her panther who had leapt onto the bed and settled herself next to her mistress's body.

"Promise me you will always be loyal to your father and mother. They need your love and support. Do not let the wicked ones poison your mind with their innuendo and half-truths. Pray to Ra, child. The

One Light is our only hope.

"Run along now and send word to Senaa to come see me in an hour. I will be able to discuss financial matters with him then.

"Promise me, Meke," the Queen said faintly. "Promise you will be loyal."

"I will, I promise." Meke kissed her grandmother on the forehead and tiptoed quietly from the royal bedroom. This was the last time they would see each other in this world.

When Senaa entered the Queen Mother's chamber an hour later, Mau-Ba raised her head from her mistress's chest and yowled plaintively.

Senaa soothed the silky panther and looked down at the Queen. He thought the dowager appeared to be sleeping peacefully. Too peacefully, he then realized, for she was dead. A tiny trickle of dark liquid oozed from a corner of her mouth.

"So, they have finally killed your mistress," he said resignedly to Mau-Ba. The Queen had, indeed, been poisoned.

She had always suspected that the dark priests would find a way to get rid of her. Their lackeys in the royal household could have gradually poisoned both Per-aa and the Dowager Queen over a considerable length of time.

The faithful steward knelt by the bedside of the woman he had loved and served throughout his entire adult life. He took her still-warm hand in his and held it to his cheek, feeling his heart break wide open. Somehow he knew they would not be this close to each other for many, many years.

With an effort, Senaa drew a long, steady breath. He rose slowly and gazed once more at the woman he would always love. Squaring his shoulders with the dignity of his office, he turned and walked solemnly to see Meke's father and mother to tell them the dreadful news.

Realizations

Visions and sensations of ancient Egypt lingered in Alana's awareness. Though she was aware of being back in the grove, she could still feel the weight and texture of elaborate wigs and jewels that had adorned the Queen's linen-clad figure. The affection she and Per-aa had shared still echoed in her heart. His promise of a secret remained unfulfilled.

"Drink this, Alana," said Ah-Lahn, gently offering her a strengthening elixir to help ground her back into the present. The expected radiance that follows a life review scintillated in her aura, yet a slightly puzzled look played about her eyes.

"What do you remember about your journey?" he asked when she appeared revived.

Alana pressed her hand to her heart.

"The Queen experienced such caring from Per-aa. He was passionately devoted to her, always affirming her position, even when he took other wives as political alliances. She was touched by how much he relied on her, especially in maintaining good relationships with key allies. She blossomed in his value of her charm and intellect and in how he encouraged her curiosity.

"They both worried about their son who would become Per-aa. The Queen felt her husband's regret over leaving her to deal with the priests of the old gods. She knew he was proud of his accomplishments, but she could tell he wondered what else he could have done for his people."

Alana looked to her husband for understanding. "Did he leave this world with a determination to come back and try again?"

Ah-Lahn nodded. "Most souls do want to try again. None of us is ever as successful in life as we had planned between lives. In the invisible world we are given insight into our human frailties, but we must overcome them in the physical world. That task is nearly always more difficult than we expect it to be.

"Few truly understand the purpose of returning lifetime after lifetime. We do the best we can and pray we are making progress. We may never know the full extent of our past failures or victories. These are life's deep secrets that must be lived to be discovered."

Ah-Lahn was serious again, his next question full of import. "What else did you notice about the Queen herself?"

Alana closed her eyes, recalling the images that were still fresh in her mind. As she remembered, she felt the consciousness of the Queen merge with her own.

"I relished my power as co-ruler. While I loved my children, my hours of greatest enjoyment were those I spent as co-ruler with Per-aa. I took pleasure in luxury. Although I realized my steward gave me wise counsel about my own expenses, I was all too happy to bask in the adulation and gifts my husband showered upon me.

"The end of my life was a disappointment. I lost my looks and, once my husband was dead, my influence declined. My son, the new Per-aa, had his own revolutionary calling that he felt compelled to pursue, despite my urging caution.

"I came to accept the truth of his visions, and I quietly embraced his new religion. But I would have been miserable without my devoted steward."

Alana paused. "My devoted steward," she repeated, looking up into the eyes of Ah-Lahn, whose gaze met hers with an intensity that seemed to will her to a new recognition.

"You were that steward. I felt such love between the Queen and Per-aa, I could not imagine that you were not the Pharaoh. But you were not. Your soul stood beside mine as Senaa. Why was that? Why were we not married in that lifetime?"

"Our roles are always the result of the choices we make," said Ah-Lahn tenderly. "In Egypt you were determined to live a life of luxury and political influence, and you succeeded, perhaps beyond your own expectations. You helped Per-aa create an enlightened reign, and you kept your promise to defend him as best you could. For that, I applaud you.

"Yet, this was not the only embodiment in which you have held me at a distance. Fortunately, in Egypt we were able to support one another —you by employing me, and I by advising you. But my love for you was stronger than yours for me. Your indifference and frequent annoyance were hard for me to bear."

Alana forced herself to face Ah-Lahn. How could she not have recognized the tie between them when she was Queen? Apparently others, like Meke, had noticed their connection.

"I am sorry, Ah-Lahn. I did feel your devotion, and so did Per-aa. I was aware of being unusually fond of my steward, but I was not going to jeopardize my position by taking a lover, even if you had offered. Please forgive me. No one could have been of greater support to me than you were."

Ah-Lahn embraced her. "Our ancient bond is stronger than a single lifetime, Alana. And we forgive each other as we forgive ourselves. What matters now is that I need you beside me as never before. Your skill as adviser to kings promises to be particularly useful.

"Some of the same individuals from our Egyptian lifetime have returned for another opportunity to play out the drama of their soul momentums. I fear a few are once again turning to the dark arts. Just as they opposed Per-aa and his Queen, they now threaten us and druíthe like Uncle Óengus.

"I am aware that my son, Tadhgan, may be negatively influenced by some we knew in Egypt. He is not a dark soul, but he is too easily led astray. There are those who would trade upon a certain dissatisfaction or restlessness in his personality. Will you help me guide him in the years to come?"

"Of course." Alana laid her head on Ah-Lahn's chest. She could feel his heart beating in time with her own.

"There is more for me to reveal to you later," Ah-Lahn said as he smoothed her hair. "We will rest now."

Then, easing her away from his embrace, he looked deeply into her eyes and asked earnestly, "Do you feel how I have loved you all these centuries? How I have waited for you all my life? How I will cherish you for another thousand years? You will always be my Queen."

"I do feel your love, Ah-Lahn, and I pray that you will always feel mine," Alana replied solemnly. She touched her lips to his cheek and whispered, "A thousand years and more will I be at your side, come what may."

Ah-Lahn lifted his wife into his arms and carried her to a resting place in a far corner of the grove. He knew she believed what she said about remaining at his side. He hoped she could keep her promise when circumstances tested her resolve, as they inevitably would.

Questing for Truth

*A*h-Lahn tucked Alana's wool cloak around her before leaving her in the grove's sacred protection. "Rest here and I will bring you some food. You have done well, mo chroí."

Alana tried to relax, but she could not rest. Her mind was spinning. Recalling the Egyptian lifetime had sparked vivid regrets she found difficult to contain. And she continued to remember.

The Queen's life after Per-aa's painful death had been traumatic. She believed she had failed to carry on her husband's legacy. In the end, she could not protect him or their kingdom from the treachery of the dark priests. And she had made troubling mistakes, especially in failing to truly appreciate Senaa.

Alana knew that Ah-Lahn was obligated to reveal more embodiments to her. Egypt was only the first. Would she be up to the challenge? Or would the records of her past failings overwhelm her ability to act in the present? When Ah-Lahn returned with their meal, she told him of her concerns as they sat outside the grove to eat.

"I am not certain I can do this, Ah-Lahn. What if I fail to learn the right lessons? I know you cannot simply tell me what they are. What if I disappoint you and Uncle Óengus?"

"You will not," he assured her. "I have faith in you, Alana. You are already a better seer than you think you are. Now, try to eat something and we will go back to our cottage to sleep. I have composed a song for you that may help to stimulate tomorrow's recollections."

Later that night, as Alana drifted off to sleep, Ah-Lahn's soothing voice carried her far across the silent sands of time.

Over the seas the great ships came
carrying beings of light and power,
bearers of art and poetry and song,
radiant ancestors, the beginnings of us,
though at the end of a mighty wave
that crashed on Éire's verdant shore.

Come from another emerald isle,
seafaring pilgrims were they all,
colonizing a new world
with knowledge and wisdom of ages past
to shine out across the centuries.

We are fruit of their seed,
bough of their branch,
and soil of the ground their magic made.

Though living now in fairy hills,
in ancient times they taught our kin
to revere Sun and Moon in stone,
in sacred mound and blazing fire,
following in their eight-fold course
across our native land and sky.

The paeans we raise are theirs of old,
sung across the blue expanse
from a people gone long ago,
vanished beneath a great deluge.

Their voices resound in our own throats,
so close are they to us in prayer.

We are fruit of their seed,
bough of their branch,
and soil of the ground their magic made.

For past is present in our rites,
the ancients live again in us,
guiding us toward An Síoraí,
though antiquity's wisdom is lost
in the watery grave of obscurity,
as my words will also vanish some day.

Memory abides deep in the soul;
its proof is in our vibrant living
that we may continue millennia from now.
Stay with me and do not doubt;
your heart is all the chalice we need,
and one day you will remember all.

We are fruit of their seed,
bough of their branch,
and soil of the ground their magic made.

Alana awoke the next morning to find herself alone in the cottage she shared with her husband.

Of course, she remembered—he would have been up since dawn.

She was still growing accustomed to his habits, adjusting her own rhythms to his, smiling to herself when she noticed him making an effort to do the same for her. At the moment, she was grateful for his absence. The solitude gave her an opportunity to contemplate what experiences might await her in today's journey into records of the past.

During the night a steady rain had fallen, leaving the world out-side their cozy thatched dwelling glistening in the bright sunlight that warmed away the morning's mist. Alana stepped out into the fresh air and deeply inhaled the earthy scents that wafted in on a light breeze.

A thousand questions swirled in her mind. She had dreamt of the lost cities and radiant beings of light that Ah-Lahn's song evoked. How would those images relate to the scenes she would review today?

What embodiment would her soul choose next? Would there be a connection with Egypt? Would the challenges be similar or different from life to life? Would she discover successes or failures? Would secrets of her relationship with Ah-Lahn be revealed?

Reviewing her life as the Egyptian Queen had left her with more questions than answers. The Queen had kept Senaa at a distance, even though she relied heavily on him. Their deep soul affection had been obvious to her granddaughter Meke.

What choices had she and Ah-Lahn made in previous lifetimes that kept them apart in Egypt? Were there other times of separation? Had she repeated those choices in her refusal to accept Ah-Lahn until An Síoraí had revealed him as her soul's twin?

Alana finally shook her head and made a decision. She would not agonize over what could not be answered until the next life review.

For the better part of an hour, she stood absorbing the sights and sounds of Nature that flowed in and around her. She was keenly aware of Sprid's presence, as if the panther's spirit were encouraging her quest for the truth of her past lives.

She missed the warm companionship of Laoch. She could easily imagine his lanky body romping around this glorious landscape. Of course, had the hound been with her, he would have gleefully chased away the curious pair of tame foxes that gathered by her cottage.

Alana smiled at the thought. Only the stately hawk that watched from the high branches of an oak tree would have escaped Laoch's eager attention.

The sun rose higher in the morning sky, casting a warm glow around Alana as she sat, rapt in her meditations.

Ah-Lahn came upon the scene as he returned from his early-morning rituals. His heart swelled and his throat caught with emotion.

How beautiful! he exclaimed to himself. She looked as radiant as an angel.

Gently, he walked up to his wife and, bending gallantly, kissed her tenderly on the cheek.

"Good morning," he said softly as she turned to him and smiled up into his eyes. "Are you ready to venture once more into the past?"

"I am," she answered simply. She did not wish to disturb the luminance that always lingered in his aura after he had performed the sacred rites required of a Ceann-Druí.

She rose lightly to her feet and added, "I must confess to being a bit apprehensive, yet I am eager to learn more."

"As am I," Ah-Lahn said warmly. "I sense that An Síoraí has messages for both of us."

He folded her arm over his as they walked the short distance to Uncle Óengus's wisdom grove, matching each other's stride and cherishing this moment of closeness before the next life review began.

Outside the circle of giant oaks, Ah-Lahn stopped and gazed off into the distance, seeing into other worlds. His voice assumed a serious tone as he spoke:

No civilization ever believes it will cease to exist, but human creations cannot long endure. Circumstance and nature intervene. Sometimes with water. Sometimes destruction comes with flame.

Collapse often appears in the guise of conflicting beliefs. And the destroyers are always determined to replace the present with a future they erroneously believe they can control.

Many humans are led by their nature to conquer, while our race's propensity leads us to wander. We are adventurers at heart. Intent on exploration, we follow the inner guide to greater heights, welcoming new ideas.

And always do we strive to inspire our fellow creatures into more refined states of inner knowing.

Sadly, even our own wise culture will not endure. Oracles assure us the destroyers of Ynys Môn will fail to physically conquer our island, but others will come to replace them and us. The master seers believe that our way of life cannot retain its present character for much longer.

Your service and mine will continue, though not as we now conceive it. I pray we will always carry in our souls the love of words and sound that create an atmosphere of unity with finer realms. This is our reason for existence and the path we have sworn to uphold.

"Is that what you wish me to discover?" Alana asked when they stepped reverently into the grove that pulsed with a life force all its own. When Ah-Lahn nodded his assent, she took a deep breath and relaxed into the numinous atmosphere.

She said nothing more as her husband gazed intently into her hazel-green eyes. They were already growing bright with the concentration that came easily upon her this morning.

Ah-Lahn placed his right thumb at the center of Alana's brow and extended his fingers up over her forehead. With his left hand at the center of his chest, he directed light energy into her mind while he intoned the sacred syllables that would unlock the gates of her memory.

At her husband's direction, Alana stared into the center of an enormous, clear quartz crystal sphere that Ard-Mháistir Óengus had used for Ah-Lahn's own life reviews years earlier.

A light-filled passage opened into Alana's mind. Her consciousness became infused with that light. As her gaze intensified, misty images began to swirl in the crystal's interior. They spun faster and faster until they coalesced with a sudden flash, and Alana stepped with her full awareness into the scene before her.

Immediately she recognized herself and Ah-Lahn from ages long lost in the veils of time. She was the priestess Treylah, and he was the priest known as Khieranan.

PART FIVE

Holding Us All Together

*Life begins anew each time
a turning point is reached,
for our past is always prologue.*

Into the Far Distant Past

Poseid was beautiful from the air. Treylah relished the view as she looked out the airship's window and stroked the silky panther curled up on the seat beside her. Seen from an altitude of 10,000 feet, the largest island in Atlantis sparkled like an emerald set between azure jewels of sea and sky.

"Look, Spirit," Treylah exclaimed to her panther. "Down there. That is where we live. Are you glad to be going home?"

To satisfy her mistress, the exquisite cat half opened her deep green eyes and turned her head to share the view. She uttered a low purr, but was otherwise non-committal as to her opinion of the sights below.

Whenever possible, Treylah arranged her flights in the morning to take in the expansive view of her homeland. She always marveled at how similar the countryside and cities appeared.

All areas of the island were covered in greenery. Myriad varieties of vegetation grew profusely on and around man-made mountains and canyons the beauty-loving Poseidii of long ago had sculpted. The island's original flat plain had simply been too dull for their artistic taste, so they had changed it.

Even the large buildings, where millions of urban dwellers made their homes, were tucked into hillsides and swaddled in trees, shrubs, and vines. Only a few government structures and temples gleamed like white beacons from the hilltops.

Mankind's landscaping genius was apparent everywhere on Poseid. Probably one reason for the general serenity of the place, Treylah had always thought. That and the well-ordered social structure the Poseidii had put into place centuries ago to ensure fair treatment of their citizens. Though not all of the island's inhabitants were equally protected, as Treylah had recently discovered.

As her airship glided silently into port in the capital city where she served as a priestess in the Temple of the One Light, she pushed the troubling images from her mind. She could not think about those unfortunates right now. Her problems were more personal.

Treylah relaxed when her feet touched familiar ground. After spending six weeks in the countryside, she was even more grateful than usual for the inventions that made urban life so convenient.

Her personal communication device worked better in the capital. The weather was more temperate here. The elaborate canal and sanitation system—that marvel of Atlantean engineering ringing the city—ensured a clean water supply and the timely elimination of waste.

There are no foul odors in the capital, Treylah observed as she breathed in the scent of home. Unless you caught a whiff of the corruption that was rumored to be festering within the upper echelons of Atlantean society. Of course, there had been rumors for centuries. Since time immemorial, oracles had been warning of impending doom.

"Exactly like the first time," they predicted, citing the legend that Poseid had not always been an island.

Treylah shook her head in denial. She could not believe that twenty-eight thousand years earlier atomic energy used to rid Atlantis of monstrous creatures created by mad scientists had caused the continent to break into the islands of which Poseid was the largest.

People would fabricate any kind of wild story to justify their own political ends. Treylah did not want to think about it. Right now she wanted only to stretch her legs and give her panther a bit of exercise on the short walk from the airship port to the temple's public entrance.

She stopped at a kiosk to check the schedule for the city's electronic transport system that glided silently above the pedestrian pavement. She could be home in less than two minutes on the high-speed conveyance, but today she preferred to travel on foot. She needed more time to bask in the exotic pleasure of Poseid's unique marriage of mankind's inventiveness and Nature's abundance. At this moment, that union felt deeply healing.

"Ahhh," she sighed—her senses exulting in the beauty of the capital city where she lived.

The island's golden sunlight seemed especially bright today as it played on the luxurious urban gardens that never failed to lift her spirits. The air cooled as she stopped to watch cleverly programmed fountains that propelled sparkling jets of water high into the air, forming sylph-like patterns of endless variety.

Flashes of color darted here and there from fantastically plumed tame birds that fluttered and soared exuberantly throughout the city. They flew unharmed by predators, for there were none. Formerly aggressive animals, like her panther, had long ago been gentled to live in peace with their fellow creatures.

Treylah slowed her naturally brisk pace to enjoy the shade of blossoming trees and shrubs that grew profusely along the main boulevard. She wished she could visit her favorite shops whose terraces were festooned with lush hanging gardens. But, for now, she would have to content herself with inhaling the myriad perfumes of tropical flowers that scented the air, while delicate melodies played by local musicians wafted through the park-like atmosphere.

The entire city was alive with sight and sound and texture that animated her senses as she mentally prepared herself for the confrontation she could avoid no longer.

What would Khieranan say to her when they met again? She certainly had a few choice words for her husband and fellow priest. They had not parted well, and Treylah still refused to believe it was her fault.

They had argued before her hurried departure. During the six weeks she had been away, they had not cleared the air. Try as she might to resolve the disagreement in her own mind, she was still angry.

Khieranan had been unyielding in his refusal to support her plan for joining her eminent teacher, Solas, and a group of his followers who were emigrating to an Atlantean desert colony that lay far to the east.

"The choice is yours, Treylah," Khieranan had said coolly. "I will not stop you. But I cannot understand your willingness to abandon me because Solas promised you a position in his administration. I thought our marriage meant more to you than that."

Saying no more, Khieranan had turned and left Treylah angry and frustrated. Why had he not given her an opportunity to explain her reasons for going with her mentor? If he had stayed another minute, she would have asked him to leave Poseid with her.

He should have understood. He had been equally devoted to his own mentor, the High Priestess Nhada-lihn. Truth be told, he had never been the same since she disappeared. And though more than two years had passed, he still spent what Treylah considered an inordinate amount of time in Nhada-lihn's deserted portion of the temple.

Unfortunately, there had been no opportunity for further discussion. Treylah had been called away to deal with a family emergency in a remote province of Poseid and had not seen Khieranan again. Since her departure, she and her husband had communicated only briefly and, then, in only the most perfunctory manner.

At last, Treylah and her panther arrived at their destination. Together they turned and looked back fondly upon the city that shone like a jewel in the late morning light. A feeling of wistful longing that she could not explain made her heart ache.

"Come along, Spirit," she said, though neither of them hurried up the perfectly cut marble steps that master masons had created centuries earlier as the temple's public entrance.

Treylah expected that her aide, Petra, would be waiting to lead her through the restricted areas where the priestess would purify herself before entering the sacred precincts of her office.

But she was not ready to resume her normal routines. Not yet. Her head was still swimming from the confusing events and circumstances she had faced in the past six weeks.

She was returning from a difficult mission "out in the world," as her sister priestesses called any locale other than their temple home. A tragedy had befallen her family. Because she was a priestess and the eldest of seven adult children, her duty had been to preside over the burial of their parents and a younger brother.

She had brought what spiritual comfort she could to her grieving siblings who had assembled from across the island to honor their loved ones. Spirit had purred and nuzzled each one to relieve their suffering, but the shock had been too great.

The entire family was stunned by the severity and abrupt onset of the fatalities. Treylah wished she could have done more for her siblings, but no one could explain what had happened.

The exact circumstances of her family members' sudden deaths were murky. Not even the usually efficient government physicians had found a reason for such relatively young persons to contract a mysterious fever and die.

Treylah's heart sank as she recalled that her parents and brother had passed away before she could reach their bedside to perform the rites for the dying. Nor had any of her other siblings been present at the deaths.

Everyone was equally confused as to why their loved ones had been living in this part of the country. After a family conference that yielded no conclusions, the youngest sister, Naihal, had asked to speak with Treylah in private.

"I know what they were doing," she had said in a nervous whisper. "I did not want to endanger any more of our family by telling them, but I think you should be aware of what I know.

"As scientists who followed the Law of the One Light, they were working to improve conditions for the slave laborers who are given fewer rights than the city's tamed birds.

"Our parents were trying to remain undetected. Unfortunately, when our brother joined them, one of his friends inadvertently alerted the authorities, who branded our family as traitors. Once that occurred, our parents knew they were doomed. I was also working with them, but they sent me away to live with our sister Yasmine so I would be safe.

"Treylah, you must be careful. I fear we may not see each other again. Yasmine has not told me outright, but I sense that her husband wants to leave all of Atlantis behind. They are probably encouraging our brothers and sisters to emigrate with them.

"Go with the One Light," urged Naihal. She looked around furtively as she took her sister's hand in hers. "Please, heed the prophecies and consider leaving Poseid. You know what I mean."

Suspicions

Treylah had known exactly what Naihal was talking about. Perhaps the oracles were right after all. Her sister had told her that more seers were predicting cataclysm. Was that why Solas and others were leaving their homes for Atlantean colonies to the east, west, and south?

The burden of these uncertainties weighed heavily on her mind as she entered the first purification area inside the Temple of the One Light. Her growing suspicion that something was amiss on a scale that extended beyond her own family was soon confirmed.

Petra was uncharacteristically eager that she should quickly remove her traveling clothes, perform her ablutions, and put on her white priestess robe so they could have a private conversation.

Despite the aide's attempt to send Spirit directly to Treylah's apartment, the panther was pacing and sniffing the air and staying unusually close by her mistress.

Petra gave up trying to control Spirit and drew near to the priestess. She looked around anxiously and whispered, "You are not the only one who has suffered a family tragedy that has taken her from the temple. Both Irosial and Elzah have recently returned from similar situations, and Zailah left yesterday after being called to her uncle's home across the mountains.

"Since you have been gone, the High Priest has been issuing new directives and consolidating many offices into his own. We are not supposed to discuss the changes, but, of course, rumors are flying. What do you think is going on?"

"I do not know," said Treylah. "I will contact Khieranan. As Second

Priest, he is certain to know what is happening."

"Be careful when you speak with him," warned Petra. "The walls have ears, and the temple is rife with suspicion."

As soon as Treylah and her panther returned to their own quarters, the priestess gathered herself in meditation. Putting aside her concerns about the unfortunate parting from her husband, she quieted her mind and emotions so she could make telepathic contact with Khieranan. Although he was probably nearby in another part of the building, this technique was a safer way for them to communicate.

When they were growing up together as neophytes at the temple, they had developed a coded telepathy that instantly joined them mind-to-mind. It also created a protective energetic shield against the prying minds of others. Since their marriage three years ago, they had both improved their communication by elevating their consciousness into increasingly refined states of awareness.

While serving side-by-side in various temple rites and ceremonies, they often joined minds telepathically to avoid outer conversation. Others marveled at the flawless synergy with which they performed their duties, but they never let on how they did it.

Maintaining clear communion with Khieranan had been difficult for Treylah during her absence. Her grief and emotional confusion invariably blocked her attunement with her husband. Even when she was relatively calm, his vibration had also seemed scattered. She supposed that he, too, was still angry. They did not use telepathy for difficult conversations.

"Contact me when you get home," he had communicated briefly when she sent him her travel schedule. "I am called away now and must obey." That was several days ago, and they had not connected since then.

Fearing detection should anyone hear her speaking, even in the privacy of her own rooms, Treylah quietly intoned the sacred syllables that would alert Khieranan to her presence. She concentrated with more intensity than usual and visualized herself surrounded in the sphere of iridescent blue energy that sealed their communion.

"I am here," she telepathed to him.

"And I," he answered immediately. He did not wait for the questions he already knew she would ask.

"Treylah, conditions in the temple are not good. The High Priest has issued an edict that we priests must surrender the sacred objects and emblems of our offices. New ones will be issued 'for those who are deserving,' as he puts it.

"The priestesses have already had to give up their talismans. If you look, I am certain you will find that any ritual items you did not take with you have been confiscated."

Treylah moved quickly to the cupboard where she usually kept the special rings, pendants, amulets, and crystals she used for the various ceremonies she conducted.

"Gone!" she all but shouted. Her body tensed. How dare someone remove her sacred objects! She shuddered at the sense of violation.

"I am not certain of the High Priest's next actions," Khieranan continued. "Several of us have noticed that the central altar flame is flickering. You know how simply being in its presence has always been restorative and uplifting? Now the flame itself feels wounded. It appears to be asking for assistance.

"Some of my trusted fellow priests have also observed others whom we thought were our friends spending a lot of time away from their precincts. We fear they are in league with the High Priest, though we do not know to what end.

"What I do know is that we are no longer safe here. I would be missed and probably pursued if I were to leave before the lunar celebration tonight, but no one should be suspicious if you are not in attendance. Send word that you are exhausted by travel and grief and wish to be excused from the ceremony.

"Several of my comrades have arranged for a vessel to take their wives and children to safety. This will be a long and potentially dangerous voyage, but I want you on that ship."

"I cannot go without you," Treylah protested. Her heart recoiled at the thought of leaving Khieranan without resolving their argument.

Forgotten was her desire to follow Solas. Her only thought was for reconciliation with her husband.

"You must go tonight," Khieranan said firmly. "Tell no one and do not be seen to be packing. Wear several layers of clothing if necessary. The weather may be severe before you arrive in a temperate location. Take nothing else."

A wave of panic rippled through Treylah's body. "Are circumstances really so bad?" she asked. "What are you going to do?"

"I will follow after the lunar festival," Khieranan said as reassuringly as he could manage. "I have a smaller vessel hidden for myself and a few others. We will slip away during the chaos of the celebration. Pray for us, my love. The High Priest has spies everywhere. This is our only option."

Treylah started to object, but her husband interrupted before she could speak.

"You must trust me in this. Hope lies across the seas. We have known for some time that the High Priest had unwholesome ambitions. You and Solas were right. We should have left months ago. I regret I did not listen to you.

"All is forgiven between us, my love," he continued earnestly. "You must do as I ask. The opportunity for escape is nearly gone. I will contact you later with final instructions."

As Khieranan closed their telepathic connection, he reassured himself that he had been right not to tell Treylah how slim were his chances of escape. He did not want to alarm her further. Getting her to safety was his first priority, even if he had to deceive her.

Obedience

Treylah sat in silence for several minutes. Her mind was racing. How could events have taken such a treacherous turn?

She had been aware that Khieranan believed the High Priest and many of his fellow priests did not adhere to the One Light. However, she had not wanted to consider the man capable of overtly evil intentions until this moment. The unthinkable now appeared to be true.

She trusted her husband's attunement and his observations. After all, he had been in the temple every day during the six weeks of her absence. Clearly, much had happened since she had been gone.

Although the changes had seemed sudden, Treylah reconsidered her own experiences. Both before and after her marriage to Khieranan, she had often felt the High Priest's attention upon her as intrusive, even vulgar. Well before her parents' death, signs of aggression from him had made her wary of his presence. Those feelings of danger now returned with alarming intensity.

Following Khieranan's instructions, Treylah sent her request to be excused from the lunar celebration. An anxious hour later, she received a curt reply from the High Priestess who had replaced Nhada-lihn that she was relieved of her duties for this one event.

However, she was to appear as usual the following morning. Several of the other priestesses were away on family emergencies, and she could not expect special treatment.

Treylah secured her remaining jewels and a few precious family mementos in a small silk pouch that she sewed into her undergarments.

She set out an extra layer of clothing for the voyage and sat quietly in anticipation of Khieranan's next communication.

As nighttime descended on the city, she was prompted to intone the sacred syllables and visualize the protective energy that would connect her with her husband. She immediately felt his vibration.

"I am here," he telepathed.

"And I," she answered.

"Treylah, events are accelerating even faster than we had feared. I was hoping we might get a reprieve, but circumstances are dire. You must leave tonight as planned.

"Our technicians have noticed some anomalies in the guidance systems of the public airships, so we are using smaller sailing vessels that have their own crystal power back-ups. They should be fairly inconspicuous. These days most people use them as pleasure craft.

"At midnight, make your way through the alley system that runs parallel to the minor canal. The alleyway will lead you to a little-used quay where your ship will be waiting.

"The women who are not priestesses and their children will already have arrived at different hours by various routes. You will be the last to board. You must be extremely mindful of your surroundings and do not delay once you have reached the quay.

"I will try to see you off, but do not be distressed if I do not appear. I will be there, one way or another.

"Joha-lihn will manage your journey. Trust him as you would trust me. We will meet on a peninsula that lies two days' voyage to the south-east. One of our colonies is located there. After collecting our ships, those who wish will proceed further east to the community led by Solas.

"We believe the High Priest has no desire to chase us. He only wants us out of Poseid. Word is that he is in league with some malicious scientists. The two groups have been working together for years to poison the minds of the people against the One Light.

"If the High Priest succeeds in taking over control of Poseid, I fear that will trigger the end for our civilization. I only wish we had escaped long ago."

"Of course you could not leave as long as there was hope for change here in Poseid. I see that now," Treylah admitted. "You were right, my love. I am sorry I was angry with you."

"I should have suspected the worst when High Priestess Nhada-lihn mysteriously disappeared two years ago." Khieranan berated himself.

"She warned us not to trust mere appearances of piety. She always taught that discerning the vibration of individuals and circumstances is essential for those who follow the One Light. Now we know why.

"I did not want to risk your being questioned, so I did not tell you why I was spending so much time away from you. I have learned some techniques for communicating with her directly.

"Lady Nhada-lihn has given me instructions that I cannot share with you at this moment. However, be assured she is doing everything possible from inner levels to thwart the evil intentions of the High Priest and those he has convinced to follow him.

"Be strong, Treylah. We must hurry. I will love you as I have always loved you, come what may."

"Come what may," she repeated.

Her heart trembled as Khieranan closed their telepathic link. She now realized she might not see her husband in the flesh for many weeks. *If ever* was too horrible a thought to entertain.

The Battle

Treylah's heart was breaking. She had to leave her panther behind. "Go to the forest, Spirit. You will be safe there," she said. Her voice caught in her throat as she looked into her panther's beseeching emerald eyes. The beautiful feline yowled a complaint and rubbed persistently against her mistress's body.

"You cannot come with me, girl," Treylah insisted as she stroked the sleek black fur. "I know you will be at my side energetically. That will have to be enough for us until I can send for you. Please understand, there is no other way."

Spirit stared at the priestess for a full minute, her expression inexplicable. Then, without warning, the panther turned and leapt out of the room's wide window that opened two floors above a courtyard that offered access to the outdoors.

The priestess rushed to the casement. Her beloved companion had made no sound when she landed, and there was no trace of where she had gone. The emptiness in the quarters they had shared was palpable.

At the appointed hour, Treylah donned an extra layer of clothing under her traveling cloak and crept silently from her rooms. Padding on soft-slippered feet down the back hallway, she made her way through a storage area to the loading dock that connected with the canal alleyway. This route was unfamiliar to her, but Khieranan had telepathed a map to make the path easy to follow.

All members of the priestly class could make themselves invisible, so invoking that technique offered no protection against those who meant her harm. Nevertheless, Treylah cloaked herself in case others might question her presence in a darkened passageway late at night. But she saw no one as she stealthily made her way to the harbor.

At last, there was the antiquated ship, as Khieranan had promised. The hooded figure on the quay must be Joha-lihn, though Treylah thought this person appeared taller and broader in the shoulder than the young man who was one of her closest friends.

Making herself visible, she approached the ship and realized why she did not recognize Joha-lihn. The figure before her, affecting a casual demeanor as he waited, was Khieranan.

"Quickly," he whispered intensely when she reached him. "Get aboard. We are betrayed and I am going with you after all. The High Priestess decided to rescind your request to miss the lunar ceremony. She went to your room, discovered you were gone, and ran to tell the High Priest.

"We had suspected he was keeping her as his mistress. Our suspicions were true. She has been feeding him information about all of us for months."

Treylah's eyes widened as she remembered how often the High Priestess had visited her quarters, posing as a friend and gaining her trust with feigned interest. The woman had even encouraged Treylah's opinion that Khieranan was spending too much time in Lady Nhada-lihn's temple precincts. Had the High Priestess been purposefully driving a wedge between the couple?

What had she done? Treylah was appalled to think she might have shared confidences that contributed to the High Priest's actions against the priests and priestesses. If Khieranan noticed she had gone pale, he said nothing. He was too focused on her safety.

"Joha-lihn has been detained by their spies. We do not know where or how he is, but we must escape while we have the chance. Go, Treylah! Go, now!"

Without a word, she sprang onto the ship. The captain was ready to cast off, but Khieranan had not yet boarded. When he turned to join the others, the temple police marched onto the quay, carrying torches to light their way, and pushing before them a bruised and bloodied Joha-lihn.

The High Priest was directing them from behind, decked out in full regalia as if he were conducting a sacred ceremony. He was carrying the Shepherd's Crook that should have been an emblem of peace and care for the weak. The mitered hat of spiritual authority was perched on his bald head. On his hands flashed some of the rings he had confiscated.

His eyes glowed red like a man possessed as he shouted menacingly, "Betray me, will you, Khieranan! This is all your doing and you will pay— as will this one!"

While Treylah and the others watched in horror, the High Priest thrust out his right arm, directing a terrible, laser-like ray at Joha-lihn. The man writhed in pain as he cast a wild-eyed, angry glare directly at his friend Khieranan.

Another bolt and then another struck with wicked force until the tortured man slumped, his body shattered by the withering energy of the crystal rays that once had been used only for healing. As weapons of hatred and murder, they were viciously effective.

"Stop!" demanded Khieranan, raising his arms to deflect the bolts of energy the High Priest began to hurl toward him.

"Take off!" he yelled back to the ship's captain, who, with his terri- fied passengers, was standing transfixed by the dreadful sight unfolding before them.

"Get going, man!" shouted Khieranan again.

The captain jumped at the command and sprang into action. He immediately launched his vessel, which powered away from the harbor with the speed of a gale-force blast of wind.

With a lightning-fast sweep of his arm, Khieranan threw off his traveling cloak, revealing himself clothed in the vestments of the High Priestess Nhada-lihn's followers. He appeared to grow in stature as his aura shimmered with fiery blue light.

"No, Khieranan, no!" cried Treylah in a panic. She would have leapt off the ship if two quick-thinking women had not restrained her.

Khieranan appeared not to hear her. Instead, he planted his feet and raised his arms to the heavens. Then he began to chant the sacred words that had not been spoken outside of the Temple of the One Light since Nhada-lihn had mysteriously disappeared more than two years earlier.

Treylah was beside herself. If only she had learned those prayers, she could assist him. But she had been too angry with the man she loved to ask what he could teach her. Now she was too late.

Sensing the power the lone priest was invoking, the High Priest and his soldiers escalated their assault, howling in rage against the shield of Khieranan's blazing blue aura that temporarily repelled their murderous energy back upon them.

Nevertheless, Khieranan realized he could not survive the brutal attack. Even with the abilities Lady Nhada-lihn had imparted to him, he had only minutes before his strength gave out. He would not allow himself to be captured and tortured to reveal the names of his compatriots. He had only one clear choice.

Abruptly, he lowered his arms and smiled at the High Priest. This move so surprised his assailant that for an instant the aggressor forgot his insane hatred of this honest man who represented everything the High Priest despised.

Taking advantage of the momentary reprieve, Khieranan summoned every erg of his remaining strength and connection with the One Light. Raising his arms again, he cried aloud, "Now!"

Instantly, a shaft of dazzling rainbow light descended from the ethers, landing between him and his attackers. The light carried within it the luminous image of Lady Nhada-lihn herself.

She was gloriously clothed in a gown of deepest ruby. Her blonde hair glistened like spun gold. Her deep violet eyes focused knowingly on this beloved priest whom she had trained for just such a moment.

Stretching forth her hands, she shot out a ray of pure white light to link with his upraised arms, creating a figure-eight flow of scintillating energy between their figures.

The connection made, Khieranan became perfectly calm. He quickly glanced back over his shoulder to ensure that Treylah was safely out of danger. Then, with an expression of sad disbelief, he looked once more at the malignant crowd gathered on the quay.

He held absolutely still for a few seconds and then raised his eyes to Lady Nhada-lihn. She nodded to him and, in a flash, a blinding ruby light blazed out in rings upon rings of fire across the harbor, causing the attackers to collapse, sightless and senseless. In that instant, Khieranan vanished from sight.

As the ship sped further away from the quay where her husband had stood only seconds before, the last image Treylah could see was the brief appearance of his blue-green eyes gazing at her through the veil between this world and the next.

"I am here," she heard him say.

Devastated, she could not answer him.

Completing Treylah's Journey

*A*lana clutched her hands to her heart to make sure it was still beating. She could hardly breathe from the shock of the scenes she had just witnessed.

She was mortified by her failures as Treylah. Instead of learning from Khieranan, she had resented him and blamed him for not spending more time with her. And she had betrayed confidences to the High Priestess.

Treylah's inner guidance had told her not to trust the woman, but she had let her mind override that subtle voice. She had been flattered by the Priestess's attention, which had seemed genuine.

Instead, her belief in the woman had compromised her attunement with An Síoraí. Anger had blinded her and made her vulnerable to the persuasion that created a deadly rift between her and Khieranan.

Alana silently rebuked herself and turned away from Ah-Lahn. What must he think of her? How could he still love her after learning of Treylah's failures?

Yet here he was, standing with his hand on Alana's back, creating a gentle pulse that warmed her heart. How could that be? She was not worthy of such kindness after how badly she had misjudged Khieranan's abilities and the High Priestess's treachery.

Alana shook her head. "Stop, Ah-Lahn. Please. I do not deserve your kindness."

He turned her around and held her firmly by the shoulders.

"Alana, look at me. Under the circumstances, Treylah did her best. Khieranan understood that. The forces they faced were too virulent for a handful of priests and a single lady master to overcome.

"Khieranan eluded torture, and Treylah escaped with her life. No one failed, except for the individuals who would have destroyed them."

Ah-Lahn spoke earnestly. "What you saw is not the end of the story. I know this is difficult, but you must return to the life review."

Gently, he led Alana to a blanket-covered seat in a corner of the grove. "Do you want to rest first?"

"I want to finish," she whispered and shuddered as she drew in a breath. "Go ahead."

Ah-Lahn handed her a cup of strengthening elixir, then sat next to her while she drank. "I will be right here when you go back. No flames or crystals are necessary this time. I am going with you as your seanchaí."

Placing his left hand on Alana's back and his right hand on her forehead, Ah-Lahn once more chanted the sacred syllables that opened the life review.

Immediately, mists swirled and orbs of light coalesced in Alana's inner sight. Without hesitation, she stepped back into her Atlantean embodiment with Ah-Lahn's comforting voice guiding the way. In the clear tones of a master storyteller, he began:

Treylah's ship made straight for a peninsula southeast of Poseid. As Khieranan had predicted, the voyage required two days, which were miraculously free of bad weather. And free from pursuit, although Atlantean airships could have overtaken the antiquated vessel in a matter of minutes.

Such was the impact of Lady Nhada-lihn's power on the High Priest and his followers that they were rendered incapable of speech or action for several weeks.

During that time, many more devotees of the One Light petitioned the government for permission to emigrate to other Atlantean colonies. All were granted safe passage, with airships provided for those who headed to the Incal lands several days' voyage to the south, the rich new western lands recently colonized, and the thriving outposts in the east.

Treylah and her companions waited much longer than originally planned, in case Khieranan had managed to escape.

When he did not arrive, they headed for Egypt.

Solas was waiting at dockside when they arrived. Treylah saw him immediately. He was wearing finely crafted leather sandals, a linen kilt, and the neme headdress of an Atlantean leader. His skin glowed a deep bronze in the afternoon sun, and he appeared more powerful than Treylah had ever seen him.

Beyond the quay she also saw a huge pyramid rising out of the desert. Here was the structure Solas was erecting to house the energy-generating crystals he had brought from Atlantis. Treylah could see from her mentor's appearance that the crystals were already having a positive effect.

'Solas!' she cried, running into his arms. 'I have lost my Khieranan! I could not help him because I did not know his prayers! I should have asked him to teach me. Instead, I was angry and allowed myself to be duped by people who were planning our destruction. I am to blame for his death.'

Solas understood her grief, though he did not share her conclusions. He had witnessed the battle with his inner sight. Fixing her with his clear grey eyes, he explained. 'Treylah, more forces than you could have known were involved in that battle.

'It is true that you and Khieranan would have been safe, had you accepted my first invitation. Unfortunately, your loyalty to me upset your husband, just as his devotion to Lady Nhada-lihn angered you.

'He was perturbed that you considered leaving him, though at that time your attunement was correct. If the two of you had not been at odds with each other, he would have seen the wisdom of your choice and joined us.

'Before I could reconcile the two of you, your family situation intervened. The timing of that event could not have been worse. I spoke with Khieranan after you left and urged him to come with us, which he agreed to do. However, you were away much longer than anticipated. I had to depart before you returned, and your husband insisted he would not leave Poseid without you.

'Because he was determined to wait for you, Lady Nhada-lihn asked him to help her reveal the High Priest's evil intentions. She believed, and I agreed, that once the man showed his true colors, many would turn from him, and he would fall from power. Khieranan knew the risks, and he was willing to take them.

'We never meant for the situation to disintegrate into a life-and-death battle. You two were caught in the middle, and Lady Nhada-lihn had no way to fully protect you.

'Treylah, you were not trained for the powers your husband was granted. I would have imparted them to you myself if you had been able to receive them.'

'I see,' she said quietly. Then a troubling thought crossed her mind. 'Was Khieranan's death inevitable?'

'The future must be lived to be known,' explained Solas. 'Free will always outweighs what may appear as destiny. However, given the circumstances, your beloved was almost certain to make the ultimate sacrifice for you and his people.

'Many were saved while the High Priest was incapacitated by the energy Khieranan and Lady Nhada-lihn released. Your husband's sacrifice was a triumph. Can you accept that?'

Treylah nodded, but she was not comforted.

Ah-Lahn paused briefly. Alana was still actively following his voice, so he continued.

After Treylah had rested for several days, Solas renewed his offer for her to serve with him. As she was a senior priestess of the One Light, he gave her a place of honor at the pyramid temple.

For the next twenty years, she worked with her mentor and others to elevate the consciousness of local Egyptians and Atlantean émigrés alike. As her own spiritual gifts increased under the intensified tutelage she eventually earned from Solas, she became aware of darker ages that were fast approaching.

With renewed determination, she counseled all who would listen to align their hearts and minds with the One Light. Her words of wisdom inspired many to greater appreciation of the natural partnership between seen and unseen worlds.

Treylah was a gifted teacher, much beloved by her students and Solas himself. Still, she could never overcome the deep sense of guilt that continued to plague her.

Khieranan did his best to reach her from the invisible world, but she would not acknowledge him. Some of the surviving Atlantean priests and priestesses often heard him call to her, 'I am here.'

Never once did she reply, 'And I.'

Ah-Lahn brought Treylah's story to its conclusion.

The Egyptian colony continued to thrive for many years. Poseid and the other islands of Atlantis were not so fortunate.

During the decade following Treylah's departure, those who opposed the One Light gained greater control over all aspects of Atlantean life. Once again, they rushed toward oblivion, creating abominations of animal life, enslaving the people, misusing cosmic energies—exactly as they themselves had done in previous embodiments, 28,000 years earlier.

Finally, the earth could bear no more and broke apart in explosive volcanic eruptions and cataclysmic tidal waves. Almost overnight, mighty Poseid and all the Atlantean islands plunged to the bottom of the ocean.

Their legacy remains a cautionary tale to all who would arrogantly seek power devoid of An Síoraí.

Alana's eyes fluttered open. Ah-Lahn gently rubbed her hands to ease her back into the present. He did not try to penetrate her thoughts as she sat staring straight ahead.

Fully five minutes passed, and then she asked, "What happened after Treylah died? Did she and Khieranan meet between lives?"

Alana found referring to them as other people less painful than equating herself with the woman she believed had failed her beloved.

"They did," answered Ah-Lahn simply. "At first, Treylah was not willing to face Khieranan. For many embodiments, her feelings of guilt continued to hold him at a distance, though they often lived in relative proximity.

"Her master guides in the invisible world encouraged her to acknowledge him, which she eventually agreed to do. Still, like each of us, she had to work out her obligations to Khieranan and others in the physical plane where she had incurred those debts.

"Treylah and Khieranan continued to reembody. Occasionally they were spouses, although those lifetimes were less conciliatory than their master guides would have preferred. Treylah's soul could not bear the inevitable pain of separation that must come at the end of life. Many times she pushed her twin soul away or fled the relationship long before either of them died.

"Oftentimes they embodied as siblings or close family members who loved and misunderstood each other in equal measure. Yet, regardless of outer circumstances, the bond between their souls could not be broken. We are those souls, Alana. Our bond is that strong."

Ah-Lahn looked earnestly into his wife's weary face. "Close your eyes and tell me what you feel."

Images swirled in Alana's mind as she settled into Ah-Lahn's strong presence beside her. Khieranan had not abandoned Treylah. After all these centuries, he was once again at her side.

Indeed, what was she feeling? She forced herself to touch troubling emotions. Confusion, regret, sorrow. Fear. Guilt. Unworthiness that dragged her into anger.

And yearning. Oh, how desperately she longed—as a wanderer does for Home—for a final reunion with her beloved twin. A key to that mystery existed, if only she could find it.

Khieranan had told Treylah that all was forgiven between them.

He had forgiven her, but could Alana forgive Treylah? Or the Egyptian Queen whose behavior had wounded Senaa?

The forgiveness of others was a beautiful gift, but Alana now knew that unless she opened her heart to receive the gift, she would suffer. And she would cause pain to those she loved the most.

She had to let forgiveness in. The only way to open that door was to welcome the other feelings as well. The idea frightened her. How could she bring herself to experience her own guilt or anger or the enmity of people like the evil high priests she had encountered in Egypt and Atlantis?

The voice of her father, Carwyn, answered from the invisible world:

There is no other way, daughter. You must take a risk if you are to resolve the burdens of your soul. Your greatest strength lies in your willingness to be vulnerable.

To be mistaken is to be human. To feel the pain of embodied life and love yourself anyway is to touch the heart of An Síoraí. Step into the fullness of life and find the forgiveness you have withheld from yourself.

Ah-Lahn and Alana sat in silence, looking out across the grove at the fire that was fading to embers. At last, she whispered, "Yes, I see more clearly now."

Carwyn's words had opened a window of understanding in her mind. Yet she could not summon the courage to accept the excruciating pain of separation which she and her twin flame had suffered again and again for eons. A fearful knowing that their souls were far from unified lurked below the surface of her awareness.

Ah-Lahn knew she was struggling.

"There will be other tests, Alana," he said softly, drawing her close. "Inevitably, we are called to deal with the same characters from our past. Momentums of thought and action follow souls from lifetime to lifetime. We have not seen the last of these challengers."

He felt her body stiffen. "Do not worry. The time may come for another confrontation, but not yet."

Ah-Lahn stood and looked at his wife with deep affection.

"Rest now while I visit Uncle Óengus. He has done us a great service by keeping the chieftains occupied for two days so we would not be summoned to attend them. The Ard mháistir is probably more than ready for us to join them."

Though weary, Alana started to rouse herself from the comfortable corner Ah-Lahn had tucked her into. He rested a hand on her shoulder.

"Stay here, mo chroí. I will let you know when you are needed."

He bent down to kiss her, instinctively closed his eyes, and got a mouth full of fur instead her lips. Ah-Lahn sputtered and stood up sharply.

Attracted by the scintillating energy generated by a life review, an eager black kitten had found its way into the grove. The little creature had leapt into Alana's lap and planted itself in front of her face where it now purred exuberantly, peering soulfully into her eyes.

"I see you will not be alone," Ah-Lahn chuckled. "Take care of her, little friend." He gently held the kitten aside so he could kiss his wife. Then, replacing the ball of fluff on Alana's lap, he went to find Uncle Óengus.

While Alana watched her husband depart, the kitten purred more energetically and nuzzled her for attention. She looked into its eyes and laughed. They were a familiar emerald green. She was not alone.

Intrigues

Shortly after their traveling party from Tearmann had arrived in Cois Abhann, Ah-Lahn had approached Uncle Óengus with a request: Would the Ard mháistir be willing to entertain Cróga and Gréagóir for a couple of days? Ah-Lahn and Alana needed to complete some vital inner work before negotiations commenced. Once talks got under way, their time would not be their own.

Óengus had readily agreed.

"Of course, my son, I will keep the chieftains busy. Just say how long, and the beer and stories will be flowing free and easy!"

"Truth be told," confided Óengus, "I have been wanting to get Cróga and old Gréagóir together outside of formal meetings to see what I can ferret out about the plans neither of them has any intention of disclosing to the other.

"I know I am bound to support Gréagóir and his Ceann-Druí whenever possible to help the Toísech make wise choices, but I have never completely trusted the man. He is too much a fox for my tastes, and his Ceann-Druí is not forceful enough to manage him.

"I would prefer that Cois Abhann had a different chieftain, but we work with what we have. I believe my added counsel keeps him out of a certain amount of mischief.

"What interests me at present is Gréagóir's obvious disappointment that Cróga brought you and Alana to the negotiations instead of his kinsman, Arán Bán. I am wary of there being too much coziness between those two, though I doubt they are actually plotting against you and Cróga. At least, not yet.

"But do not worry. I will keep the chieftains busy while you two get on with your inner work. Let me know when I can release them from my very friendly clutches."

Óengus knew he had more than kept his promise, regaling Cróga and Gréagóir with tales of his early days as a roving bard nearly fifty years earlier, broadening his brogue to suit the occasion.

Oh, I was a wild one, I was! Goin' to war with the chieftains. Barterin' songs fer supper. Flirtin' with all the pretty girls. Workin' a bit o' magic to entertain the royalty in any court that would have me.

Then I met my darlin' wife, Seanait, bless her soul. She settled me right down. Never been happier in my life than I was with that sweet lass—gone now these many years, she is. She was too fine for earth to hold her.

For two days, Óengus had spun his druí magic, carefully loosening the tongues of the wary chieftains until Cróga and Gréagóir were convinced they had been friends of old, met again to renew agreements to benefit them both. Meanwhile, the Ard mháistir watched and listened to uncover the secrets each kept from the other.

"Uncle, have you run out of stories yet, or shall we give you another day with the chieftains?" Ah-Lahn called out cheerfully as he entered the Ard mháistir's cottage.

"You can have them back now," replied Óengus, not hiding the relief in his voice. "I am not as young as I was. Used to be I could sing and tell stories for a week straight. Now I am finished after a day.

"However, before we commence with the horse trading, I have some observations to share with you and Alana. Is she ready for a conference?"

"She is," said Ah-Lahn. "Shall I ask her to join us?"

"Let her rest a while longer. Then come again this evening after your supper. There is intrigue afoot that you both need to know about."

The grand old oaks that circled the grove where Alana lay with her eyes half closed looked upon her with a solemn approval that she would have found odd for them to bestow on one as young as she.

However, they had known her in ages past and often spoke to one another of the adventures she had seen as well as those yet to come. Not all agreed on the outcome of those adventures, though all remembered that she was made of the stern stuff of mighty druíthe. The lass would do her best, of that they could be certain.

They watched with interest as she relaxed in her cozy bower in the Ard mháistir's grove and slipped, unaided, into another life review.

Encore

Once more, Alana was walking beside ancient buildings made of stone that glistened in the bright sun. The architecture was familiar, with colonnades and temples whose inner sanctums were reached by climbing long flights of masterfully carved steps.

However, compared with the precision grandeur of Poseid, this town appeared rugged, even a bit haphazard. Nestled in a river valley, surrounded by mountains that were easily visible over the one-story buildings she passed, the area had a distinctly rural feel to it.

A vigorous breeze swirled, kicking up fine dust, carrying the rich aroma of livestock and green fields. Produce was grown nearby. The marketplace was filled with vendors hawking fruits and vegetables of admirable variety.

Few of the shops or other building façades were decorated with more than a coat or two of whitewash. There were no street musicians playing for the public's enjoyment. Nor were there brightly plumed birds or exotic animals roaming the streets.

Children were running freely while men and women went about shopping and casually chatting with one another. Horse-drawn carts and chariots maneuvered for position along wide, stone-paved streets.

The most remarkable sight was the presence of magnificent soldiers. All wore the same short tunics and scarlet cloaks, their muscles rippling under immaculate leather and bronze armor. These were dignified men whose strength was obvious to anyone who watched them.

She could call most of them by name and they all knew hers. For Alana was once more a queen, and this was Sparta, the rough-and-ready land upon which the future of Greece now depended.

The Queen had left the palace to go for a walk. She was determined to stroll where she pleased. She was safe enough with the guard following at a discreet distance. The King's orders, not hers.

She needed to clear her head. The terrible prophecy was impinging upon her life in a way she knew she could not forestall. Sparta and its allies must confront the wretched Persians and, in all likelihood, her husband would not return. She simply could not bear the thought of life without him.

She had always adored him. When she was too young to think of being anyone's wife. When he had been married to that sad woman who perished while he was still a young man. When he had questioned her if being married to a mere soldier would content her. He had never expected to become King.

Life had moved on. She had grown up, they had married, and she was now his Queen. She was honored to be the mother of his son and proud to work at his side as an adviser whose counsel he valued. Neither of them cared a whit that others thought she often spoke out of turn.

That smart mouth had gotten her into trouble many times in her youth, especially at the school where boys and girls were similarly educated. Both sexes learned mathematics, music, art, astronomy, philosophy, and ethics. They became fully steeped in their own laws, which they believed had been handed down from the gods themselves.

The headmaster at their school had been a discerning and highly disciplined person who was always just and focused on developing intelligent citizens. Spartans were thoughtful, not blindly obedient.

He enjoyed conversing with the young royal who was his student, for the Queen had also been born the daughter of a King. Unfortunately, some less enlightened instructors had complained that she was rashly opinionated. The headmaster had been forced to admonish her while trying to hide his amusement at her quick mind and sharp wit.

"Princess, you must learn to keep your opinions to yourself when addressing your elders. Privilege at court does not apply here."

"But my father the King lets me speak my mind," the girl had protested. "What will become of me if I am not allowed to think for myself? You may say that no man will have a contentious wife, but I do not plan to marry. So what is the matter?"

"Balance, child, balance. And diplomacy, especially in the face of those with whom you do not agree. One day you will need more self-control than you can even imagine. And do not be certain that you will never marry. Your stars, though difficult, are promising. Be careful not to gainsay the blessings that await you.

"Come, walk with me and tell me your thoughts on today's lesson. 'Can a ruler ethically exile a competitor who has demonstrated selfish motives, or must the ruler tolerate insolence for the sake of the state?' "

The Queen thought fondly of those days at school. She wished she could roll back the years to a simpler time before her husband had become King, to a time before they had been compelled to live in that dreary palace whose thick walls and obligations of statecraft were more onerous with every passing day.

For as each morning dawned, the Queen felt as if her own death drew closer, though she knew full well that she would not be allowed to die with the man she loved more than life itself. He needed her to live, to protect their son until the boy reached majority and could assume his father's throne.

She must carry on. Duty was the Spartan way and she was, above all, a Spartan woman, born of royalty and married to the most splendid of all their kings. She would not dishonor his sacrifice with cowardice, no matter how desperately she wanted to run away into a different life.

The sun was high and hot in the summer sky when she returned to the palace. The King, her husband, was in their quarters. Dressed in the light tunic that identified him only as one of many soldiers, he looked up with obvious relief as she came in.

"I have been worried about you," he said, crossing the room swiftly and firmly closing the door. He never used to worry about her safety. These days he imagined enemies lurking around every corner.

"I went for a walk," she answered evenly, trying not to be defensive when he was merely expressing his care for her. She did not like being fussed over or confined, but she understood his concern. She actually shared it, though she dared not let him know.

"The guard was always close at hand. And I did not tarry except to walk by the school to remember better times. I was thinking about our headmaster and how fortunate we were to study under him, though years apart.

"Today's youngsters do not know what they are missing. The curriculum has not changed much, but the atmosphere of the school seems to lack the depth of inquiry he brought to our lessons."

The King knew she was making small talk to avoid the subject they must discuss. Smiling and opening his arms to her, he enfolded her in his powerful embrace. As she clung to him, the inevitable tears got the better of her and ran down her suntanned face.

"I am sorry," she said, choking back those infernal signs of weakness she had vowed not to show him. "I will not disgrace you in public, but I cannot accept that you must leave us. Surely Sparta needs you more as a live king than a dead martyr. Is there no one else to lead in your place?"

Silence filled the room.

The King held her away from him and looked into her eyes as if he would will her to let him go. His own expression threatened to betray his desperate wish to avoid the bitter destiny he knew was fast approaching.

"Have you had your final say?"

The Queen took a deep breath and let it out slowly.

"Yes, my love, I will not trouble you again. I know my duty and I will do as you wish. I will . . ."

"Alana!" Ah-Lahn called out eagerly as he stepped into the oak grove where he had left his wife.

He had expected to find her awake and ready for their evening meal. He was not prepared to find her rubbing her eyes and looking at him with a glazed expression. She did not appear well.

"Oh, Ah-Lahn," said Alana, sitting up slowly. "I was in another life-time and I saw Solas." Words came fast as her memories tumbled out.

"He was a Greek King, and I was his Queen. We both knew he was going to die, yet I could not prevent him from going to battle. I was ter-rified. I knew I would never see him again. Where were you, Ah-Lahn? Why could you not stop him?"

"Come here, mo chroí." Ah-Lahn put his arm around her and held her close. "The next life review was eager to come through, and you did not need my help. I am sorry I broke in on your recollections."

He gently turned her to him and placed his hands on her shoulders. He looked into her hazel eyes that reflected the struggle she was experi-encing and urged her to continue. "Can you tell me what you saw?"

"I was in Greece, in Sparta. Again as Queen, and Solas was there as a great leader—a powerful, yet humble King." Alana's attention drifted off into other scenes.

"What else do you remember?" Ah-Lahn prompted. He must keep her focused on the Greek life review. There were details only she could discover for herself.

"The King was going off to war, and he was not coming back. I was frantic because I knew this was the last time we would be together and there was nothing I could do to change the rush of events that were about to overtake us. I remember waking up and being angry that you were not there to stop him."

Alana did her best to check the unreasonable emotion threatening her memory. Ah-Lahn was not to blame for the King's decisions, but she could not help feeling he should have advised against such rash action.

Then a light dawned.

"But you could not have been with us. You were already dead when the King decided he must face the Persians. I saw you earlier when I was only a Princess.

"You were the old headmaster at our school. That is why you were so good to me when the other instructors thought me a nuisance. We knew each other for such a short time. Why was that? I grieved when you died."

Ah-Lahn shared her grief. He remembered how the headmaster had regretted having to leave the Princess while she was still young. Their times of separation were at least as painful for Ah-Lahn as for Alana. Perhaps more so, because he always seemed to recognize her while she either could not or would not acknowledge him as her soul's twin.

"As in other lifetimes, we had unique obligations to life, separate paths of service. I have always been a teacher and a philosopher at heart. You have been drawn to political power. We may eventually arrive at one another's perspective, but that journey is a long one. I suspect we are far from truly understanding each other.

"The heart knows its ultimate destiny, but the mind insists on its own way of getting there. And I often find yours particularly stubborn, mo chroí."

Ah-Lahn winked at Alana as she sat up to protest.

"I know, I know. I am set in my ways. Still, you must admit, I have had some experience with the fickle nature of kings and queens.

Still smiling, he helped her to her feet. "We must go now. The evening meal is being served, and Uncle Óengus wants to see us as soon as we have eaten. He is including you in all of the deliberations, and he wants us both to be fully prepared."

Alana was silent as they walked to the Ard mháistir's cottage. What was important about the Greek embodiment that caused it to push through to her outer awareness?

What was she not understanding about Treylah and the two queens? What did they have in common? What was her soul trying to tell her in choosing these lifetimes?

Events were moving quickly now. She would have to meditate on the lessons that still were not clear in her mind. Was her mind being stubborn while her inner guidance already understood the reason for these life reviews, as Ah-Lahn suggested?

Alana hoped that the present would reveal the answers to the past.

New Relations

Dark clouds had gathered over the túath. The air smelled of rain and promised cold, but the Ard mháistir's earthy home was cozy inside. The spacious thatched cottage looked older than the man himself, so often had its roof and timbers been patched and repaired.

Yet, to those with eyes to see, its nooks and crannies held secrets of the ages in the souvenirs and sacred objects Óengus had collected from years of traveling across the land he called home and from his little-known journeys back and forth between this world and the next.

Due to Alana's impromptu Spartan life review, she and Ah-Lahn arrived later than expected at Óengus's dwelling. He had a fire going against the nighttime chill and immediately went to the point of their conversation. He spoke as softly as his big voice allowed, lest unwanted ears should overhear their discussion.

"I must say I have done my work well, for an old druí." Óengus chuckled at his boast. "Cróga and Gréagóir are now bosom friends. After a few beakers of beer and the ease laughter brings, they have begun to share confidences. Last night I overheard Gréagóir suggest to Cróga that he should keep an eye on you, Ah-Lahn."

"On what grounds?" asked Ah-Lahn, surprised that his integrity should be questioned by any person, especially the tribal chieftain he had grown to think of as a friend.

"At first, Gréagóir asked Cróga if he trusted you, to which your man answered in the affirmative."

"As well he should," Ah-Lahn said firmly. "I have been nothing but loyal to Cróga since he became Toísech."

"Now, do not go worrying just yet," Óengus smiled and raised a reassuring hand. "Cróga said exactly that and wanted to know why Gréagóir would ask.

" 'Oh, no particular reason,' says he. 'Just something my kinsman Arán Bán mentioned when he was here nearly two years ago studying with Óengus. Something about Ah-Lahn having ambitions to take over your position as Toísech.' "

"Patently untrue. Arán Bán and I were here as colleagues. Why would he have been talking behind my back even then?"

Ah-Lahn felt his temper rise at this revelation. He had supported Arán Bán's elevation to prominence within the wider community of the druíthe. He had even suggested that his colleague should assume the role of Acting Ceann-Druí after Cróga's adviser, Old Quin, died.

This apparent betrayal of his generosity stung Ah-Lahn—a man for whom loyalty was vital. Considering recent events regarding Arán Bán's behavior toward Alana, he was not entirely surprised at the man's mendacity. But this report of ill will harbored against himself long before Óengus named him permanent Ceann-Druí came as a shock.

Óengus brought Ah-Lahn's attention back to the conversation.

"Cróga dismissed Gréagóir's suspicions, but I could tell the idea had begun to work on your chieftain's mind. I can see where he might be swayed by idle talk, unless you can persuade him otherwise during this conference."

"What do you suggest, Uncle?"

Óengus could see that Ah-Lahn was more troubled by this revelation about Arán Bán than he had expected him to be. Speaking as the druí's mentor, he sought to steady his friend.

"Formal negotiations begin in the morning to determine how our leaders can best defend themselves and each other against the young chieftain whose túath lies between our two territories.

"Be in the Great Hall early and have everything in order as Cróga prefers. Deliver your best invocations and ask your bards to sing their highest praise of his leadership.

"Gréagóir's Ceann-Druí will be doing the same for his man, and I will make certain everyone is treated with mutual respect and cooperation. Show yourself attentive, efficient, and competent without any sign of doubt in yourself or Cróga.

"Alana, you will attend all meetings as an observer and a participant if needs be. I am sure you will enjoy watching the chieftains and their advisers try to outwit each other."

Óengus winked at her, then put his arm around her husband's shoulder.

"Ah-Lahn, my guess is that Arán Bán tried to prejudice Gréagóir's mind against you to enhance his own position with Cróga. Even though his whisperings took place two years ago, we must take precautions while you are here."

The Ard mháistir stood and picked up his staff. "That is all we need discuss tonight. We have much to accomplish over the next few days, and tomorrow requires an early start."

"Uncle Óengus," said Alana, softly touching his arm, "may I offer you a simple verse that has come to me?"

"Of course, my dear." His blue eyes twinkled to hear her call him 'Uncle'. "I am never too tired to receive a new poem."

"I want you to feel how much I appreciate your kindness," Alana explained. "I know my father was your good friend before he died in the massacre at Ynys Môn. In meeting you, I feel I have gained a new parent. These lines express what is on my heart."

When the gods sent their children
to live on Earth,
they knew they would need a guardian
to help them make their way
and not falter as they grew
from innocence to maturity.

To teach the young ones dignity,
honor and integrity,
the gods fashioned a friend,
a model of their love

and the strength of their authority;
the very essence of themselves in man.

They called their creation *Father*
and were glad to see
how the children honored him
and cherished him
all the days of their lives.

"Thank you, daughter, for so you shall always be to me," said Óengus more quietly than usual. He embraced her warmly in his big-bear arms, then released her to Ah-Lahn's care.

"Now, take your husband home and sleep well in the surety of our affection."

Impeccability

AT THE NEGOTIATION TABLE, TOÍSECH GRÉAGÓIR'S GREAT HALL

Even if Ah-Lahn had not been her husband, Alana would have deemed him impressive in the performance of his duties as Ceann-Druí.

He served Toísech Cróga admirably throughout the negotiations, and demonstrated such respect and honest deference to Gréagóir that the old chieftain found himself doubting the truth of anything Arán Bán had implied about this knowledgeable adviser.

Alana was fascinated by their discussion of the challenges of dealing with their fractious neighbor, Toísech Farrell, who was known to encourage cattle raiding on his borders with both their territories.

She was amused, though not surprised, when, after the second day of deliberations, consensus favored teaching the annoying young chieftain a lesson by attacking him on both flanks at once. Alana's father had been an able swordsman as well as a druí, so she was well acquainted with the tendency of fighting men to encourage one another to resolve differences with force rather than philosophy.

When the two tribal chieftains simultaneously pounded their fists on the thick oaken table where they were seated, agreeing that they "could take that young upstart in a single morning," she ventured to suggest another approach.

"May I ask a question?" Alana's clear young voice rang out above the general din. Each leader's entourage was also present for the deliberations, and most of the men were clamoring for a battle. However, accustomed as they were to fighting alongside female warriors who were equally as fearless as they, the company fell silent.

"Of course, Alana," answered Óengus, who then addressed Cróga and Gréagóir. "Gentlemen, may we hear what our young guest would say? You did agree that she might participate when appropriate."

As neither chieftain wished to appear inhospitable, they both nodded their assent. Óengus motioned for Alana to proceed.

"Thank you. I was wondering if anyone had spoken to Toísech Farrell." Amused at the grumbles that swept throughout the hall, she continued: "Do you suppose there might be reason for common cause between the three of you?"

Ignoring the furrowed brows around the table, she went on.

"My husband, Toísech Cróga's Ceann-Druí, has mentioned to me that some of the northern Brigantes have historically launched raiding parties that attack your lands at harvest time. Perhaps Toísech Farrell would prefer to protect his own harvest with an alliance between your three territories. You might also attract other neighboring chieftains into the pact, so you would all be stronger. You could end up promoting peace among all of the Brigantes."

"Well said, Alana." Cróga spoke first while Gréagóir nodded in agreement. And then they immediately ignored her, putting their heads together across the table to hash out plans for sending a joint delegation to Farrell.

Within minutes, the idea was all theirs, and they had convinced their entourages of the great wisdom that could be had when two intelligent chieftains turned their very bright minds to a difficult problem.

Ah-Lahn and Óengus did their best to stifle broad smiles as they surreptitiously winked at Alana. She was annoyed at being instantly forgotten by the two chieftains who continued to congratulate themselves on their wise plans. But she could tell from Ah-Lahn's expression that she had suggested exactly what the druíthe would have done. He and Óengus were satisfied with the outcome.

Two days later, following the final evening meal held to celebrate the conference's successful conclusion, Gréagóir took Ah-Lahn aside.

"I am sure you have noticed that I rely more on Óengus's guidance than I do on that of my Ceann-Druí. He is a good man, but he is not the Ard mháistir. I fear I may outlive my best adviser. Would you consider becoming my Ceann-Druí, in the event Óengus heads for Tír na n'Óg?"

"Sir, you honor me with this offer," Ah-Lahn answered honestly. "For the foreseeable future, I am Cróga's man, though none of us knows what lies around the next moment's bend. But please accept my gratitude for your hospitality and my best wishes for your prosperity and the success of our mutual ventures."

"I can see why Cróga values you so highly," replied Gréagóir. "I, likewise, wish you and Alana safe travels."

"My wife will be pleased to be included in your good wishes," answered Ah-Lahn with a firm handshake that hid any trace of misgivings he might have felt about future interactions with Gréagóir.

Emerald green hillsides glistened as if touched by fairy magic in the bright morning sun that rose over Cois Abhann. A gentle breeze blew from the north, promising a good day for navigating An Bhearú south to the sea.

After all parties had said their official fare-thee-wells and Toísech Cróga had boarded his currach boat, the crews unfurled the enormous sails on each of the three crafts. Óengus held Ah-Lahn and Alana back for a final bear hug.

"Be wise, my dears," he said without hiding the emotion in his voice. "Keep a weather eye on all the goings-on within Cróga's circle. You have many friends there, but sometimes only a single determined adversary can start rumors and infect weak minds with innuendo.

"Look to your own house, Ah-Lahn. Take care with those closest to you, and be mindful of what is not said as much as words spoken to your face.

"I may not see you again," the Ard mháistir said with an especially tender glance toward Alana. "Remember me in your prayers, as you will be in mine. You are dearer to me than my own children, should the gods have dared to give me any."

Óengus chuckled and then added, as much to himself as to the couple before him, "They likely knew I would love the bairns too much and forget I was supposed to discipline them.

"Be off with you now, and let an old druí get back to his grove. I will send you fair winds to see you safely home. What happens when you reach that shore, I cannot control."

With a wave of his hand and a wistful smile on his lips, Ard-Mháistir Óengus turned and walked steadily up the verdant slope to the cottage he had called home for more than seven decades.

Ah-Lahn and Alana stood with their arms around each other and watched him in silence. Then, with a mutual sigh, they turned toward the river and boarded the sturdy craft that would take them home to meet the challenges Óengus had foreseen.

PART SIX

The Essence of Being

*We cannot predict
to what or whom
we will be called.*

The Voyage Home

*A*n Bhearú carried those who sailed her peaceful waters as effortlessly as a mother who has borne many children. Those who made their home along her lush, tree-lined banks were grateful for her unhurried pace that nourished all manner of wild and human life.

Those, like Ah-Lahn and Alana, who only visited the river's fertile shores, would long for the day when they might return to this mighty waterway that shimmered with the blessings of Ard-Mháistir Óengus.

They could not know when that day might come. For not even skilled mariners can see exactly what lies ahead. The sea must be sailed to be known.

"Are you ready to return home?" Ah-Lahn asked Alana as their trio of currach boats swung easily into the river's wide channel.

She looked out across the water at the flax growers—entire families of them—bending over the tall stems of their plants, gathering and pulling large handfuls out of the ground. Others would tie the stems into standing bundles that looked like rows of ladies with golden hair and green skirts dancing in the fields.

The harvest was just beginning and promised to be a good one. Alana could hear the families singing as they worked. She could not help envying their togetherness.

Remembering the agony of lost family and community in Atlantis, Egypt, Greece, and Ynys Môn, she shuddered as a wave of apprehension washed over her.

"I am not ready to return to situations that threaten to separate us," she said in a low voice.

Ah-Lahn regarded his wife pensively, his eyes going deep and bright as he heard An Síoraí's inspiration. Alana met his expression with a long, level gaze, doing her best to align with his consciousness as he spoke with the soft power of his inner guidance:

Rise above the schemes of others, Alana. They cannot touch what they cannot see.

Though dark forces oppose us, we persevere. The higher up the mountain we climb, the narrower the path becomes, and the more determined are the foes that oppose An Síoraí in us. But they will not find us where they look, for we are forged of one pure spirit that minor villains cannot un-join.

Our joys are born of that spirit, in moments of reunion when all the world is one, and we are enfolded in that one-ness—unique as a star held in the firmament's embrace that knows each twinkling flash of light as itself.

Our journey is never-ending, no matter what may intervene. Remember me when days grow weary and challenges seem too hard to bear, for I am with you every moment.

I am your guide to other realms, swaddling you in love's protection that will not wilt from opposition to your mission or to mine.

We earn our dark nights, beloved—those moments when all seems lost, when we feel abandoned, cut off from life and all who cherish us. And yet, those initiations come only to those who care enough to trust their inner guidance.

Voyages will always remind you of me. And of how we fit together, traveling across wide valleys, fording streams, climbing hills, or resting beside calm waters. Larger joys await us and will come true when we honor our shared purpose.

Shine your light where darkness hides. Be steadfast, Alana, and you will become one with the essence of unity that holds us all together.

Though July's sun shone warm and bright, Ah-Lahn shivered. He drew his cloak about his shoulders and sank into a deep reverie. Alana put her arms around him, pondering how the inevitable confrontation with darkness would play out once more in their lives.

Currach boats did not sail after dark, so the crew pulled into a secluded cove that first night, putting up shelters for the travelers, building fires for warmth and cooking, and serving a perfectly reasonable stew.

After a warm meal, Alana was very tired. She went right to sleep, wrapped in her warmest cloak on a bed of woolen blankets that kept the chill of damp earth from interfering with her rest.

But Ah-Lahn could not sleep. His discourse to Alana had astonished him. Was this a prophecy of coming troubles? He had never considered that someone on the path of the druíthe might earn the ordeals that tested his soul. As he contemplated his desire to lead a life of integrity, he felt his heart quicken with a longing for An Síoraí which he had never experienced with such fervor.

This yearning surprised him. For the past several years he had been longing for union with his twin flame, Alana. Yet this new inner hunger was deeper still. How strange to long for trials, he mused.

Ah-Lahn stepped out into the clear night air. As he looked up at the Milky Way and its billions of stars shining overhead, his soul spoke to him in verses born of an exquisite desire to overcome any sense of separation between himself and the essence of An Síoraí that lived in his own heart.

Give me my dark nights.
Let me be broken on the wheel of loss,
Stripped of reason and safety,
Fed to the beasts of pride.

May I suffer the injustice of human treachery,
And taste the bile of disappointed dreams.

When hope flees and despair howls
In the depths of my brokenness,
Then, and only then,
Will I be clay malleable enough
For the Potter's hand.

I would earn this annihilation;
Though it catch me by surprise,
Arriving in the stead of accolades
Expected by an ego basking
In the world's acclaim.

Neither sacrifice nor ritual
Can free my soul to be her perfect Self.
Only from darkness are we born.
And so I seek the void
Whose mysteries cannot be known
In seeking or in thought.

My striving wearies me.
Why do I try to make roses bloom?
O, An Síoraí, take me to your Self
And teach me to surrender
Strife of my own doing.

I am still afraid of the dark.
Yet all the resurrected parts of me
Call out to you for trials of moonless nights,
Dark caverns, and the plunging abyss
Where Spirit's purest alchemy takes place
In the furnace of your sublime transfiguring fire.

Return & Reactions

*A*ngry black clouds obscured the late afternoon sun as ferocious winds blew sheets of ocean spray against the fleet of currach boats, rendering sails unusable and oars a necessity.

The seamen were challenged to keep their boats upright as they made steadily for their home cove. Fortunately, once they reached the shallows they were able to land safely with their passengers and possessions intact.

Casting his eye to the water-blackened precipice above the shoreline, Ah-Lahn caught sight of Arán Bán standing on the cliff edge, his cloak blowing in fierce gales that appeared to emanate from him.

Feet planted, arms akimbo atop the hundred-foot-drop, he stared down at the ships, a grim smile upon his pale lips. Next to him, expressionless and thinner than usual, stood the Ceann-Druí's son, Tadhgan.

So the confrontation begins, said Ah-Lahn to himself.

He nodded slightly to the looming figures, betraying no suspicion of any negative intention behind the two men's greeting. Then, taking care that all passengers should arrive safely back at their cottages, he guided the travelers up the steep stairway that long ago had been carved into the rocky cliff face.

"Alana, will you see to the safekeeping of the gifts we brought back from Gréagóir's túath?" Ah-Lahn directed calmly as they reached the top of the treacherous drop.

"Of course. Shall I meet you at home?" she replied evenly. Her husband's simple nod told her all she needed to know of what might be about to transpire.

Fully aware that Arán Bán and Tadhgan were watching his every move, Ah-Lahn turned to Toísech Cróga and addressed him with the confidence of frank conversations they had shared on the voyage home.

"Thank you again for your camaraderie and trust."

"We understand each other, Ah-Lahn," the chieftain answered, warmly shaking his Ceann-Druí's hand. "Let me know if you need my help."

"Of course." Ah-Lahn instinctively looked to where Arán Bán and Tadhgan stood.

"Alana, will you walk with me?" offered Cróga, adding quietly with a sly smile, "We should give our audience something else to chew on."

"I agree," said Alana, taking his arm in a show of unity.

Their departure was suddenly interrupted by a loud purr and a flash of sleek black fur as Alana's panther, Sprid, appeared and began rubbing affectionately against her mistress's legs. The big cat was instantly followed by a wildly excited wolfhound bounding up to greet them.

Cróga instinctively stepped in front of Alana. He had raised Laoch from a puppy and was all too familiar with the consequences of the big dog's exuberance. Without the chieftain's quick intercession—that now had Laoch standing to his full height, happily licking his former master's face—the great grey beast would have flattened Alana.

Instead, Laoch rolled over so she could rub his belly. Then he flipped onto his feet and began whining and barking and galloping in circles around her, Cróga, and Sprid, who, as was becoming her custom, rolled her deep green eyes at her incorrigible canine companion.

When the travelers were out of hearing range, Ah-Lahn visualized a sphere of blue light around his body and approached Arán Bán and Tadhgan.

"Arán Bán, I did not expect to see you here to greet us. I trust all has been well in our absence." Ah-Lahn extended his hand in greeting to the man he was beginning to view as a dangerous adversary. The gesture forced Arán Bán to return the courtesy.

Ah-Lahn then turned amiably to Tadhgan and put an affectionate hand on the young man's bony shoulder.

"My son, I am pleased that you are here to meet our arrival. I trust your studies are going well with Ollamh Gormlaith. I bring you greetings from Uncle Óengus with an invitation to visit him soon. He was cross with me for not bringing you along on our mission, despite the interruption your absence would have caused in your preparation for investiture as a bard."

Tadhgan flinched at his father's touch. Instead of returning Ah-Lahn's greeting, he shot a furtive glance toward Arán Bán. His companion jumped in to answer.

"Tadhgan is doing splendidly—better than many have given him credit for. I have been mentoring him myself and can say I have rarely observed such talent in one so young. I expect him to surpass even those who have been pushed beyond their natural gifts."

Ah-Lahn was shocked that Arán Bán was tutoring his son. Ignoring the obvious insult aimed at his wife, he stepped back from Tadhgan and stood face-to-face with Arán Bán.

"And have you also taught him not to answer his elders when asked a direct question? I know that Ollamh Gormlaith instructs her students to show respect to all members of our community."

When Arán Bán did not respond, Ah-Lahn turned to address his son directly.

"Tadhgan, if you require the oversight of a druí to complete your training, perhaps you would have no objection to studying with me. As your father, I would like to evaluate your readiness, which I am certain, as your friend here affirms, is more than satisfactory."

When the young man only nodded, Ah-Lahn looked him in the eye and said pointedly, "When the Ceann-Druí addresses you, Tadhgan, you are to give verbal answer. So I will repeat—Do you have any objection to my supervision?"

"I have no objection," Tadhgan lied, realizing he was cornered.

"Thank you, my son. I will expect you at my grove tomorrow following your morning meal.

"Arán Bán, will you meet me before the students have eaten? I would like to hear more about Tadhgan's progress so I do not repeat lessons he has already mastered."

"As you wish," replied Arán Bán flatly.

"We all have much to accomplish tomorrow, so I will bid you both a good evening." Ah-Lahn bowed slightly to the two men and left them brooding in icy silence.

When Ah-Lahn entered the cottage he shared with Alana, she leapt to her feet, peppering him with questions.

"What happened? Did you have to confront either of them? Were they rude or combative? I could tell they were up to no good. And how strange to see Tadhgan standing like a lackey to Arán Bán. How did he behave toward you, his father?"

"One matter at a time, mo chroí," Ah-Lahn answered with a smile.

His heart was suddenly moved by the profound care he read in her eyes. Laying aside his cloak, he quickly crossed the room and cupped her face in both his hands. He kissed her warmly, drinking in the sweetness of her affection that poured out from her soul.

Alana put her arms around his waist and held him close, her head on his breast. She could feel his strength and prayed that she might lend him hers. *Oh, that we could stay this way forever,* she thought.

Ah-Lahn reluctantly released her from his embrace and took a seat at the table where she had laid out a light meal. As he ate, he unfolded the earlier scene to his wife and dearest friend.

"There was no overt confrontation. More like adversaries taking the measure of one another. Arán Bán could not help telling me that he has taken over mentoring my son, and Tadhgan could not bring himself to speak to me until I challenged him to respect my office as Ceann-Druí.

"I will speak with Arán Bán first thing in the morning to see what I can make of his intentions. I may let slip that Gréagóir questioned Cróga about my fitness as Ceann-Druí, or I may save that information for another time. I do not want to precipitate a war of words, or arms, if Arán Bán can be dealt with diplomatically.

"As for my son, I see that I will have to handle him carefully. He looked like a steaming volcano ready to erupt. Triggering an explosion may be the best way to clear the air between us and get him back on track, but that depends on his behavior tomorrow.

"I do not believe Tadhgan is a danger to any but himself. And yet, I am profoundly troubled by how thoroughly Arán Bán seems to have inveigled himself into the lad's mind."

Ah-Lahn pushed back his chair and rose from the table. He crossed the room and sank wearily upon their sleeping platform that was comfortably covered with woolen blankets.

"Enough of intrigues for tonight. Come, embrace me, mo chroí, and tell me, Are you glad to be home?"

"I am glad to be wherever you are," whispered Alana. She fell into his outstretched arms and joined her lips to his in a kiss as deep as the sea they had just crossed.

Tadhgan stomped off to his cottage, determined to push past anyone he might meet on the short walk back to his unkempt student dwelling.

Though he no longer studied with Ollamh Gormlaith, he was still allowed to stay in a small hut located on the edge of her school's property. As no one greeted him, he made his way home before his surly expression betrayed him to curious faces.

He tossed his cloak on the floor with a dozen other pieces of clothing and flopped onto a chair at a rude table for the meager meal a fellow student had left for him. But he was too agitated to eat.

He stood up and began pacing around the dank room that reflected the chaos of his mind as plainly as if he had carved the word into the hut's mud walls. And muttered as he walked the floor.

How could his father have embarrassed him before the only person who had ever given him credit for having natural talent!

Arán Bán was right. His father did not love him. His father thought him a fool. His father did not respect him.

Why else would he have elevated that "slip of a girl," as his mentor called her, to a position of importance that he—his father's heir!—should have received?

"I will appeal to Toísech Cróga!" he cried aloud to no one but the spiders that lived in the corners of his lodging. "I will prove my worth. Then everyone will see how unjustly I have been treated."

He pounded his fists on his thin chest so hard he coughed.

"The Ceann-Druí will pay for his insults."

And yet, Tadhgan had to admit, there was one other person who believed in him. Ollamh Gormlaith knew he wanted to be an accomplished bard, like she was. And she had supported his intention, though with a caveat that he could not now remember.

However, he did remember that Gormlaith knew he wanted to be nothing like his father. Surely, she would have conveyed that message to other druíthe who might have suggested the lad pursue another course of study.

So why had Arán Bán whisked him away from Gormlaith's school? Neither Tadhgan nor the Ollamh had understood the abrupt change. In the past, Arán Bán had only taken on students who wanted to become druíthe. The matter was too confusing.

At last, exhausted from his peripatetic pacing, the lad threw himself upon his straw sleeping mat that was covered by a single, rough wool blanket. He snatched his cloak from the pile of clothes where it had landed and tossed it gracelessly about his narrow torso.

Wrapping himself against the chill that no outer garment could dispel, he fell into a fitful sleep, dreaming of vengeance and glory.

At the same time as Tadhgan was wrestling with his inner demons—some of which Arán Bán had nurtured himself—the druí relaxed in his comfortably warm cottage. Una was away visiting a sick relative. She had taken their children with her, so he was alone and glad of it. He needed his wits about him right now.

He quickly ate the rich stew an aide served and then put his feet up by the fire that crackled invitingly on the cottage hearth. Calmly reflecting on the day's events, Arán Bán plotted his next actions.

His eyes narrowed as he spoke to the image of Ah-Lahn he conjured in his mind. "Oh, you are a cool one, Ceann-Druí, but you do not intimidate me. You have no idea what is in store for you and your ambitious little bride now that you are back in my territory.

"A few well-crafted insinuations suggested to a few susceptible minds can work wonders." With a smirk, Arán Bán spoke aloud the words that had become for him a mantra.

Satisfied that events were unfolding to his liking, he stretched out on his softly cushioned sleeping platform, pulled up a finely woven wool blanket and drifted into a dreamless slumber.

Father & Son

The morning dawned bright with promise amidst the earthy aromas of nearby livestock and ripening fields of oats, barley, and wheat.

Ah-Lahn had risen early to pray that he might bring an open mind to the meeting with his son. He wanted Tadhgan to succeed. He was determined to place no obstacle in the way of the young man's finding his vocation as a bard, or in whatever capacity his talent and desire should lead him.

Arán Bán had sent a message that he was not well and would be unable to meet the Ceann-Druí after all.

Just as well, thought Ah-Lahn as he walked through the túath.

Obedient, at least in form, Tadhgan arrived at the Ceann-Druí's grove at the appointed hour and stood silently at the entrance.

"Come in, Tadhgan," said Ah-Lahn, assuming an even tone. Do not let the lad's surliness rankle you, he reminded himself.

"This morning I would like to observe you in the role of seanchaí. The latest story you have been memorizing will be a fine choice. You will not need your harp for this exercise. We want to concentrate on the flow of the words themselves."

"As you wish," said Tadhgan without emotion. Taking his place in front of his father, the young man squared his shoulders, took a deep breath, and began to recite the legend called *The Lady from the East:*

Long ago, in ages beyond memory, there rose up a great tribulation in the land known as the 'Queen of the Sea.' Civil war was brewing, sending scores of her inhabitants out in astonishing ships that sailed on air or water, seeking safety for themselves and their children.

Many of them passed by our shores, preferring warmer climes in the desert lands to the east. But some liked the look of Éire, for their home had also been an emerald isle. They embarked upon a new life, bringing with them wondrous talents for building and shaping the land as few local tribes had ever imagined.

A thousand years elapsed, and distant origins were forgotten as the newcomers merged with the rich earth of Éire, delighting in her lakes and streams and sacred wells that in those yesteryears held a powerful magic.

All seemed content in living as the landscape insisted. For the land was ensouled with an interior intelligence that taught those who would thrive here to walk softly and cherish all living things, regardless of their place in the web of life.

Many years later, a new wave of travelers arrived from the East. They said they were refugees, fleeing persecution that threatened the very existence of their civilization.

Among them was a maiden of such fair visage that all who saw her marveled at her radiant beauty. They thought she was a goddess, for so she seemed in both aspect and demeanor.

Her ship had been seen emerging from a heavy mist that spawned a double rainbow as she came ashore. So the rumor spread that she had been sent by the gods to bless our land and bring healing to our people.

And that she did. Very soon after her arrival, she took up residence in a remote woodland cottage.

Sheltered by oak and hazel trees, she spoke in mellifluous tones that sounded more like song than mere words. She urged her enthralled listeners to embrace all living creatures, as does An Síoraí, the Eternal One.

The lady was greatly esteemed by the people who adopted her. For many years she advised them in their squabbles, encouraged them in their personal challenges, and healed them of their diseases of body, mind, or soul.

Her work seemed to make her happy, yet there lingered a sadness about her that would creep in upon her face when she thought no one was looking. And, though she did her best to conceal the feeling even from herself, there was an unresolved anger that lurked beneath the surface of her emotions, threatening to overwhelm her when she witnessed injustice being practiced against any part of life.

They said she had lost her family during her escape from oppression in her homeland in the desert lands to the East. The loss had broken her heart in places that refused to mend, despite her generous service to others.

Though many worthy men of Éire would have gladly taken her to wife, Meke chose to live alone in her grove, tending to those in need.

Ah-Lahn stood and held up his hand, indicating the young seanchaí should pause for instruction.

"Your technique is very good, my son. I notice the influence of Arán Bán, who is also a skilled technician. What I am missing now is feeling."

"Feeling?" Tadhgan's tone was defensive. "My recitation was full of feeling. Did you not notice how my voice dropped to indicate the lady's sorrow?"

"The vocal drop was quite noticeable," Ah-Lahn agreed. "It offered a convincing simulation of a certain emotion. However, my sense is that you did not actually experience that emotion. Your performance came from outer technique rather than inner, personal integration with the characters."

"I disagree," Tadhgan reacted. "I felt energy moving in me. But Arán Bán says: 'A skilled bard should never lose control or grow so involved in the performance as to become unaware of the dignity of his office.' "

"The level of emotional engagement is a fine line, of course," replied Ah-Lahn, choosing to ignore his son's self-important repetition of Arán Bán's teaching.

How ironic, Ah-Lahn remembered in that moment. He had had this same discussion with Alana. But, forgetting that she had erupted in anger that day, he pressed on.

"Remember, Tadhgan, the duty of the bard is to become inspired as well as to inspire. Your personal response to the story brings it alive and renders it fresh with each telling. That aliveness will inspire you to greater heights in composing your own stories, poems, and songs."

Warming to one of his favorite subjects, Ah-Lahn began walking enthusiastically around the grove, spontaneously raising the energy in the sacred space.

"Your craft is becoming well honed. Now I am asking you to step away from technique to embrace the art of your profession. Do you understand, Tadhgan? We are not the doers. We are only agents of An Síoraí. Our purpose is not outer perfection. We strive for inner connection with the Spirit of the Eternal One."

"I thought that is what I was doing," said Tadhgan, clenching his jaw and fists.

Ah-Lahn felt his soul trying to reach across an ancient abyss.

"You are on the cusp of a breakthrough, my son. Achieving the next level always feels like a failure in the phase you are leaving behind. You are in transition—an uncomfortable place to be. However, that phase can be temporary, if you will allow me to assist you. Will you give me leave to nudge you toward the goal you are seeking?"

"I suppose so," agreed the young man, though his expression was anything but receptive.

Ah-Lahn offered Tadhgan an encouraging smile. "I have traveled this road where you are now and where many other young bards have trod.

"Many years ago, I composed a poem about a mentor and a student in this very situation. I would like you to speak these lines with me. The piece becomes a chant when two people give it together. Each repetition elicits a deeper meaning."

Tadhgan hesitated. His father was so annoying. "As you wish," was his only response.

Ah-Lahn took a breath and began: "Why would you not trust me?"

"Do you mean to insult me?" objected Tadhgan.

"Indeed, I do not. This is the first line of the poem. Please repeat after me: Why would you not trust me?"

"I do not believe you composed this years ago."

"I have told you the truth. This is your lesson today, as the piece has been for many others. Let us begin again: Why would you not trust me?"

"Why would you not trust me?" Tadhgan repeated glumly.

"My heart broke, knowing you doubted that I love you."

"My heart broke, knowing you doubted that I love you." Tadhgan choked on the words.

"I tried so hard to share with you the glories I have seen." Ah-Lahn spoke these lines with a tenderness that misted his own eyes. He had conducted this lesson with other initiates, but none so obstinate and none so dear. Surprised by the intensity of his own emotions, he took a deep breath and waited for his son to respond.

"I tried so hard . . . ," Tadhgan began. But then years of pent-up anger erupted before he or his father knew what happened.

"I have done *nothing* but try hard!" he exclaimed. "And I *have* loved you! But I have *never* been good enough for you! Arán Bán was right. You have never cared about me as a father should. Certainly not as the Ceann-Druí should care for his son."

"Tadhgan, I . . . ," Ah-Lahn tried to explain, but his son barreled on.

"I am your heir! And what do you do? You marry a girl who is barely older than I am. And then you expect me to accept her in the place of my mother? How could you!"

"I never meant for my marriage to Alana to hurt you," said Ah-Lahn, as he struggled to control a devastating rush of emotion that came out of nowhere, blinding him to An Síoraí's warning.

Why would the lad not understand that this challenge was for his own good? Frustration got the better of the Ceann-Druí, and he bore down on his son with an intensity he would later regret.

"We should have discussed this situation long ago, and we will do so after this session. In the meantime, my function here is that of mentor, not parent. We are in the midst of an important exercise.

"Will you please control yourself and explain the difference between your earlier recitation and your experience of repeating these few lines?"

"I will not!" retorted Tadhgan, planting his feet with his hands on his hips, as he had seen Arán Bán standing at cliffside only yesterday. His face was red and flushed. His breath came fast and ragged.

"Arán Bán told me to watch out for your tricks. You want to woo me back to your household so you can keep me under your thumb. My mentor told me I should have higher ambitions than you would ever let me consider. And I intend to pursue them!"

Ah-Lahn now realized he had no choice but to pose the question it pained him to ask. "Do you wish to be released from my instruction?"

"I do!" shouted Tadhgan, turning toward the grove's exit.

"As you wish, my son," answered his father. "Go in peace. You will always have my love, no matter what you believe."

Uttering a cry like the howl of a wounded animal, Tadhgan rushed from the grove into the darkest part of the oak forest, cursing the gods who had saddled him with such a father.

Ah-Lahn watched his son flee from him, perhaps forever. He faced where the young man had stood before him and spoke with profound emotion the verses he had long ago titled "Trust."

Why would you not trust me?
My heart broke, knowing you doubted
that I love you.

I tried so hard to share with you
the glories I have seen.
But you would not come along.

I see you were not able then.
Until you learn to trust yourself,
you cannot trust another.

And human care is not enough
to bridge the gap between the outer
and the inner Self.

Lonely Trials

When Ah-Lahn failed to appear for their evening meal, Alana grew anxious and sought him out in his grove—the first place she knew to begin looking for him.

There she found him, staring into the fire in deep concentration. She had seen him in this meditative state before, but there was something different about this setting. His face was grim in a way she had never observed. His shoulders were slumped, as if he carried a burden of immense weight.

Reticent to disturb him, she stood silently. Unless his consciousness was far away, she knew he would acknowledge her presence. But he did not. Even when she accidentally kicked a small stone against one of the oak trees, he did not stir.

Breathing a silent prayer for his safety and support, she crept away in profound realization that this mighty druí was wrestling with an initiation that he must face alone. She could send him her love and come to him when he called, but he was on an inner voyage that only he and An Síoraí could navigate.

Ah-Lahn had sensed Alana's presence. How could he not know when his soul's other half approached?

Yet he had chosen not to respond to her. He was not ready to discuss the abrupt severing of the tie between himself and his son. The pain was too deep, and he saw no immediate remedy.

In this moment, Ah-Lahn could not welcome his wife's desire to alleviate his pain. The grief he felt had to be experienced, explored, and listened to, for the lessons he might find there.

He trusted that Alana would not interrupt his meditation. Nevertheless, he was aware that her caring nature often made her overly sympathetic. That particular human tendency was not helpful when he was intent on discovering a solution that would lead to the highest good for all involved.

He remembered how, in the first days of their marriage, he had been unexpectedly troubled by an old shoulder injury, suffered years earlier in a friendly wrestling match with some of his fellow druíthe. Puzzled that the injury should bother him again, he had engaged in a deep conversation with his body about the true source of the pain.

He had been seated on the sleeping platform he shared with his wife, his brow furrowed in very focused concentration. Entering their cottage and seeing him in what appeared to be great discomfort, Alana had walked over to him.

Gently wrapping her arm around his shoulders, she had said, "My poor Ah-Lahn. I am so sorry you are hurting. What can I do for you?"

Startled out of the interesting insight his shoulder was sharing—that he was taking on too many burdens—Ah-Lahn had said sharply to Alana, "Do not call me poor."

He had instantly regretted his tone. And because he was always a teacher, he was inspired to offer her an explanation, speaking in the voice of his inner guidance:

Do not pity me. I am not poor or weak in my humanness.

What you see is a man working out his destiny, striving to come up higher, to reach into the invisible world so he may blend this realm of time and space with what is unseen, though profoundly felt.

Do not pity one who journeys, who marks his life by milestones of loving surrender—not merely of a mulish will, but of lesser voices that would render him complacent when labor is required.

For entering and leaving earth are both arduous tasks, as is living all the intervening years. I am grateful for the sweat I have spent in striving. I have a path to show for it.

Be glad for me and all who climb mountains of An Síoraí's alchemy. We are happy warriors who rejoice in our adventures.

We harbor no regrets to spoil our arrival in that fair place where land and sea and sky convene—our destination that hides, all shrouded in mist until the final hour of our travels.

How grateful we will be to walk in that fine realm where pity is impossible.

Alana also remembered this event and Ah-Lahn's profound outpouring from the depths of his soul. She was aware that her husband was once again venturing into new levels of awareness, so she let him be.

Strategies

The following day was a blustery one, perfectly reflecting the whirlwind of emotions whipping through the túath.

There were few secrets in this collection of cottages, schools, fields, and groves. By mid-morning everyone from druí to farmer had heard about the argument between the Ceann-Druí and his son. Natural seanchaithe to the core, each one had felt obligated to retell the tale with increasing elaboration

Of course, Arán Bán had made certain to spread the story after Tadhgan had feverishly sought him out to confess the confrontation. Relating the event to appeal to his mentor's opinion, the young man had cast his father as the villain, himself as courageous victim.

"You would have been proud of me," boasted Tadhgan, puffing out his thin chest. "I stood up to him. I told him I would not recite the ridiculous poem he lied about composing years ago.

"He said my delivery lacked emotion. *Ha!* I showed him plenty of emotion when I demanded that he release me from his instruction. You were right, Arán Bán! He is a bully. Will you take me back and finish preparing me to be a proper bard?"

"Of course," replied the druí in his most sympathetic tone, stifling a smirk. "Your departure from my tutelage was only temporary and was not your fault. I know that. And because you have displayed such courage in the face of insufferable disrespect, I am going to teach you some advanced techniques that even Ah-Lahn's little wife does not know.

"Let us return to my cottage. You will stay with me under my protection, and we will begin anew. There is no better balm for suffering injustice than learning skills that will surely set you apart from others who are less deserving."

Ah-Lahn did not immediately go home. Instead, Cróga and Riordan had sought him as soon as they had learned of Tadhgan's stormy behavior.

"What does this mean?" asked Riordan. "Shall we take action against Arán Bán or Tadhgan?"

"No, but thank you," Ah-Lahn answered hoarsely. Fatigue from a sleepless night was evident in his usually resonant voice.

"Let them be. Tadhgan has made his choice, and I must respect it. I am more than a little responsible for his decision. I took a risk yesterday by provoking the pent-up anger I observed in him on the cliffs when we returned from Cois Abhann.

"I knew he could not make further progress in his studies as long as that emotion festered under the surface. I had hoped to guide him through an exercise that has been effective for other initiates, but we both lost control. The result was as you have heard.

"Tadhgan's feelings have more to do with me personally than with his training. But, clearly, he cannot learn from me. Indeed, I seem to have learned a difficult lesson from him."

"Do not blame yourself, Ah-Lahn," said Cróga. "The boy's mind has been infected by Arán Bán. Only last night I learned that for some time our sly druí has been doing his best to poison others against you. He appears to have taken advantage of our recent absence to work considerable mischief throughout the túath."

"I know you do not wish to hear this, Ceann-Druí," continued Riordan, purposefully addressing Ah-Lahn by his office. "However, for the good of our community, the Council of Druíthe must ensure that Arán Bán's influence is reduced. Do you have any suggestions?"

"I do." Ah-Lahn had spent most of the night considering how they should proceed. "First of all, I would like to request that we delay the investiture of initiates for three months, until Samhain. This will allow the túath residents to shift their full attention to preparations for the upcoming festivities.

"And I recommend that we invite Tóisech Gréagóir to attend along with the Ard-Mháistir. I know that Óengus's school has prepared several druíthe for investiture at Samhain. Combining his ceremony with ours should present no major inconvenience. I believe both he and Gréagóir will welcome the invitation."

"Agreed," said Riordan and Cróga.

Ah-Lahn continued: "May I also request that you, Riordan, and members of the Council speak directly with Arán Bán? For obvious reasons, I will have no further interaction with him. However, you could apprise him of your knowledge of his recent malignant insinuations about me and others within the community."

"Of course," Riordan reassured his friend. "Your colleagues understand that you were the one most willing to help Arán Bán succeed."

"I am glad of their support," said Ah-Lahn. "I suggest you let him know that he is authorized to mentor Tadhgan, as that is the young man's decision. However, he is not to approach any other initiates.

"Gormlaith and Dearbhla will continue mentoring their bards and fáidthe. And, with the Council's approval, I will resume guidance of the few students I have been preparing to work with Ard-Mháistir Óengus."

"This is an excellent plan," answered Cróga. "I will let it be known through my trusted warriors that Arán Bán has been given the honor of concentrating his considerable talents on the preparation of the Ceann-Druí's son to avoid any appearance of special favors to that young man."

"Excellent," said Ah-Lahn with a deep sigh of relief. "I am in your debt. Do you wish me to extend your invitation to Gréagóir and Óengus?"

"There is no need. I will send a messenger myself," said Cróga. "I have some personal thoughts to convey to them. Of course, I count on you both to see that all preparations are made for the Samhain investiture ceremony. Such an event will bring great honor to our túath."

Riordan and Cróga extended the double handshake of true friendship to the Ceann-Druí. As they watched this man they both admired walk purposefully to his cottage, concern for his well-being showed clearly on their faces.

Father Minus Son

*A*h-Lahn and Tadhgan could not stop ruminating about one another. Though they were busy with preparations for the investiture ceremony, in idle moments each man wrestled in his own mind with the conundrum of their relationship.

Try again! Tadhgan badgered himself. He furrowed his brow and set his jaw in defiance of the ineptitude he felt at the moment. He was having trouble remembering a complicated history whose memorization was a key requirement for his designation as a bard.

If he did not get the lines right, he would not receive his bronze bard's branch. He desperately wanted that honor. Once he was accepted as a bard, the community would recognize him as a person of consequence, not merely the Ceann-Druí's son.

Tadhgan blamed his father for the worm of bitterness that had burrowed into his heart, leaving only disappointment to feed the resentment that had festered in his childhood mind and that still tormented him with nightmares of his inadequacy.

If only his father had been there when he was born, his mother might not have died. Ah-Lahn would have known how to save her, but he had arrived too late. For that and more, Tadhgan despised the Ceann-Druí with the deep-seated conflict of one who both loathes and craves his parent's affection and approval.

As Ah-Lahn worked through his day's obligations as Ceann-Druí, he could not help thinking that everything about Tadhgan's appearance seemed hungry, almost desiccated. From his son's stringy, unwashed hair to his pinched lips and spindly legs, the lad looked like a scarecrow. He should have been building up the athletic body those engaged in practices of the druíthe took care to develop.

Ah-Lahn blamed the lack of nurturing on the absence of the boy's mother, Lile, who had died on Tadhgan's second day on earth. He could not help that his own time and attention had been taken up with his studies and duties as a young druí. Nevertheless, he realized the boy had likely felt like an orphan, despite having a devoted nurse throughout his infancy.

As a father, Ah-Lahn still regretted that he had blamed his son for the death of the boy's mother. He would have been at the birth if the bairn had not insisted on being born two weeks early—impetuous, even in the womb.

He had rushed home the minute word reached him of the birth and Lile's illness. Unfortunately, by the time he reached their cottage, his son was alive and his wife was dead.

Lile was never strong, Ah-Lahn remembered with a pain that stabbed him still. She was as delicate as the gold leaf her family of artisans had used to create fine jewelry and ornaments. Her skin was smooth as a pearl, her consciousness as pure, for she spoke ill of no one. Flowers bloomed profusely for her, and in her presence the sun always seemed to shine a bit brighter.

Ah-Lahn had loved her since they were children together. Everyone assumed they would marry, which they did, when he was twenty and she was eighteen. Lile spent her days praying for him and their people, for devotion to the light of An Síoraí was her service to the community.

Something had troubled Lile throughout her ill-advised pregnancy. Though she would not confide the reason, Ah-Lahn could read in her face the worry that wore upon her day after day. Or was her expression one of fear?

"I will not leave you in this condition. The birth is too close." He had all but begged her to let him remain at her side, but she had urged him to fulfill his other duties.

"You are needed at the border, Ah-Lahn," she had insisted. "The chieftain and other druíthe rely on your support to win this war. The baby is not due for another month. I will be fine. Do not worry."

But he had worried. In his heart he knew something was amiss. Lile should never have borne a child. Yet after his return the previous year from a several-week's campaign with Cróga's father, who was chieftain at the time, Lile had so fervently insisted that Ah-Lahn give her a child, he had relented. She had conceived immediately.

That was a decision Ah-Lahn would rue till the end of his days. He did blame the child and was deeply sorry that his feelings should be mixed toward the infant who had sprung from his own loins.

The little boy was as familiar as an old friend and yet strangely foreign to Ah-Lahn. Tadhgan did not resemble him in appearance or temperament, though he did have his mother's dark brown eyes and sensitive mouth.

The entire sequence of events had been a puzzle Ah-Lahn could never resolve. Why had Lile been eager to have a child, then inexplicably burdened throughout her pregnancy, which, in the end, proved fatal?

And why had she been emphatic that he should be away at the border? Had she not wanted her husband present for the birth of their son?

The midwife who tended the mother and newborn told Ah-Lahn the virulent infection had taken hold quickly, resisting remedies from even the most skilled fáidthe. Lile appeared to have given up on life. Despite their considerable efforts to save her, she did not try to survive. Instead she slipped away without a word, her expression inexplicable as a single tear trickled onto her pillow when she passed.

Ah-Lahn still remembered the devastation that had hung about him like a shroud for nearly twenty years. The persistent sorrow had lifted only years later on that magical day when he first saw Alana for the first time and recognized her as his twin flame.

Now, with her presence in his life, he felt resurrected, as if the previous events had never occurred. Though, of course, they had occurred. And Ah-Lahn feared he would never be entirely free of the belief that he had served neither his son nor the boy's mother well.

A Seer's Insight

*A*lana was certain she heard fairy voices as she gradually wakened from a misty slumber. The dreamtime radiance that lingered in her mind glistened like sunlight on butterfly wings, promising hope and insights beyond her imagination.

She was once again lodging on the grounds of Dearbhla's school. With Ah-Lahn's encouragement, she was completing advanced training as a seer that included many hours of meditation meant to deepen her intuitive and prophetic abilities.

In this important initiation, she would focus on the mirror-like surface of a large chalice that had been filled with water and placed on the altar at the west side of the Banfháidh's own wisdom grove. The chalice had been carved from a single piece of green marble whose size and weight required two people to move it into place.

The stone's subtle vibration spoke to Alana of mysteries past, present, and future. For today's exercise, Dearbhla's only instruction was that she should use her intuitive skills to see with the eyes of her soul.

As Alana stirred in her cottage, a nine-year-old neophyte quietly entered to serve a breakfast of porridge and honeycomb. After enjoying this simple meal, she dressed and made her way to meet Dearbhla, who had risen earlier to prepare for the day's meditation.

The ground was cool beneath Alana's bare feet, for she seldom wore shoes when opening her inner sight as she was about to do. The autumn grass was still damp with morning dew that gently bathed her steps like angel kisses as she entered the wisdom grove. Earthy fragrances of mistletoe, moss, and fern wrapped the clearing in a vibration of peace and safety.

Dearbhla began the session with a powerful invocation to spirits of protection. Alana joined her in a rhythmic chant, reciting the sacred words that had come down through generations of seers in centuries of devoted practice.

Thus prepared, Alana sat on a bench in front of the chalice and focused inward. With soft eyes, she peered deeply into the still waters.

Some moments passed without event, and then she began to feel the presence of a young man.

Here was someone well known to her—a person she had loved with a child's pure devotion and a friend of times gone by. He was a companion with whom she had shared adventures. And then an adversary who bore her ill will—as best she could tell, through no fault of her own.

Who is he? Alana asked her soul as the image came into focus. Her acquaintance with the young man felt ancient. Yet he was agitated like someone of more tender years and troubled in his mind, which whipped back and forth between thoughts of affection and angry projections.

Inhaling deeply, Alana allowed herself to absorb his vibration. As she took in the young man's energy, she let it rest in a sphere of violet light which she visualized over and around herself. She meant to let his energy remain in that sphere until she perceived the chaos had been consumed. Only then would she exhale the transformed substance back to the image that was rapidly becoming clearer.

But then a shocking thing happened.

When the violet light contacted the young man, his image shuddered and rejected it. To Alana's complete astonishment, Tadhgan appeared to be standing before her.

He was furious that she had penetrated his consciousness, for in that moment, he had been seated in meditation in Arán Bán's grove. Their simultaneous openness had created a link that neither had anticipated and that Tadhgan vehemently resented.

Instantly, Alana's connection with him was broken. She careened backward off the bench and would have tumbled to the ground had Dearbhla not caught her. Profoundly shaken, she leaned on her aunt's arm as the Banfháidh led her away from the chalice.

"Did you see him?" cried Alana. "Tadhgan was here. Why would he appear in my meditation? Something or someone wanted me to see him, but why?"

"Calm yourself, Alana," said Dearbhla gently. "Your soul knows the answer if you will receive it. Take a minute. Settle into your body and then speak the story your inner guidance wants to tell."

Alana closed her eyes and concentrated on her breath. In a couple of minutes the story began to flow from her as if the events were still fresh in her mind:

> Many years ago, before our forefathers' memory, three friends grew up together in a land long gone, sunk beneath the waves in water and flame.
>
> They were a playful trio, two boys and a girl, loyal to each other and the best of friends. They were smart, ambitious, and yet deeply spiritual in the way of children who commune freely with angels and faeries.
>
> Attracted by the mysteries of the invisible world, they decided to become priests and priestess. Though young, they were enthusiastic. Something about their innocence appealed to the High Priestess, Lady `, who accepted them as novices, overruling the objection of the High Priest who thought them frivolous and naïve in their devotion.
>
> As they strove in their novitiate, one of the boys and the girl discovered a synchrony of heart and mind that the other boy did not share. Though they did their best to remain friends, when the one boy and the girl professed their love to each other, a rift developed.
>
> For the other boy also loved her, though he had kept his affection a secret. When she wed his friend, he fell into a depression that none could understand.
>
> One day, the High Priestess discovered him sitting alone in an isolated precinct of the temple where they served together. Understanding why he suffered, she asked him a question:

'Which of your friends do you love better?'

'Neither,' said the young priest, surprised to see her seated next to him. He had not heard her approach.

'Which of them would you want to love you more than they love each other?'

'Neither,' he answered again, hanging his head. He could not begrudge them their extraordinary connection.

'How do you suppose they feel since you have begun to avoid them, especially she whom you profess to love?'

'I am sure they are hurt and confused by my behavior.'

'Which is more precious, the loyalty of a true friend or the affection of a lover?'

'They are equally precious. Though different, they are both essential to our happiness in life.'

'Do you believe we are deserving of only one type of love?'

'I believe everyone deserves both.'

'Then,' said the High Priestess, 'do you not also believe that if you open your heart to your companions in true friendship, you might also attract a romantic partner with whom you are perfectly matched?'

'I do believe that to be true,' the young priest confessed.

Suddenly Alana broke off the story. "Oh, Dearbhla," she cried, "that young man was Joha-lihn, Khieranan's friend from Atlantis—the one who was tortured by the High Priest before Treylah's escape. He died such a terrible death. And I know he blamed Khieranan."

Alana's heart was beating so fast she could hardly breathe as images of those events came rushing back to her memory. Dearbhla listened intently as her niece relayed what she saw.

"Joha-lihn believed his fellow priest had left him to be captured and tortured. But I am certain that was not true. I remember Khieranan saying he did not know where Joha-lihn was. I saw his face in my life review. He agonized for his friend, and so did Treylah."

"But the young man left embodiment believing that his friends had betrayed him," said Dearbhla. "Such trauma can scar a soul. Although explanation is given between lives, when a soul reembodies, it picks up where it left off. Relationships wounded in time and space must be healed there.”

“And Joha-lihn is now Ah-Lahn’s son.” Alana stated what she knew to be true. “But Ah-Lahn told me he thought Tadhgan was the Queen’s son in Egypt because of their headstrong natures. Perhaps we were not together in that lifetime.”

“Look deeper, Alana,” suggested Dearbhla. “There are more clues for you to discover.”

Alana closed her eyes and directed her attention into the past. She was quiet for several seconds.

“My impression is of one I loved as a brother. Such was Treylah’s affection for Joha-lihn.” She paused.

“Of course, the Egyptian Queen’s brother, Anen. They had been close as children, but a rift developed in their relationship. I remember now. Anen resented the Queen’s adviser, Senaa. He believed his sister preferred her steward over him, her brother. The soul of Joha-lihn felt rejected by his friends once again.”

“And he died with that resentment never spoken or resolved,” explained Dearbhla. “What about Tadhgan? Do you understand why your inner guidance would show him to you?”

“I believe so. When I first arrived here with my mother, I noticed an immediate connection between us. He was friendly then and treated me almost like a long-lost lover. I thought he was sweet, though rather immature. At the time, I paid him little attention. I was too overcome with grief from losing my family to think of anyone else.

“And then Ah-Lahn swooped into my life a year later. After that, Tadhgan was hostile whenever I attempted to speak with him. The only thing he ever said to me after his father and I married was, ‘You are not my mother. Do not try to act like you are.’ Naturally, I respected his wishes and let him alone.

“Aunt Dearbhla, what is to become of the three of us? Clearly, our souls need resolution. Is that possible after all these centuries? And what about Arán Bán?”

Alana’s mind was again flooded with images of the past.

"Oh-h-h." The single word sighed out in a troubling realization.

"I saw that man in my life reviews of Egypt and Atlantis. He was always practicing the dark arts and always a virulent enemy of our twin souls. Is Arán Bán capable of such violence in this life?"

"I hope not," said Dearbhla, "but we cannot be certain. He is consumed with hatred for your husband and you. I recently learned he has told everyone who will listen that you betrayed him.

"What worries me most is his influence over Tadhgan. I understand Ah-Lahn's decision to respect his son's choice of mentor, but I fear he made a mistake by leaving him with Arán Bán.

"We must share all we have learned with Ah-Lahn. His determination to help his son may have blinded him to the records of how badly circumstances have unraveled in the past."

"I trust your intuition, Alana, and yours, Dearbhla," Ah-Lahn agreed reluctantly as they met in his grove.

Their insights confirmed his suspicion that his son's antipathy stemmed from more than this lifetime. He was surprised their relationship had been hidden from his own life reviews. Perhaps he had not wanted to see, or the time had not been right for the truth to be revealed.

"I am grieved to know that the soul of my dear friend Joha-lihn should have carried such a burden of anger and misunderstanding for so many lifetimes. I should have done something to alleviate his suffering.

"Unfortunately, there is little we can do until after the investiture ceremony. In the meantime, we can only let events play out. Plans are made and the stage is set for Samhain.

"Óengus and Gréagóir arrive shortly with their candidates. Riordan, Cróga, and I will consult with them to finalize arrangements, though nothing major can be changed now. However, I will confer with Óengus privately. He may have an idea we haven't considered.

"I will speak with Tadhgan after Samhain. Surely, if I explain to him what really happened between Khieranan and Joha-lihn, we can put to rest these ancient misunderstandings."

Samhain

Not since the Ceann-Druí's wedding had such excitement rippled through Tearmann. The local residents had been hard at work for over two months so all would be in readiness when their guests arrived from Cois Abhann.

Samhain was a complex, three-day celebration that marked the onset of winter and the beginning of the new year. This festival was also the most richly spiritual of the four seasonal gatherings. At autumn's time of dramatic change, the veil between this world and the next became transparent.

During Samhain, spirits of ancestors, heroes, and heroines from ages past gathered among the living, creating the opportunity for enhanced communication between the unseen and the seen. Enormous bonfires were planned for the hilltops as symbols of purification and regeneration. And everyone looked forward to the brief abolishment of time when acceptable chaos might reign.

The ceremonies would be held on the Buaicphointe, the highest point in Tearmann. Here hundreds of people could enjoy a good view of the fascinating presentations that would take place.

Should the chill winds of autumn force the festivities inside, the túath's spacious lodge could be used. So far, thanks to some special weather-related invocations by Ard-Mháistir Óengus, the temperature was unseasonably warm, the breezes gentle, the sun unusually luminous.

Since dawn, small groups of residents and guests had been making their way up the hill to claim the best viewing spots. As the opening ceremony approached, scores more could be seen hurrying to find their places. Drummers, pipers, and harpists played familiar tunes, and the crowd sang merrily while they waited.

At last, the hour arrived for the grand procession to begin, led by Ollamh Gormlaith. She was wearing her deep blue robe and finest gold torc. In her hands she carried her Ollamh branch, its golden bells jingling, calling the audience to attention.

Other senior and junior bards followed. They vigorously shook their branches whose gold, silver, and bronze bells combined with the joyful music to set the audience's hearts to pounding in anticipation of the promised spectacles.

Gormlaith's six candidates for the first order of bards followed, including an unusually cheerful Tadhgan. Their faces were shining in expectation of receiving recognition for their years of intensive study.

They wore simple blue cloaks over plain tunics and leggings. None of them carried bronze branches yet. Their final demonstration would earn them that reward. There was great honor in achieving this first symbolic branch of office. Once earned, more years of training would follow for them to be awarded silver or gold branches signifying advanced skill.

The Brigantes held their bards in high esteem, regardless of their individual mastery. However, the idea of being less than brilliant in front their neighbors and guests had some of the candidates quaking beneath their cloaks.

Next came the fáidthe, led by Banfháidh Dearbhla. Threads of gold and silver had been woven into the fabric of her rich green robe and glistened in the sunlight. On her head a wreath of oak leaves crowned her shower of white-blonde hair that flowed over her shoulders and down her back.

Many hoped that she would speak a prophecy on the second day of the Samhain festivities, though there was no guarantee.

Dearbhla was followed by eight male and eight female fáidthe who walked in pairs. All wore similar green robes with oak leaf circlets on their heads. Their cloaks were fastened with golden brooches and each one wore at least one ring that had been passed down to them from an elder fáidh.

As they passed by, a murmur rippled through the crowd, for these men and women were less frequently seen in public than the bards or druíthe. Having dedicated themselves to the mysteries of healing and prophecy, they quietly ministered to community members who were sick or in need of guidance.

Many fáidthe sought anonymity and were glad to work behind the scenes. Indeed, Gréagóir's senior fáidh had remained behind to tend to some of his people who were ill.

Only three fáidh candidates followed: Sorchae and a married couple from Dearbhla's school. They wore long green robes and beautifully wrought golden pendants, but no wreaths, as those would be bestowed upon their investiture. All three had passed rigorous examinations conducted in private by their tutors. The Samhain ceremony was more a public acknowledgement of their accomplishments than proof of their mastery.

Finally came the senior druíthe, led by Ard-Mháistir Óengus. The spectacle of these white-robed figures, twelve men and women from each túath, hushed the crowd to awed silence. Their regal bearing sent chills up and down the collective spine of the congregation.

Again, there were only three candidates for investiture, all from Óengus's school for druíthe.

When all participants had taken their places, Óengus solemnly stepped to the center of the clearing. Raising his staff, the Ard mháistir began his invocation:

> *O Spirits of East and West, South and North, give ear, we pray, to our supplications. Angels of our world and the next, bless this assembly with your protection and inspiration.*
>
> *Beloved An Síoraí, may the words of our mouths and the deeds of our hands bring health and abundance to all our people and safety to our homes, our leaders, and those we love both near and far, here with us and in gracious Tír na n'Óg, Land of the Ever-Living.*

Pausing briefly, his eyes penetrating the veil between that which is seen and that which is not, the great druí swept his staff vertically in a full circle around his own body and then again horizontally, turning around to encompass the entire crowd.

At his signal, Gormlaith and the senior bards began beating their bodhrán drums, creating a soul-stirring rhythm that reverberated across the Buaicphointe. When the crowd was fully caught up in the numinous atmosphere, the Ard mháistir stepped forward.

He intoned a single note and began a powerful chant. As his voice grew deeper and louder, a soft white mist swirled around his body, and his shape began to shift with every line.

> I am the salmon wise and sleek
> I am the stream in which it swims.

Suddenly, the mist became a waterway where a huge salmon vigorously surged up against the current and splashed back down, spraying drops of water on the delighted spectators nearest the apparition.

> I am the song of Lughnasa
> I am the verse writ by the wind.

The mists turned into golden fields of ripened wheat, and a warm breeze wafted across the Buaicphointe, carrying the sound of pipes.

> I am the spirit of the bards
> I am the tales they long to tell.

Once again the mists shifted, coalescing into scenes of famous heroes acting out the legends that the Brigantes loved to hear while Óengus's voice carried over the powerful sound of drums.

> I am the secrets still untold.
> I am the mystery you know.

Now the mists grew thicker and began to glow with a pearly luminescence as a chorus of angel voices sang the next lines of the chant.

> I gather here in mystics' glen
> To bid you seek me all the more,
> To slip behind the screen of time,
> To slip behind the screen of time.

Seamlessly, singers and bodhrán drummers picked up the music's pace until the entire crowd began repeating the final phrase.

> To slip behind the screen of time,
> To slip behind the screen of time.

As all watched, the mists dissolved, revealing a magnificent golden hawk whose outstretched wings and sleek body shone like the sun.

With a cheerful cry, the wonderful bird flew around and around the Buaicphointe, creating an enormous spiral pattern in the sky. Up and up it flew until it disappeared into the mist that settled like a blessing on the enchanted spectators.

For a moment, the audience held its breath and looked up to where the hawk had flown. Then they began to clap and cheer, for the mists suddenly cleared. Standing where they had last seen him, was Ard-Mháistir Óengus, once again in human form.

He smiled broadly at his beloved Brigantes and then nodded to Gormlaith to bring her candidates forward.

Investiture of new bards would be the longest of the three ceremonies, as the six initiates would be joined by bards from each túath in a dramatization of the four primary seasonal festivals.

Because Samhain honored the spirits of all gods, goddesses, heroes, and heroines from ancient times to the present, the participants had agreed that each bard would portray his or her favorite being or aspect of the seasons.

A great noise of drums, harps, whistles, bells, and bellowing horns announced the entrance of two dozen players of all ages. The audience laughed and pointed as they recognized May Queen, Green Man, Brigid, and the Harvest God, Lugh.

Some bards portrayed warriors complete with shield and sword. Still others had bedecked themselves with symbolic greenery—vines for protection or prosperity, rowan for healing, willow for romantic love, and alder for spirituality.

At Arán Bán's insistence, Tadhgan had been given the role of the legendary bard, Amairgen. After the dazzling flash of color and sound that summoned all performers to their places, the Ceann-Druí's son strode confidently to the center of the clearing.

He carried a staff and walked with great dignity as three harpists accompanied his presentation. Beginning at once in a clear, strong voice, he sang his solo with dramatic effect.

> A figure appears in twilight's glow
> to answer your hearts' longing
> for comfort and recovery
> of the lost traditions you once knew.
> Or are they truly gone for good?
>
> Stepping into Dreamtime at his gestured call
> you discover them unspoiled by time:
> heavenly powers and earthly guides
> that carry you to seers' realms
> where such ones as he abide.
>
> Amairgen is my name,
> poet-sage of ancient Éire,
> inspired judge who claimed this land.
> I commune with all living things
> and often shift into their shapes
> to expand my knowledge and my care
> for all beings in my purview.

> I take my place with staff upraised
> and part the veil to other worlds
> blessing all with lightning force
> and honeyed eloquence of speech.
>
> O soul, give ear as our songs ring out
> that all here might be entertained.

Amidst thunderous applause and shouts of appreciation, Tadhgan swept his cloak grandly around his shoulders and hurried off as the next performers took their places.

The other five initiates intoned a prayer to the Goddess Brigid as the young female bard portraying her stepped forward in a gown she had created from fabrics in every color of the rainbow. She held up her hands to the sky as she swirled around the Buaicphointe, bestowing her Imbolc blessings on the crowd.

Next came the May Queen and Green Man, who danced and sang an enchanting duet to signify Bealtaine's aspects of courtship and bringing forth new life. The two were newly engaged and bowed repeatedly as the crowd cheered them.

A stocky young bard from Gréagóir's túath reluctantly made his entrance as the Harvest God, Lugh. His costume of wheat sheaves had been hastily constructed and had not survived the commotion of other players pushing their way into place following Tadhgan's introduction.

Clothed in little more than his homespun tunic, the young Lugh stood in silent embarrassment until his friends came to his rescue. All the performers who were trees, bees, crops, and other representations of agriculture rushed in to surround the lad and sing with him the song he himself had composed to celebrate an abundant harvest.

As a grand finale, the heroes and heroines, who had been anxiously awaiting their turn, marched out in two groups. They faced off in a slow-motion battle that had the audience on their feet as the Brigantes men and women defeated their adversaries in an inspiring demonstration of courage.

At the end of the battle, all knelt to honor the "dead" and then carried them solemnly around the Buaicphointe as a choir of male and female bards intoned a paean of praise.

The entire congregation then joined in a final song dedicated to all souls in the invisible world. As they looked up to the sky, the fluffy clouds that had formed over the green now took on the shapes and faces of the departed who had gathered to bless the initiates and their fellow bards.

Cheers once more rang out as the performers who were not initiates hurried back to their places in the audience, some still playing their instruments as they rejoined the exultant crowd.

By this time everyone was more than ready for a hearty meal. Óengus reappeared to close the day's rituals and to bless the branches with bronze bells that were then bestowed on the new, first-order bards. The six stood solemnly, trying not to show their eagerness to receive their well-earned accolades.

Once the bonfires were lit as a sign that the feasting could begin, the new bards rushed to the meeting hall where they were exuberantly fêted well into the night by the entire community.

Ah-Lahn noted that Arán Bán had been absent for most of the day, appearing only for Tadhgan's solo performance and then vanishing into the afternoon's lengthening shadows.

As the Ceann-Druí could discern no particular meaning from that occurrence, he erased the thought from his mind in hopes of enjoying the celebration. His only disappointment was Tadhgan's failure to look in his direction when he tried to catch his son's eye to signal his approval of the young man's performance.

Prophecy

Owing to the previous late night enjoyed by most of the residents and guests and the abbreviated performance planned by the fáidthe, the second day's festivities began after midday.

Newly installed bards enthusiastically shook their bells to call the crowd to assemble on the Buaicphointe. The presentation area had been set up with seats for musicians who would accompany the Dance of the Elemental Spirits the fáidthe would present.

To begin the day's events, Ollamh Gormlaith and Druí Riordan stood smiling together at the center of the clearing to offer the day's opening invitation for all those gathered to lend their hearts as well as their attention to the celebrations that were about to begin.

As the couple accompanied themselves on harp and drum, their voices rang out in a song of deep affection for each other and for all the beings, seen and unseen, who would attend today's festivities.

Their song and their presence together filled the crowd with joy and promised a delightful day.

Come dance with me!
Spin 'round and 'round
where time turns into timelessness
and forever spirals on life's great wheel.

Male and female are we now,
flame and water, water and flame.
You are the spark; I am the tinder.

I will be the sun, you be the moon,
for we are souls that sail to sea
across the ocean of An Síoraí.

What a lively dance is this:
spinning into luminous realms,
weaving garlands 'round our shoulders
opening our hearts to playful spirits
who come to puncture pompous displays,
and carry us off on clouds of laughter,
singing songs only the faeries know.

Come dance with me in life's sweet play!
Your smile's been tucked away too long.

The crowd cheered as Gormlaith and Riordan exited holding hands.
No doubt, another wedding was on the horizon.

With a dramatic introduction of pipes and drums, the full complement of musicians began the powerful accompaniment for the Dance
of the Elemental Spirits. Nine pairs of fáidthe, including the married
candidate couple, ran to the center of the clearing.

Each pair carried brightly colored ribbons to signify one of the four
elements—green for earth, yellow for air, red for fire, and blue for water.
The ninth couple carried all four colors.

As the men and women spun around the clearing in complex patterns, the energy of dance and instrument built until everyone in the
audience was on their feet, clapping and cheering at the inventive steps
and swirling ribbons.

Finally, a single banfháidh walked regally into their midst. The audience was delighted to recognize this figure as Sorchae. She performed a
graceful dance to represent the unifying spirit of An Síoraí that brought
all the elements together. The nine couples gathered around her and the
dance concluded.

The audience applauded enthusiastically, the dancers bowed and
stepped back a few paces. Sorchae then asked for quiet and brought the

audience to attention as Banfháidh Dearbhla entered the clearing. Earlier in the day, she had felt that no prediction would be forthcoming this afternoon. But the passionate dance of her brother and sister fáidthe had summoned An Síoraí's spirit of prophecy. Taking her place before the crowd, she raised her arms to the sky and began to speak powerful words of which she had no foreknowledge:

Hearken, all who will heed my words!
Who among you will tempt the Fates?
Who will walk through the Golden Gates?
Who will sorrow bring to their knees?
Who will fly home on victory's breeze?
Who will stay to save the child?
Who will travel through forests wild?
Who will lead by Spirit's call?
Who will heal us one and all?

Dearbhla stood looking out intently upon the gathering. The thrilled crowd wondered—Will she speak again? What does the prophecy mean?

After several minutes, she departed, the fáidthe following her in silence. Those who could see such things would later report that the fáidthe had appeared to melt into the afternoon mist that hugged the túath like a mother swaddling her bairn.

The Ard mháistir rose from his seat. Sweeping his staff in a wide circle around the entire Buaicphointe, he sealed the blessings the day's rituals had invoked and then addressed the crowd:

"Thank you, friends, for your appreciative attention this afternoon. All are heartily invited to partake of the magnificent feast prepared. Enjoy yourselves as you contemplate the words of the prophetess.

"May the gods and goddesses and the spirits of our ancestors guide you on your way. Tomorrow's rituals begin at noon."

Excited conversation immediately erupted as the crowd hurried from the Buaicphointe to the meeting hall. Here the hearth-fires were burning warmly and the bountiful meal was set out on long tables containing generous platters of salmon, beef, the finest cuts of pork, wild fowl, sausages, breads, and a mouth-watering array of vegetables and fruits. Of course, many revelers headed straight for the hard cider and beer they always looked forward to at these feasts.

No one came forward with a solution to the prophecy, but that did not discourage countless suppositions about its meaning. That night, more than a few went to their beds with riddles on their minds and curious images in their dreams.

Challenges

The Ard mháistir's weather magic faltered on the final morning of celebrations. Fog shrouded the Buaicphointe, obscuring it from view, making the day's activities impossible to hold at the summit.

A conference of túath leaders was called and a decision made to conduct the final acceptance of new druíthe in the meeting hall, which was hastily put back in order after the previous night's revelries.

Several program adjustments were required. The senior druíthe had planned some spectacular exhibitions—though of what exactly, they would not say. They regretted that these displays would have to be curtailed, at least until the weather improved. If the sun made an appearance in the afternoon, one final demonstration might be possible.

Nevertheless, everyone was pleased with the festivities. The candidates had done well, and, judging by the amount of food and drink that had been consumed, both residents and visitors had thoroughly enjoyed themselves.

Word spread that all who wished to attend the investiture of druíthe should gather in the hall at midday. Near the appointed time, bards spread out across the túath, ringing their bells so that none, except perhaps those suffering from too much celebration the night before, would miss the festivities.

When all were assembled, Óengus gave the opening invocation. He was about to begin the morning's events when Arán Bán burst through a side entrance, pushing a grim-faced Tadhgan before him.

The druí wore his finest ceremonial torc. He was clothed in his most resplendent robe and cloak that was fastened with an enormous gold brooch. Hanging from his neck was a brilliant silver pendant that flashed when he moved.

His blue eyes were wild with excitement as he strode forward and loudly proclaimed, "Ard-Mháistir! A moment, if you please!"

Not a soul moved in the hall.

"A special offering, if you will! To honor our esteemed guests with a demonstration of remarkable ability by one newly accepted as a bard. And yet, not merely a bard, as you will see. For this young person has studied diligently and, under my guiding hand, has gained mastery beyond his years.

"Friends and visitors! Let us celebrate youth's potential! Let there be acknowledgement that long years of tedious study are not necessary when one has exceptional talent!"

Óengus was stunned by Arán Bán's audacity. He started to object, but the druí continued, forcefully gesticulating toward his protégé.

"This young bard has been belittled in public by his own parent, Ceann-Druí Ah-Lahn. Will you deny him the opportunity to redeem himself in the eyes of his túath? Surely such denial would be unjust."

Ah-Lahn and Óengus exchanged a worried glance. They had not expected a direct challenge from Arán Bán.

"What say you, Toísech Cróga?" demanded Arán Bán. "Will you tolerate such injustice practiced against one so deserving of respect?"

He had calculated that an insinuation of unfairness would shame the chieftain into saving his own reputation in the presence of his guests. The gamble worked. Though Cróga could not pretend to miss the warning he detected in Ah-Lahn's eyes and furrowed brow, he felt obliged to give his permission.

"Very well, Arán Bán, you may offer a demonstration. We appreciate your desire to honor our guests. We trust you also understand that the day's ceremonies must proceed following your student's performance."

"Of course," answered Arán Bán, bowing low. Then, thrusting out his arm toward Tadhgan, he turned to the audience, his voice rising in dramatic authority as if he would command them all.

"My friends, you see before you a young druí in all but name. To prove his worthiness to bear the title, he will match the Ard mháistir's shape-shifting with the same lines recited yesterday."

The crowd murmured and then fell silent. Tadhgan glanced at his mentor. The druí nodded and said to him in a stern whisper, "Proceed! Speak as I taught you."

Stepping to the front of the hall, Tadhgan squared his shoulders and began to recite, accompanying himself on a bodhrán drum to increase the rhythmic effect. His voice grew stronger, louder, and more confident with each line, entrancing the congregation and himself as he spoke.

> I am the salmon wise and sleek
> I am the stream in which it swims.

To the astonishment of everyone in the room, a misty shape began to form around the young man.

> I am the song of Lughnasa
> I am the verse writ by the wind.

A strong, cold wind suddenly blew through the hall, causing those assembled to wrap their cloaks tighter around their shoulders.

> I am the spirit of the bards
> I am the tales they long to tell.

An unearthly voice began to moan as the temperature in the hall dropped further. People in the audience began to shiver and hold each other close.

> I am the secrets still untold
> I am the mystery you know
> To slip behind the screen of time . . .

The young man paused, and the audience held its breath. What was happening? Surely this was magic, though not any kind they had ever witnessed. Then the scene erupted as Tadhgan began to repeat the phrase over and over, beating his drum faster and faster, his voice rising until he was all but shrieking.

> To slip behind the screen of time,
> To slip behind the screen of time,
> To slip behind the screen of time.

Without warning, a monstrous, winged shape materialized in full view of the entire congregation and hovered over Tadhgan. Viciously, it breathed out a hideous black mist that enveloped him. He appeared powerless to resist inhaling the mist as his drum beat faster and louder and his voice raised to fever pitch.

> To slip behind the screen of time!
> To slip behind the screen of time!
> To slip behind the screen of time!

With a thundering boom and a blinding flash, the terrible specter flew out across the terrified audience. Tadhgan's body shuddered violently in a demonic spasm. Then uttering an otherworldly cry, he collapsed, lifeless on the floor.

With a collective gasp, the audience dropped back as the black mist swirled around the young man's body and then shot up through the building's thatched roof.

Ah-Lahn rushed to Tadhgan's side and fell to his knees. Sobs erupted from the Ceann-Druí as he cradled his son's body in his arms and rocked the young man as if he were once more a child.

"Tadhgan, can you hear me? My son, do not leave like this. Tadhgan, I love you. Do not go!

"Óengus, do something!" cried Ah-Lahn as the Ard mháistir knelt to examine the lifeless form. "Bring him back, I beg you! Surely he did not mean to die. Quick, Dearbhla—a potion, some herbs to revive my son!"

"Ah-Lahn, there is nothing we can do," said the Ard mháistir shaking his head and steadying himself with his staff as he rose back to standing.

"Intentional or not, Tadhgan created the opening through which he slipped into the next world. I can say prayers for his soul, but I cannot force his return to this plane."

"Let him go, Ah-Lahn," said Alana as she helped her husband to his feet. Facing him, she brushed the hair from his eyes and embraced him with all her strength. "Uncle Óengus is right. There is nothing you can do. Tadhgan is gone."

Ah-Lahn lowered his eyes, allowing the awful truth to penetrate his consciousness.

"Joha-lihn, my friend," he murmured, looking down at the form lying at his feet. "I would have helped you through the records of our past, but you would not have it. Why would you not trust me?"

Then, sensing movement to his right, he turned in time to catch sight of Arán Bán. The druí was trying to slip away.

"You! Arán Bán! Stop!" Ah-Lahn shouted with a power that halted his adversary in his tracks.

"You did this! What were you trying to prove? How could you goad an inexperienced student into such a display? You have killed my son!"

"Ah, there you are wrong, Ceann-Druí," sneered Arán Bán as he sauntered back toward Ah-Lahn with an oily smirk. "Tadhgan was never your son. He was mine."

"What do you mean?" demanded Ah-Lahn.

"Have you not always wondered why he bore so little resemblance to you?" continued Arán Bán. "Of course, he had his mother's look, but he had the disposition of his father. Do you understand, or must I spell out the truth for you?"

Not giving Ah-Lahn the chance to reply, Arán Bán puffed out his chest and declared, "I took your darling wife in your bed while you were out proving your manhood with a minor chieftain. What a delight she was, lying fragrant and delicate in my arms."

"You lie!" cried Ah-Lahn. He would have choked Arán Bán on the spot, had Riordan not stepped forward to hold him back. "Lile would never do such a thing. We loved each other!"

"Oh, she tried to rebuff me at first when I visited your cottage to comfort her in her loneliness. But she soon found me irresistible, thanks to a little help from one of Una's spells.

"I was very persuasive. After I had thoroughly pleasured us both, I threatened to kill you if she confessed the deed. Of course, the naïve lass believed I would do it. I knew I had planted my seed in her that very day. And, by the time you returned from gallivanting around the countryside, she also knew.

"So she begged you to give her a child and then never let you near her afterwards. She was ashamed. Regret grew in her mind as surely as my bairn grew in her belly. And to make certain she suffered, I came around often so she would remember my touch every waking moment of her pitiful life."

The crowd stood like statues, holding each other, hands to their hearts or covering their mouths, unable to look away. Arán Bán's voice took on a triumphant tone.

"Then you were away again when the bairn came. Not too soon, as you thought, but RIGHT ON TIME!

"Did you never wonder at his strength for an early-born babe? Lile was not alive to tell you, so the secret died with her, just as the bastard dies today with you!"

Several druíthe who had gathered sprang to stop Arán Bán as he whipped a dagger from his waistband. With the strength of ten demons, he wrestled from their grasp and rushed at Ah-Lahn, aiming for the unarmed druí's heart, though he succeeded only in stabbing the Ceann-Druí in the right hand that he automatically raised to defend himself.

For an instant, no one moved. Arán Bán seized the moment. He turned and raced out the hall's side entrance, heading for the shore where he had hidden a boat in the event of trouble.

An intelligent move, indeed, he congratulated himself.

As he ran, he rehearsed in his mind how skillfully he had manipulated Tadhgan into believing he wanted to be a druí—a vocation for which the lad possessed no talent whatsoever.

The boy was certain to make a mess of his big opportunity, which played right into Arán Bán's plan to humiliate the Ceann-Druí. That bit of the plan had been too easy, except for having to endure Tadhgan's incessant whining about Ah-Lahn. But that was a small price to pay for such sweet revenge.

He had nearly reached the cliffside steps that led to his waiting craft when Ah-Lahn and a half dozen druíthe caught up with him. They halted as one body just as Arán Bán approached the treacherous descent down the hundred-foot drop to the sea.

Hastily turning to face them for one last exultation of victory, he lost his footing and slipped. He would have plummeted to his death, had Ah-Lahn not instinctively reached out to catch him.

But the hand that caught his enemy was the hand the malevolent one had stabbed. Ah-Lahn's grip weakened and grew slippery with his own blood. Despite his heroic desire not to let go, he could not will the strength to hold the man for whom he now experienced the strangest of emotions—compassion.

How can I feel compassion for this person who has destroyed my family? Ah-Lahn asked himself in the flash of recollection that sprints through a man's mind when disaster looms.

And yet, in this moment, all he felt for Arán Bán was sorrow that the druí had made such terrible choices in so many embodiments.

For, indeed, in a rapid-fire review of their ancient relationships, Ah-Lahn saw that this man had opposed him and his loved ones as the High Priest on Atlantis, in Egypt, and in countless other lifetimes. And here they were again, on the cusp of life and death.

"Arán Bán, I will not let you die!" shouted Ah-Lahn to his former colleague. "You must not carry this hatred into one more lifetime. Let me help you."

"I do not want your help," snarled the High Priest of old as he slapped away Ah-Lahn's hand. "Do me no favors, Ceann-Druí." He spat out the title he still believed should have been his.

"Let go and leave me to my fate. Do not insult me with your spiritual pabulum. My blood is on your head, just as Tadhgan's is on mine. We are even."

Violently shaking loose from Ah-Lahn's grasp, Arán Bán made not a sound as he fell silently, landing with a sickening thud on the rocks below. His mangled body mirrored the condition of his warped soul, which took flight into the darkness he had chosen once again.

The Departure

$\mathcal{A}$lana cried out in alarm and rushed to her husband as his fellow druíthe carried him into the hall.

"He collapsed on the way back," Riordan called out. "His wound did not seem that bad, but now he is feverish and cannot speak."

"Let me see him," commanded Dearbhla, pushing aside the crowd to reach the men. They quickly laid their leader at her feet.

"As I feared, he has been poisoned. Arán Bán tainted his dagger to do his deadly work, even if he missed the heart. Carry Ah-Lahn to my cottage. I will do my best to save him."

For the next three days Ah-Lahn hovered between worlds, his dreams haunted by visions of a druí whose name he could not remember falling into an abyss from which he could not save him.

Or he would see himself with his beloved Alana, walking beside crystalline streams in a brilliant green, high-mountain valley under stunning azure skies. He was reassuring her that he was well and that she had no need to worry.

Then he would struggle back to consciousness where he saw her dimly through a dark mist that clouded his mind. She was sitting at his bedside, holding his left hand as she prayed for him not to leave her. Or she was bathing his feverish brow, urging him to drink an herbal tonic Dearbhla had prepared.

Day and night he sensed her presence, for Alana refused to leave the side of her husband, even to sleep or eat.

Yet, somehow in his confusion, Ah-Lahn knew he could not stay. The pain in his body was too great, the strength to fight all but gone, the will to remain with his wife ebbing, though he knew she would be devastated without him.

"Alana, mo chroí," he whispered to her on the third morning after the attack, "I wanted to stay for you. I meant not to leave you this time. But the gods seem to say otherwise. I love you as I have always loved you—as I will love you again, when e're we meet."

And then, because Ah-Lahn was a lover of words, his final thoughts were a poem, now heard only by the angels who gathered to bear him home, his verses spoken into the invisible world as he faded away from his soul's heart-broken twin.

> How odd to feel one's life diminishing,
> not for lack of intention,
> but merely for its natural course
> of sands trickling slowly
> to the bottom of the glass.

> Fear is absent in this sifting.
> It has already been wrung out
> in living and in proving
> trepidation's powerlessness.

> Peace reigns in this moment,
> and joy permeates the atmosphere
> of the earthly dwelling
> I am leaving behind.

> Is this wishful thinking?
> To be done with life's toils,
> no longer to fret over
> holding time and space together?

I think not.
I do not wish to die,
but neither do I care so much
for staying in this troublesome world.

The final push is the hardest,
and I am weary in the working,
though I know I have help
and strength enough
to plot my course to its rightful end.

My friends will be surprised to see me gone.
Yet, some will understand
why this is my time to go.
And they will wish me well
on my journey.

PART SEVEN

To Be One

*As travelers through time
let us trust the path
to carry us forward
from life until life.*

Transitions

Sprid and Laoch lay in a circle, nose to nose and tail to tail, around Alana as she warmed herself by the fire in the tidy cottage that was now her home in Toísech Gréagóir's túath.

Uncle Óengus lived only a short walk away. He spoke with Alana when she needed human conversation and let her be when the inner world of contemplation was the only solace she required.

Ever since her animal companions had come to live with her, they had taken upon themselves the task of guarding her meditations, lest she become distraught or melancholic.

"She must grieve, but she must not wallow. Keep her focused on living, my friends," the Ard mháistir had instructed them. "For the time being, you can do that better than I."

Laoch had wagged his enormous tail enthusiastically, and Sprid had purred knowingly, her green eyes fixed on the wise man who truly appreciated her many gifts. She knew when Alana was slipping away into despair and did her best to keep her mistress anchored in the physical world she must inhabit now without her beloved Ah-Lahn.

Alana was grateful for the animals' presence and for Óengus's trust in them and her. "They seem to know I will find my way, even on days I am filled with doubt," she commented to the Ard mháistir when they sat by the fire in her cottage late one sunny winter morning.

"As do I," Óengus assured her. "Tell me, Alana, what do you hope to find along that way?"

"I want to be like Ah-Lahn. He was wise and calm and kind. He lived his spirituality as I have never quite managed. He seems far removed from me now. Perhaps, if I become more like him, he will return."

"A worthy goal, indeed, my daughter. And I should tell you—Ah-Lahn was not always the balanced druí you married. When he first came to study with me, he had a wild side. He was fiercely competitive in tests of physical strength and a playful tease to those he loved. Though he avoided violence, he was not afraid of a fight.

"And, as you say, he possessed an ease with An Síoraí that set him apart, even from his fellow druíthe.

"Ah-Lahn's spirituality was inspired by the sea. His people being fishermen and sea-faring traders, he learned to read wind and wave before he could speak a full sentence. Flowing with Spirit was as natural to him as catching the tides.

"Your husband was a lover of word and song, as you know, and he found beauty in every dimension of consciousness. I counseled him to keep his eyes and ears open in life, to discern when others did not share his awareness. Still, he tended to view those he met through the perception of his own generous nature.

"His was a noble way of being in the world, and for that Arán Bán most despised him—as he had in lifetimes past." Óengus sighed, remembering Arán Bán's unwillingness to take the hand of friendship Ah-Lahn had extended to him.

"I cannot help being angry with all of them—Arán Bán, Tadhgan, even Ah-Lahn—for bringing such sorrow into my life," Alana confessed.

"Why does the past have to intrude on the present? Why can we not work out our obligations to one another between embodiments instead of dragging ancient wounds into another lifetime? Sometimes I cannot bear living in this world."

"I know, mo mhuirnín," Óengus agreed. "Detecting anything of worth is hard when your soul's other half leaves this world. I felt the same loss when your mother, Enfys, died.

"However, I must tell you—as I listened to my grief, I came to realize that I had experienced greater separation between us when your mother was alive. For she was happily married to your father, and we lived on opposite sides of Muir Éireann.

"Thankfully, the veil between seen and unseen worlds is much thinner than a sea that must be crossed in boats. After Enfys died, I discovered her alive in my heart, closer than if we had stood physically together.

"Even when I perceived her off in other worlds, continuing the work of a bandruí that does not end with the body's death, the fine silver cord I saw connecting us did not sever. It merely stretched. I had to learn to appreciate this world without her in it and to continue serving all who are in my care. Yet, Enfys is with me always."

"You give me hope, Uncle," said Alana with a sigh.

"We must always have hope, mo mhuirnín. Hope is the essence of life. Without it, we end up believing the lies dark forces whisper in our ears when we are not paying attention. Arán Bán turned his back on hope and lost his way."

Óengus closed his eyes for a moment, touching into his memories and sensing a way forward for the young bandruí before him.

"Alana, until I say otherwise, I want you to meditate on the spark of An Síoraí that lives within you. This is the key to your becoming like Ah-Lahn. He was ever a bright student, yet not until he focused on the eternal flame within him did he become a master druí.

"I know you believe him to be far away, but he is right here with us. When you experience An Síoraí alive in your own being, you will see Ah-Lahn as clearly as you see me standing here before you.

"You will gain much knowledge as a bandruí. But if your understanding does not transform into wisdom's loving-kindness, it will serve no one. That was Arán Bán's downfall. He could think of no one but himself and, even then, his self-regard was brittle and unkind."

Images of Alana's former mentor came to her mind. She was amazed when tears sprang into her eyes and a wave of profound compassion for the man who killed her husband washed through her, dissolving anger and replacing it with sorrow for the man's choices.

Immediately, the Ard mháistir received an insight he had anticipated might come soon.

"You have reached a turning point, Alana," he said, standing and asking her to face him. "The druí's pathway is a perilous one, as you know all too well. Will you accept the hazards along with the blessings?"

"I will," said Alana.

"I will," answered Óengus. For that solemn moment had arrived in their lives when master and student are called to pledge their sacred honor to one another with greater commitment than had been possible even moments earlier. Better than Alana could know today, the Ard mháistir understood the depth of her promise.

He paused for a moment as they absorbed the scintillating energy that drifted down upon each of them like a luminous cloak—a blessing and a protection their pledge had evoked from An Síoraí.

"Now take Sprid and Laoch to the grove," Óengus said at last. "I will send for you when your next practice presents itself to me. More likely, it will come to you first. For your inner guidance is the director of your studies, not I. Your soul knows where she is going. You and I must simply follow her promptings.

"Now, I must be off to tell your aunt that you are well and moving forward. She has not wanted to interfere with your life here, nor has she used her abilities to intrude upon your sanctuary. Yet, as your guardian, she cannot help being interested in your progress."

Óengus gave the young bandruí he cherished as a daughter an affectionate kiss on the cheek and walked away from her cottage.

Alana felt a warm glow in her chest as she watched him go. And, for an instant, she was aware of Ah-Lahn's blue-green eyes twinkling at her. Then, ever so faintly, she saw him turn and follow Óengus into the mist that drifted across the path leading to the Ard mháistir's cozy dwelling.

Conversation Between Worlds

December, AD 62 to Spring, AD 63, the Ard mháistir's school

When Óengus reached his cottage, he carefully laid aside his cloak and settled into his seat by the fire.

The sun had been unusually bright this morning, prompting him to stroll around the túath before visiting Alana. Home now, his old bones thanked him for not staying out in the air too long, and he gratefully accepted the bowl of hot soup a young aide served.

The Ard mháistir smiled over his simple meal. Today's walk had been a pleasure. He did not venture into winter's chill as often as was once his habit. This morning the túath children, and many who had grown up under his watchful care, had greeted him warmly and asked for his blessing, which he readily gave to all.

Later that afternoon he beamed his greeting to Banfháidh Dearbhla. Nostalgia was the theme of their conversation.

"Ah, Dearbhla, what a prophetess you showed yourself to be in speaking those few short lines at Samhain last autumn," Óengus said affectionately. "I believe I have solved the riddle you posed that day."

> Arán Bán and Tadhgan tempted the Fates.
> Ah-Lahn walked through the Golden Gates.
> Sorrow brought Alana to her knees.
> The new graduates flew home on Victory's breeze.
> I, myself, stayed to save the child.

"And who knows," he declared, "Alana may heal us, one and all. She has nearly as much promise as Ah-Lahn at her age. And, like her soul's twin, she yearns for realms of higher consciousness where she will learn to lead by Spirit's call, just as you prophesied."

"I, too, have pondered the prophecy, Óengus," Dearbhla beamed back her agreement. "I believe you have the truth of it."

Throughout the colder months, Óengus watched and listened. To his delight—songs, poems, stories, and invocations began to pour out of Alana as she intensified her meditations on the eternal flame within her.

When winter's grey gave way to springtime's jubilant green, he was not surprised to observe that she heard the voice of her beloved, speaking to her over the silver cord that linked them, soul to soul.

Ah-Lahn

You will know we have connected when tears come, the tears that tell true, dissolving separation in an instant. Doubt does not exist where I am.

Come sit with me awhile and learn a secret: Our souls' destiny is a vision held in the hand of An Síoraí, the Eternal One.

Alana

I still reach for you in the night, to touch your invisible hand, even as I feel your thoughts speaking into mine. Deep is where I have to go to find you and high above where I had flown before our days of loving.

After the rain you came to me, to dry my tears, to hold me safe. Come find me again. The weather has been stormy, and I am weary in walking. Though I hear your footsteps in my mind, I look around and find myself alone.

Separation is an illusion that feels real until I remember lying in your arms, feeling the strength of your spirit and your will to be my husband forever—though I could not hold you close enough to keep you from your destiny.

Has my heart grown large enough to merit our reunion? Forever feels too short a time for me to count the million ways I love you.

Ah-Lahn

I am right here, beside you, around you, eager to help you every hour. I am the watchman on the wall of your future, a willing participant in your life, the gentle nudge you often feel.

I urge you forward on a path that narrows as it climbs, clearing obstacles as you go.

My love for you is a fire that blesses you and draws you all the way to where I am. For I am nearer than your breath, perhaps more vital to your journey Home.

Alana

How can I possibly live in this world? Only in your presence do I feel myself alive and worthy to speak of Love's delicacy or its power to remove mountains of human willfulness.

While walking in the desert of loneliness on days when I do not feel you here, I wonder: What about me causes you to come and go? These are secrets I long to learn.

Ah-Lahn

We cannot know life's mysteries all at once, Beloved. Not until we have fulfilled our reason for being, which may require more light than we have yet garnered in our souls.

The future stretches far ahead for us, mo chroí. I will see you in my dreams and in my waking. And part of me will always be alive in you, as you will always be alive in me.

Predictions Fulfilled

Nine years had passed since Alana came to live and study with Uncle Óengus. Today, she was being invested as a bandruí while the túath of Cois Abhann celebrated the festival of Samhain.

During the small ceremony, held this year in the privacy of the Ard mháistir's grove, when Óengus placed the wreath of oak leaves on Alana's head and hung about her neck the gold medallion that had belonged to Ah-Lahn, he looked back on their time together.

She had proved herself to be one of the brightest and most accomplished bandruí his school had ever produced. And he had raised up many superior druíthe in his time. Óengus was certain of that.

The nine years of study he had insisted she must complete had prepared her well for the rigors she would face as a bandruí. And, yet, there remained about Alana a cloud of uncertainty that only a druí with the Ard mháistir's refined perception might detect.

For several years, he had believed she still grieved for Ah-Lahn. And, of course, that grief had been compounded when she mourned the loss of her wolfhound, Laoch. The great beast had succumbed to the advancing age that not even the most beloved canine can escape.

Alana had not wanted to believe that her dog might also leave her. So she had been unprepared for the day when he stiffly ambled over to lie down beside her while she sat in the sun outside her cottage.

With his head in her lap, he had looked up at her soulfully, sighed, and closed his big brown eyes forever.

Again, Alana had wept for days. And again, Óengus remembered, time had passed.

Eventually, as these and other experiences opened Alana's heart to the tribulations suffered by all of life, the Ard mháistir realized the self-doubt that sometimes slipped into her speech was born, not of grief, but of a deep-seated regret that she was not ready to face.

Nor was he permitted to confront her with an element of consciousness that only An Síoraí could reveal, possibly not even in this lifetime.

Today, as Óengus watched Alana being congratulated by the many Brigantes who had come to love and respect her, he heard the voice of inner wisdom commenting on the aspect of her progress that pleased him most:

Alana is growing in the wisdom that knows when to intervene
on behalf of souls struggling through life,
and when to love those souls enough to let them find their own way.

Her ability to sense that difference was the sign Óengus had been waiting for.

Early one crisp November day, the elderly Ard mháistir discovered Alana in the wisdom grove where they often meditated together. He eased himself onto the blanketed seat beside her in a corner of the sacred space and looked around. To his mind, the grove had never appeared this brightly illumined with the rich reds, golds, and oranges that gilded the oak leaves in their final glory at autumn's end.

Alana opened her hazel-green eyes, surprised to see his crystalline blue ones glistening with emotion.

"Uncle, what troubles you? Are you ill? Has something gone wrong in the túath?" She knew he still maintained a watchful eye on local goings on.

"Nothing is amiss, mo mhuirnín. Truth be told, I have received a welcome premonition: I am soon to pass through the Golden Gates. I am called to Tír na n'Óg, Land of the Ever-Living.

"My race is run in this world, Alana," Óengus continued, not hiding the tinge of weariness he now allowed himself to admit. "Do you understand what that means?"

"I do," she answered softly. Of course, she knew that being called to Tír na n'Óg was the goal of any life.

"I am thrilled for you, Uncle," she said bravely. Then bringing his wrinkled hand to her cheek, she could barely speak. "And I will miss you every day."

"I know, mo mhuirnín, and leaving you is my only sorrow. You may have many years remaining in service here on earth—though I suspect this world may not hold you quite as long as you believe it will. Whatever your future, I know you will embrace it, come what may."

"Come what may," she agreed, tenderly wrapping both her arms around him. Only then did she notice that he was slipping away, etherealizing, as he had once called the process. His body, mind, and soul were already passing over to Tír na n'Óg, the eternal world that soon would be his permanent home.

Alana rose early the next morning and, obeying her inner guidance, dressed in the white robe and gold torc of a bandruí.

Wrapping herself in her warm woolen cloak, she went immediately to the Ard mháistir's wisdom grove where she built a fire in the central hearth and seated herself on a bench before the flames.

She welcomed the fire's heat on this chilly morning. As she had done on countless occasions in the past, she gazed into the cheery flames and focused her attention on the light of An Síoraí within her.

Almost immediately, her inner sight quickened. Standing before her was the form of Uncle Óengus. In that moment, Alana knew he had passed away in the night. He had walked through the Golden Gates and was now come to bid her farewell.

Here, indeed, was her beloved teacher. He wore his finest torc and other gold ornaments that signified his office as Ard mháistir.

Alana nearly called out to him, but, reading her intention, he slightly shook his head. Something in his presence prevented her from breaking the profound silence that enfolded him. He was the same and yet not the same as she had known him only yesterday.

Though possessed of the full mastery of his years as Ard mháistir, he now appeared to her as a robust young man. His hair and beard were once more dark brown, and his eyes sparkled with youthful vitality. Pure white light shimmered all around him, and sparks of gold danced in his aura.

Alana stepped forward to embrace him, but he held up his hand for her to stop. They stood for a moment, their souls radiating the deep affection each held for the other.

At last, Óengus stepped toward her. He reached out his right hand and placed it on the top of her head. With the fingertips of his left hand touching the center of his chest, he intoned a single sacred syllable. A waterfall of light fell all around her. And then he was gone.

Alana did not move. She wished only to absorb the profound peace that lingered in her aura from the Ard mháistir's blessing.

Focusing her attention intensely on An Síoraí, she looked more deeply within. There was Óengus, walking away from her along a path that sparkled like crystalline sand and rose up an incline into a mist.

She could see the white light around him growing brighter. A circlet of golden light surrounded his head. As she watched, his form became almost transparent.

As the master was about to disappear from view, the mist parted and a radiant female figure stepped forward. She was crowned with a similar golden circlet and surrounded in the same brilliant white light. Here was Alana's mother, Enfys, come to greet her beloved Óengus.

Alana saw them join hands and face each other. Instantly, the light within and around their forms increased and began to merge. Intricate spirals of iridescent light were now spinning around them, moving faster and faster, until the two figures were enveloped in a milky white radiance.

Sparks of gold were shooting out in all directions from enormous rings of light around their heads. Alana could feel herself being lifted into a higher plane of consciousness where she could see them.

Rising as a unit, yet still distinct from one another, these two, who had been created from a single spirit spark in the white fire of An Síoraí, began to rise into the mist.

Alana's heart bloomed with gratitude that she should be witnessing such a scene. She was overwhelmed by the immense bliss that emanated from Óengus and Enfys.

As they rose higher and higher, Alana saw the mist thin. Ever so faintly, she could detect the barest outline of luminous temples that she knew must be Tír na n'Óg.

She was breathless with anticipation. Would she see them enter in? Would she witness the union of twin flames?

The second that thought crossed her mind, she heard a tone sound as if from far away. Instantly, Óengus, Enfys, and the glistening buildings vanished in a flash of light. A mighty burst of energy illuminated the grove as if ten thousand suns had landed in that sacred space.

At the same time, an immense release of unspeakable joy swept through Alana. Tears streamed down her face and she fell to her knees. Unable to contain the enormity of light and emotion flooding her entire being, she lost consciousness.

When she awoke some moments later, she found herself seated once more before the fire that burned as if recently lit.

The grove sparkled with the light of a million tiny diamonds. The ancient oak trees had turned green and vibrant in a second springtime.

Waves of ecstasy continued to ripple through Alana, bathing her in the energy of the Land of the Ever-Living.

She exulted as sensations of light and love and joy permeated her body and took up residence in her heart.

Here was a gift from Óengus and Enfys—a glimpse of Tír na n'Óg's glorious radiance. Alana felt that vision as a promise of what she might experience in her own soul's eventual union with Ah-Lahn, whenever the two of them might find a way to be together forever.

For days following the ascension of the twin flames, Alana's feet barely touched the ground. She remained so enraptured by her experience that performing even simple physical tasks was difficult.

In order that she might linger in the wisdom grove's still-rarified atmosphere, she delegated many of her duties to others. She knew such levels of bliss as she had experienced could not long remain in the realms of time and space. Yet she was determined to keep hold of them for as long as possible.

Inevitably, the necessities of daily life intruded upon her reverie, and she was called back to the many responsibilities she was now expected to assume following the departure of the Ard mháistir.

Alana knew she would never be the same after witnessing the final reunion of Óengus and Enfys. However, as days slipped into weeks, and months into years, she found remembering the fullness of the glorious event she had experienced an increasingly difficult challenge.

Until one day, without realizing she had made the choice to do so, she forgot.

The Slide

Sarah and Kevin were standing together outside a gorgeous palace whose translucent walls glinted like rainbows in the sunlight.

He was telling her something very important, something she needed to remember, when they heard a voice announce over a loud speaker, "Please make your way to the exit."

"What a shame," said Kevin, casting a final glance at the crystalline buildings they were being asked to vacate. "I was getting used to this place. At least the ride back will be quick. Come on, Sarah, we don't want to be late."

"Okay," she acquiesced. She did not want to leave. She believed she had not completed an important task, though she could not recall what it was. Perhaps she was meant to buy a souvenir of their adventures. However, the gift shop was closing, and Kevin was urging her to hurry.

They walked over to where the tour bus was supposed to be waiting for them. Instead, they saw a long row of personal-sized bobsleds, each one marked with a name painted on the side in gold letters.

"Take this one." Kevin pointed to a sled with a name that was not hers as he selected a sled that did not bear his name. Sarah started to object, but he insisted. No one else claimed those sleds, so they pushed off and headed for home.

The mountain top was not steep and the trail was wide, so they were able to ride side-by-side for nearly half a mile. Then without warning, the trail began to divide.

"Sarah, take my hand!" Kevin shouted.

But she did not hear him—or else, she chose not to.

Whatever the reason, Sarah was intrigued by the trail before her. She could see her husband gesturing to her, but she turned away, determined to follow her own way back home.

She split off from him as her trail wound through a stand of tall, slender pine trees. She could feel her sled picking up speed, going faster and faster down the trail that grew steeper and steeper until it ended at the edge of a precipitous cliff.

Sarah's sled flew off into space. She tried to hold on to it, but it slipped from her grasp. She was airborne for what seemed like an hour, or was it an instant? And then she landed on an icy track that wound its way down the mountain.

She was sliding back and forth, around sharp curves. Many of the curves held a clear orb that showed scenes of people going about their daily lives. Sarah instantly recognized herself at every turn, though too briefly to do other than realize she had been embodied as many different people and to experience a flash of what their lives had been like.

A thousand emotions swept through her. She felt both joy and pain while living as courtesan, prince, nun, alchemist's apprentice, medieval scribe, Victorian poet, actor. For an instant, she lived as man, woman, child. Conqueror and conquered. Illiterate and intelligentsia.

There was no time to name the people she had been. She could tell that none of them knew her as she sailed by, and few of them recognized each other.

Each lifetime began in forgetfulness and most remained that way.

She was careening through different periods of history and flying past ages dark with ignorance or illuminated with enlightenment.

Down, down, down she slid along the track, until she arrived at a civilization built of glass and metal. Here, at last, she landed with a thud and a ringing in her ears so loud it could wake the dead.

Recalling

Sarah groped for the cell phone that blared on her nightstand. "Hello?" she croaked in a daze.

"Sarah? Is that you?"

She winced as a voice shouted from the other end of the line.

"Hon, it's Kevin! Are you there? Sarah, answer me. I know it's late, but I caught the first flight I could."

"Kevin?" She finally recognized his voice. "Where are you?"

"Outside the village pub. I thought I'd better call before coming over. What cottage are you in?"

Sarah rubbed her forehead and thought for a minute.

"Uh, number 10. And don't knock. I'll let you in. Other people are sleeping." She huffed out a breath. "What are you doing here?"

"I had to see you. I'll tell you everything when I get there."

What *am* I doing here? Kevin asked himself as he stuck his cell phone in his jacket pocket and put the rental car in gear. He guessed they would find out together.

Time held its breath as Sarah padded down the cottage hallway in her stocking feet and quietly opened the front door. A bracing sea breeze shocked her fully awake. She inhaled the cool, salt air and waited for Kevin to arrive.

Yes, Kevin! The husband she had been ready to divorce only days earlier was now driving around the village in the dark of night to see her. In Ireland, for goodness sake! This was not the man she had left behind in New York.

Sarah tried to clear her head. And talked out loud to herself, hoping to figure out why she was standing outside, without her shoes, wearing yesterday's clothes.

"How long have I been asleep? My phone says seven hours. Can that be right? I feel like I've been out for centuries.

"What happened? Oh . . . the seanchaí happened. The atmosphere he created was so powerful—and familiar. Like that flash of recognition when our eyes met." She paused, retracing what little she recalled.

"I know I left dinner early. I came back to my room. I meant to write in my journal. But then . . . I must have passed out on my bed. Now it's 2:00 in the morning, and Kevin is turning his car in to my driveway. I don't know if I'm awake or still in some crazy dream."

Sarah held a finger to her lips for Kevin to be quiet as she led him through the cottage's cozy living room where last night's turf fire had gone out, though its earthy fragrance lingered on a rustic hearth.

"Nice," he commented when Sarah ushered him into her room.

"Yes, the furnishings are perfect for one person," his wife said flatly and claimed the higher ground of the cushioned window seat.

"What's going on with you? The last I knew I was married to a man who didn't fly across oceans. And now you show up in Ireland in the middle of the night, in the middle of my lovely retreat! *Explain* yourself."

"I intend to. And please stop looking like you want to murder me. I wouldn't have tortured myself for the last twelve hours to get here if I didn't have good reason."

"Fine, you have my full attention," grumbled Sarah. "I promise not to murder you until you've had your say, and I've had mine."

"That's fair." Kevin sighed and pulled up an arm chair to face her. His experience had been powerfully clear, but now he was fumbling for words. "I felt you. I felt you calling me."

"I didn't call you," she insisted. "I've been leaving my cell phone in the room while the tour is out exploring. I forgot to turn it off last night and then I fell asleep in my clothes."

"So I see." Kevin suppressed a laugh as he explained his meaning.

"You didn't call me on the phone, Sarah, you called me in my mind. And then I saw you, but not as the person you are now. You were different, and yet you were definitely the woman I married.

"You were wearing a full-length dress or robe of some kind and your hair was long and wild. There was a giant wolfhound nearby, asleep under a tree. You were sitting beside a pond, deep in meditation, and you were compelling me to come to you. When I did, the sensation was like being pulled through a knothole or a tunnel. And then I was beside you, holding you as if my life depended on it."

Sarah furrowed her brow, but did not answer. Kevin began speaking more confidently as vivid memories carried him.

"I was frightened I would lose you again. I knew we had been together, but then separated many times in the past. All I knew for sure was that I had to reach you now, here, in this time, in this place, so we didn't destroy our relationship.

"The message kept coming to me that this would be our last chance to break the pattern. I can't explain the experience more clearly. The images were extremely vivid."

Kevin's body ached from hours of travel, but he knew he had to tell Sarah everything he remembered. He plumped a cushion behind his back and faced her wary expression as he began the story he found hard to believe himself:

The visions started the weekend after you left. I know this sounds bizarre, but I was watching television when, out of the blue, the temperature in the living room felt like someone had opened a window and let in an icy breeze. Which makes no sense, because it's July in New York.

Still, I was freezing. I turned off the AC and the television, and switched on the fireplace. I pulled on a sweater and drew up a chair in front of the fire to get warm.

I sat there for quite a while, watching the flames. At some point, they started to swirl and grow brighter. Then they began to form into spheres that looked like translucent crystal balls that contained images of people moving around in them.

Then I heard a voice in my head saying, *Pick one and step in.* So I did. Instantly, I was in a Greek academy that looked like that painting in Athens. Except I was in Sparta.

"I have no idea what you're talking about, but go on," said Sarah, yawning and rubbing her eyes.

Anyway, I was in Sparta, living and teaching at the academy, and I was very old. You were one of my private pupils, and you were much younger, probably about ten. I was working with you individually because the other instructors found you too precocious.

Sarah wrinkled her nose at him and shrugged. "Are you sure you weren't just having a nightmare?"

"No, I was wide awake. Not too far into this vision, I realized I was in a life review. The scenes were unfolding like a movie of actual events, the way I've heard life reviews described. I know I didn't make these things up."

In Sparta you wanted to learn about science and leadership. You felt you had a destiny, but one that was very different from the other girls your age. Most of them looked down on you. They were jealous of your quick mind and accused you of being conceited because you were a princess.

I knew you were only trying to find your place, and I wanted to help you. Unfortunately, I died of old age before I could teach you the lessons that would have helped in your marriage to the King and that would have supported you after he died in a terrible war.

Sarah felt an inexplicable wave of sadness pass through her. Kevin noticed her shudder, but he did not comment. He could only hope his story would trigger her memory. He went on.

That was the end of the Sparta life review. The images faded, and I was suddenly sweating in front of the fireplace, in July, when no one in their right mind would be burning a fire. But the thing is, I felt very much in my right mind to imagine us in Greece.

That was Saturday. On Sunday afternoon the same thing happened. Cold breeze. I'm freezing, turning on the fireplace, watching the flames morph into translucent orbs, and picking another one. Except that Sunday there were more scenes.

First, there was Egypt, and I was having a dream that I've actually had in this life when I was a kid. I was riding with you on a royal barge on what must have been the Nile. Everyone in the scenes that followed wore elaborate costumes and gold jewelry. You were the Queen, and I loved you with all my heart, though we weren't married. Instead, I managed your estates.

You weren't unkind as the Queen, but you took me for granted, which was hard to bear. I helped you as much as you let me, but I was never able to tell you how much I loved you. And then you died.

Sarah, we kept dying—one of us leaving the other behind. Sometimes you went first, as in Egypt. But I recall going out of embodiment in some spectacular departures. One of the most dramatic was on the island of Poseid in Atlantis. And we were married this time.

As soon as Kevin said "Poseid," a shiver ran up Sarah's spine and she started to tremble. She clutched her hands together on her lap and stared at her husband. She could see a strange glow began to shimmer around him as he spoke.

We were a priest and priestess in a huge temple in a large city. We each worked with our own teachers and were devoted to them. I studied with a woman who had been High Priestess, but was now a lady master. She had mysteriously disappeared.

I was learning some amazing powers from her. But before

I could share them with you, an evil high priest attacked me as we were trying to escape the island. That's when the master shot out beams of light from her hands. She knocked out the priest and his soldiers and then whooshed me up into the light.

I remember looking back at you from that light and regretting that I could not explain to you what had really happened.

You blamed yourself for my death because we had argued before the attack. And I couldn't resolve things between us, even after several embodiments had passed. You were always pushing me away.

We still hadn't settled our relationship when we came together in Ireland nearly two thousand years ago. Though we discovered more about our relationship than we had in the past, we weren't finished.

Kevin paused to catch his breath and take a few bites of the granola bar he pulled from his jacket pocket. He was starving, but there was no stopping now.

"Keep going," said Sarah. Her voice was taking on a dreamy quality and she no longer glowered at Kevin.

"The first time I saw you in that Irish embodiment, I recognized you as my twin flame, exactly as I did this time. Initially, you rejected me, but after you almost died . . ."

"I almost died?"

"You don't remember a witch casting a spell on you?"

"No."

"Well, she did, and after I helped heal you, you changed your mind about me. We were married briefly, but then the man who had been the evil priest on Atlantis murdered me."

Kevin could see that his wife was frowning again and yawning.

"Hang in here with me, Hon. I have one final vision to tell you about. This may be the most important of all because it was a prophecy of what might happen if we don't make different choices than we've made before."

Two nights ago, I dreamed we were with the lady master from Atlantis. She took us to an auditorium where we watched a movie that showed us in this life, but we were divorced. You had pushed me away again, and we were both very angry.

The pain of that separation was terrible, and the feeling stayed with me all day. Then last night, I heard you calling me, and I knew I had to get to you.

Kevin clasped Sarah's hands and looked intently into her eyes. "I don't know why you push me away, but we have to break this pattern. Do you have any idea how much I love you—how much more I could love you, if you'd let me?"

Suddenly, a cloud came over Sarah's face, and she snatched her hands back from her husband's grasp. Kevin felt a cold breeze blow through the room as his patience deserted him.

"You're doing it again. Why do you pull away like that? Why did you leave me, Sarah?"

"If you don't know, I can't tell you. You wouldn't understand."

"Try me."

"Don't bully me, Kevin. You broke my heart. That's all the explanation you're going to get."

Kevin's mouth fell open and his eyes went wide. Like two actors repeating lines in a play, he and Sarah were speaking the words he had heard in his dream. The cloud he had seen mask his wife's face intensified as the prophecy's warning reverberated in his mind.

"No! We are not doing this!" he cried. "We are not falling back into this pattern, Sarah. Come here."

Kevin leapt from his chair and dropped on to the window seat to her right. Without hesitating, he placed his left hand on her back behind her heart and his other hand on her forehead.

"What are you doing?" she exclaimed, her body stiffening.

"I'm bringing you back," said Kevin firmly. "Keep your eyes open and stay with me. We save each other here and now, or we lose each other forever."

Coming Home

Sarah could feel Kevin's hand on her back, creating a pulsing energy that was like a heartbeat. He held his right hand gently on her forehead and began taking slow, even breaths. Gradually, Sarah's jagged breathing grew smoother, and she inhaled deeply.

She could hear Kevin intoning a note that sent soothing waves of sound through his hands into her body. Her mind began to let go as she felt unusual strength flooding into her from her husband.

She had never known him like this. Or had she? There was something familiar about the wisdom and power she sensed streaming from him. Had those qualities been in him all along and she had never noticed? Or was he accessing a part of himself he had never needed until now?

They sat together on the window seat for several minutes, saying nothing.

At last, sensing that Sarah had relaxed into the vibration he had set in motion, Kevin moved back to his chair facing her and, once more, took her hands in his. She could see his eyes had gone deep and serious. He fixed her with an intensity that held her more firmly than his embrace had ever done.

"Sarah, look at me and tell me exactly what's going on inside of you. If you can honestly say that you do not love me, we will end this conversation right now and I'll fly back to New York."

"I'm afraid . . . ," she began haltingly. "I'm afraid I can't be what you want me to be." Her voice cracked as a dam broke inside of her, and centuries of sorrow and regret came flooding out in tears that would not be denied.

Kevin leaned in to her, incredulous. "What could I possibly want you to be that you are not?"

"I feel like you want me to be nice all the time, even-tempered, not volatile or sharp. More spiritual. Less arrogant, selfish, materialistic. You don't like what you see when you look at me."

"Did I ever say those words?"

"No, but you've thought them. Sometimes I think I can read your mind, and I don't like what I hear." Sarah dug a tissue out of her pocket and blew her nose.

Kevin brushed a strand of auburn hair out of her face and rested a hand on her shoulder. "Shall I tell you what I see in you?"

"If you must," she answered weakly.

"When I look at you, I don't just see, I feel you. I feel your inner fire, your caring, your quick mind, your laughter, your courage, your ability to move people with your words. I sense your willingness to adapt to difficult circumstances.

"I perceive those qualities in you because I contain them. My own unique aspects, perhaps, yet the same. Sarah, we have sprung from a single root. We are more alike than not. Focusing on differences makes us foreign to ourselves.

"I cannot look at you without seeing myself. When you let yourself ease into your love for me, I feel as if our original separation eons ago never occurred. And a hundred thousand years of lifetimes evaporate."

Sarah willed herself to stop crying and look at him.

"Do you know why I have a hard time with those moments when you are abrupt or unkind? When you are afraid—which is where those behaviors come from. When you're like that, I don't only lose the real you, I lose me."

"I don't know what you mean."

"Let me ask you a question," said Kevin. "Do you believe we are twin flames—the other half of one another?"

"Yes," Sarah said without hesitation. "I have felt that connection since our first meeting in the library all those years ago. I thought you had forgotten. I left last week because you were the one pulling away from me. Why did you do that, Kevin?"

"I thought I made myself clear," he said firmly. "You changed when you went to work for A.B. Ryan. I haven't recognized you in months. You seemed to be running away from yourself, into a career that wasn't really you. Even when you were affectionate toward me, I felt like you were trying to make me into somebody else.

"I guess I was protecting myself from the fear I sensed in you. And your fear was killing me. You were hurtling off a cliff, and I couldn't stop you. The pain of watching you slip away from our commitment to each other was unbearable."

"And I got angry when you dared to tell me the truth," was all Sarah could say.

"Ours is not a fairytale romance, no matter how miraculously we got together. We are the other half of each other. How we treat ourselves is how we treat each other," Kevin said fervently.

"You have no idea how hard it was for me not to follow you over here as soon as you left. But I had to care for myself enough to let you go. I knew you could never truly love me until you decided to know your-self—to see yourself as you really are.

"I've had to do the same. Witnessing those life reviews helped— which is why I was bold enough to fly over here."

"Maybe we shouldn't have married each other," Sarah said wanly.

"Our marriage is not a mistake. If you think that, you negate us both. Please, stop pushing me away. You're only reinforcing lifetimes of sepa-ration."

Kevin got up and began pacing. As he spoke, both the energy in the room and his voice grew more powerful. He turned and looked at his wife. His eyes were flashing with intensity.

"I love you, Sarah, with my whole heart—because that is where I hold you. Where I have held you for millennia. Our reunion is only a breath away. This chasm between us is an illusion that fear has taught us to believe.

"I live in your heart. You cannot lose me, not even by refusing to remember who we are. You can pretend I am a stranger, but inside you know: I am your Ah-Lahn and you are my Alana.

"I will tell you a secret," he continued, looking off into the distance as songbirds outside the cottage window greeted the sunrise. "In all of our lifetimes you have missed me the most when I have been nearest. When you yearn and weep, that is when my soul is leaning into yours.

"Absence is not what makes you cry. Tears are soul signals that what An Síoraí, the Eternal One, has joined together, no human can destroy. We are lost only if we think we are. The mystery is how we can imagine being anywhere other than together."

Sarah drew in a sharp breath. Dawn was not the only radiance beaming into her room. The aura around Kevin was growing brighter as he spoke. He was bathed in a luminescence that looked like a long white robe. The light intensified as he turned and poured out his heart to her.

"Let me love myself in you, as you love yourself in me. That is how we weave ourselves together, no matter where we are in cosmos. The idea of loving yourself in your partner is important for any couple. For us as twin flames, it is a matter of life and death."

Sarah could bear no more. She jumped to her feet and cried out, "But our being together—loving that much—has meant your death, as Khieranan and Ah-Lahn and probably many others!"

"You do remember!" Kevin rushed to his wife and pulled her into a joyful embrace.

"Wait!" She put her hands on his chest and, again, pushed him away. "Kevin , will you not see the truth? People die around me. Alana's family and ours. I had two miscarriages. Our babies died because the people I love are not safe!"

Uncontrollable sobs shook Sarah's body as the ancient belief behind her fear poured out, and memories of last night's dreams flooded her awareness. She buried her face in Kevin's chest and felt her heart crack open in the vulnerability she had hidden from them both for ages.

He folded his arms around her and gently stroked her hair.

"Hon, sooner or later everybody dies. One of us will likely leave this world before the other, but that does not mean we are not safe to be together now, today, in this moment, and for many years to come.

"Love is not the force that kills. Fear is what pulls the joy out of life. Separation comes from our belief in the lies fear tells us. You and I do not have to live that way.

"Come be whole with me, Sarah. The forces that are terrified of the oneness of twin flames will always try to make us afraid. There is no escaping that fact. Our strength is in our union, in our determination to love consciously—to help one another overcome our weaknesses and faults. And to love the people around us.

"Be that love with me, Hon, and see what we can make of this life. Our marriage can be a great adventure. When we are in harmony, we are like the warp and woof of a beautiful tapestry.

"Our lives are a weaving. When a thread gets pulled or a stitch dropped, a gap appears. If we are not careful, we fall through. But we can repair the holes we have made in our tapestry. We are meant to be woven together, and we will be forever if we remember who we are."

Sarah looked up and gazed into Kevin's blue-green eyes. In that moment she felt her soul accept the love he was pouring into her from the depths of his being. She felt him alive in her heart. And she understood the mystery of their twin souls as she had not done in a very long time—perhaps not in ten thousand years.

In her mind's eye, she could see the holes in their weaving being mended. As the chasm between Sarah and her beloved closed, she heard her voice of inner wisdom vow to An Síoraí, the Eternal One:

From this day forward, I will treat Kevin and myself with loving-kindness. I see now that only in such tenderness will we thrive in one another. Only in that unity will we build a bridge to the oneness of our origin as twin flames.

At last, Sarah spoke the words her husband longed to hear: "I do love you, Kevin. And I promise to stay with you forever. I know I have broken that promise before, but I will keep it this time, come what may."

"I know you will," said her beloved, holding her tight and kissing the top of her head. "And so will I."

Long past the hour when dawn broke over the Irish Sea, painting the water and sky with brilliant pinks and golds, husband and wife slept peacefully in each other's arms. The sun was high overhead when they finally woke up—happy and starving.

Laughing as they threw on some clothes, they hurried to eat lunch where a very surprised gathering of Sarah's fellow writers welcomed Kevin and encouraged him to join their group.

Later that afternoon, these same friends smiled as they caught sight of the couple walking hand in hand along the pathway that looked out across the sea. Sarah and Kevin knew they had sailed those waters in many a lifetime. They kept hold of one another well into evening and dreamed that night of the starlit realm where their souls had been born.

When the sound of birdsong woke Sarah early the next morning, she heard the words that had been spoken to Alana by Ard-Mháistir Óengus as he made his way to Tír na n'Óg. Alana had not understood his message then. Today Sarah did.

> Your soul already knows
> its origin and its destiny.
>
> Be still and feel the rhythm
> of reunion's sweet alchemy
> that unlocks Love's deep mysteries
> in the heart's secret chamber,
> where nothing may disturb
> beloveds in their oneness.

"Kevin, wake up! I hear another calling. A dog and a cat are waiting for us at the animal shelter back home. We're going to be a family after all."

Epilogue

Sarah laughed as the kitten and puppy rolled around on the floor at her feet. She and Kevin had meant to adopt mature animals, but that plan had dissolved almost instantly once they explored the animal shelter.

"How about I go look at canines and you check out the felines?" Kevin had suggested.

Sarah liked the idea and headed into a large windowed area off the lobby where dozens of cats were lounging and playing. The sheer number and variety of adoptable animals was overwhelming, yet none caught her eye until she spotted a British Bombay kitten with green eyes.

"You look like a mini-panther, you little cutie," Sarah cooed. She bundled the tiny ball of black fur into her arms, where the baby immediately settled and began to purr.

As they walked back to the lobby, Kevin emerged from the canine area with a sheepish grin on his face. He was carrying a puppy with the wildest coat of mixed grays, whites, and browns Sarah had ever seen. The pup's hair stuck out in all directions, as if he had been napping.

"I know we said we'd only look at adults, but this little guy woofed at me, and I was a goner," Kevin admitted. "He followed me with his eyes until I picked him up. Can we keep him?"

"We can take him home as long as we can keep this little girl," said Sarah, laughing as she held out her kitten for Kevin to see that she had also succumbed to a baby.

"But look at the size of your puppy's feet. He's going to be huge. We may have to get a bigger house."

In less than an hour, the adoption paperwork was complete and

Sprite the kitten and Hero the puppy were on their way to live on Long Island. As Sarah and Kevin drove home from the shelter with their new family, they joyfully agreed that life would never be the same.

They beamed their thanks to Ireland for its part in that dramatic change. The ancient oak trees that yet lived on the Emerald Isle felt their gratitude and nodded graciously in acceptance.

In the quiet of her home office, Sarah took up her journal. After returning from Ireland, she had decided not to go back to her job in the city. Somehow, she was not really surprised that only her friend, Debbie, had expressed disappointment in her resignation.

Finances would be a bit tight until Sarah found a more suitable occupation, but she and Kevin would manage. And they would be much happier.

> Today I am starting to write my novel and I am not stopping
> until the book is as complete as it needs to be. This is a promise
> I am making to myself and to Kevin.

As she wrote those words in her journal, Sarah affirmed that she was finally willing to face the fears, sense of unworthiness, and guilt that had blocked the book that was now leaping out of the notes she had been squirreling away for a decade.

The people, the places—the sights, sounds, aromas. The textures and the tastes of foods sweet to savory, simple to exotic. They were all available to her now. Her senses tingled as she imagined putting into words the myriad images that surged into her mind, demanding that she write them.

She was awash with the story that had waited for centuries to finally come alive. Or had it always been alive in her, but she had been afraid to be the seanchaí and allow the story to break through the distractions and avoidance that had muffled her until now?

Regardless of the reason, she would delay no longer. She would not faint before the task. This was her moment of truth. She would dare to tell the story of her past and Kevin's.

Opening her laptop, Sarah stretched her arms overhead and inhaled the unmistakable fragrance of apple blossoms that wafted gently into her office from far across a timeless sea. She cast her mind back nearly two thousand years and began typing:

ÉIRE'S SOUTHEASTERN COAST, MID-APRIL, AD 61

A barefoot young woman walked carefully along the water's edge, avoiding a patch of broken shells and bits of seaweed tossed up on the coarse sand by the latest high tide.

Her name was Alana. She was twenty-two years old and troubled about her new life in the land of the Brigantes tribe. The clear future she had grown up expecting was lost to her here in this foreign place.

Turn the page for a preview
of the first exciting new sequel to
The Weaving

The Ancients and The Call

Twin Flames of Éire Trilogy - Book One

by Cheryl Lafferty Eckl

One

Ugh! Sprite! Stop!" grunted Kevin, waking to the intensity of two bright emerald eyes peering into his face. His wife's black mini-panther kitten was sitting on his chest, purring vigorously, and licking him with her raspy little pink tongue.

At Kevin's exclamation, Hero, the wire-haired pup who was still growing into his enormous grey and white feet, jumped up on the bed, whining and dancing on the covers. He nosed Sprite out of the way and began slurping his owner's face and hands.

"Okay! Okay! I'm awake!" Kevin groaned, pushing back fifty pounds of bouncy canine so he could sit up. Rubbing his blue-green eyes, he looked at the bedside clock. 6:00 a.m. He'd been asleep for only a couple of hours. However, his four-legged housemates held tenaciously to their own schedule. Even on a Saturday, they insisted that 6:00 a.m. meant doggie business in the backyard for Hero and breakfast for everybody.

Clearly, no rest for a sleepless man. That was weird because his wife was the one who sometimes had insomnia. Where was Sarah? Her side of the bed was empty.

Oh, right, he remembered as he shuffled into the kitchen, let the dog out, put on a pot of strong coffee, and fed the cat. His wife had taken a morning flight to Boston yesterday to visit her family in Braintree, narrowly missing the early November snow storm that had howled like a banshee across New York on its way to Massachusetts.

Good thing Sarah was going to be away for a few days, Kevin said to himself. He needed to get his head straight.

Hero did his doggie duty faster than usual and bounded back into the house with a happy "Woof!"—all wagging tail and clumsy feet that sent his empty metal food dish clattering across the tile floor.

Sprite, who was enjoying her fancy canned tuna on the counter, looked up disdainfully and rolled her eyes at Kevin as he filled the dog's dish and set it down on the floor before the eager hound.

"Yeah, I know. Hero's a goofball. But you don't fool me. I know you two snuggle at night when the wind is up."

Talking to his animals nudged further back in Kevin's mind the troubling images that had kept him awake until 3:00 a.m. and then given him nightmares. But as soon as he sat at the kitchen table to drink his black coffee and eat a bowl of cold cereal, the memory of his experience in the swamp of mediocrity came rushing back.

He tried reading the sports page in the morning paper, but his mind was too full of "what ifs."

"I need a plan," he said to Sprite and Hero as he took a large swallow of coffee. "At least I've got a few days to come up with something before Sarah gets home."

He had declined his wife's invitation to accompany her to Braintree. He liked her family, but they could be a noisy bunch, and right now he needed quiet. Only a few months earlier, Sarah would have pushed him to go with her, even though she knew he didn't always enjoy the Callahan family's exuberance.

When she hadn't insisted this time, he'd been a bit surprised. Could she tell he needed a break? Or did she need one, too?

Although they'd reconciled after their big blowup last summer, now, in early November, signs of strain were once more troubling the harmony they had promised each other after returning from Ireland.

Kevin grimaced at the memory of July's emotional separation. After nearly a year of frequent misunderstandings and arguments, Sarah had angrily packed herself off to a writer's retreat near Dublin—with no promise of returning home to her husband.

One night, while caught up in the Emerald Isle's liminal atmosphere, she had dreamed of past lives that she and Kevin had shared—in first-century Ireland as the druids Ah-Lahn and Alana, on the continent of Atlantis before the flood, in Egypt at the time of the pharaohs, and in ancient Greece during the fifth century BC.

The magic had not been confined to Sarah's dream. While she was in Ireland, Kevin was experiencing similar recollections in their home on Long Island. Vivid memories of the same past embodiments had kindled in his mind when he'd slipped into a state of lucid dreaming.

He had never encountered phenomena like these life reviews. He didn't know what to do with them until he was shown a prophecy that he and his wife could permanently lose their opportunity to stay together if they did not do the deep, personal, inner work necessary to resolve the antagonisms that had separated them in many former lives.

Spurred by this dire possibility, he had rushed to Ireland where he poured out his heart to Sarah—the woman he couldn't live without.

They were twin flames, he had passionately reminded her—souls created together in the beginning as two halves of the same whole. They belonged to each other as they could belong to no one else.

Fortunately, his fervor had sparked Sarah's waking memory of all she had dreamed, and the truth of their shared destiny had moved her to reconcile with him.

He had stayed with her through the end of her writing retreat, and they had come back home to Long Island where they once more relished their time as a couple—walking on the beach, laughing at their animals' antics, finding renewed affection in one another's arms.

Throughout most of the summer, these reembodied druids had held each other even more fervently than in the first days of their marriage. Because now they knew that love could be lost. The full horror of that possibility had left its imprint on them, lest either man or woman should stumble again.

Unfortunately, in recent weeks, an obstacle to their oneness had resurfaced.

When they'd returned from Ireland, they had agreed that Sarah would resign from her position as a marketing writer for prominent Manhattan politician A. B. Ryan so she could work full time on the novel she was inspired to write about their past embodiments.

That meant Kevin would be their only wage earner. A small price to pay for getting her away from A. B.'s negative influence, he thought as he put aside the newspaper and set his bowl of half-eaten cereal in the sink.

At the time, the arrangement had seemed like a good idea. But now Kevin was beginning to wonder if they'd made the right decision—not for Sarah, but for him.

She was thriving in her work as a novelist. "The chapters are just pouring out of me," she often exclaimed. "I'm amazed at how much I'm remembering about our past lives." And when she couldn't recall certain details of the lifetimes they had shared, Kevin often did.

He was glad to help her fulfill her dream of being a novelist—that is, as long as he didn't compare her enthusiasm for her work to his boredom with his.

He used to enjoy his job as manager of accounting at Nordemann Financial Services, the successful mid-size firm he had joined ten years ago. But now, after all he'd learned about who he used to be as the druid Ah-Lahn, his life was beginning to feel like the nightmare of life-sucking mediocrity whose image still lingered in his mind.

Exploring his lifetime as a powerful druid had been a revelation. In that embodiment he'd been a skilled master healer, a wise arbiter of the law, an inspired poet. In many ways, Ah-Lahn had out-pictured the inner genius of Kevin's True Self that nowadays he only occasionally tapped into.

"If I was so advanced in ages past, why am I still embodying?" he asked Sprite and Hero. "Did I commit some terrible error that caused me to backslide? Did I totally miss the mark in other lifetimes? Why am I so much *less* today than I was centuries ago?"

The animals offered their full attention, but no ready answer.

"A decline like that would keep anybody awake at night," Kevin grumbled as he padded into the bathroom and stood at the sink. He looked in the mirror and winced. The image that stared back at him was not a pretty one.

His dark brown hair needed a trim—a chore he'd been putting off along with several others that were just too much effort right now.

Yesterday's whiskers grizzled his chin, tempting him to let his beard grow for a couple of days.

Dark circles under his blue-green eyes told the story of last night's sleeplessness and of the gathering emotional storm he could feel near to breaking on the shores of his domestic life.

Kevin stood staring in the mirror for several seconds, wondering if he could live in his sweats until Sarah got home. Then Hero bumped open the bathroom door and Sprite jumped up on the sink with an inquisitive, "Meow?" that snapped him into action.

"Come on, MacCauley, you can do better than this," he admonished himself and stripped down for a shower. Once under the steamy hot spray, he automatically lathered up, shaved, and washed his hair. Finally feeling less like a fairytale troll, he toweled off and pulled on a clean pair of jeans and royal blue turtleneck sweater.

With a clearer head, Kevin decided to meditate—something he hadn't done for a while. He'd let his practice slip. Another behavior that wasn't like him.

He had always said that when he meditated, he knew who he was. Without that clarity, he'd been avoiding the conversation with Sarah that was becoming absolutely crucial to his own survival.

No more procrastination, he vowed. When she returned home from Braintree, they would talk about their future.

Kevin poured himself a second cup of coffee and carried it into the living room. If he could meditate anywhere in his house it would be here in this room that he and Sarah had redecorated to look like a quaint Irish cottage—ironically, he observed, a full year before their adventures on the Emerald Isle.

In the past, the coziness of this space had put him in touch with a wise inner part of himself. He hoped it would again. If he was going to avoid the stifling mediocrity that he felt closing in on him like a nightmare, he needed that internal stability.

Acknowledgements

Every life is a journey through many planes of existence, both seen and unseen. Every person, place, or event we encounter on that journey is a teacher. Their lessons may bring us exquisite joy. Or they may challenge us to the very core of our beliefs about ourselves and others.

All are equally valuable because they form the warp and woof of the tapestry we weave that becomes the fabric of the life we create.

Gratitude for life's ups and downs allows us to observe the threads that belong to our partnership with the spirit of An Síoraí, the Eternal One, that lives in the deepest part of us. And, if we are wise, we will also acknowledge the many threads that others have woven into this miraculous creation we could not have fashioned alone.

The Weaving reaches far back in time and points to a future still unfolding, which gives me the opportunity to gather several millennia of thanks and send them out to countless teachers and mentors for all the lessons, including more than a few dark nights.

Boundless thanks to Theresa McNicholas, without whom this novel would never have come to fruition. And to Michael, who is deserving of particular thanks for accommodating the long hours of his wife's time this book required and for contributing valuable insights along the way.

I am blessed with an extraordinary publishing team that includes James Bennett of Symmetry Design, Paula Kennedy Kehoe of Lightwave Communications, and Larry Stanley of Montana Wedding Photographer.

Special thanks to Dónall Ó Héalaí, founder and director of Celtic Consciousness, and his father, Dr. Pádraig Ó Héalaí, for their priceless assistance with the Gaelic terms that speak to the beauty of the ancient Irish culture that inspired *The Weaving*. To learn more about their work, please visit their website at www.CelticConsciousness.com.

I have done my best to make faithful use of their suggestions. Any errors in spelling, usage, or pronunciation are mine alone.

I also am grateful to the masters, sponsors, and hosts of spirit beings who have walked with me throughout my lifetimes. The story of twin flames belongs to all of us. Thank you to Mother for letting me tell one small part of it.

And to my beloved Stephen, whether together or apart, I live in you as you live in me. Thank you for helping me finally understand what that means.

The author wishes to express her gratitude to Owen Ó Súilleabháin of Turas d'Anam, Larry Stanley Photography, 123rf.com, pixabay.com, pexels.com, dreamstime.com, and bigstockphoto.com for images used throughout *The Weaving*.

We know that we are cherished here.
So may you also understand
and go lightly on your journey.

An Invitation to Twin Flames

Your story is hidden
deep in mysteries of ages past,
yet uniquely visible
when you care to see.

Learn your story,
see yourself as a hero.

What or whom
have you feared
to embrace?

Only loving-kindness
can build a bridge
'twixt self and other,
creating unity of mind and heart.

Invite mutual resonance
to arise in your breast.

You, who once were close,
but drifted apart
in turbulent waters,
revive compassion
for those struggles,
and forgive the chasm
that opened
between you.

In truth,
you have walked
together for eons,
though you may not remember.

Understand this as
Love's greatest gift,
which you once knew
and now must learn again:

All of life is one
with all of life,
and Reunion marks
the end of fragmentation
so wholeness may prevail.

Go, be fearless
and feel Unity resounding
in every corner of your psyche.

That is how you may regain
the Oneness of your origin.

Cheryl Lafferty Eckl has played many roles since she began her career as a singer-actress in musical theatre—award-winning author, mystical poet, professional development trainer, life coach, inspirational speaker, and subject matter expert on end-of-life issues and grief.

These days, her favorite role is *seanchaí*. That's Irish for storyteller.

If you ask, she'll tell you that it's her love of Ireland—its people, language, land, and culture—that continues to inspire characters and stories in thrilling novels that follow the trials and triumphs of twin flames who sometimes struggle and often succeed in unlocking Love's mystery.

Learn more about Cheryl's books, and enjoy her extensive library of articles, audios, videos, and blogs at www.CherylLaffertyEckl.com.